Eternity

He brought his mouth to hers, and they shared a long, deep kiss. His lips trailed warmly along her cheek, then downward along her neck. He didn't often kiss her on the neck, and she began to take shallow, quick breaths in anticipation as he neared her pulse point.

The delicate skin above her artery was scarred with two small, barely noticeable marks . . .

PRAISE FOR LORI HERTER'S MAGNIFICENT NOVELS OF SENSUAL HUNGER . . . OBSESSION . . . POSSESSION . . . CONFESSION . . .

"ANNE RICE FANS . . . BEHOLD ANOTHER LOOK AT VAMPIRES . . . SENSUAL AND PROVOCATIVE."

—Heartland Critiques

"WONDERFUL! . . . LORI HERTER HAS GIVEN THE VAMPIRE MYTH A FRESH NEW TWIST THAT LEFT ME THIRSTY FOR MORE."

—Norma Beishir, bestselling author of Solitaire and Dance of the Gods

"A WORLD OF DARK FANTASY . . . SEXY."

—Kathleen Creighton

Berkley Books by Lori Herter

OBSESSION
POSSESSION
CONFESSION
ETERNITY

LORI HERTER

ETERNITY

A Berkley Book/published by arrangement with
Kamin & Howell Entertainment, Inc.

PRINTING HISTORY
Berkley edition/December 1993

For information address: The Berkley Publishing Group,
200 Madison Avenue, New York, New York 10016.

ISBN: 0-425-13978-6

BERKLEY®
Berkley Books are published by
The Berkley Publishing Group, 200 Madison Avenue,
New York, New York 10016.
BERKLEY and the "B" design are trademarks of
Berkley Publishing Corporation.

PRINTED IN THE UNITED STATES OF AMERICA

10 9 8 7 6 5 4 3 2 1

To my readers
with much appreciation

I saw eternity the other night
Like a great ring of pure and endless light,
All calm, as it was bright;
And round beneath it, Time, in hours, days, years,
Driven by the spheres
Like a vast shadow moved; in which the world
And all her train were hurled.

Henry Vaughan
1622–1695

1

You miss our old ways, don't you?

DAVID DE MORRISSEY opened his eyes slowly as he awoke from sleep. Perhaps it was a remaining instinct from former days, but the smell of dawn always alerted him. That remnant fear of approaching daylight that had always made him retreat into the protection of darkness still had an effect on him, even now.

On the other hand, it might have been the mischievous tabby kitten who had just jumped on the bed that awakened him. Tabitha always had extra energy at daybreak. And though she had the entire Oak Street mansion to roam, she chose the bedroom in which to chase her tail at dawn, or jump from floor to antique dresser to bed and back again. Or climb the expensive new drapery.

David reached to stroke her fur as he sat up in the dim light. The half-grown cat began to purr and turned to lick his thumb. He couldn't help but smile and be profoundly pleased to experience this small feline gesture of affection. Not more than six months ago, no animal would have gone near him. If pressed, it would have hissed and scratched and jumped away to protect itself as if from a deadly predator. But today, this kitten wanted only to be his playmate.

Turning, David looked down at the delicate, peaceful form of his wife, still sound asleep beside him, her long dark hair spilled luxuriantly over her slim, white shoulder and the pillow. Her exquisite face took on an ethereal quality in the pink light of sunrise, which gradually brightened the room through the open window. Lips slightly parted, dark eyelashes closed over her smooth cheeks, the sweetness of her face, as always, moved David. Her arm lay across the sheet over her abdomen, one small breast almost exposed. Beneath the cover she was naked, as was he—a reminder of their ardent lovemaking at midnight before they had drifted off into contented sleep. She'd seemed satisfied. David hoped she was. More than anything he wanted to keep his wife happy. Veronica remained the center of his universe, as she had been since the very first night he met her.

Veronica was once the child-woman who had surrendered both her deep emotion and her untouched body to the lure of a mesmerizing, powerful male—an immortal creature of the night. He possessed the ability to transfix her with his penetrating gaze, make her delirious with his touch on her neck, satiate her desires as no ordinary man ever could. So Veronica became the devoted, even obsessed, young woman who had willingly waited many long, empty years for that superhuman man she had loved to the point of worship. She wanted nothing but to be united with him forever.

But Veronica now found herself married to an ordinary mortal. David wasn't a vampire anymore. He had been cured of his supernatural malady by drinking a rediscovered ancient gypsy formula. And while David was profoundly happy with his present condition, he wasn't always sure his wife was.

He reached out to touch her hair on the pillow, stroking the silky strands beneath his fingertips. A feeling of tenderness gathered within him, causing a twinge deep within his chest, a tangible symptom of his all-involving love for Veronica. He wanted to gather her up in his arms and caress her with a kiss. But she was sleeping. She always seemed to need an hour or two more sleep than he, they'd discovered in their six months as husband and wife. So he let her be. For now, he told himself with a little smile.

He got out of bed carefully so as not to wake her, grabbed his pajama pants from the floor and put them on. In one corner of the room, near the door, lay several packed suitcases ready to go. David ignored them, didn't even want to think about that just yet.

He walked out of the bedroom, located on the third floor of the Romanesque mansion, built in the late 1800s and considered one of Chicago's best historic homes. Tabitha followed him into the hallway that connected a ballroom at the rear of the mansion to the living room at the front, with doors opening to smaller rooms in between on each side, one of which they had made into their bedroom. Veronica spent enormous amounts of time planning and overseeing the refurbishing of David's largely neglected home. Now every room—except the living room, the huge ballroom, and the oval entry hall—reflected her touch, her increasingly refined taste.

Tabitha chased after David's bare heels as he entered the living room, plushly carpeted with a colorful Aubusson rug he'd installed years ago when he bought and moved into the house. The rug blended with the twined flower-and-insect pattern he'd chosen for the upholstery and drapery, and complemented the rich oak furnishings and marble-manteled fireplace. David had told Veronica she was free to redecorate this room, if she wished. She'd told him she loved it as it was, that it would upset her to change even the smallest thing.

David had been touched by her sentiment, yet an unspoken fear that perhaps she was too attached to the room made his heart uneasy. This room contained a lot of history for them. On the very loveseat he was just now passing, Veronica, in her former job as a writer for a Chicago magazine, had once interviewed David, who had been and still was a renowned playwright. A few weeks later, again on the loveseat, she'd told him, trembling with shyness and inexperience, that she was willing to make love with him. Days later, in this very room, Veronica had discovered he was a vampire and run out of the house in terror. She'd later come back to him and told him, as they stood in front of the fireplace, that she wanted him to take her blood, to initiate her into his vampire world so she would be under his power.

This room and the ballroom, both of which Veronica wanted left so absolutely unchanged, were filled with the vivid memories of their strange love affair, when they shared a vampire bond that took their relationship, sexually and spiritually, just beyond the human realm. Perhaps it was that superhuman relationship she wanted to be reminded of, did not want to let go of, missed in her life, now that David was a man just like any other.

He walked out the living room door onto a landing and bounded down a spiral staircase that took him past his vast second-floor library. When he reached the ground floor, he walked across the oval entryway, painted creamy white, covered high above with a domed ceiling, and bordered with elaborate molding. His bare feet sunk into the pile of another plush Oriental carpet.

On the other side, where a locked door used to be, was now an open passage. It led to a formal living room filled with antique furniture that Veronica and he had selected from the cluttered collection of old furnishings David had saved over his four centuries of vampire existence. The room was a showcase now, with eighteenth-century tables and chairs cleaned and refurbished with new upholstery. Majestic drapery hung from the high, arched windows.

He crossed the room and walked down a hallway that led to the kitchen, remodeled with imported tile and new cabinets, and equipment all in working order. It was incredible to think of what Veronica had accomplished in six months. When she moved in, the first-floor rooms had served as storage for the decaying furniture he'd brought with him from Europe; and the kitchen, which he'd totally neglected, had been in complete disrepair. Vampires don't require food.

David helped out with plans for remodeling when he could, but he was busy reworking a screenplay and exploring ideas for a new play. So Veronica had taken on the responsibility to oversee all the work that needed to be done. Frankly—and he suspected Veronica knew this—David didn't have a head for such details, nor did he enjoy dealing with workmen and designers. He was glad to be able to remain in his familiar upstairs living quarters, holed up in his office or in the living room writing, while the remainder of the house was emptied, cleaned, and refurnished. And now he felt proud and grateful that Veronica had created for him such a remarkable home. He loved being in this house, especially now that he was no longer alone. He hated the thought of leaving it.

Down a short hall from the kitchen, in the back corner of the house, was a small room, originally servant's quarters, that had a window overlooking the backyard. The backyard used to be merely grass and trees, but Veronica had had a flower garden planted, making a charming view. It was here David had decided to install a personal gym. He'd taken a keen interest in fitness soon after becoming a mortal again, because he no longer had the superhuman strength and agility he'd possessed as a vampire. It was, perhaps, the one thing he missed; he'd come to take his former superior muscle power so much for granted. Now he had only the strength of an average man, and he felt vulnerable.

Seeing Arnold Schwarzenegger in a movie had given him the idea. He hired a personal trainer, a young man who came once a week to monitor his improvement, and bought all the necessary equipment. He now had a four-day-per-week workout schedule that covered cardiovascular conditioning and weights.

David got on the treadmill, positioned to face the window, and watched the remaining sunrise as he reached a pace of four miles per hour. Tabitha jumped onto the windowsill and chattered at a bird on the lawn. This had become David's favorite way to begin a day.

He frowned as he kept up with the pace of the treadmill. His comfortable routine would be disrupted when they arrived in London. Why had he let them talk him into going?

A half hour later, Veronica opened her eyes lazily at the early morning sunshine and stretched. She could see through the high window that the sky was blue and the weather clear. A good day to fly, she thought, looking forward eagerly to their departure for London late that afternoon. She'd never been to London. She'd never been outside the United States. This trip promised to be so exciting! Not only would she see London, but she'd get to see the movie version of David's musical being filmed. She just wished David were more enthused.

She looked over at his side of the bed and wasn't surprised to find him gone. He had his routine, and she knew where he was. Tabitha, *her* cat, had probably followed him down. The kitten found it more intriguing to see David pull weights up and down than to watch her sleeping. Veronica couldn't blame the cat. She liked to watch David pump iron, too.

Veronica got out of bed on David's side, picked up his striped cotton pajama top and slipped it on. After pausing to comb her hair, she hurried down to the first floor, to the weight room.

There she found her husband sitting at the bench press, pulling down steel bars extending on either side of him and geared to lift a column of weights behind him. His broad shoulders and chest made a V shape toward his waist, his rib cage and pectoral muscles protruding as he breathed with each movement, the muscles of his arms and shoulders working. Though she sometimes wondered why he was so obsessed with lifting heavier and heavier weights, she didn't object. He looked magnificent! She drew in a long, admiring breath as a sly smile came over her face.

David noticed her standing in the doorway. "Up earlier than usual," he said with a grin.

"There's a lot to do before we leave this afternoon."

David lost his smile. "Did you have to remind me? I'd put that out of my mind and was enjoying myself."

"Poor baby." She walked up to him.

"No respect," he mumbled, his voice strained as he pulled the weights. "No sympathy. What's a man to expect from his wife?"

"Adoration?"

He looked up, blue eyes brightening. "That'll do. God, you look beautiful in the morning. You make my pajama top look like high fashion."

Veronica smiled and stepped closer as he let go of the machinery to reach out and touch her bare thigh. She lifted her foot sideways across his feet and sat astride him, on his lap, facing him, her hands resting lightly on his muscular shoulders.

He made no further attempt to continue his exercise and gazed at her with contented amusement. "You're disrupting my routine."

"Sometimes it's good to break a routine. Keeps you from getting in a rut." Veronica caught the sleeve of the pajama, which was too long for her, in her hand. She used the excess cloth to blot perspiration from his forehead and neck.

David's handsome, aristocratic face with high cheekbones and narrow nose looked the same as when she'd met him several years ago. He'd only been mortal six months, not enough time to show signs of aging yet. His eyes were a vivid, translucent blue, marvelous to contemplate. Though they no longer showed any hint of the cobalt vampire glow that used to appear with intense emotion, they could still mesmerize her with their wisdom and sensitivity.

"I like my rut," David told her, though he seemed to be enjoying her ministrations.

"Good thing we're leaving for England then," she replied.

"Why are you so happy with the idea of leaving here? We've just gotten our home in order. We're together and settled for the first time in our lives. *I* don't want to go *anywhere*. I just want to stay here and live quietly with you."

"I wouldn't have chosen to go away just yet either," she agreed, "but since they need you in London right now, I don't really mind." David's hugely successful stage musical, *The Scarlet Shadow,* was being filmed in London, starring the same actor, Matthew McDowall, who had created the title role onstage. There were script problems, and David had been called to the set for rewrites. "I'd love to see the city where you once knew Shakespeare," Veronica continued. "Think of all the things you could tell me about the past."

"I don't want to be reminded of my past." David leaned his head against the back of the narrow, vinyl-cushioned seat. "Seeing the place where I studied with Will Shakespeare would only make me sad. Remembering where, why, and how I made the decision to travel to Transylvania to become a vampire is not something I wish to do. I just want to be an ordinary man and forget my ill-chosen path into darkness. I love only the sunlight now. And you."

"But you'll see *London* in the sunlight now! For the first time in four centuries. And I'll be there with you. Instead of shutting away the past, I think you should reflect on it, make peace with it."

His sad eyes took on an indulgent quality, and he smiled. "You sound very wise nowadays."

"I had a good teacher," she whispered, feeling tears start at the back of her eyes. David's eyes warmed, and he ran his thumb down her cheek, apparently moved by her sincerity.

David meant so much to her, had taught her so many things about life when he was a vampire and she was a young dreamer who didn't fit into the world around her very well. Perhaps because he'd had to live only by night, cut off from the everyday world, he'd come to reflect on life and relationships more than any other man she'd ever known. And he'd gained incomparable wisdom from his long centuries of observation and his unending study of literature and history.

But now he was a normal man, a part of the mainstream of life again, and she wanted him to enjoy his new life. She wanted him to be a part of it. Instead, he seemed to have a tendency to continue living as a recluse. Was it just a habit he couldn't break, or were there other reasons? She wasn't sure and she was beginning to worry.

"It's not only dealing with the past," David said, as if looking for further reasons not to go to London. "I don't like to fly."

"But this time you can sit in a seat on the airplane, not have yourself shipped in a coffin. It'll be fun. You'll be able to look out the window."

"It sounds tedious to me. A dozen hours sitting in one place with a bunch of strangers? Looking out to see the earth far below?"

Veronica was reminded at least once a day that David wasn't yet a modern person. In some ways he was still a sixteenth-century man, and apparently the idea of flight for humans seemed unnatural to him.

"What if there's an accident?" he continued. "Traveling by any means is risky. Just last night on the news there was a five-car crash on the expressway and a plane crash in Mexico."

"That's always the chance a person takes. Air travel is safer than traveling by car or train. But you've traveled all over the world in the centuries you've lived. I would think you'd be more used to the idea."

"I always found travel inconvenient at best. And, you forget, when I was a vampire, I was indestructible. Then I could survive a disaster, so I had no fear of accidents. Now I could get killed just as easily as anyone else." He lowered his eyes. "Perhaps you're used to that risk. I'm not. Mortality is new to me. And I'm having trouble accepting that one aspect of being a normal man. I'd grown used to thinking of myself as unable to die. It's not that I'm not willing to die someday—I wanted to be mortal, to have a normal life span like everyone else. But I'm afraid of dying too soon, of being separated from you again, because of some accident or disease."

"Everyone is afraid of that," Veronica said.

"You say it so easily. You've accepted the risks. How?"

Veronica felt puzzled. "I don't know. We all follow advice about eating right, using seat belts, getting regular checkups, and so on. That's the best anyone can do, so why worry? If you worry so much about what *might* happen, it spoils the life you have."

"I can't even visit a doctor," David said, his expression growing more morose. He seemed to have missed her point. "Who knows what a doctor might find doing a simple blood test? He might suspect my history is different from other people's."

Veronica shook his shoulders. "No wonder Darienne always thought you were so awfully serious! What would she say if she were here now listening to you go on in such a morbid way?"

David's expression grew sardonic. "I hate to think. She'd tell me to stop complaining or go back to being a vampire." He turned to look out the window and squinted at the bright morning sunlight now flooding the room. "I wonder where she is."

Darienne was a vampiress who had known David since they were mortal adolescents of about the same age in France in the late 1500s. She could have taken the same herb formula David used recently to revert to the mortal state, but she'd had no wish to. Darienne loved being the glittering, seductive, creature of the night that she'd been for centuries.

"She might be in London," Veronica said, remembering the last time they saw Darienne, six months ago, soon after David had become mortal. Darienne had had a long affair with Matthew McDowall, who had not realized that his sensual blond mistress was a vampiress until just before their relationship ended. Matthew left her then, saying he was going back to his ex-wife. Veronica remembered how devastated Darienne had looked, though Darienne had tried to cover her hurt feelings. "Wasn't she going to London to try to find Matthew's son?"

David leaned his head back against the seat again, as if tired. "I hope she didn't follow through on that impulse. But she seemed intent on it, and there was no way I could stop her. She probably found and seduced that young fellow to try to turn him into a replacement for his father. I'm afraid she may have transformed him into a vampire to satisfy her insatiable needs."

"Now that she doesn't have you anymore?" Veronica said, lifting her eyebrows.

Darienne had had an on-again, off-again, sexual relationship with David spanning four centuries. Darienne's superhuman sexual needs could be fully satiated only by another vampire. Veronica had heard that she'd tried to turn the man she loved, Matthew, into a vampire against his will. It was at that point, apparently, that Matthew had left Darienne for good. And now that David was "a puny mortal," as Darienne had put it, she wouldn't be returning to David for sex anymore. Which was just as well, Veronica thought with some sense of security, now that David was married to her. She actually liked Darienne and had come to understand and accept Darienne's past history with him. But she did not want to share her husband under any circumstances, not even with his oldest friend.

"No, she doesn't have me anymore, thank God," David was saying, his eyes on the kitten as it crouched while watching a bird outside the window. "And she doesn't have Matthew, either. She doesn't have anyone, unless she's found Matthew's son and had her way with him." He looked at Veronica. "That's another thing. If we go to London, Darienne may be there, Matthew has started filming there, his ex-wife will probably be with him, and Matthew's son lives there—well, what a mix-up that could turn into! Darienne might even try to revive her relationship with Matthew. She could cause no end of trouble."

"But those aren't your problems," Veronica said.

"But they'd come to me for advice, don't you see? Both Matthew *and* Darienne. Separately, of course. But they've both come to me in the past. Darienne never listens to what I say, yet that has never stopped her from coming to me whenever she pleases to hash out everything. And Matthew would come to me because he knows I understand what Darienne is like. I no longer have the superhuman strength that one needs to deal with such people and such problems. If she tries to attack Matthew again, I can't rescue him. She's stronger than me now."

"But it's *their* problem, David. Matthew rescued himself last time. You didn't even know she'd attacked him until he told you afterward, when it was all over. If one or the other asks you for advice, well, tell them what you think, and then let it go. You have your own life now."

"But how could I not get involved?" he argued. "It's naive to think I wouldn't—*we* wouldn't. It's inevitable. That's why I don't want to go to London, Veronica. This trip may bring us nothing but trouble—arguments with the director about my script, Darienne's endless entanglements, and besides all that I hate to travel!"

Veronica had trouble keeping her patience. Sometimes it seemed she'd married a worrywart. When David was a vampire, he used to worry, too. Indeed, he was filled with angst about his vampire existence and pondered constantly over his guilt and the morality of his every action. But perhaps because he had superior strength, he carried his grief gracefully, with a dignity that made him heroic. He used to have a sense of perspective. But now . . . sometimes Veronica felt as if she were married to an ordinary man, the sort of morose husband who worried about health, taxes, and crabgrass, who had lost the perspective of the wider world around him, of philosophy and poetry. David rarely quoted Shakespeare anymore. He used to, all the time.

She wouldn't ever ask him to be a vampire again—not that she would mind if he was one. But he'd been so unhappy as a vampire; for his sake she didn't want him to return to that state. Yet he didn't seem altogether happy being mortal either. All she wanted was for him to be the *man* he used to be, that he still could be, immortal or not. The man she had fallen in love with.

"But David, we have the plane tickets," she said, running her hands over his shoulders and down his biceps, "our bags are packed, and they're expecting you in London. We have to go. So what's the use of fretting about it?" She moved her hands inward, sliding her fingers over his pectoral muscles, then downward over his rib cage, enjoying the feel of his firm, manly body. "Why not just relax, go with the flow?"

He did seem to relax and looked at her with deepening eyes. Placing his hands on her thighs astride him, he murmured, "If you keep this up, we'll never leave the house."

"No, no." She smiled. "We'll leave on schedule. But we have a little extra time . . ." She unbuttoned the pajama top and let it slip down her arms to the floor.

He breathed in while his eyes scanned her bared body. His warm, large hands slipped around her back, and he pulled her closer. "I love you," he said with feeling just before he kissed her. His mouth on hers grew more ardent as he locked her in his strong embrace, pulling her so close her breasts crushed against him and the breath was pushed out of her lungs. She loved being made to feel weak and overwhelmed by his strength. The feeling was akin to how she'd felt with him when they first knew each other, when he was superhuman.

But she kissed him back with every ounce of her own strength, winding her arms around his neck, tangling her fingers in his thick, dark hair, which was exactly the same shade of brown as her own. His mouth left hers, and he bent his head to kiss her collarbone. She closed her eyes at the feel of him, and smiled when he lifted her slightly so he could slide kisses down to her breasts. When she felt him tease her nipple with his teeth, then the arousing tug of his lips suckling her, she gasped with delight and began to breathe faster. She wanted more. That old obsessed feeling of wanting, knowing, needing, nothing but David that had overpowered her for so many years, returned, and she found she still craved the sensation.

She missed that intimate vampire bond they'd had, that had begun when he'd taken her blood and she'd fallen under his power. Their supernatural bond had disappeared when he became mortal. And now there wasn't an hour of any day when the remembrance of it didn't cross her mind, however fleetingly. Making love with David, being turned on by him sensually, made her feel obsessed with him again, at least until the lovemaking was over. And Veronica had grown addicted to feeling obsessed years ago.

She felt his arousal against her inner thigh and smiled with eagerness. While he continued to nuzzle and kiss her breasts, she reached down to unsnap his pajama pants. When the engorged length of him was freed, she fondled him between her hands for a few moments, anticipating her own joy.

When he chuckled, she looked up. "What?" she asked with a grin she was sure revealed her excitement.

"We just did this in bed six or seven hours ago. And now you've got me all fired up again. This isn't how married people are supposed to behave."

"How do we know? Neither of us has ever been married before."

"True. Still, I thought wives were always supposed to claim they had a headache. But you want this—me—all the time. I'm not complaining, mind you." He gave her a quick, enflamed kiss on the mouth. "I'm just impressed, and happily mystified."

"I enjoy wanting you," she said. Her voice dropped to a needy whisper. "I love to feel you inside me, to feel as though I can't get enough of you, be close enough with you."

His eyes grew serious and sad. He was about to say something, but she kissed him on the mouth quickly to prevent him. While they kissed, she rose up slightly, then came down, taking the velvet length of him within her pulsing body. The sensation made her feel delirious and rich with emotional fulfillment. His flesh filled the empty space she'd saved for him alone for so long. Wanting him had become a worshipful ritual in the long years they were separated. And now appeasement was like a sacrament for her, and a powerful, tangible reminder of the otherworld relationship they once shared.

David's breathing had grown fast, and she let go of the kiss so they both could breathe easier. His gaze locked with hers, his eyes as luminous in the sunlight as blue stained glass. She looked back at him, easy and comfortable with such an intense, silent eye contact, while their bodies moved together in a gentle back-and-forth rhythm.

When they'd had their bond, they could feel each other's feelings, even at a distance. In fact, she'd been able to feel his mind in hers and hers in his. And this, this cerebral and physical coupling during sex, was almost like sharing each other's feelings again, the way it used to be. It was why neither felt any wish to look away, or even blink; they could engage in such direct eye contact with no sense of self-consciousness or shyness or intimidation.

This was a depth of intimacy few mortals were willing or able to experience. But for Veronica it was something she'd grown used to during the early years of her relationship with David, and it could never feel strange. This was the legacy of their bond, this ability and willingness to fuse her soul to his for these few moments without fear or inhibition. Since she could no longer have the bond, she'd content herself with this. It was more than most couples had, and she was grateful.

The sensations within her began to build as they writhed together with sweet sensuality. When he brought his long fingers down between their bodies to touch the quick of her, she gasped, a sound between a sob and a laugh, and closed her eyes for a moment, the sensation was so pleasantly shocking. When she opened her eyes, he was still looking at her, smiling with adoration as he studied every nuance of her passing expressions, every small reaction to his caresses of her body.

He seemed to delight in giving her pleasure, and the knowledge of that brought a sheen of tears to Veronica's eyes. He'd always been this sensitive and caring, this focused on her and her alone, as if no other woman had ever mattered to him. This was why she never worried about his past experiences with Darienne, or other women he might have known over the centuries. There might even have been a woman in his life while they were separated, a relationship that probably developed out of his loneliness without her. But when he looked at her this way, she knew he wasn't comparing her in his mind to anyone from his past, not even voluptuous Darienne. His eyes and being seemed to be filled only with her, as if there were no room for even a thought of anyone else, just as her mind and body were filled with him alone. No other man had ever adored her this way. She wondered if there were many women in the world who had such a man to love them, a man capable of knowing and showing his feelings so directly and without reserve.

"Oh, David," she breathed, smiling as she used her thigh muscles to move against him while he continued to touch her intimately. "I love to make love with you."

With his free hand he stroked her hair at the side of her face down to her shoulder, where it fell past her collarbone, almost reaching her breast. He cupped her breast with his hand, rubbed the nipple with his thumb, and watched as she inhaled a long breath of deep arousal. "How sensual and beautiful you are," he whispered. "You respond to me so sweetly. You make me feel male through and through. I want to give you everything, make you happy, keep you near me." A shadow came into his eyes. "Don't ever leave me."

She touched his face. "Why would I leave you?"

"Just don't." He brought his mouth to hers, and they shared a long, deep kiss. His lips trailed warmly along her cheek and jaw, then downward along her neck. He didn't often kiss her on the neck, and she began to take in shallow, quick breaths in anticipation as he neared her pulse point.

The delicate skin above her artery was scarred with two small, barely noticeable marks. These were the marks David had made when he first took her blood, marks which were slow to heal, in fact were not allowed to heal, because she would beg him to drink from her again, and sometimes he did. The ecstasy of feeling him take her blood, the knowledge that she was nourishing him, the spell of being so fully under his vampire power, were memories Veronica would cherish always.

And now the sensation of his mouth moving downward to touch her there again made her ready to weep with anticipation of a fulfillment she could no longer have. Still, she so badly wanted him to place his lips on her scars, just to have a small experience again of what it was like . . .

His mouth fixed at that point on her neck with heat and tenderness, sending a shudder through her soul and making her weep. "David," she whispered on a little sob. "Oh, David."

He drew away and looked at her, tears welling in his eyes. "You're shaking. You miss our old ways, don't you? You wish I was still a vampire."

She wanted to say no, but would he believe her? She wasn't exactly sure what she would want, if she could have anything she wanted. "I do miss the way things used to be, sometimes. I wish I could give you my blood again, that you would take that from me as well as possess my body. There was nothing like that experience." She wiped away a tear with her hand. "But I like what we have now, too."

"But it's not the same for you, is it? What we have now is commonplace. An ordinary marriage. I can't give you that superhuman ecstasy we once shared. I don't want to ever be a vampire again. Yet it grieves me to know that I'm disappointing you."

Veronica didn't know what to say. She wanted to reassure him, and yet what he said held a lot of truth. "I don't think our marriage is ordinary, David. I think we're closer than most men and women ever get in a relationship. And when we make love like this, you *are* still the same man I fell in love with years ago. No one could thrill me the way you do."

"But I used to thrill you more."

She made a little shrug and stroked his face. "Maybe, but I'm happy with what we have. Do I complain?"

"No," he said, lifting her hair away from her face. "You're too sweet to complain. And I know you love me. But, among mortals, love doesn't always last. There's no bond to keep us obsessed with one another. You may grow weary of me one day."

"No, David. Would you grow weary of me?"

His eyes grew startled. "Never. But it's different for me. I chose you after knowing hundreds of women over hundreds of years. You've only known me in your little lifetime. How do you know there isn't some other ordinary man who could make you happier than I can? Someone who's more carefree than I, less of a chore to be with."

This made Veronica laugh. "A chore?"

"Well, I know I grumble about traveling, while you look forward to it. I'm overly concerned about things . . ."

"That just makes you lovable."

"You mean, like some old curmudgeon?"

"Except you don't look nearly as old as you are." She kissed him and moved her body against his sensually again, picking up where they'd briefly left off. "And you're far too sexy for me to get bored with you. If your worrying gets on my nerves, just caress me. I'll forget in minutes." As the need for physical fulfillment began to grow strong, she looked at him, allowing all her love and need to show unashamedly in her eyes. "You still have power over me, David. It's a little different, less overwhelming and easier for me to cope with, but it's there . . . it's there. When you make love with me, I still worship you . . ." Her voice left off in ragged breaths as she held on tightly to his shoulders. His hands moved to her hips and pressed her body more firmly against his as she moved up and down over him, his flesh deep inside her.

"I worship you, too," he said, his voice husky with passion. "My precious little wife. You're everything to me . . . everything . . ."

Veronica could say no more, for the sensations of their lovemaking overtook all thought and made her aware only of the coming fulfillment with David. She began to breathe in deep gasps, almost sobs, growing desperate for the moment to arrive. And then that brief instant of quieting came, and she felt suspended, looking into David's eyes as if for eternity. Together they shared the anticipation, and then the bliss. She held on tight to him as her body shuddered with deep, consuming climaxes and she cried out his name. She felt his body stiffen as he, too, cried out. And then they both relaxed.

It wasn't the flight into the stars, the world of ethereal lights and freedom he'd taken her to during sex when he was a vampire. But it was wonderful, and she was more than satisfied. She ran her fingers through his hair as he moved his hands over her back soothingly.

"See?" she said with a little grin. "Do I look unhappy?"

He smiled at her. "No, I must say, you don't look the least bit unhappy."

"Neither do you, now. You know, we can still do this when we're in London, too."

"I hope so! I'll need you to help me forget I'm there."

She mussed his hair. "You might enjoy London after all. Try thinking positive!"

"I'll try. But it's rather a foreign concept to me."

Lovemaking had transcended his mortal mind-set and for a few moments had brought him out of himself, had made him more like the man he'd used to be. Now he was falling back into his usual self. But Veronica had patience, and hope. He'd only been mortal for six months. Eventually, he'd regain his old perspective and renew his wisdom. He just needed time and her love. This she was happy to give. If only he believed in himself the way she believed in him.

As she moved off of him and picked up the pajama top she'd discarded, the scent of semen came to her nostrils. She slipped her arms into the pajama sleeves and went over to the window to pick up Tabitha, who was dozing on the windowsill. Tabitha had followed her home one day when she'd run out to do some shopping. David had no objection to keeping the kitten, so Veronica named her and fed her. But often the little cat preferred David's company, which amused Veronica. Tabitha was like a toddler who liked Mommy well enough, but whose eyes lit up when Daddy came home from work.

"David," she said, scratching the kitten behind the ears, "now that you're a normal man, do you think you're normal in every way?"

David's eyes moved back and forth, obviously confused as to what she was asking. "I assume I am," he said, putting up his hand as he looked toward her to shield his eyes from the bright sunlight coming through the window behind her. "What do you mean?"

"Well," she said, walking up to him, still carrying the kitten, "before, you . . . you couldn't have children. But now . . . ?"

"Do I have active sperm, you mean?"

"Yes. Can I get pregnant? I hadn't thought of it till now. I was so used to not having to think about that possibility in the past. For some reason, it just occurred to me."

His eyes took on a new aspect as he stood and turned to her. "I have no idea. Vampires are sterile. But now that I'm mortal, all my other bodily functions have gone back to normal. I suppose that may have, too." His gaze focused on her face. "Do you want a child?"

The question frightened her a bit, gave her a sense of awe. "I don't know. I haven't thought about it. Do you?"

His shoulders seemed to fall, as if weighted by a new

burden. "I've never thought about being a father. Except perhaps when I was first a mortal four hundred years ago. But then, I wasn't married and was preoccupied with pursuing other goals. And after I became a vampire, there was no point in thinking about it. It wasn't possible or even desirable."

"Well, I suppose it's something we should think about. In the meantime, maybe we should take precautions until we're sure what we want to do."

He smiled. "Us, take precautions about sex? That'll be a novelty."

She grinned and pushed her hand against his rib cage. "We better go have breakfast and get dressed. My cousin will be here in a couple of hours to pick up Tabitha." She pressed her cheek to the cat's fur. "Poor kitty. I hope she won't be scared away from home."

"She already knows and likes Harriet. She'll be all right." He reached out to tug Veronica's hair. "I can see now, if you become a mother, it'll be you who turns into a worrywart."

She made a face at him. "Would not."

"Would, too."

She began to laugh and was glad he was in a fun-loving mood. "Go get dressed. We have a plane to catch!"

That afternoon, as they got into a hired shuttle van to take them to the airport, David felt tense and had a headache. Veronica had given him some aspirin, but it didn't seem to help much. The sunlight seemed unusually bright and hurt his eyes, even though the sky had gotten somewhat cloudy. David pulled out his sunglasses as he gave the driver directions. Veronica watched him and asked, "Does the sun hurt your eyes? I noticed you were squinting this morning, too."

"Hasn't it seemed bright to you today?"

"Not that bad."

"It *is* midsummer. A lot of people wear sunglasses," he said, adjusting them on his face.

"Yes, but I thought your eyes had grown accustomed to daylight as well as mine are. The last week or so, it seems to bother you again, the way it did when you were first cured." His eyes had been so unused to sunlight, from living only at night as a vampire, that the sun had hurt his eyes for a few weeks, until he'd fully adjusted to daylight.

"Shh." David indicated the driver in the seat ahead of them, who could certainly overhear.

Veronica nodded and spoke more softly. "And you've been getting headaches sometimes." Her eyebrows lifted, as if with a new thought. "Maybe it's tension. Worry about this trip."

"That must be it," David said, refusing to think it could be anything else. "Did you pack aspirin and that stuff you buy for indigestion?" He had to rely on Veronica, who knew her way around a drugstore, to choose the over-the-counter remedies all mortals used for their everyday ailments—colds, headaches, muscle aches, stomach upset. David still had trouble getting used to all these little nuisances. Other than an occasional headache, he'd never gotten any such symptoms when he was a vampire.

"I brought everything along," Veronica said. "Besides, I'm sure they have drugstores in London."

"No doubt."

"Is your stomach bothering you?" she asked. "You didn't eat much for lunch."

"No, no, I'm fine. I just wasn't hungry."

He'd noticed a lack of appetite for food lately and didn't know what it stemmed from. Vampires, of course, had no desire for food, only blood. And they couldn't endure sunlight. David knew these facts from centuries of experience. He also knew that when he took the cure, Herman, a Swiss vampire scientist he'd consulted by phone about the remedy, had told him that there was a five to ten percent chance that the cure wouldn't last, that David could revert to his vampire state. The question of whether he should tie these facts together or not played in David's mind as the shuttle sped them to the airport.

Another reason for not wanting to go to London, which he hadn't told Veronica, was his niggling fear that the squinting at sunlight and his lack of appetite might be the first signs that he was reverting. If this were true, it wasn't a time to be away from home. David had kept his coffin, still locked in the secret room in the basement of the Oak Street mansion, just in case he did not remain mortal. He hoped to God he would never have to use it again.

But David was sure that his symptoms were only everyday human maladies anyone might get. They probably meant nothing at all. As Veronica said, they were only a result of his tension about this blasted trip to London he'd been talked into. He'd do what was needed and come home again, fast as he could.

Veronica took his arm and snuggled up to him, laying her head on his shoulder. He tried to put his worries out of his mind and took hold of his wife's hand. Thank God for Veronica. Everything had to work out all right, for her sake.

2

Strawberry Hill

THE PLANE landed safely in London the next morning, after a smooth flight. David's nerves were frayed nevertheless, and he was glad to step off the aircraft into Heathrow Airport. The airport was a hub of activity. The noise, the confusion, the crush of people made David's head swim. When they reached customs with their luggage, David pulled out his passport, which he'd paid a large sum of money to have forged some years ago. Vampires who are hundreds of years old cannot show a birth certificate to obtain such documents. David did not want to do anything illegal, but he had no other choice. Veronica displayed her own quite legal passport, her very first, which listed her new, married name, Veronica de Morrissey.

After passing through customs, they took a taxicab to Claridge's in the handsome Mayfair district, which David knew well and had watched develop over the centuries. He remembered the yearly cattle market in the late 1600s, which for decades was held every year in May in this area. The fair thrived and drew every huckster and sideshow from the adjacent, growing London metropolis. He could still remember the sounds, smells, and sights, for the fair bustled with activity even after dark. But by the 1730s the fair had been stopped because of the development of the "Mayfair" area by a consortium of builders. Mayfair was turned into an aristocratic quarter whose well-planned streets became, by the latter part of the eighteenth century, lined with splendid homes. Here, for example, Handel had lived on Brook Street for nearly forty years. David was a well-known playwright in that era, too, and he'd been privileged to meet the composer. Nowadays, many of these buildings served as embassies, the headquarters of international airlines, and other offices.

David had chosen Claridge's not for its historical setting, however, but for its reputation as "the most discreet hotel in London." The protection of guests' privacy included fending off the curious and discouraging the news media, which made the hotel a favorite of those in the public eye. As the multiple-award-winning creator of *The Scarlet Shadow*, which was still playing in many cities throughout the world, David had become more famous as a playwright than he'd ever been in past eras. He'd become known as a reclusive celebrity, who refused interviews from *People* and other magazines and TV shows. He'd even declined to be interviewed by Barbara Walters. Though he was mortal now and could walk about in daylight as readily as anyone else, in his mind the secret of his dark past hung about him, and he still feared discovery. David had stayed at Claridge's as a vampire in decades gone by, and he chose it again now for the same reasons he'd chosen it then.

Veronica gasped as they entered the handsome lobby, with its checkered marble floor pattern, high ceiling, and polished staircase. David experienced a moment of alarm when he noted his wife was wearing pants, but then remembered that Claridge's had finally, though not so long ago, agreed to allow women in trousers. Darienne had once been barred entry several decades ago because she'd arrived in an outfit similar to one Marlene Dietrich had made headlines wearing. In a huff, Darienne had vowed never to return to Claridge's again. And this made another reason why David wanted to stay at this particular hotel.

They registered and were shown to their suite, an elegant bedroom, bath, and sitting room with a working fireplace and decorated with antiques. They had barely begun to explore it when a hotel staff person arrived to deliver a message. It was from Nolan Wolf, the director of *The Scarlet Shadow* film. The phoned-in message said he and the crew were filming today with Matthew McDowall at Strawberry Hill in Twickenham.

He hoped David and his wife would come this afternoon, if they weren't too tired from the long flight. Nolan needed his help with the script as soon as possible. The studio would provide transportation, and a phone number was given for David to call.

"Already?" David said with a sigh.

"I'd love to go," Veronica said, "if you're not tired."

"Aren't you?"

"I managed to sleep on the plane."

"I wish I had," David said. "All right, we'll go. I might as well see what snares await me."

They arrived sometime later at Strawberry Hill, on the outskirts of London. As they left the limousine and walked up to the location, David confided quietly to Veronica that he remembered the place well. This was Horace Walpole's famous house, he told her, built during the 1700s into a Gothic villa, which Walpole had furnished according to his imaginative and educated taste. Walpole, who was the Earl of Orford, was an English wit and writer. David remembered particularly the occasion, in 1757, when he'd established his own private printing press at Strawberry Hill. Here he printed not only his own works, but those of others, including a book of poems David had written. The edition had sold at a very high price, because of the small number printed, but it had been a mild success within literary circles.

"Do you remember any of the poems you wrote?" Veronica asked, eyes wide with interest.

David thought a moment. "Not even a stanza," he replied with a dry smile, thinking his poems couldn't have been terribly profound or he would have remembered something of them. Plays had always been his forte.

Strawberry Hill now served as St. Mary's College, and from all David could see, they had with scrupulous care kept the place preserved in all its ornate splendor. Arrangements must have been made by the studio well in advance in order to film here.

When David and Veronica entered, they found the cameras and crew at work in a long, impressive room with a parquet floor set in a diamond pattern. The room featured a high cathedral ceiling the plaster of which was molded into an intricate design of interlaced spoked circles, which rose in graceful curves from the upper part of the walls to form a great arch. Numerous large paintings covered the walls, and a tiled fireplace was recessed into one wall. Antique chairs and cabinets had been rearranged for the filming. David was instantly brought back to that early era of his long life, recalling in particular a gathering he'd attended one evening in this same room. He and others had been invited to read selections of their own works to a party of elaborately adorned aristocrats and literary elite.

David brought himself back to the present, looked past the cameras and lights, and saw Matthew McDowall standing by a chair, playing a scene with another actor. It apparently was the brief scene David had put into the script in which Sir Percy Blackeney, the English nobleman who was secretly the Scarlet Shadow, was receiving news of revolutionary France. David's musical, of course, had been based on the storyline of *The Scarlet Pimpernel* by Baroness Orczy. In David's version, however, Sir Percy was a vampire.

Matthew was dressed in a blond wig and an elaborate eighteenth-century costume with a lavender satin coat and long lace at his neck and wrists. Nolan stood near the camera, watching as they finished the scene. Apparently satisfied, Nolan gave the actors a break while they set up for the next shot. Matthew's stand-in was called.

Matthew smiled when he saw David and Veronica, and he hastened over to the doorway where they were standing. "I'm happy to see you," he said, shaking David's hand. "And you, Veronica. You look lovely. Marriage obviously suits you!"

Veronica smiled back. "It sure does!"

At that point Nolan, a handsome, fiftyish man with graying brown hair and glasses, came up to David, hand outstretched. David had met him briefly in Chicago after Nolan had been selected as director by the studio that was making the film. Nolan had come to Chicago to discuss the script with him. David had found him pleasant enough but rather difficult to communicate with.

"I'd like to go over some things with you," Nolan said after they'd greeted each other. "I'll be free in about ten minutes."

He left, and David turned back to Matthew. "How are you?"

"Well enough," Matthew said. It was difficult for David to tell if this was true by looking at the actor, for he wore a great deal of makeup to make him appear blond, pale, and a bit younger than his years. Matthew was in his late forties now and might have been passed over for the heroic, romantic leading role if he had not made such a memorable hit onstage as Sir Percy. He also possessed a magnificent singing voice and brilliant acting instincts born of experience, which would have been difficult, if not impossible, to match in a younger actor. David would have settled for no one else.

Matthew motioned them to another room, so they could talk without disturbing the crew. "I was really happy to hear of your wedding. Are you content now with your life . . . I mean, being a normal man again?" Matthew was one of the very few who knew David's secret history.

"I'm very happy, although I would have preferred to stay in Chicago," David told him with asperity as they sat down on some folding canvas director's chairs that looked incongruous in the eighteenth-century library.

"David doesn't like to travel," Veronica said.

"I wish I could have stayed in New York," Matthew said, bowing his head a bit. "My leaving to film this movie upset Natalie." He was referring to his ex-wife, with whom he'd reunited six months ago, when he'd broken his relationship with Darienne. "She said I was putting my career ahead of her again. That's why our marriage failed twenty years ago."

"But she's here with you, isn't she?" Veronica asked, looking puzzled. "A gossip column in the paper said she was coming with you."

"At first she was going to. But at the last minute she changed her mind," Matthew told them, sadness in his voice. "I was studying the script and getting preoccupied with making the movie. She said she could see I hadn't changed, that she was still second place in my life, and she wasn't going to come to London with me. In fact, she said she didn't want to try anymore to rekindle our relationship."

He paused and drew a breath. "She was right. It wasn't working. You can't always revive a love that's gone through as much wear and tear, and anger, as ours has. We're different people now. I have to accept that. It's just sad, that's all. I'd hoped to have someone permanent in my life, for a change. I'd hoped it would be her." He lifted his broad shoulders in a resigned shrug. "Maybe I'm meant to be single."

"I'm sorry," David said, feeling empathy for the actor. He knew what it was to be alone, to have no one.

Matthew nodded. "I envy you. I wish I had your happy marriage and beautiful bride," he said, smiling again at Veronica. "I had that once, when I was too young to appreciate it. Now I can't get it back. Too set in my ways, too ambitious for my career."

He stretched restlessly in the chair and glanced toward the doorway, as if waiting for someone to call him back to the cameras. "I'd forgotten what a bore it is making a movie. You spend more time sitting around than working. And when you do work, you have to reshoot a scene dozens of times before they're happy. Onstage, it's once straight through, like riding a roller coaster. When you're done, you're exhilarated and satisfied. And you hear applause." His eyes took on a warm, faraway look.

David could see Matthew was deeply dissatisfied, both with his life and his work. He liked and admired the gifted actor and wished he could help. "How long have you been in London?"

"Three weeks. I arrived after filming had started, and there have been squabbles about the script since before I got here. It's Solange, mainly," he said in a whisper, referring to the French actress chosen by the director to play Marguerite. After insisting on Matthew for the film, David had agreed to allow all other parts to be cast by the director and the studio, since David had little knowledge of actors and their availability. "The lines you wrote for Marguerite just never seem to work for Solange," Matthew continued in a humorous, sarcastic tone. "Marguerite wouldn't say this or that, she's constantly informing us. She complains she hasn't enough lines, either. But she has Nolan's ear. In fact, she has a lot more of him than that, but that little nugget hasn't hit the tabloids yet. He's married."

"I see," David said with a sigh. "Perhaps if I explain her character to her in French, it would help."

"Anything's worth a try. She pays no attention to my insights, even though I did the stage show and understand your concept. Maybe you'll have better luck. You have longer experience than I at handling a narcissistic French beauty." David guessed Matthew was making a reference to Darienne. "Solange isn't on the set today. Tomorrow, she will be, though. We'll be shooting here again."

At that point Nolan came in to speak to David. He was carrying a script. Matthew rose to go. "I probably need my makeup retouched. How about dinner together tonight?" he asked, looking at David and then Veronica.

Veronica smiled and nodded.

"A great idea," David readily agreed and suggested the Causerie at Claridge's, where Matthew was also staying. He wanted to talk to Matthew about Darienne.

David spent the rest of the afternoon arguing about his script with Nolan, leaving Veronica to wander about the historic house and watch Matthew complete his day's work in front of the camera.

Two hours later, when David had finished with Nolan, he found Veronica in one corner of the library, on tiptoe, looking at an upper shelf of books.

"Find something?" he asked, placing his hand on her shoulder as he came up behind her.

"Is that your book of poems?"

David peered up at the small volume, bound in aged leather, that she was pointing at. "Good Lord, it is!" The spine of the book read, *Poems by D. de Morrissey.*

"Can we take it down and look at it?" she asked.

David mentally debated the matter. "These old volumes are very fragile. I don't think we should risk injuring them by trying to pull this one out. I have my own copy of that edition—somewhere. When we're home again, I'll find it for you."

"Okay," Veronica said, sounding a trifle disappointed. "I did see a caretaker peeking in here a little while ago."

David slipped his arm around her as they headed toward the door to go back to Claridge's. "That was sweet of you to look for my book. I'm amazed it's still here."

"I'm amazed I'm married to someone like you." Veronica looked up at him with admiration. "You've had artistic influence in ages past, and you do now, too."

"Yes, well, my influence on this film has been tenuous at best. Now I have an ambitious actress and a love-smitten director to rescue my script from. Even if you live long, life doesn't get easier."

At dinner that night in the Causerie, Veronica and David sat across from Matthew at a spotless linen-draped table with sparkling china and wineglasses. The actor's makeup had been removed, and he appeared rested and well, David thought. Matthew might look his age, but he made the age look enviable. David wondered if he himself would hold up so well a dozen or more years from now, when he'd attained Matthew's biological age. The deep lines around Matthew's eyes seemed to have lessened, and his color was ruddy and healthy, erasing the stark, exhausted look he'd had from overwork when David last saw him. The actor's graying brown hair curling over his broad forehead gave him a sporty, fun-loving appearance that had suited the comic roles that had first made him famous.

They ordered from the menu. Veronica voiced some concern when David ordered only a salad, but he simply wasn't hungry. "Jet lag," he told her.

Matthew studied him, brows drawn together. "You do look tired, David. Better get some sleep."

David smiled, rather amused. Matthew himself was notorious for pushing himself far beyond his limits while doing his stage role. Darienne had constantly been concerned about him. Which reminded David of what he'd wanted to say. "I don't mean to bring up a touchy subject, but I must ask—have you seen or heard from Darienne?"

"Not since the night I left her in Chicago and flew to New York." He gestured toward David. "You and Veronica were there. That's the last I know of her."

David nodded, considering how much he should say. He didn't want to cause unnecessary alarm.

"How was she after I left you all that night? Was she upset?" Matthew asked, glancing at Veronica. David noticed, as Matthew must have, how troubled her expression had become.

"I think she was devastated," Veronica said. "She tried to keep her chin up and pretend she'd get over it, but . . ." Her voice trailed off.

Matthew seemed to grow uncomfortable. "She attacked me," he said in a slightly defensive tone. "She wanted to transform me, to make me . . . ," he glanced around as if aware he was in a restaurant and couldn't speak too freely, "to make me what she is," he finished in a lowered voice. "Frankly, she scared the hell out of me. I was with her for three years and never knew her secret. Then she told me everything and wanted to transform me, so I could be immortal, too—have superior strength and so on. Of course, it intrigued me at first." He looked at David. "You remember the long discussion you and I had."

"I do," David said, recalling the night Matthew had come to him for advice, without Darienne's knowledge. "I did my best to talk you out of it."

"Indeed you did. What clinched it was when she showed me her *coffin,*" he said, whispering the word. "It upset me so much, I felt ill and almost blacked out. As I tried to get away, she followed, still trying to convince me. Finally, she had me pinned against the door. I actually felt her teeth at my jugular. The only way I escaped alive was by telling her that if she transformed me, I'd stay up until the sun rose and destroy myself. I'd commit immortal suicide. That stopped her. She said she couldn't bear it if I weren't somewhere on earth, whether alive or undead. And that's when she told me she loved me."

Matthew toyed with his wineglass. "That threw me. She'd never said that before. We'd agreed from the beginning our affair was supposed to be without commitments. No big emotional thing. I'd admired her independence and I was tired of women who clung to me, wanting more than I could give. She admitted she'd been in love with me all along, but she'd never told me because she was afraid I'd leave."

He drew in a long breath. "Well, I did leave her." He looked at David, then rested his eyes on Veronica, as if he felt he had to justify himself to her rather than to David. "Funny way for her to show she loved me, to attack me like that, against my will. Don't you think? Like a man who rapes his girlfriend, then claims he did it because he loved her."

Veronica's expression softened. "I hadn't thought of it that way. Darienne shouldn't have tried to do what she did." She leaned across the table toward Matthew in an earnest posture. "But she *did* stop. In the end, she didn't harm you."

Matthew's expression grew harrowed. "It was a pretty close call!"

"Were you in love with her?" Veronica asked.

The actor's eyes widened, as if the question took him off guard. He seemed at a loss for words for a moment. Finally, he said, "I'm not sure I know what love is. When I was young and met Natalie, I was sure I was in love then. I don't know what I feel nowadays. For anyone, including Natalie." He paused as a thought seemed to come to him. "A British actor, Sir Cedric Hardwicke, once said that anyone who has been an actor for any length of time doesn't know whether he has any true emotions or not." Matthew shrugged. "Maybe I've been an actor too long."

Veronica looked wistful. David was watching with interest her passing facial expressions. He turned, ruefully, to Matthew. "I think Veronica feels sympathy for Darienne. They're fond of one another, even though they're so different."

"Darienne was always on my side when you and I were apart for so long," Veronica explained to David. "I feel bad that she's unhappy now."

"But how do we know she is?" David said. "No one has heard from her. Or knows where she is."

The waiter delivered their food. Both Matthew and Veronica had ordered Beef Wellington. David had a shrimp salad.

"Wherever Darienne is," Veronica continued when the waiter had left, "I'll bet she still misses Matthew." She looked across the table at the actor. "I could see in her eyes how crushed she was at losing you that night. I've never seen her look that way before. It's not something she'd get over quickly. It would be like me trying to get over losing David."

Matthew studied Veronica a moment, the lines about his eyes deepening with thought. Then he looked down at his plate, saying nothing.

David reached to take Veronica's hand and kissed it. He wanted to be sensitive to Veronica's trusting point of view. But he'd known Darienne for four hundred years. True, Darienne had been devastated, but she'd probably gotten over it. David just worried *how* she'd gotten over Matthew—and with whom.

He poked at his salad with his fork. "Matthew, I think perhaps you should be aware of something Darienne hinted at after you left us to catch your plane that night. We stayed with her for an hour or so to be sure she was all right. And she was. But just before we left her, she suddenly said she was going to fly to London. I had the feeling from her conversation that she'd gotten a brainstorm to come here and look up your son."

"Larry?" Matthew's brows drew together in an expression of alarm. "Why?"

"To replace you, I'm afraid."

"Replace me. How do you mean?"

David hesitated, not wanting to spell things out here in the dining room. "How do you think?"

A look of understanding crossed Matthew's eyes, but then he seemed perplexed again. "But Larry's a kid."

"Isn't he about twenty-five?" David asked. "He may seem young to you because he's your son. But a handsome man of that age is certainly fodder for Darienne's lusts. And I hear that . . . well, that he looks like you. I just had the feeling that she was thinking, If I can't have Matthew, I'll take the next best thing."

"My God," Matthew said under his breath. "She wouldn't attack *him,* would she?"

"I don't know," David said. "I'm sure she's not above seducing him sexually. I'm past being surprised by anything she might do."

Matthew looked agitated now and lost interest in his meal. "I wish I could have a good, long conversation with Larry. But he never wants to talk to me. Natalie and I flew to London together about four months ago especially to see him. It was Natalie's idea. She wanted my son and I to meet, and she convinced Larry to let us visit him. Larry blames me for the bitter divorce Natalie and I went through, and the fact that she was left to raise him alone." He lifted his shoulders in a shrug. "But that was Natalie's choice. When he was five, she kidnapped him from my custody and fled to Scotland, where they lived until he went off on his own to college in London. Though my son never saw or talked to me in all those years, apparently he always felt everything was my fault. He believed his mother wouldn't have taken such a drastic action if I hadn't been a neglectful father and husband. Maybe he's right. I don't know."

Matthew paused to collect his thoughts. "Sorry, I'm digressing. Anyway, Natalie and I flew to London and I met Larry. It didn't go well, mostly because Larry didn't like the fact that his mother, at that point, had accepted me back into her life. He vented all his feelings and opinions, said that I was selfish and self-centered and never gave a damn about either of them. I tried to give some explanations, but he wouldn't hear them. All his rancour eventually contributed to Natalie and I breaking up again, this last time. We both began to realize that we could never create a trusting family between the three of us. After she and I returned to New York, things began to go downhill. My doing this movie was the straw that broke the camel's back."

Matthew looked self-conscious, as if he felt he was saying more than he meant to. Then his expression brightened. "But while we were in London, we did meet Larry's girlfriend, Sheena. She's a raven-haired Scottish girl, a drama student, about twenty-two. They seemed very much in love, though she wasn't living with him. I think she keeps old-fashioned values. Natalie and I both liked her. Natalie hoped they'd get married, though I was afraid she might be jumping ahead a bit. Still, if my son did marry Sheena, I'd be pleased for him. Not that he'd give a damn what I thought." Matthew picked up his knife and fork and began to cut his meat.

"So he had a girlfriend as recently as four months ago," David said, realizing that might mean Darienne *hadn't* made any appearance in the young man's life.

"Sheena is still his girlfriend," Matthew said. "I phoned him when I arrived in London and then again about a week ago. Larry wasn't anxious to talk to me, and our conversations were brief. But both times I asked about Sheena, and he said she was fine and that they were still going together."

David began to relax. "If Larry has kept up his romance with Sheena, then it's unlikely Darienne has interfered. Unless he's cheating on Sheena."

Matthew's expression grew wry, and he shook his head. "Sheena's something of a Scottish spitfire, and I don't think she'd put up with anything like that. She even took Larry to task for giving me backtalk. That's why Natalie and I like her. She has a sense of fairness, and solid, old Scottish Presbyterian ideas of what's right and wrong. Natalie thinks Sheena can give our son some stability, which he didn't get from us. Or from me, anyway."

"Well, then, Darienne may never have even come to London!" David said with relief. He speared a shrimp with his fork. "I'm sorry now I worried you."

"No, I'm glad you told me. If she shows up somehow, somewhere, I'll know to be on guard, for me and my son."

"Is Larry an actor, too?" Veronica asked.

"He's been a radio announcer for the BBC for a few years, while he studied drama on the side. He wants to be a Shakespearean actor," Matthew said, glancing at David, who he knew had a special interest in Shakespeare. "In fact, he's shunned a couple of opportunities that came his way to do some modern comic roles. He doesn't want to follow in my footsteps, it seems." Matthew smiled sadly. "Larry even changed his name when he started his acting career. He's Laurence McFarland now. He didn't want to use his real name, McDowall."

"That must be painful for you," David said.

"I'm beyond pain." Matthew picked up his knife again to cut another bite. "If he winds up happy in his life, if he can manage to pursue his career and hold on to someone like Sheena, even start a family and keep it together, then I'll be thrilled for him and not mind if he never has much regard for me. He'll have accomplished more than I ever did."

They continued talking about other things, mostly script problems and gossip about Nolan and Solange, for the rest of the dinner. Afterward, David and Veronica retired early for a good night's sleep.

The next morning at Strawberry Hill, Matthew approached David and Veronica. Veronica had come along to watch the shoot and be with David, though she was feeling slightly ill.

Apparently the dinner last night had unsettled her stomach. She'd skipped breakfast.

"I decided to phone Larry last night, after dinner," Matthew told them, his eyes bright with excitement, "just to see how he was. Sheena answered. She was at his place decorating for a party. She said Larry was out rehearsing for a production of *Hamlet* at a small theater, and he had the title role. He never mentioned it to me. Tonight is his opening night, and the party is afterwards. I don't intend to crash his party uninvited, but Sheena said she could get me tickets for the play. I'm planning to go. He's refused my invitations to come to the set to see me, but he can't stop me from seeing *him* perform! Would you and Veronica like to go with me?"

David glanced at Veronica, who smiled and nodded. "Be happy to," David replied.

When Matthew left them to study his script, Veronica sat down in a nearby chair. "Still not feeling well?" David asked.

"I'll be okay. I just can't figure out what I ate that's bothering me. Matthew ate the same thing, and he seems fine. I hope I'm not coming down with the flu."

"Is there something you can take? Something I can get you?"

"Maybe some soda to drink."

David walked outside to the catering truck, which had provided various refreshments for the cast and crew. The bright sun hurt his eyes, so he got his sunglasses out of his shirt pocket. He carried them with him constantly during the day as protection from the sharp pain he felt at the backs of his eyes whenever he was outdoors, or even indoors by a window with sunlight flooding through.

The English girl who operated the small white van, with sides that lifted to display food, suggested ginger ale for an upset stomach. David had never heard of it. He hadn't gotten used to soft drinks yet. Bubbles on his tongue made him wince. But he brought the ginger ale back to Veronica, hoping it might help. He was concerned about his wife. In the six months they'd been married, he'd never known her to be sick. It was always he who complained of muscle aches from his exercise routine, and headaches. He'd even come down with a cold a few months ago, which Veronica never caught.

She'd been the one taking care of him all this time. He had no idea how to take care of her, not if she was sick. He knew how to give her emotional support, but physical illness he had little knowledge of.

Well, it was probably nothing. Something she'd eaten that "didn't agree" with her, as people always said—as if foods were capable of agreeing or disagreeing.

As he handed his wife the bottle of ginger ale and a paper cup with ice, he said, "The young lady recommended this. Is it all right?"

"Oh, thanks!" Veronica said, taking it from him. "I forgot about ginger ale. My mother used to drink it if something didn't agree with her."

David smiled at the phrase he'd just been thinking of. He stroked her hair. "Will you be all right?"

"Sure. Don't worry."

Her tone sounded reassuring, and David tried to relax. He had his script to argue about and Solange to deal with. The auburn-haired French beauty was pouting, much as Darienne would, because David had told Nolan he would not add any new dialogue to Solange's part in the scene they were getting ready to shoot. She was in the corner of the room, in costume, speaking to Nolan now, stamping her foot, choice French phrases shooting from her rouged lips.

David took in a long breath and prepared to walk over to them. The day was only beginning and already his headache was back.

3

Or perhaps it was spite

DARIENNE TOOK the ticket Larry had given her out of her handbag as she walked up to the small theater. It was 7:30 P.M., and she was arriving early for the play, since she'd had nothing else to do after rising from her coffin at dusk. It was a fine summer night. She'd walked the mile distance to the theater from her exclusive home in Belgravia, where London bluebloods resided. She'd owned the home for over a century, but seldom used it.

After presenting her ticket to the doorman, she found her way upstairs to the balcony and took a seat in the front row. She adjusted her white silk suit jacket, buttoned now to cover the revealing camisole underneath. She smoothed the tapered hair at the back of her head, still not quite used to her new haircut. Throughout her four hundred years of existence, she'd always worn her honey-blond hair long. But two months ago she'd called a local hairstylist to her London house one evening and asked the woman to cut off all her wavy tresses. She'd meant the drastic cut to be a purge, a way of pushing aside the past and starting anew.

Or perhaps it was spite. Matthew had loved her long hair; he used to run his fingers through it, pull gobs of it forward and frame her face with it. So she cut it to prove to herself that she no longer wished to attract him. Matthew had done something to her no other man ever had: He'd broken her heart. Darienne hardly knew she had one until she met him. And now she had no heart at all, for he had certainly destroyed it.

Matthew had walked out on her without even a pretense of regret that their three years of sensual passion were over. He'd left her for Natalie, his ex-wife, an attractive, but mortal, woman. Natalie could never give him what Darienne had; *no* ordinary woman could give him the superhuman eroticism Darienne offered. Yet he'd chosen Natalie. Darienne had had to endure seeing photos of them together in *People* and other magazines, in the newspapers and on TV entertainment news shows. She knew Matthew was in London now to make the *Shadow* movie and that Natalie was with him. The London newspapers had reported it, though they hadn't shown any photos—which was just as well. Darienne didn't think she could endure one more photo of Matthew with his arm around his slim ex-wife with her stunning silver hair.

Every night Darienne vowed to forget Matthew and concentrate on replacing him with a man who could prove to be an even better choice: Matthew's son, Larry. Larry was younger. More handsome. Not aging and shopworn like his workaholic father, she told herself. And he was still malleable, unlike Matthew, who always had such a strong will of his own. Oh, Larry had spirit, all right, but young men were always putty in Darienne's hands. Inexperience and their youthful hormone level made young men especially vulnerable to a woman with her physical credentials and vast knowledge of men.

When Darienne had first come to London, it had taken her a few months to locate Larry. She didn't know that he had changed his name. When, finally, she saw him at a distance, leaving the BBC building after working late one evening, she was disappointed. He did indeed look like a youthful Matthew with his curly brown hair, ruddy, pleasant face, and intense eyes. He was taller than Matthew but lacked his father's magnificent chest, which Matthew had developed from singing. Larry was slim with an angular physique, and he walked with a smooth masculine stride that carried a sense of purpose.

But compared to Matthew, he looked so young and damp behind the ears. Darienne understood for the first time that what had attracted her most to Matthew was his maturity.

Still, she convinced herself, Larry could be trained. She would let him grow a bit older before she made him immortal, and that would solve the problem. Time, after all, was on her side. She could easily wait to have just what she wanted—Larry, who looked so much like Matthew, as a vampire who would have the stamina to quench her superhuman sex drive even better than Matthew could as a mortal. Ideally, she'd wanted Matthew to become a vampire. That would have been the best of all worlds. But Matthew had rejected that idea, and rejected her as well.

Catching Larry's attention had been child's play. Unknown to him, she'd observed him for a while, learned where he lived, what his habits were. He often went to a pub near his home in the evening, if he didn't have a rehearsal to do or a play to perform in. Darienne began frequenting the same pub. She always ordered port, the only thing besides blood she could consume. Larry liked to play darts, so she challenged him one evening and beat him. After that he bought her a glass of port and sat down with her. He seemed quite impressed, and not only with her dart-throwing skill.

She made sure to see him at the pub regularly in the months that followed. Though she sensed that he found her highly attractive, as all men did, he never made any sexual advance. She wondered why until one day his pristine Scottish girlfriend turned up. Then Darienne understood. He was being true to Sheena.

Darienne doubted Larry was getting all he would have liked from Sheena, and she knew he could easily be distracted by a voluptuous blonde offering him everything. She gave Sheena credit for having a fiery, if prim, personality and comely looks, but Darienne knew she could break up their old-fashioned romance whenever she wanted. In fact, she could tell that Sheena was already growing nervous, becoming increasingly tart-tongued whenever Darienne appeared.

Darienne was biding her time for now, observing Larry's slow progress into more mature manhood and waiting for the optimum moment to make her move on him. That's what she told herself anyway. Sometimes she wondered if she were afraid—afraid that sex with Larry would be disappointing, because he wasn't his father. She was even more afraid, though she rarely admitted it, that even if she made Larry a vampire, he still wouldn't match Matthew's lovemaking. Only Matthew could be Matthew . . .

Straightening in her chair, Darienne ran her hand through her short hair and told herself to snap out of it. She was finished with Matthew! Reminding herself of the callous way he had treated her after she'd told him how she loved him, she insisted to herself that she never wanted to see Matthew again. Better to have a younger version of him whom she could train.

Yet it was the fact that she couldn't wind Matthew around her finger that had so attracted her in the beginning. Tears stung her eyes suddenly as the memory of Matthew flashed into her mind so real it was as if he were near. Dabbing at her eyes with impatient fingers, Darienne tried to be firm with herself. She must forget the past. It was only because she knew Matthew was here in London that she'd been relapsing into her sorrowful doldrum state again. Ever since she read in the paper three weeks ago that he'd arrived here with Natalie, Darienne had lost some of the ground she'd gained. Just knowing he was in the same city gnawed at her equilibrium. She had to fight her intense desire to go to him, try to see him once more, an urge which would be foolish and humiliating if she acted on it.

With a resolute air, she opened the program she'd been given to distract herself. She found a photo of Larry inside and studied it, noting how his eyes held a whimsical expression. And warmth, intelligence, and perception. And then she closed the program, realizing she was seeing Matthew's eyes in the photo more than Larry's.

She gazed as if lost over the theater seats below, which were beginning to fill with people. What was she to do? How could she forget Matthew once and for all? No matter what she did, how hard she tried, his image, the remembrance of his sensual touch, always found its way back into her mind. Sometimes she wondered how she could survive without him. She'd used to adore being what she was, a worldly vampiress. But lately, her existence seemed so empty. She realized how David must have felt without Veronica during the years they were separated. But David at least had had the hope of getting her back. Darienne was certain Matthew would never take her back. Not after she'd attacked him, nearly made him a vampire by force. How stupid she'd been! How could she have lost her head that way? She'd grown desperate, sensing she was losing him. And now he was with Natalie, the first woman he'd ever loved. There was no chance he'd want Darienne in his life again. So she had to make do with Larry, she repeated to herself like a ritual meditation, her personal mantra. Surely Larry would develop the same sensual touch, the same nurturing sensitivity his father had. Larry was Matthew's offspring. They had the same genes; they looked alike. Larry would be her consolation.

Darienne opened her handbag and took out a handkerchief. She'd begun carrying one since she was so prone to tears lately. She hated her emotional states, but didn't know how to stop them. Psychologists said it was healthy to cry. She'd often read that. But she didn't know what good all these falling tears and sniffles could be doing her. She used to be tougher than this, much more resilient. The idea that she was growing emotionally weak upset her further. She wished she could talk to David. He might understand and help her get over this unbecoming state she'd fallen into. Really, this was beneath her, all this sentimentality.

She was wiping her nose when she happened to look down at people moving into their seats on the main floor below. To her astonishment, she thought she saw David. Maybe it was because she was just thinking of him, but . . .

My God, it is David! she thought as she looked again. And Veronica was behind him! They were walking along a row, moving slowly so as not to step on people already seated as they found their places.

Darienne crushed the handkerchief against her mouth as her eyes fixed on them in astonishment. She was so happy to see them. David must be here because of the film. It hadn't occurred to her he would come to London, too. Tears started in her eyes again as she saw David slip his arm around Veronica when they sat down. He spoke in her ear and seemed concerned. Darienne smiled at the obvious tenderness between them. At least *they* were finally together and happy. Right now it lifted Darienne's spirits to know *someone* was content with life, even if David had given up immortality to have that contentment. It wasn't a choice she could ever make, but she was glad for him, and for Veronica, whom Darienne thought of almost as a sister.

As Darienne put away her handkerchief, she began to wonder, Why had David and Veronica come to this small theater? Perhaps because David revered Shakespeare and wanted to see *Hamlet*. Or did they know that Laurence McFarland was actually Larry McDowall, Matthew's son? If they'd come to see Larry, then why weren't Matthew and Natalie here to see their son's opening night as well? She'd asked Larry, casually, if he had any relatives coming to see him perform, and he'd said, *No!* in a rather sharp way. Sheena had said, chiding him, that Larry had refused to tell his father about the play, so Darienne assumed Matthew didn't know. But if David knew . . .

Darienne's heart seemed to stop when all at once she saw a barrel-chested man with curly graying hair walking up the aisle. He wore a well-tailored light gray jacket and carried himself with the same erect singer's posture Matthew used to. When he turned down the row David and Veronica were sitting in, Darienne got a better look at his profile. It *was* Matthew! He moved down the row and took the empty seat next to David. The seat on the other side of Matthew's was taken by a man. Where was Natalie?

Darienne's hands began to tremble as she raised her fingertips to her mouth. Her entire nervous system grew alive and alert. And yet she had a feeling of weakness in her abdomen. She was in the same building with Matthew. She was looking at him! For months she'd dreamed of just being able to look at him again, and suddenly here he was. The woman sitting next to her glanced at her, and Darienne knew she needed to calm down. The last thing she wanted was to be noticed. She needed to think what to do.

Fortunately the theater lights dimmed. In a moment the curtain rose. She heard actors on the stage begin to deliver lines of Shakespeare, but her eyes were fixed on the back of Matthew's head. How should she handle this situation? she was asking herself. She dared not make her presence known to Matthew. Or to David, either. They might intuit and interfere with her designs on Larry. And yet she longed to speak to them, to hug David and kiss Matthew. But she must avoid them. If they even guessed she were here . . .

On the other hand, she thought, pausing as a new line of logic began to form in her mind, what if Matthew knew of her goal to make his only son a vampire? That would certainly get Matthew's attention, wouldn't it! What might he do to save his son? Should she even contemplate the possibility? Should she gamble on the chance that she might find a way to have Matthew after all?

Why hadn't she thought of this before! Instead of spending all these months weeping, licking her wounds, planning to make do with Larry, she could have been laying plans to get what she really wanted. And why shouldn't she have what she wanted? David did. Veronica did. Why should *she* be left out? Was she not Darienne Victoire? She deserved the best! And the best was Matthew McDowall. She gazed down with kindling desire at his broad shoulders and the curled brown-and-gray locks that used to feel so springy between her fingers when she kissed him.

No substitute would ever do.

The play continued, and Larry did a professional job in his role as Hamlet. He looked young and handsome enough. His voice, Shakespearean now in tone and enunciation, resonated in the small theater, and he commanded the stage easily. Yet he dimmed in comparison to her memory of Matthew onstage. He had not yet developed or perhaps would never have Matthew's innate charisma, his mesmerizing presence before an audience.

All at once, while the play was still in progress, Darienne saw Veronica get up from her seat. David began to rise, too, as if concerned, but Veronica shook her head as if telling him not to follow her. She began edging down the row of seats toward the aisle. Darienne guessed she was leaving for the ladies' room. This was an opportunity to speak to Veronica alone, Darienne quickly realized, and in a flash she was out of her own seat and rushing down the steps to the lower level of the theater. As she hurried toward the ladies' room, she wondered if she were wise to make her presence known to Veronica. But she had to find out what was going on, why Matthew was here without Natalie. Veronica and she had always confided in each other in the past; she felt she could take the risk and trust her.

When she entered the rest room, she found Veronica sitting in a chair placed at one end, beneath a window that was open at the top. Veronica was holding a wet paper towel to her forehead, her eyes were closed, and she appeared to be feeling ill. The ladies' room was empty, and she didn't look up when Darienne came in.

Darienne approached her carefully, not wanting to startle her if she wasn't well. "Are you all right?"

"Just a little queasy," Veronica answered, then opened her eyes. She stared, then took the towel away from her forehead. Her eyes widened. "Darienne?"

"*Oui,*" Darienne said with a smile. "I'm sitting in the balcony. When I saw you walk out, I followed, hoping to have a few minutes alone with you." She bent down and took Veronica's hand. "I'm so happy to see you! I've missed you."

Veronica leaned forward, and they gave each other a hug. "You look so different! You got your hair cut." She looked Darienne over with delight. "I never imagined you with short hair, but it's fantastic. Wait till David sees you!"

Darienne glanced down at the tiled floor for a moment. "I'd rather you didn't tell David I'm here just yet."

Veronica seemed puzzled. "Why?"

"I . . . noticed Matthew is here, too. If David knew I'm in London, he'd warn Matthew and . . ." She left off, not quite knowing how to finish, hoping Veronica would understand.

"Oh. Well, sure. I won't say anything." Veronica grinned. "It'll be hard keeping it to myself though. They *have* been talking about you."

"Have they?" Darienne stood and leaned against a sink. "What did they say?"

Veronica paused, looking up at Darienne with a winsome slyness. "I suppose I'm breaking a confidence. But I don't care. It seemed to me they weren't very sensitive to your point of view. In fact, I spoke up for you. David told Matthew he thought you might come to London to pursue his son. Matthew got quite concerned. But since Larry still has a steady girlfriend, they both decided maybe you had given up the idea."

"I see," Darienne said, pleased with the report. She was also touched. "It was sweet of you to speak up on my behalf. What did you say to them?"

"Well, my comments were mostly to Matthew, actually. He asked us how you seemed to take things after he left, that last night in Chicago."

"He asked about me?" Darienne repeated with surprise. "I'm amazed." Her tone grew acerbic. "He walked out of my life like Rhett Butler. I wouldn't have thought he gave a damn."

"I had the feeling he did care, at least a little," Veronica said, throwing the wet paper towel into the nearby wastebasket. She looked much better than when Darienne had come in. "I told him that I thought you pretended to get over it quickly, but that you were really very hurt."

"Did Matthew say anything more?"

"He described how you . . . well, he said you 'attacked' him. I wasn't sure what to believe about that, but whatever happened between you, it seemed to have genuinely frightened him."

Darienne bowed her head and nodded. "I wanted too much from him too fast. I was losing him. I did frighten him, and I ruined everything."

"I pointed out that you *did* stop, that you didn't harm him."

Darienne gazed down at Veronica, feeling deeply touched. "That was so kind of you to stand up for me."

"I know you loved him. I know how desperate a woman can feel when you love someone you fear you may lose. I spent years feeling desperate over David."

"I knew you would understand. I'm sure they think I'm grasping and dangerous. I'm just in love—for the first time in my existence. I don't have enough experience to know how to handle the situation very well. I've made mistakes."

Veronica seemed to ponder Darienne's words. "It was interesting—last night Matthew said that when you told him you loved him, it really threw him. It was as if that shocked him almost as much as your trying to make him a vampire."

"I imagine it did," Darienne said in a dry tone.

"So I asked him, 'Were you in love with her?' "

Darienne grew very quiet, almost stopped breathing. "What did he answer?"

"He said he wasn't sure he knew what love was. He quoted someone who'd said that anyone who has been an actor for a long time doesn't know whether he has any true emotions or not. And then he said, 'Maybe I've been an actor too long.' "

"Obviously he has!" Darienne said, trying for a flippant tone, though a lump of deepening emotion gathered in her throat.

"But," Veronica pointed out, "he didn't say he wasn't in love with you."

Darienne was afraid to be hopeful. She tried to swallow and asked, "Did he say anything else?"

Veronica thought a moment. "It was then that David told him he was worried you'd go after his son, and Matthew got concerned." She looked up at Darienne, worry coming into her ingenuous brown eyes. "Are you going after Larry?"

Darienne felt guilty suddenly. "I've insinuated myself into his life," she admitted. "Don't judge me too quickly for that. I needed someone to ease the pain and loneliness, and Larry seemed a logical choice. But I may have an alternate plan now, depending on. . . . I noticed that Matthew didn't have Natalie with him. I thought she—"

"They're not together anymore," Veronica told her in a hopeful tone. "Matthew said that when she saw him get wrapped up in the *Shadow* movie, she didn't want to take second place in his life again. So she broke off the relationship."

"But the newspaper said—"

Veronica shrugged. "Maybe Matthew's agent or publicist didn't know she'd left him and gave out the wrong report."

Darienne's heart was beating with excitement at the news, yet she couldn't help but say, "Natalie is a smart woman. I honestly admire her. She knows when it's wise to let go. I don't know if that's a lesson I could ever learn."

Darienne realized that she'd been going on about herself and Matthew. "Are you feeling better?" she asked Veronica. "What was wrong?"

"I felt nauseous, but I'm much better now. The theater seemed so stuffy to me. The fresh air from the window," she said, pointing behind her, "and seeing you again have made me feel a hundred percent better." She put on a smile that seemed a little nervous.

Darienne wondered if there were something she wasn't saying. "Are you sure?"

"Oh, yes. I'm fine!"

Darienne didn't want to press her, so she changed the subject. "How's David?"

Veronica smiled quietly and seemed a little wistful. "He's fine, too, I think. We're married now." She showed off her wedding ring, a wide gold band set with diagonal rows of glittering diamonds.

"What a beautiful ring. So you did get married! When and where?"

"About a month after David was cured. We had a quiet ceremony in a church chapel. Since then I've been fixing up David's house—our house," Veronica corrected herself with a smile.

"David must be very happy with his new life."

"He is," Veronica said, "*but* since he's become mortal, he's grown nervous and even fearful. He knows he can die now, so the possibility of accidents and illness upsets him. I suppose he'll adjust, but it's hard for him. He's even taken up bodybuilding because he feels weak now."

"He's lost his vampire strength altogether?"

"Yes. Physically he's just like any other mortal man."

Darienne hesitated to ask, but she sensed something subtle in Veronica's wistful face and voice. "And lovemaking? He's grown ordinary that way, too?"

Veronica looked up at her, then glanced away. "David could never be ordinary, but . . . well, it isn't quite the transcendent experience it used to be. I miss his taking my blood. I miss the bond we used to share."

Darienne thought of a simple solution. "I can transform him back into a vampire, if you want."

Veronica's eyes darkened with surprise that was laced with desire. But she shook her head and said in a poignant tone, "No, Darienne. He was so unhappy when he was a vampire. He made me wait for him all those years because he wanted me to take the time to be sure before I made a decision to become a vampiress. To him, being a vampire was a terrible, loathesome thing, and he didn't want me to have to become one, too, so we could be together forever. How could I want him to go back to being something he so utterly despised? How could I make him hate himself again?"

Veronica smiled. "Remember how happy he was when he was cured? He was thrilled just to be able to look at me in the sunlight instead of by lamplight. He's having some trouble now adjusting to mortality, but I'm sure that will pass. I could never want him to go back to what he was."

"But what about you, your desires and needs?" Darienne asked.

"I'll adjust, too." Veronica sounded quite sure of herself. "I know I will. I'm happy just to be with him, after all those years apart. And I have the memory of our former bond. When we make love, it almost seems to return for a few moments." She smiled again, with new tenderness. "We're closer than most married couples, I think."

"As long as you're happy, I won't interfere. But if you ever change your mind—"

Veronica firmly shook her head. But an odd, unsettled look crept into her face. "I can't change my mind—I think I'm pregnant."

Darienne stared at her, dumbfounded. She studied Veronica's wide, awed eyes. "You are? Are you sure?"

"No," Veronica answered with a nervous little laugh. "The idea just occurred to me this afternoon. I've been feeling queasy off and on for no reason. Especially in the morning. I thought maybe it was something I ate or a flu bug. And then I remembered that I'm very late this month."

"Late?"

"You know, my monthly period."

Darienne had to think what she meant. "Oh. Oh, that. I'd forgotten."

"You mean, you don't . . ."

"Not since I died. It was one of the blessings of being transformed. So you've missed a month and you're feeling sick to your stomach. As I recall, those *are* the classic symptoms." Darienne had to steady herself a bit. This news seemed almost incredible to her. "Then David is no longer sterile," she said with wonder.

"If I *am* pregnant, I guess not! I was wondering about that the last time we made love. The idea just came into my mind.

Maybe because I already was pregnant."

Darienne nodded, half listening. She was thinking: If David was going to be a father, then he must remain mortal. If he were to become a vampire again, he would outlive his own child, or else have to make that child a vampire, too. Either choice would be heartbreaking for him.

Darienne felt solemn now, and sad. She'd kept a little hope that David might change his mind one day and want to become a vampire again, that she would have him as her ageless friend once more, as they'd been for hundreds of years. She'd hoped Veronica would want to become a vampiress, too—perhaps Veronica might have even coaxed David into becoming immortal again so they could be together forever. That way, Darienne would have had them as friends for eternity. And if she could have somehow managed to transform Matthew, too, they might have all been together for all time.

But if Veronica was pregnant—well, she and David were grounded in mortality then. Even Darienne felt the need to protect the child, so he or she would grow up healthy and happy, with two normal parents. And then she wondered—the thought came upon her totally unbidden—if she took the formula David had taken and became a mortal again herself, could *she* become pregnant? Could she have Matthew's child?

Mon Dieu, what a thought! That was something she'd need to ponder a few decades at least. She couldn't imagine herself as a mother—never had had the least desire to be one, even when she was mortal. Besides, she'd need to get Matthew back first. And despite Veronica's hopefulness, Darienne wasn't very optimistic.

"What does David say? Have you told him you may be pregnant?"

"No. He knows I've been feeling queasy, but he just assumes it's indigestion or flu, like I did. I don't think I'll say anything until I'm sure. It would only give him more to worry about while we're here in London. It would be better if I tell him once we're settled back home in Chicago and after I've seen a doctor."

"Will you be all right until then?"

"We may be here only a few weeks. I wouldn't know what doctor to see in London anyway. And it would be hard to get away without David wondering where I was going."

Darienne felt uneasy. "You really don't think you should tell him?"

Veronica shook her head. "I know him. He'd be frantic worrying about every step I took. He's already under a lot of stress. He doesn't like to travel. There are arguments with the movie people about his script. He's been getting headaches and hasn't been eating well. I can't load him down with one more big thing to worry about."

Darienne nodded, not knowing what to say. Pregnancy was one area in which she had no expertise at all.

"Besides," Veronica said, "maybe it's a false alarm. Maybe my monthly cycle's messed up because I've been so excited about traveling abroad. And maybe I've caught some flu bug. It would be a shame to worry him about something that may not even be true."

"Whatever you think is best," Darienne said. She took Veronica's hand in hers and patted it. "Just take care of yourself, all right?"

Veronica stood and gave Darienne a hug. "I will. You've acted just like a tonic on me. I feel fine now. I'm glad you followed me in here. But I'd better go back, or *David* will follow me in here!"

Darienne chuckled, then squeezed her hand. "You won't say you saw me . . ."

"I won't. I promise."

Darienne hesitated, then added, "Just so you know—if you hear that I'm seducing Matthew's son, I'll only be doing it to get Matthew's attention."

Veronica's delicate brows drew together. "Do you have to resort to such an extreme measure? I hear he has a girlfriend."

"Yes, he does. But a little experience with an older woman won't do him any harm before she ties him down for life. The point is, I don't think Matthew would see or talk to me for any other reason but to protect his son, do you?"

"I don't know," Veronica said, looking worried. "You could try some other approach."

Darienne angled her chin. "I don't like the word *try*. I like the word *do* much better. And I do what I think will work. I may be wrong. Sometimes I go too far, I admit. But it's never my intention to hurt anyone, not really. Do you believe that?"

"I believe you." Veronica smiled in a bemused way. "I could never be like you, but I've always envied the way you play by your own rules and set your own values. You're calculating sometimes, but kind."

"I like the way you put that," Darienne said, feeling a sisterly fondness for Veronica. "You *are* different from me. But we've always understood each other, as only women can. Thank you for listening. I hope to see you again soon. Take good care of yourself."

Veronica walked out of the rest room first, then motioned to Darienne that the coast was clear for her to leave, too. Darienne waved good-bye to Veronica and rushed back up to the balcony. She quietly took her place again and stayed there till the end of the performance.

But she didn't hear a single word of Shakespeare. Veronica had given her too much to contemplate.

A speck of dirt in your mind, as well!

WHEN THE play ended, Darienne waited in her seat and watched below as Matthew, David, and Veronica made their way out of the theater, following the crowd. Only Veronica looked up at the balcony. She gave Darienne a secret smile, then glanced at David and Matthew, who were talking to each other as they slowly moved along the aisle. Apparently ascertaining that she wouldn't be observed, Veronica looked up at Darienne again and mouthed the words *dressing room*. Darienne nodded that she understood and winked a thank you.

So Matthew apparently had decided to see his son in his backstage dressing room. Perhaps he sensed Larry had noticed him in the audience. And Larry would have to be polite if Matthew brought David and Veronica with him. She decided to figure out where the actors' dressing rooms were and go there, too.

When she found the small hallway at the side of the stage where the dressing rooms were situated, she passed some of the exhilarated actors and their friends, ready to celebrate a successful opening night. She kept a sharp eye out for Larry, Matthew, or David, so she could back out of sight quickly and not be seen. When one young actor, still in costume, asked if he could help her find someone, she told him she'd come to surprise Larry. "His dressing room's the last one on the right," the fellow said. "I just saw Matthew McDowall go in. He was in the audience tonight!"

Darienne smiled. It was natural the young, largely unknown cast would be impressed that a famous theatrical star had come to see them perform. Perhaps they didn't know he was Larry's father. Matthew had played *Shadow* in London to adoring crowds and had won the Olivier award for his performance, in addition to the Tony award he'd won on Broadway. Remembering the adulation that surrounded Matthew for the three years he'd played that role made Darienne feel proud and sad, suddenly. Oh, to have those years back again. They'd been the happiest of her existence.

She approached Larry's dressing room carefully. When she drew near to the doorway, she could hear the voices within as the other actors in the hallway moved off in another direction to break open a bottle of champagne. The theater was old and the dressing rooms, she noticed as she passed one, were small and dingy. The room next to Larry's was empty at the moment. She slipped in. The walls were thin, the doors open, and she could hear every word.

"It was good of you to come tonight."

Darienne closed her eyes, almost with pain, thinking she was hearing Matthew's voice. But then she realized the voice spoke with a Scottish brogue, similar to Sean Connery's, and she knew it must be Larry. He'd been raised by his mother in Scotland after she'd left Matthew, so he'd picked up an accent. But the timbre of Larry's voice was so similar to Matthew's, it caught her off guard, knowing Matthew was in the room, too. Her stomach began to feel weak.

Next she heard David's educated, French-accented voice. "We enjoyed your performance immensely. I'm something of a Shakespeare buff. Your Hamlet compares with the best of them. You have your father's sensitivity for character."

"Thanks." Larry's voice was terse.

"Well . . . ," David said, as if realizing too late that he'd said the wrong thing to the wrong person, "it's time I take Veronica back to the hotel."

"Oh, no. You all must come to Larry's party." Darienne recognized the high voice, also with a Scottish accent. It was Sheena. "We'll be going to his place as soon as he changes out of his costume. You will come, won't you?" she invited eagerly. "Mr. and Mrs. de Morrissey? Matthew?"

"Sheena," Larry said with rigid politeness. "We shouldn't impose on them."

"Thank you." It was David's gracious voice. "But Veronica has a touch of the flu, and she needs to rest."

After that, there followed a flurry of kind regards and good-byes. Darienne backed behind the open door in her room when she heard David and Veronica's footsteps in the hallway as they left.

Then she heard Sheena's voice again. "You'll come, won't you, Matthew?" Her tone was sweet and imploring.

"I don't think he'd enjoy it," Larry said.

"Of course, he would," Sheena insisted. "Your father should meet your friends. They'd be thrilled to meet him."

"This is Larry's night." Matthew spoke now. "If I were there, it would draw attention away from him."

Darienne shut her eyes tightly. The resonant, clear, reassuringly familiar sound of his voice was painful to hear. She'd missed it. She often played tapes of the songs he'd recorded, but that wasn't the same as hearing him speak. Besides the American accent, there was a maturity in his tone that Larry's voice didn't have. Matthew's manner of speaking conveyed patience, understanding, and humility.

"It's very kind of you to invite me," Matthew said, "but I don't think I should come tonight. I would like to see you both again while I'm in London, though. Would you like to see the movie sets at the studio? I'd be happy to show you around."

"That would be lovely!" Sheena replied.

"We'll think about it," Larry said in a hurried manner that indicated his mind was already made up.

"Good enough," Matthew replied in a pleasant tone. "I won't keep you from your own party any longer. I'm staying at Claridge's. Call me soon, will you?"

Larry did not reply, at least not verbally.

Sheena said, "I'll call you." Her voice grew a bit muffled, and Darienne guessed it was because she was giving Matthew a hug. They exchanged final good-byes, and then Darienne heard Matthew's footsteps in the hallway. When he'd passed by her doorway, she peeked out. She saw him a few feet down the hall, walking away alone, his broad shoulders squared, but she detected a sadness in his step. She wanted to run to him and comfort him, to tell him *she* loved him even if his son didn't. Instead, she ducked back into the empty little room, afraid she might act on her impulse. She sat down in the makeup chair to collect herself.

"How can you be so unfeeling?" she heard Sheena saying to Larry. "Can't you see he wants to make it up with you? He cares for you. He wants your love."

"He didn't give a damn all the time I was growing up. How could he? He was never there!"

"Maybe he wanted to be. Your mother said he tried to keep in touch. She said she wouldn't take his calls and refused to keep any money Matthew sent her."

"She didn't want his money," Larry retorted. "She wanted *him*—she wanted a real husband and I needed a real father. Now she's left him again after they tried to get back together. I told her it wouldn't work. She gets blinded by his appealing looks and manner, like you and all the other women who think he's so wonderful. But I see him for what he is—a selfish bastard who doesn't give a damn about anything except pleasing himself."

"But then why would he make the effort to see you and try to get to know you the way he has? How was coming here to see you play *Hamlet* selfish?"

"He's pushing fifty. My mom just dumped him. He's probably worried about growing old and being alone. So now it's convenient for him to have a son."

"You're so cynical!"

"Look, you came from a happy, stable family. It's easy for you to look at everything through rose-colored glasses. If I'd had your father, I'd probably have a forgiving attitude, too."

Sheena chuckled. "If you'd had my father, you and I would be brother and sister." Her voice grew soft and nuzzling. "I wouldn't have been happy about that. I much prefer you as my boyfriend."

There was silence, except for a whimpering sound from Sheena. Darienne guessed they were kissing. She sighed and stood up. Time to go to work. She walked out, turning toward Larry's dressing room. Indeed, she found Sheena in Larry's arms, kissing as they stood in the middle of the small room.

"*Bonjour, chéri,*" Darienne said as she paused in his open doorway.

Sheena abruptly broke their kiss and turned. "Oh," she said. "I didn't know *you* were here tonight." The friendly cordiality she'd given Matthew had vanished.

Larry, however, smiled and took a step toward her. "So you came!" He looked dramatic and broodingly handsome in his black *Hamlet* costume and makeup that hollowed his cheekbones. His hair had been combed back flat against his head at the sides, while the brown curly hair on top hung over his forehead in traditional youthful fashion.

"You were wonderful, Larry! I wouldn't have missed your opening night for the world." Darienne took the liberty, in front of Sheena, of hugging him and giving him a kiss on the cheek. She could see Sheena bristle.

Sheena had dark brown, straight, shining hair, which she wore lately in a Buster Brown style with bangs and a blunt cut at chin level. The haircut set off her large black-brown eyes, which, Darienne had to admit, were quite stunning. They held a great deal of energy, and when she was angry, as she was now, they seemed almost to emit fiery sparks. She was not tall, perhaps five foot four at most. But she appeared to have a fine, fully developed figure, which she usually kept hidden under colorful but modest dresses or pants and sweaters. Sheena had said once that she came from a small town in the west of Scotland. She'd gone to Edinburgh for college, then on to London to study drama, which had taken her interest. It was in a drama class that she'd met Larry. But though she'd spent several years in big cities, she seemed stubborn about holding on to her rural values. Darienne could tell from looking at her, reading her eyes and face, that in Sheena's mind, a proper young woman did not flaunt her body, did not drink, did not sleep with a man until she was married to him. Which made things almost too easy for Darienne.

"Coming to the party at my place?" Larry asked.

"I adore parties, *chéri,*" Darienne purred. As she drew away from embracing him, she casually allowed her hand to move from his shoulder slowly down his chest. "Of course, I'll come!"

Sheena snatched up her handbag from the corner where she'd left it. "Then we'd better leave and let him change," she said tartly to Darienne as she walked out of the room.

Darienne lowered her eyes and followed in a polite manner. Larry closed the door, and Darienne waited in the hall with Sheena. She supposed it was fair to give the young woman some warning, a bit of advice.

"If I were you, Sheena, I wouldn't be so quick to leave when a man is changing clothes. Men secretly like to have a woman watch."

"Do they indeed?" Sheena said in a clear, confident, but impatient voice. "No doubt you know *that* from personal experience."

"Exactly what I'm saying, *chérie*. You need to allow yourself to get some experience. You're playing in the major leagues now."

Darienne bided her time at the party, talking to the forty or so friends, an equal mix of young men and women, whom Larry had invited to his small flat. Knots of men tended to gather around her, but she gracefully extricated herself, wanting to be free to make her first real move on Larry. Sheena tried to stick close by him, apparently taking some heed of Darienne's warning, but acting as hostess for him often brought her back to the kitchen to make more punch and put out more food.

During one of these intervals when Sheena was occupied with washing piled-up dishes, Darienne saw Larry go into his bedroom to look for a new music tape to play. She followed.

"There you are," she said as she walked into the bedroom, as if she'd been searching for him. She silently pushed the door almost closed behind her. The bedroom was small and cramped with a double bed and a dresser. Posters advertising Shakespearean plays from years past covered the walls.

He was looking through a group of tapes on a shelf when he turned at the sound of her voice. "Hello! I didn't mean to ignore you," he said with a grin.

"I didn't think you were. You're just a busy host. It's a wonderful party."

"Thanks."

She sat down on the end of the bed, near him, and watched as he continued to look through the pile of audio cassettes. His profile was like Matthew's, too. Except the line of Larry's chin was so smooth and young, he looked almost innocent. A baby compared to Matthew.

"Ah! Here it is!" he said. "Scottish bagpipes."

"That's what you were looking for?"

"Don't tell me you don't like them."

"Well . . ." Darienne was reluctant to reveal her dislike of the mournful sound. "I'm surprised you do. You told me once that you're American by birth."

"I try to forget that," he said in a flippant tone. "I spent most of my life in Scotland."

"And your girlfriend is Scottish."

"Right. So bagpipes it is."

Darienne chuckled. "Are you going to marry her?"

His expression changed, almost grew sheepish—a young man shy to confide his feelings. "Don't know. I might."

"She's very pretty. Bright, too. And . . . untouched."

He lowered his eyes.

"You're a handsome young man. You could have your pick of women, you know. Why do you choose such a chaste girl, when you could be having fun instead?"

"I said I might marry her."

"All the more reason to . . . test the waters."

"No," he said, a surprising, grim anger coming into his face. "You mentioned I'm American by birth. America—where morals are decaying, and single parenthood is practically the norm. My mother was from upstate New York and only eighteen when she met my father. He was a few years older. *They* didn't waste any time testing the waters. She got pregnant and they got married, all within a few months of meeting. It was a miserable marriage. A bitter divorce. My mother was forced to kidnap me away from him when I was five. She took me to Edinburgh and became a single mother who supported us by working as a secretary. I grew up without a father, in a foreign country, with a lonely mother who worked hard to give us a meager life. I've always hated my father for deserting us, and I'm often angry with my mother, because she has a recurring tendency to forgive him."

He pressed his lips together and tapped the plastic cassette case against his fingertips. "All of this pain could have been avoided, it seems to me, if my parents had managed to keep their knickers on while they were dating. My mother wouldn't have had to marry an unsuitable man to avoid having an illegitimate kid. And then she wound up raising me alone anyway."

"Maybe they loved each other."

"You see, that's the thing," Larry said. "If you bring sex into the mix too soon, you don't know if it's love or lust. Maybe they were in love. Or maybe they just had the hots for each other. It's better to wait and know the difference."

"So you're willing to wait for Sheena."

"It's not as if my yearnings don't get the better of me sometimes. But she's got good, strong moral values. She's got common sense, and she keeps me in line if I get out of hand. Maybe it seems strange nowadays, but I admire that. I don't want to repeat my father's mistakes and wind up with a kid somewhere who hates me because I couldn't get along with his mother."

Darienne felt a bit weighed down by Larry's grim logic, the sadness of his childhood. She felt hesitant now to insert herself into his life situation. But she had her own mission to accomplish, her own happiness to regain, and she needed to use Larry, briefly, for her own purposes. She hoped he wouldn't be hurt. But if he was, well, she'd just have to feel guilty about it. She wasn't going to change her plans now, not when she had this singular chance to get what she wanted.

"I think it's very wise of you to want not to make bad choices in your life," she told him. "In fact it's refreshing to find a young man who respects his girlfriend, the way you respect Sheena." She blinked and smiled. "But . . . don't you find yourself feeling a little constricted, letting your needs go unmet? Or do you have some way of dealing with that?"

His face colored with embarrassment as he shifted his weight from one foot to the other. "Of course, it's frustrating, but . . ."

"You do without then?"

He didn't seem to know where to look and in particular did not want to look at her. He glanced at the door, then at the carpet. "Why are you asking such personal questions?"

Darienne crossed her legs. This drew his wandering eyes and held them captive, since her short skirt hiked up, revealing almost the full length of her smooth, slim thighs. She injected a frivolous tone into her voice and thickened her French accent a bit. "I live by a different philosophy, Larry. I believe in *joie de vivre*—the joy of life. And a natural part of life is sex. So your point of view interests me. It's unusual, especially for a young man who looks very much in his prime, with healthy and plentiful hormones."

Larry, who was still looking at her legs, cautiously raised his eyes to her face, as if beginning to suspect what she was about. But instead of disapproval, she saw the sly light of wonder creeping into his eyes. "My hormones are healthy all right."

"*You* aren't a virgin, are you?"

"Of course not!"

"So you aren't aiming to be a saint. You just want to be . . . careful."

"Y-yes."

She began to unbutton her suit jacket. "Suppose you met a woman, a slightly older woman, who had some experience with life and relationships. Suppose this lady had taken a permanent measure which prevented her from getting pregnant—a woman who enjoyed sex purely for the joy and sensuality of it." The buttons undone, she let the jacket come apart, revealing her plump, upturned breasts covered only with a lavender satin-and-lace camisole, through which the contoured tips of her nipples could be detected. She rose to her feet and stepped up to him. "This woman is quite independent." She smiled as she fingered a button on his plaid shirt. "And discreet. She requires no commitments, no strings from a man she admires. All she wants is a little of his time for some private moments, to explore the chemistry between them." She ran her hands up his chest. "What would you think, if you met such a woman?"

Larry's breath was shaky. "I'd think I was damned lucky."

Darienne smiled. "You have met her, *chéri*. You are lucky. And so am I."

"Do you really mean this?" Larry asked, eagerly raising his hands to her waist, then dropping them to his sides again in confusion. "I've thought about being with you ever since I saw you. But I didn't think a sophisticated woman like you would be interested in me." The lights in his eyes dimmed, and he looked guilty. "And I didn't want to be untrue to Sheena."

"You wouldn't be untrue, *chéri,*" Darienne said, placing her fingertips against his mouth as if to silence the thought. "Not really. What we would have would be purely physical. Your heart would still belong to Sheena. And she wouldn't have to know."

"But she might find out."

"Not if we're careful. And if she does, well . . . you aren't married or even engaged. It's not as though you'd be breaking a vow."

He laughed as if almost giddy. "This is incredible! You really want to be with *me?* Why?"

The question pained her, but she smiled and stroked his angular jaw. "I like your face. You're the image of my ideal. I can't resist. I know I'm wicked to sneak in between you and Sheena this way. But I can't help it," she whispered, making her voice grow wanton. "Touch me," she said, running her fingertips lightly over her camisole.

His young hand was shaking as he lifted it to her breast. But he hesitated only a moment. He touched the plump inner curves of her cleavage.

"God, you're beautiful!" he said in a husky whisper. "You're so sexy."

"Yes, I am," she purred as she leaned up to kiss him lightly on the mouth. She lowered her hand to his belt and below. "Oh, my," she said with admiration, gliding her fingers down the swollen length of him through the cloth of his pants. She was getting excited now, too. "It's going to be *so* good—"

"When?"

"I don't know yet. Not here. Not tonight. Sometime when Sheena's gone. I'll meet you at the pub and we'll talk about it."

"All right." He hesitated, then boldly leaned in to kiss her. She closed her eyes, entwined her fingers into his curly hair and kissed him back, pretending for a moment that he was Matthew.

Both were breathing fast with excitement as they drew apart. She ran her hand over the smooth contours of his cheek and jaw, so like the more mature face she loved. "I can't wait!" she said.

They were gazing into each other's eyes when suddenly she heard the sound of the door creaking and then a sharp female voice. "What is going on?"

Larry's eyes jumped from Darienne to the doorway in back of her. "Sh-Sheena. Nothing. I had a speck of dirt on my face. Darienne was rubbing it off."

Darienne smiled at his quick improvisation as she buttoned her suit jacket back up before turning around to face Sheena.

"Perhaps you had a speck of dirt in your mind, as well!" Sheena exclaimed, her *r*s trilling with emphasis. "What else would she like to rub for you?"

"Sheena! It's . . . it's not what you think," he lied.

His high moral values were quickly disappearing, Darienne noted, feeling a little guilty, knowing she was corrupting him. Oh, well, she'd never been known for her virtue, in any era of her time on earth. Seducing young men had always been her specialty. But because he was Matthew's son, she felt remorseful somehow, knowing she was toying with someone Matthew loved.

She dismissed her troubled conscience for now and attended to the problem at hand—being discovered already by Sheena. "He was going through the cassettes on the shelf, looking for bagpipe music. I was helping him look," she explained to Sheena, not really expecting the young woman, if she were smart, to believe her. "You know how men are—they never dust. He got dirt on his fingers and fingerprints on his face. He couldn't see them himself, so I had to remove the smudges for him."

Sheena looked suspicious, but either because she wasn't sure, or because there was a party going on in the next room, she said nothing except "I think you should get back to your guests, Larry." She waited until he left Darienne's side and walked past her out of the room. She closed the door then, looked directly at Darienne, and said in a firm, yet somehow sassy voice, "You'd better look for dirt on someone else's face from now on. For your information, I dusted that shelf the other day myself. Take your saucy French airs, your naughty lingerie, and advertise elsewhere! Larry's taken."

Darienne smiled. "You'd do better not to act as if you were his mother, cleaning for him, reprimanding him, setting rules. He'll rebel one day."

"Will he now!" Sheena said. "Thanks for the advice. Now you can *leave*."

"All right." Darienne decided it was better to acquiesce. She really had no quarrel with the young woman, who was perfectly within her rights to try to keep her man. Actually she had to admire Sheena. She didn't fall apart, didn't dissolve into tears or throw a tantrum when she saw her prospective husband alone with another woman. She took control and dealt with the situation—exactly what Darienne was doing to try to get *her* man back.

Darienne left the party quietly without saying anything further to Larry. She walked the streets of London for a while, wondering what Matthew was doing tonight and laying her plans for his future. Once her plans fell into place, she would never wander aimlessly like this or wonder about him again.

5

Our lives are so fragile

"I NEED to call Harriet," Veronica told David, raising her voice so he could hear. He was in the bathroom taking a bath while she was getting dressed in the bedroom of their hotel suite.

"Why?" he called back.

"To ask how Tabitha is doing," she told him. Her real reason was to ask Harriet for advice regarding her possible pregnancy. Her cousin was the mother of two children, who were almost grown now.

"Veronica," her husband said in an indulgent tone, "I'm sure the kitten is fine. But if you want to make an overseas call and bother Harriet at who knows what time it is in Chicago, then go ahead."

"How long before you're ready to leave for the studio?" she asked as she hurried to comb her hair in front of the mirror.

"Twenty minutes."

There was a phone in the sitting room as well as the bedroom. She walked to the other room, sat on the sofa, and reached for the phone. The hotel operator put through the call, and soon the phone was ringing in Chicago. Veronica was relieved when she heard her cousin's sleepy voice say hello.

"Harriet? It's Veronica in London. I'm not calling in the middle of the night, am I?"

"It's about three A.M. Are you okay? I didn't expect to hear from you till you got back."

"I'm sorry. It's mid-morning here. Shall I call back later?"

"I'm awake now. What's up?"

"I wondered how Tabitha is."

Harriet chuckled. "She was scared and hid under the bed for a few hours when I first brought her home, but she's fine now." Her voice grew distant as she seemed to turn away from the phone for a moment. "It's Veronica. Go back to sleep." Then her voice came back on the line again. "Ralph complains when she sleeps on the bed with us. But he wants to be the one who feeds her. Maybe I should buy him a pet for his birthday."

Veronica smiled. "And you're okay?"

"Yeah, everything's fine. Did you have a bad dream or something? Why were you worried?"

"Well, actually, I had another reason." She sighed from nervousness and lowered her voice. "I think . . . I may be pregnant."

"No kidding!" Harriet exclaimed.

"Don't get too excited. I'm not sure yet. That's why I'm calling, to ask you about it. I'm late and I feel queasy. And my breasts are starting to feel tender."

"Sounds like you're going to be a mommy!"

"Is there any way to know for sure?"

"See a doctor. You should anyway."

"I'm in London, Harriet. I don't know any doctors here."

"I know—those home pregnancy test kits. They must sell them in England, too."

Veronica felt relieved at the suggestion. "Of course. Why didn't I think of that?"

" 'Cause you never had to before. I hear they're not a hundred percent accurate, but I guess they're fairly reliable."

"Okay, I'll get one. What did you do about morning sickness when you were pregnant?"

"Nothing worked for me. You just have to get used to going around feeling sick half of the time. It usually lasts only about three months, though."

"Oh." Veronica didn't find this comforting.

"Have you told David?"

"No." She leaned over to look through the door, to see if he was still in the bathroom or in the next room. She heard water running in the bathroom. "I'm afraid to worry him. You know how he's been since he was cured." It was Harriet who'd helped them find the formula to cure David of being a vampire. "He's even more anxiety-prone here than he was at home. He's had a lot of stress on the movie set, too. He's been getting bad headaches and the sun hurts his eyes."

"The sun hurts his eyes? He's not . . . You don't think he could be reverting, do you? That scientist in Switzerland said there was a small chance he could change back again."

Veronica grew quiet, afraid to say that the same idea had been lurking in her mind. "But, if I am actually pregnant, then he must have been normal a few weeks ago, when I conceived. And if I remember right, he was already complaining of headaches then."

"What about the sun sensitivity?"

"As far as I know, that's only been the last week or so."

"Is he eating normally?"

"No." Veronica's voice quivered slightly. "He just doesn't seem very hungry. I think he's losing weight."

"Maybe you two should come home."

"But the film people need him here because of script problems. And David feels he needs to protect his work. The lead actress wants a bigger part, and they keep changing scenes, and . . . I don't know, it's just a constant mess."

"Does David have any craving for . . . blood?" Harriet asked, as if not wanting to be blunt, but not knowing how else to put it.

"No," Veronica was glad to report. "In fact, he hasn't even ordered red meat lately in restaurants. He sticks to salads, seafood, and chicken."

"Well, maybe that's a good indication that he's okay. If he's stressed out, that could account for headaches and a weak appetite."

"What about sun sensitivity?"

"Well . . ."

Both were quiet for a moment.

"Gosh, I feel kind of helpless here on the other side of the world. You've got to take care of yourself and David, too."

"I'll work it out. Thanks, Harriet."

Veronica slowly hung up the phone. This trip to London was beginning to seem like a nightmare. She wished now that she hadn't been so anxious to go. David might have talked her and himself out of the trip, if she hadn't wanted to see London so much. Then at least they would have been home, where their separate medical problems could have been more easily attended to. She felt guilty now.

Veronica took a long breath. Well, they were here, and she had to deal with the situation. The first thing she needed to do was get out to a drugstore. That shouldn't be difficult, but she had the feeling David would pose a problem.

She got up and walked into the bedroom. David was buttoning his shirt in front of the mirror. She noted that she could see his reflection, which indicated he was still mortal and no vampire. The elaborate window drapery was closed, and the room seemed unnecessarily dark. She went to the window to pull the drapes open.

"Did you reach Harriet?" David asked.

"Yes. Everything's fine," Veronica said as she pulled on the drapery cord. Sunlight filtered into the room.

David glanced at the reflected window in the mirror and squinted slightly at the brightening light, but he made no objection. "Tabitha's oriented herself to her temporary home?" he asked in a teasing tone, which indicated he was in good spirits this morning.

"Sounds like it," Veronica said with a smile. "Harriet asked how you were. How *are* you feeling today? Still have a headache?"

"Not now. But I often start out without one and then it comes back by the end of the day."

"I hope it doesn't," she told him in a sympathetic tone. She fingered her wedding ring for a moment. "David, would you mind if I spent some time shopping?"

He turned and looked at her. "Shopping?"

"I haven't gotten to see much of London yet. Except Strawberry Hill. But you'll be at the studio again today, and . . ."

"And you're getting bored."

"Not bored. It's interesting seeing a movie being made."

"It's interesting for a couple of hours, and then it's like watching paint dry unless you're involved in it." He walked up and put his arms around her. "I'm sorry."

"No, don't apologize."

"Are you feeling well enough to go off shopping on your own?" he asked, his blue eyes carrying a worried aspect.

"I feel pretty good today. Maybe I'm over that flu or whatever it was." Actually, she felt about the same amount of queasiness she'd been feeling every morning. As Harriet had suggested, she was already learning to live with it.

"London's a big city. You won't get lost?"

"I have a map and a diagram of the Underground. I probably won't go too far from the hotel today. If I get tired, I can always catch a cab back."

"I wish I could go with you," David said fretfully.

This was just what she didn't want at the moment. "I'll be all right."

"Maybe I can arrange to get the afternoon away, so we can go sight-seeing together. Why don't you come with me to the studio this morning, and then—"

"But I'd like some time to shop on my own. You'd get bored looking at dresses with me."

David seemed unsettled. "But I don't like you going about on your own in a city you've never been in before, in a foreign country."

She smiled. "I'm a grown woman, not a little girl, remember?"

He raised his eyebrows in a self-deprecating expression. "I guess you do need to remind me of that."

"And this is England, a civilized country that uses the same language we speak," she gently chided him. "You're beginning to extend your anxiety about safety to me, too, David."

"Well, of course," he retorted. "You're more important to me than anything else in the world."

She settled her hands on his chest. "But we can't live in a protected cocoon."

"I know." He sounded impatient with himself. "I still can't get used to being mortal. Life seems too precarious to me, now."

"But you didn't worry about me this way when you were a vampire. I was as mortal then as I am now. You weren't this overprotective then."

"Because I didn't realize then how dangerous being a mortal is. I never thought about it until I became one again myself. Our lives are so fragile, Veronica. I don't think you understand that. I didn't when I was a mortal youth, either. You just don't realize how delicate life is."

She held him close, hoping somehow to comfort him. In an impish tone, she raised her mouth to his ear and whispered, "Nevertheless, this fragile female is going shopping."

"But if you wait, maybe we can go together this afternoon," he argued, still afraid, apparently, to let her go alone.

Veronica thought quickly. "I'll phone you at the studio from wherever I am just before noon. If you can get away, then we can meet somewhere, have lunch, and sightsee. Okay?"

She could see how reluctant he was to agree. Nevertheless, he apparently wanted to please her. She was counting on that.

"All right." His tone was a bit edgy. "Be careful, though. When you cross the street, look to your right first, not the left. They drive on the opposite side of the street here."

"No, really?" she teased, poking him in the stomach.

David pressed his lips together in a confounded expression and seemed a little embarrassed. "I didn't mean to insult your intelligence."

"You'll have to put some trust in my judgment."

"How can I?" His blue eyes had a twinkle. "You married me. That shows a lack of good judgment right there."

Veronica laughed and kissed him. "Best decision I ever made!"

After he left, Veronica asked the Claridge's concierge where she could find a "chemist," as she was informed drugstores were called here. She found the place recommended quite easily and returned to the hotel with a pregnancy test kit. She sat down on the bed and read the directions with shaking hands, then went to the bathroom to set out the little plastic vials included in the kit. After reading the directions twice more, for she was so nervous she was afraid she wouldn't get it right, she began the test. When she'd finished filling the test vial with urine, she had one minute to wait to see if the color in the center of the little well turned pink. If it did, it meant she was pregnant.

She checked her watch, then walked into the other room to try to make the minute pass faster. Her heart was thumping and her mouth felt dry. Wandering over to the dresser where David had stood earlier, she studied her reflection in the mirror. It was odd—her face seemed to have a new luster to it, as if her body knew something that she didn't yet. She wasn't sure what to hope for. With David so anxiety prone and his worrisome physical state, she felt it would be best if she weren't pregnant. But then, she sensed that part of her would be hugely disappointed if she weren't going to have a baby. The idea of motherhood frightened her, but it excited her, too.

She looked at her watch again. Five more seconds. She took a long breath for courage and walked back into the bathroom. After counting the remaining seconds, she held her breath and peeked at the center of the little well.

Pink!

She felt faint then and sat down on the edge of the bathtub.

David hurried to an office off the soundstage where he'd been watching Matthew try out new dialogue he'd quickly written as they worked on a scene. A production assistant had told him he had a phone call from his wife.

He picked up the phone in the office. "Veronica? Where are you?"

"At Claridge's."

"I thought you'd be calling from Harrod's, laden down with purchases."

She chuckled. "I just walked to a few places close by and then came back again. I didn't buy anything."

This struck David as unusual. Since their marriage, Veronica had taken on a heightened interest in clothes, now that she had a more plentiful budget for them than she'd had when she was single. He'd never known her to go out shopping and come back empty-handed. "Are you feeling all right?"

"Sure," she replied, perhaps a little too quickly. "Can you leave the studio and have lunch?"

"Things seem to be going reasonably well here. Solange is busy being fitted in wardrobe today, so that automatically makes everything easier on the set. I think they can get along without me for the afternoon."

"Good," Veronica said. "Want to meet me at Claridge's? We can have lunch and figure out what we'd like to do."

When he got back to the hotel, he found Veronica looking quite well. Her face even seemed to have an extra glow, and he did not ask again how she was feeling. But her manner seemed distracted, and he wasn't sure why. He put his sunglasses back on, and they went out to a pub to have lunch. His appetite was back and he enjoyed his meal. David found he had to do most of the talking, though, since his wife was strangely quiet.

They decided to visit the Victoria and Albert Museum, which occupied the greater part of the afternoon. After that they took the Underground to Harrod's, because Veronica said she'd heard it was the "department store to end all department stores." Here they browsed through the expensive men's and women's clothing departments, the china, perfume, and other departments in the huge store. Eventually they wandered inadvertantly into the arcaded Food Halls, which were magnificent, with cathedral-like ceilings and vast tiled counters sumptuously filled with raw cuts of red meats, poultry, and seafood on display.

At first, David was impressed with the sheer opulent indulgence of the place. But then the rich smell of blood reached his nostrils. His eyes were peculiarly drawn to the meats, the raw roasts and steaks that trickled with red running down the white suet edges. A harrowing feeling gripped him. His gaze could not escape the dark crimson all about him. He felt riveted to the floor. The marrow in his bones seemed to vibrate. Memories of bared human necks with blood running from two puncture wounds at the artery—wounds he'd inflicted—flashed through his mind. He suddenly felt quite ill. But before he could say anything, Veronica had taken his arm.

"David," she said, her voice weak, "I have to get out of here. The smell of the meat makes me sick."

He turned to look at her. Her hand was at her stomach. But when she saw his face, she gasped. "You're white as a sheet," she said. "What's wrong?"

He grabbed her arm. "Let's go!"

They raced out of the Food Halls and found their way out of the store, to busy Brompton Road. The bright sun shot pain into David's eyes. He shut his lids tightly, felt his pocket for his sunglasses, and put them on.

The fresh air seemed to revive Veronica. But David's head was reeling. The color red stayed before his eyes, and the smell of blood seemed to hang about him. He felt like running, to escape his darkest fear. He began walking up Brompton Road toward Hyde Park, pulling Veronica along by the hand.

"Are you all right?" he thought to ask, distractedly, as they moved along.

"Yes," she said, barely keeping up with him. "It was the smell of the meat and fish. Did it bother you, too?"

He didn't answer.

"David?"

Before long they came to Albert Gate on the edge of the vast park. They crossed South Carriage Drive and began to walk along a footpath into the park, amid sunny summer greenery. But the cheerful peacefulness of the park was lost on David.

"What's wrong?" Veronica asked again. "Tell me."

He wondered what to say. He must be straightforward, he decided. "Veronica, I'm . . . I'm afraid I'm reverting."

"Y-you are?" she said. She sounded deeply concerned, but he sensed that the news didn't surprise her.

"Herman said there was a small chance this could happen," he reminded her, striving to sound calm for her sake, but failing. "I tried to ignore my sensitivity to light. I told myself it must be due to something else. And the headaches—I don't know why they plague me, except that it must be another indication that something's going wrong with my body. When I saw the blood on the meat—" He stopped speaking as the harrowed feeling came back on him at the memory.

"You craved the blood?" Veronica looked up at him with wide, scared eyes.

"I must have. It had a profound effect on me, wracked me to the core. I saw vivid flashes of my vampire days when I'd fed from people—I saw their necks bleeding. The terror of it, Veronica—" His voice grew choked with the horror of his future. "I can't go back to what I was. I'd rather die today!"

Veronica clung to his arm. "Don't say that, David! Don't even think it! Whatever happens, I'll love you. I'll stay with you. Just don't say you want to die." She grew hysterical and began to cry. "I don't know what I'd do. Especially now. I don't know what I'd do!"

He took her in his arms. "Shhh," he said, stroking her back as she sobbed. "Don't cry. I . . . I didn't mean that. I won't do anything rash. We have to think this through. I don't know what to do, either."

She wiped her eyes and looked up at him. "Are you sure you're reverting? You seemed better today, until now. You ate well at lunch."

"My headache came back after I ate," he told her. "I didn't say anything to you, but my head's throbbing now, and the light is blinding without sunglasses. Herman said a remnant of what he called the vampiric agent might be left in my body. I imagine it's trying to take over. When I'm feeling better, perhaps my body is overcoming it temporarily. But then the vampire force rises and takes over again, and my symptoms return."

"We should go to Switzerland and see Herman. Maybe he could help you somehow."

David looked at her through his sunglasses. "That's an idea. But I don't have his phone number with me. I don't know his address. Being a vampire, he's probably unlisted. How could we contact him? If only we knew where Darienne was. She could tell us."

Veronica paused, as if a thought were going through her mind. Then her shoulders slumped. "We don't know where she lives here, do we?"

"Decades ago, she used to have a place in Belgravia. I don't remember the street. But she'd be unlisted, too. Besides, she hasn't surfaced. I don't think she's in London."

Veronica's face brightened. "Harriet might know! Darienne gave her Herman's address, so she could send him samples of the ingredients to analyze." She was referring to the herbs that comprised the ancient gypsy cure she and Harriet had obtained from their great-great-aunt in Czechoslovakia.

"It's worth a try," David said.

When they got back to the hotel, Veronica called Harriet again. This time it was almost midnight in Chicago. After a brief phone conversation, Veronica hung up and seemed subdued. She told David, "Harriet reminded me that she gave the slip of paper Darienne had written the address on to me, and she didn't keep a copy of it. I wish we'd given her a key to our house. She could have gone over and looked for it, then phoned us back." She gazed up at David, her brown eyes distraught. "I wish we were home. At least you'd be near your coffin, in case—"

"The change seems to be taking place slowly," David said, hoping to reassure her. Though he didn't feel very secure himself. "I think there's time. Everything will work out, somehow," he promised her.

But he didn't know if he could keep the promise.

6

Exactly, *mon amour*

THAT EVENING Darienne walked into the quaint, cozy pub in Knightsbridge where she'd first stalked Larry. Since it was Larry's night off from *Hamlet,* Darienne expected to find him at his usual table. She wondered whether Sheena would be with him, or if they'd had a falling out after the girl had caught him with Darienne. But Sheena seemed quite proprietory toward her boyfriend, and Darienne wasn't too surprised to find her sitting at the table with him, as she often was when Darienne arrived.

They were arguing, however. And Darienne was a bit miffed when she quickly discerned, as she casually approached them, that they weren't arguing about *her*.

"Why do you insist on shutting him out?" Sheena was saying. "All he wants is to get to know you."

"My relationship with my father is my business. You had no right to interfere. Calling him up and inviting him to go out to dinner with us!"

"He asked us to call. I told him I would."

"Well, you can have dinner with him if you like. I won't be there."

"Oh, you're so stubborn!" Sheena fumed. "You can't wallow in past hurts forever. The man wants your forgiveness. It's the Christian way to forgive those who have wronged you."

"Then consider me an agnostic."

"What will it take for you to get over this? Are you going to hate him all your life?"

"If I want to."

"You're such a child sometimes—" She left off, realizing Darienne was standing by their table.

Darienne had been there for nearly half a minute, but they'd been so involved in their argument, neither had noticed. "*Bonjour,*" Darienne said with a smile. "Am I interrupting?"

"Yes!"

"No, of course not," Larry said, his voice competing with Sheena's for prominence. His eyes took on a new light as he rose from the table. He moved over a chair so Darienne could sit next to him. As Darienne took the vacated seat, she gazed across the table at Sheena, whose dark eyes were glowering.

"You were saying that Larry is a child?" Darienne prompted Sheena to carry on where she'd left off.

Angry, sharp lights played in Sheena's eyes, but she said nothing.

"He looks quite grown up to me," Darienne said, filling the silence as she gave Larry an admiring gaze. Larry drank it up rather smugly.

His hair was combed in its usual casual way with short, curly tendrils allowed to go in all directions. He wore a denim shirt and jeans and leaned back in his chair, looking at her with warmth in his eyes that was growing hotter by degrees. It wasn't hard to guess what was in his mind, after what Darienne had promised him at his party.

Sheena apparently noticed the heat in his gaze, too. "The measure of a man's maturity depends on what you're looking for," she said, shifting her eyes from Larry to Darienne. "And it's always easy to guess what *you're* looking for." She turned her head back to Larry, gazing at him squarely in the eye. "And what is it you're after? A roll in the hay with a worldly Frenchwoman? Would that make you feel like a man?"

"Sheena!" Larry's eyes showed angry embarrassment.

"I'm just asking: What's going on between you? Do you think I'm so naive? I may not be as experienced as she, but I'm not stupid! Maybe you're not ready for a real relationship yet. You refuse to have one with your father. Maybe I'm expecting too much to think you're ready for a permanent one with a woman. You want to sow some wild oats? Is that it?"

Larry's jaw clenched. "I won't be forced into a relationship with anyone, not if I don't choose it."

"I thought you'd chosen me." Sheena's tone was firm, though her eyes were bright with gathering tears.

"I had. But all of a sudden you're starting to run my life."

"Acting like a mother?" Sheena glanced at Darienne, obviously remembering what she'd said at the party. "Guess you were right. Well, I'll tell you what, Darienne. If you're so hard up for a conquest, you can have him! *I* want a man who deals with his problems. Not an adolescent who nurses his anger and builds walls to keep away those who might love him."

Darienne listened, admiring Sheena for her spunk and secretly siding with her. Darienne wanted Larry to forgive Matthew, too. At the same time, here she was, planning to use Larry to ensnare his father. She felt torn inside, wondering if she were doing the right thing.

Of course, she knew she wasn't. But she had never been burdened with Sheena's idealism and unyielding morality. Sheena was risking losing her young man in order to make her point, clearly hoping he would see she was right. Darienne wouldn't have the courage to do that. It was safer to find some scheme to undermine your man. Appealing to male intelligence and reason was too risky—they didn't always have any at hand.

Larry, meanwhile, had seemed quite taken aback at Sheena's words to Darienne, *you can have him.* Darienne could guess that Sheena had never been so tough with him. But youthful pride made him feign a callous attitude.

"I'm not yours to give away," Larry said, his brash tone not quite covering the shock in his voice. "I choose who I want to be with."

"Well, what's your choice then?" Sheena asked. "Darienne or me? You can't have us both, you know. I don't share. I expect a boyfriend to be true to me!"

Larry was silent, though his breaths were coming a bit fast. He seemed not to know how to handle the situation. Darienne decided to stay out of the fray for the moment, since things might work out to her advantage without her pushing the situation. If they decided to split up on their own, Larry probably wouldn't blame Darienne. Then she could play the role of comforter for him—an ideal balm to soothe him at the final, critical moment, if he had any last-minute reservations.

"Can't you make up your mind?" Sheena chided him. "Would you like us to find you a coin to toss?"

Larry's eyes darkened. Darienne couldn't help but smile, enjoying Sheena's wit in the face of potential humiliation. She was rising above the situation, and Darienne admired her for it.

Sheena glanced at Darienne, caught her amusement, and seemed to resonate with her for a millisecond, then fell back into a glare. "Do you really want a man who can't decide if he wants you or not?" she asked Darienne. "Well—I don't!" Sheena got up from the table. "You two deserve each other."

Larry straightened up, alarm in his face. "Sheena—"

She turned. "Yes?"

"Just like that, you're going to walk off?"

"What would you suggest I do? Sit here and watch her seduce you?"

"You've got it all wrong. Darienne and I are just friends."

Sheena shut her eyes in exasperation. "And I'm the Queen Mum! I used to think you were honest. We used to have all those philosophical conversations about how we valued truth. But you men forget that kind of talk at the sight of a big-chested blonde! I thank God I've learned 'the truth' about you. I won't waste any more of my precious time on a two-timer! Good-bye, Larry. Look me up when you've grown up a bit. I'll be married with six kids by then!" She turned from the table and walked away.

People at nearby tables were chuckling and applauded her as she strutted by on her way out.

"Sheena!" Larry called after her, rising from the table. Sheena kept walking and soon was out the door of the pub. Darienne pulled on Larry's arm, urging him to sit down again.

"People are looking," she told him as he took his seat.

"Let them look," he said, angry. "She's embarrassed herself, not me! If she thinks I'm going to let her tell me what to do, who to see, what to think—"

"Shh." Darienne placed her hand on his shoulder. "She's gone now. You held your ground. You didn't give in. Don't be so upset."

"Right." He was silent for a moment and took a drink of his beer. "I'm glad she's gone. Can you imagine? I was thinking of marrying her! What a henpecked husband I'd be."

"You certainly avoided that," Darienne said, needing to affirm him for her own purposes, even though she wasn't impressed with the way he'd handled himself.

"And she wouldn't believe me!" he blustered on. "Practically called me a liar."

Darienne sighed with growing impatience. For a man of twenty-five, he had a lot of growing up to do. Perhaps it was because he never had a father in his life to pattern himself after and guide him to maturity. On the other hand, Darienne had always known, long before it was stated as fact by psychologists in recent times, that men matured much more slowly than women. She'd met some men past fifty who still behaved as if they were five.

"Larry," she said in a gentle tone, "you did lie to Sheena." Darienne felt obligated on behalf of her gender to point this out.

"What? How?" he asked defensively.

"You told her there was nothing going on between us."

"And there isn't." When she stared him down, he added, "Not yet anyway."

"Isn't that a technicality? You've already told me you want to go to bed with me. She could see what was on your mind when you looked at me. Denying what's obvious only makes you look foolish."

"What is it with you women? Always correcting and finding fault. What do you think I should have done then?"

"What you should do is become a man who tries to see things from a woman's point of view. That way you might avoid offending a woman or insulting her intelligence."

Larry laughed out loud. "I haven't met a man yet who understands women!"

Neither have I, Darienne thought to herself in a wistful, sardonic mood. David came close. And Matthew—Matthew didn't understand women really, but he had an instinctive sensitivity . . . Reluctantly, Darienne let the thought go. She had his rambunctious son to deal with right now.

"Then maybe I can teach you a few things that would be useful to know about women," she said, sliding her hand up and down his arm.

He lowered his eyes and looked guilty suddenly. "If we go through with this . . . I don't think Sheena will ever take me back."

"But you just said good riddance to her."

He nodded. "I know I did."

"Well, then . . . ," Darienne said in an inviting tone.

Larry raised his eyes to hers. He looked so young. There were no lines about his eyes to give him an air of experience and wisdom, as Matthew had. Yet just now Larry had the same piercing inquisitiveness in his eyes that she'd often seen in Matthew's, that sense of pulling everything out of her mind that he could by focusing on her.

"Why do you want me?" he asked. "Sheena said you were seducing me."

"I told you at your party, I'm attracted to you. You're the image of my ideal in a man."

"Me?" His eyes narrowed with an inkling of humor. "I'm not dazzled when I look in the mirror. I'm fair-looking, not ideal. A woman like you could have anyone."

"I don't want just anyone. I want you specifically."

He shook his head. "But why? I don't understand why you've singled me out."

"Who can understand what attracts a woman to a man?" she replied, taking a philosophical tone. "I saw you and I wanted you. That's why I challenged you at darts that night we first spoke to each other. I'd seen you at the pub a few times, and I decided I wanted to know you—in all senses of the word."

"You even beat me at darts, too. You came, you saw, you . . . conquered."

"Not yet, *chéri*." She moved her hand up his shoulder. "But I'm hoping."

"I'm giving up a lot for this."

"I can make you forget Sheena. After a night with me, you'll forget any other woman you've ever known or wanted."

His eyes took on a strong sensual glow. "You're awfully sure of yourself."

Darienne chuckled. "*Oui,* it's a lifelong trait. I know what I want, and I always give myself what I want. It's my secret for happiness. And when I'm happy, whoever is with me is happy, too. I guarantee it. Why don't you follow my example? You want me. I know you do. Give yourself a gift. Take me home with you. You'll make us both happy."

He stared at her, his unblinking eyes shining with desire and awe. "All right. Let's go."

By the time they had walked to his flat and proceeded into his bedroom, Larry had grown nervous. Darienne wasn't sure if it was from performance anxiety or if he was still concerned about losing Sheena.

She eyed him and smiled, swishing her long cotton-gauze lavender skirt as she moved toward him. She breathed in, making her breasts rise and the cleavage plump above her low-cut peasant blouse. As she drew near, sliding her arms about his neck, he said, "Maybe we should think about this—"

"What's there to think about?"

"B-blood diseases for one thing." He began pulling her arms from his neck.

The mention of blood automatically made her focus on the artery that was pulsing slightly in his throat. She quickly ordered the thought out of her mind. She wasn't here for that and mustn't let herself think of it. Drinking from Larry would form a bond with him, make him her slave. He'd only be in the way then, when she went after her real quarry, his father. It was Matthew's blood she craved. Not that Larry's wouldn't briefly quench her never-ending thirst. But she'd drunk from her supply of blood bags at home before she came, just so she wouldn't be too tempted. She'd wait for Matthew's blood, which would quench her soul.

"I have no diseases, I promise you, *chéri.*" She thickened her earthy French accent. "From me you'll get only pure, healthy, lusty sex. Hours of it. Don't you want that?" she asked in a languid tone as she stroked his face.

Larry swallowed. "I . . . want that. But somehow I have the feeling I'm not ready for you."

"Oh, I'll make you ready," she assured him, sliding her hand below his belt.

"I didn't mean that literally," he said, backing away slightly.

Darienne closed the small space he'd put between them. She parted her knees and captured his thigh between hers, pressing him as she arched her breasts against his chest. "You've never met a woman as unabashedly sensual as I am, have you?"

"No." His voice was husky and breathless.

"You don't quite know what to do, how to cope with me, do you?" she asked with delight.

"No."

"I'll tell you what you should do then: Whatever you want."

His eyes widened slightly, but he seemed frozen.

"You have an imagination, *chéri*. I'll bet it's running wild right now. What do your impulses tell you to do?"

He hesitated only a moment. "Rip off your dress and throw you on the bed."

"Do it," she whispered in his ear, then hotly kissed his jaw. She slid her knee upward, against his groin. "I won't mind."

He shifted his feet to keep his balance. "But—"

She sighed. "Another inhibited modern man. I've given you permission to do anything you like with me. Why hesitate?"

"It doesn't seem right to just pounce on a woman. Women want foreplay and so on. Don't they?" He seemed confused.

Darienne smiled. He was really rather sweet. He had potential. With another twenty years' experience, he might even develop the sublime, sensual sensitivity his father had. But Darienne didn't want to wait twenty years.

"Yes, most women want foreplay. Sometimes I do, too. But I'm so excited just being with you, that I'm ready now." She pressed her cheek to his and whispered in his ear again, "Appease me! My body aches for you."

This wasn't quite true. The real reason she was hurrying him was that he was hesitant and she didn't want to risk his changing his mind. Once he was initially seduced, she'd have all night to play with him, if she wanted to.

She slid her mouth across his cheek to his lips and kissed him. When he kissed her back, she was pleased. Still, he seemed rooted to the spot on which he was standing. He made no effort to urge her, push her, or carry her to the bed, which was only a few feet behind her. She thought he would enjoy being the aggressor, but apparently he was overwhelmed by her superior experience. Yet she wanted him to be the aggressor, so that later he couldn't claim she'd forced him against his will. In his mind, she wanted this to be completely his choice, so that if the time came, as it might, that he regretted what happened between them, he'd have himself to blame as well as her.

She drew away from him, let go of him entirely, and stepped back to the bed. Climbing on it, she shifted her legs beneath her and sat on her heels, knees well apart. She pulled her gauzy skirt to her upper thighs, letting the material fall between her legs to keep her most feminine area tantalizingly hidden. Purposely, she'd worn no undergarments tonight. Her low-cut blouse buttoned in front, and she began unbuttoning it slowly, watching him. She was pleased to see him staring at her with mute, helpless desire.

When she was finished unbuttoning the blouse, she pushed apart the two sides a few inches, so that the deep inner curves of her large, firm breasts were entirely revealed. The blouse edges rested softly over her upturned nipples.

"I want you, Larry," she said with longing. Crossing her arms, she cupped her hands over her breasts beneath the blouse, fondling herself. "I need to be touched." She injected a little anguish into her tone. "Help me . . ."

Suddenly, so fast it took her by surprise, he rushed toward her, unbuckling his belt. As he pushed himself over her, each hand on the bed on either side of her, her blouse slipped back, and he began devouring her bared breasts with his eager mouth. While he was thus occupied, she took the precaution of unzipping his pants, freeing him, to make sure there were no further delays.

She lay back on the bedspread then and pulled up her skirts. Spreading her knees, she encircled him with her legs. Breathing hotly, he lifted himself up a bit, then entered her.

"Ohh," she sighed with pleasure, relaxing now that she'd accomplished her goal. Larry had been seduced! Whatever happened now was icing on the cake.

He pumped heatedly back and forth inside her, breathing hard. The strong masculine thrusts felt good. She closed her eyes and moved her hands over his back to twine her fingers into his curly hair, imagining for a moment that he was Matthew.

But just as she was about to moan with desire, she felt the telltale quivering of his member within her. He stopped his thrusting and recovered his breathing.

After a moment, he said sheepishly, "Sorry. I was so excited—"

"I know," Darienne said, stroking his shoulder in a comforting manner. This wasn't an unusual occurrence. Most men were overexcited the first time they were with her. She took it in stride, saw it as a compliment to her expertise. "You're a virile young man, and it's been a long time for you. Next time, you'll pleasure me even more."

He raised himself up on his elbows and looked down at her. "Next time?" he said, still panting a bit.

"In a few minutes, when you're ready again."

He smiled, then laughed a little. "All right!"

"Thought you'd be willing. You must have liked it."

His expression took on a look of awe. "You're incredible! I've never been so turned on. You're the most sexy woman I've ever seen."

"Thank you. Shall we take our clothes off? Make it easier? Or do you like me half-dressed? It's up to you."

He looked at her, a bit perplexed. "You do everything to please a man. Almost like a . . . a . . ."

"Prostitute?"

"I didn't mean to say—"

She put her fingers to his lips. "It's all right. I'm not offended. I do like to please men. But just so you understand completely—I never charge for my favors. I sleep with men to please myself, and them, too. And I never go with a male gigolo, either. Sex should be given freely, with joy and abandon, I believe."

"What about diseases? Aren't you worried?"

"I'm immune, *chéri*."

"How can anyone be immune?"

She hesitated. "I have a peculiar body chemistry. I never get sick. My immune system is so efficient nothing can harm me." Her immune system, of course, was death. Being technically dead, she couldn't catch the diseases humans who were truly alive could. But she couldn't explain all that to Larry. She hoped he would never learn her secret.

"That's amazing," he said, as if wondering whether to believe her. "Have you been checked by doctors?"

"I've been analyzed at a lab in Switzerland," she said, thinking of her visits with Herman and expanding on the truth a bit.

"I see. If health isn't a worry, what about the old idea of settling down with one man and keeping yourself to him alone?"

She smiled at him, half seeing another face very like his. "That would take a truly special man for me."

He took a deep breath. "I'd like to be that man."

"Would you?" She stroked his face, thinking how quickly he'd forgotten Sheena. "We'll see. First I'll need some more exposure to your male prowess," she said with a mischievous grin as she ran her hand downward along his abdomen.

When she reached his swollen member, she chuckled. "That didn't take long!" she said with cooing admiration. Placing her hands on his lower back, she urged him to enter her. "We'll take our clothes off later. We have all night."

"Oh, God," he murmured as he slid into her. He laughed a little even as he moaned with sensuality. "Will I survive?"

"You'll survive," she assured him, wrapping her legs about him again. "I'll need you later."

At about four A.M., she quietly got dressed and left his apartment as he lay sleeping and exhausted from a night of sex. After he'd gotten past his initial overeagerness and slowed down, she'd taken time to teach him a great deal about using sexual expertise to enhance pleasure. He turned out to be an apt student, and he improved with each coming together. She'd enjoyed her time with him well enough, even if she hadn't found it totally satisfying. But she'd improved him for some other woman, possibly Sheena, and so she felt she'd contributed something to make up for her manipulation of him. She owed him and Sheena that much. But she owed herself more. And this night she'd merely layed the groundwork for her own ultimate fulfillment.

As she walked home down London's dark and nearly deserted streets, she thought of nothing but Matthew. Soon she'd be with him, she promised herself with determination. If he didn't come willingly, then she'd make him come to her. But Matthew would be hers, one way or another.

Matthew sat in the small theater, waiting for the curtain to rise. He'd come to see his son play *Hamlet* again. It seemed to be the only way he could see Larry at all.

Matthew was on his own tonight. David and Veronica had not wanted to come. They'd seemed distracted somehow at the studio today. David could hardly concentrate on the script, and Veronica sat off on her own most of the time looking pale and upset. Matthew didn't know why and didn't want to pry, fearing it was some marital problem. But he liked them both and hoped whatever the issue was, they could work it out.

Matthew also thought of the phone call he'd gotten late last night from Sheena. She'd called to say their proposed dinner out together was canceled, explaining that she'd just broken up with Larry.

"Oh, no!" Matthew had exclaimed, completely dismayed. "Why?"

"He's found a buxom blonde he likes better."

Matthew felt his stomach tighten now in the theater just thinking of their phone conversation. He'd asked Sheena if she knew the woman's name.

"Darienne," Sheena had replied. "Don't know her last name. She's French. Claims she lives in Belgravia, but she's your basic tart, if you ask me."

So Matthew knew now that what David had feared had actually happened. Darienne had shown up in his son's life—probably seduced him already, if he knew Darienne. And he certainly did. She'd gone to extensive lengths to try to seduce Matthew when he first met her. She'd failed, but in the end, Matthew gave in to his own desires and agreed to sleep with her on his own terms—no commitment, no expectations of a relationship. He hoped his son had some sense about handling such a predatory woman, but he feared Larry didn't. And Larry had no idea, as Matthew hadn't for years, that Darienne was a vampiress.

He would have talked to David about Larry's apparent predicament, gotten some advice, if David hadn't seemed so upset and withdrawn. Matthew had no one to turn to for help.

And Larry had no one to protect him except his father.

But Larry would call it interference. Matthew could imagine him objecting already. All he could do was hope that Darienne had somehow failed to seduce him.

The play began, and Matthew could instantly see a difference in his son as soon as he appeared on stage. Larry seemed to have increased energy and youthful exuberance. In fact, he seemed slightly out of control. Later, in the third act, in a scene with Ophelia, he delivered his slightly bawdy lines with an earthy enthusiasm he hadn't displayed the previous night Matthew had seen him perform. He lay down on the stage floor at Ophelia's feet, which was in the script. But, reaching out, he took hold of her ankle beneath her long dress, which he hadn't done before. There was playful sensuality in his every syllable.

HAMLET

Lady, shall I lie in your lap?

OPHELIA

No, my lord.

HAMLET

I mean, my head upon your lap?

OPHELIA

Ay, my lord.

HAMLET

Did you think I meant country matters?

OPHELIA

I think nothing, my lord.

HAMLET

That's a fair thought to lie between a maid's legs.

The young actress playing Ophelia was blushing through her makeup by the time the short scene between them was finished, a scene she'd handled with stylish aplomb a few nights ago. She was reacting to the change in Larry.

Matthew bowed his head and felt tears sting his eyes. Darienne had gotten to Larry, he was certain of that now. The boy had been awakened to the higher level of sensuality only Darienne could bring to a man. He felt that his son had been corrupted, that he was in danger, a danger greater than Larry even knew existed. Matthew looked up then and tried to focus his eyes on Larry's throat, which was left bare by his tunic costume. He couldn't see any marks on his son's neck. Not yet. Matthew had to get Larry away from Darienne before she did any more damage, before he lost his son to her forever.

All at once it occurred to Matthew that Darienne might be in the theater tonight, watching the play, too. She always used to watch Matthew perform, so she might carry on her tradition with Larry. Matthew looked about him, but couldn't see a comely blonde with long hair anywhere in the audience. He even turned to glance up at the balcony, but did not recognize anyone there, either. Of course he couldn't see the far corners of the theater well, and those sitting in front of him he could see only from the back. There was one woman in the front row in a yellow dress that drew his eye, but she had short blond hair, cut shorter than some men wore their hair. Since Darienne always made it a point to emphasize her femininity, this couldn't be her.

A renewed memory of Darienne filled Matthew's mind—the exquisite, deceptively winsome face; her frivolous, throaty voice; the thick, honey-blond hair that he used to unfasten so that it fell about her face and shoulders and tumbled downward over her warm, voluptuous breasts . . . the way she used to smile at him, as if he were the only man she'd ever known . . .

Matthew clenched his jaw, hating himself for still wanting her despite what she was and what she'd done to him and now to his son. She was a predatory, immoral—yes, evil—creature, deathly seductive and dangerous to the core. He had to remember that. He had to convince Larry of that.

When the play was over, Matthew remained in his seat for a moment, waiting for the audience to clear. He hadn't decided yet what approach to take with Larry, how to warn him he was in danger, and he almost wanted to avoid going backstage to see his son. He knew Larry would be angry with him. He still hated Matthew because of the past. What would he think of his father trying to advise him about his love life? He'd probably tell Matthew to go to hell.

After a few minutes, Matthew got up from his seat and made his way backstage. He had to do something. When he reached Larry's dressing room, he found to his surprise that his son was with the short-haired blonde he'd noticed before. She was standing in the doorway, in her slinky yellow dress, leaning against the door frame while she talked to Larry. As Matthew came up behind her, he heard her voice and stopped short. No other woman possessed that inimitable husky feminine voice laced with a French accent. The blonde *was* Darienne, after all.

Matthew's heart started to beat fast as he wondered what to do. He hadn't expected to find his son with her tonight. He'd hoped to be able to warn him without her there to defend herself or to try to manipulate them both, which he wouldn't put past her.

He looked over her shoulder into the dressing room. Larry was sitting at his mirror, on the side wall, taking off his makeup. Matthew understood why Darienne was staying by the door. If she went further inside, she risked *not* being seen in his mirror.

Matthew caught Larry's eye as Larry turned to respond to Darienne. His son stared at him for a grim half second, then said, "I thought I saw you in the audience. You needn't try to be such a dutiful father. You can't make up for lost time."

Darienne turned then and stared at Matthew. She drew in a quick breath and seemed taken off guard that he'd been standing so close behind her. Her green eyes were huge—and a puzzle. She didn't look totally surprised; he had the feeling she might have been expecting him somehow. And yet she seemed curiously rattled, even at a loss for words—highly unusual for Darienne. But then he could see the otherworld glow turn the green of her eyes iridescent, and he knew her feelings were running deep. He used to see that glow in her eyes when they made love. He didn't know at first that it was a sign she was a vampiress.

She lowered her eyes and seemed to try to compose herself. She looked so different with her hair cut short. Why had she done it? And why wasn't she saying anything? Was she going to pretend she didn't know him?

Perhaps that was best, Matthew decided, thinking quickly. Larry wouldn't want to know he'd slept with the same woman his father had been with. Yet how could he warn Larry unless he revealed that he knew her?

The silence seemed to have made Larry conscious of his manners. "Sorry, I should introduce you. Darienne, this is . . . my father." He said the last word with reluctance. "Matthew McDowall. Maybe you've heard of him."

"Of course. I recognized you immediately," Darienne said to Matthew in what seemed to be a careful voice. "I . . . wasn't sure what to say to such a famous actor."

Matthew merely nodded.

"Women are always so taken with you," Larry said sarcastically.

"Is Darienne your new friend?" Matthew asked, ignoring the sarcasm.

Larry chuckled smugly. "She's a bit more than a friend now." It was as if he was showing off to his father.

"I see." Matthew wondered how to handle the situation. There was no neat way to do it. This would be a messy scene no matter how he played it. He glanced at Darienne. She was smiling quietly at Matthew now, her expression as smug as his son's. This infuriated Matthew and plunged him onward. "You need to be careful who you get involved with, Larry. This woman is . . . older than you. Far more experienced. She might be dangerous."

Larry's mouth dropped open. His eyes flared with anger. "How dare you insult her! Who are you to barge in here and say such a thing!"

Matthew held his ground and raised his own voice. "I'm telling you, she's dangerous. She's not like other women."

"How the hell would you know?"

Matthew felt like caving into himself. He wished he could disappear from this scene. But he had to stay and take on this battle. Changing tactics, he turned to Darienne and said to her, "Why on earth did you cut your hair?"

Darienne's eyes lost their inner brightness. Her face looked thunderstruck. Apparently tongue-tied again, she looked away.

Matthew realized he'd hurt her feelings, and irrational guilt threatened to undermine him for a moment, until he remembered why he was there. Why in the world should I feel sorry for her! Matthew chastised himself.

Larry, meanwhile, looked confused and suspicious. "Darienne, do you know him?"

She nodded stiffly. "We've met."

"When?"

"When Matthew was playing *Shadow* on stage. I supplied some of the money to back the show when it began in Chicago."

"You never told me," Larry said.

"You never told me he was your father," Darienne replied coolly.

"But she knew," Matthew said. He turned to Darienne. "Didn't you?"

Darienne hesitated, then admitted, "I knew."

Larry's eyes moved from one to the other as they stood by the doorway. He didn't seem to know what to make of the situation.

"She's a dangerous woman, Larry," Matthew repeated. "She's after you for her own purposes."

"Why?" Larry shot back. "What could she get from me? I'm not rich or famous yet."

"No," Darienne said, seeming to regain some of her self-composure. "He's young and handsome and pleasant to be with. That's all I want."

"He also happens to be my son," Matthew said, pinning her with his eyes. "Odd you should choose *him* for your boy toy."

Larry began to laugh. "I see what he's upset about now: He's jealous! Growing a bit long in the tooth to get beautiful women the way you used to, dear *old* Dad?"

Darienne gazed at Matthew, eyes sparkling, taunting him. "*Are* you jealous, *chéri?* Wishing it were you I was with last night?"

Anger got the better of him. "Bitch!" Matthew snarled at her under his breath.

For a moment Darienne looked stricken. But like lightning, the iridescent glow lit her eyes. "You can't stop me," she retorted in a low hiss. "He's mine! Forever."

"Over my dead body!"

She gasped softly and then seemed to vibrate with inner lust. "Exactly, *mon amour*."

Matthew felt himself growing pale. He knew now what she really wanted. She was playing a game of emotional blackmail. She was counting on the fact that he loved his son enough to sacrifice himself in his stead to her deadly embrace—and then arise as a vampire.

There had to be some other solution, Matthew told himself, beginning to sweat, some way to save both Larry and himself from Darienne's unholy clutches.

But Larry was drawing conclusions of his own. "You two seem to know each other very well, to fall into a heated argument so fast. You have a past together, don't you?" He looked from one to the other, but neither answered. His eyes settled on Darienne. "Did you have an affair with my father?"

Matthew glared at her, daring her to answer with the truth.

"Yes," she admitted quietly, apparently quelling her inner, raging emotion. "Matthew and I were lovers for three years."

Larry swallowed, as if he felt nauseated. "Three years?"

"I . . . told you," she said in a gentler tone, "you're the image of my ideal."

"So that's why you singled me out—because I'm his son!"

"Yes."

"You see how cunning and duplicitous she is?" Matthew said to Larry. "I told you, she's dangerous. It took me three years to figure it out. Don't be as stupid as I was."

Darienne shot Matthew a sudden, unexpected look of admiration. "You were never stupid, *chéri*. And neither is Larry, just because he took advantage of my offer to spend an evening with him. And I'm not duplicitous. I've just admitted everything, haven't I?"

"Have you told him what you are?" Matthew asked.

Darienne dropped her gaze, then coyly looked up at him again. "If you think there's something he ought to know about me, then you tell him."

Matthew remembered how hard it had been for her to convince him, when she finally told him she was a vampiress. Larry would think his father had gone crazy. Darienne seemed to hold all the cards; Matthew didn't know how to outwit her.

"She used to be a prostitute, is that it?" Larry said, looking pleased with himself that he'd guessed what they weren't saying. "I could tell that. And you know what? I don't care! She's a magnificent woman, and I don't give a damn who she's been with, including you."

Darienne smiled at Larry. "Thank you, *chéri.*" She appeared to blink back tears and added in a choked little voice, "Matthew can be so cruel sometimes."

Oh, God, Matthew thought. Darienne was clever enough to take anything he might say and turn it to her favor.

Larry rose from his chair and slipped his arm around her shoulder. "Don't worry. I won't let him be mean to you." He glared at Matthew. "Get out and leave us alone."

"Larry," Matthew said in desperation, "you don't know what you're getting into!"

"I said, get out!"

Matthew drew in a breath, trying to hold his ground, trying to find some other avenue of approach. "All right, I'll go. But I want to talk to Darienne alone before I leave."

"She doesn't have to talk to you," Larry said with bravado, his protective arm tightening about her shoulders.

But Darienne was staring at Matthew, looking tentative and perhaps nervous. "It's all right. I'll talk to him. What more can he say to insult me?"

"You don't have to," Larry argued.

"I want to. It will be all right." She reached up and squeezed Larry's fingers at her shoulder. "Don't worry." She edged out of his embrace and stepped toward Matthew, her eyes watching him as he warily observed her. They walked out into the hall. Darienne pointed to an empty dressing room a few doors down. They went in and she closed the door.

"Speak softly," she told him, her eyes still as she gazed at his face. "The walls are thin."

"I want you to leave my son alone."

"I don't want to," she said simply.

"He's just a kid."

Darienne stood motionless for a long moment, like a beautiful statue, her eyes clear, silently speaking volumes. Then in a voice that was almost childlike, she said, "I'd rather have you, Matthew. I still love you. Come back to me and I'll leave your son alone."

To his chagrin, Matthew almost felt tempted—and not just to save his son. But he said, "No way! I want you out of both our lives."

"No, Matthew. I intend to have one or the other of you. It's your choice." She reached out to touch his chin, her fingers trembling. "Oh, I've missed you." Tears, real tears this time, filled her eyes, making them glassy and jewel-like. The emerald green shone from them, deep and unfathomable. Her voice reduced to a heartfelt whisper, as if her throat were constricted with emotion. "How I've needed you. I cut my hair just to spite you, to try to forget you. But I can't. Every night I long for you. If you'd come back to me, I'd do anything for you, give you anything you want. I'd try so hard to please you. Oh, Matthew, give me another chance. Please take me back."

Matthew was thrown by her sudden meekness, her begging him to return. But when she slowly, almost shyly, drew her lips near to his to kiss him, the memory of her attack on him flew into his mind. He remembered the feel of her sharp teeth at his jugular. Panic overtook him. Flinching, he drew back, pushing her away at the same time. "Get away from me! I don't want you near me. And stay away from my son!"

Darienne stumbled, but recovered her balance. She blinked in confusion. But as a tear ran down her cheek, her expression hardened. Her voice sounded brittle when she spoke. "Or you'll do what?" she taunted. "I once made you very happy. But you tossed me aside, as if I never meant a thing to you. I've decided I want Larry instead, and he certainly seems to want me. He values me more than you ever did. Why shouldn't I have him? Your son is mine, Matthew—for eternity!"

Matthew's breath shook in his throat from dread. "Y-you intend to make him a vampire—?"

She gave him a telling look, but did not answer. Head held high, she walked out, leaving Matthew alone in the dressing room, at a loss and terrified. He must speak to David! David was the only one who might know how to help.

He hurried out of the theater, on his way to Claridge's. Maybe David could find some way out of this dilemma, this choice between life or living death for his son. And for Matthew himself.

Darienne paused in the hall, having just seen Matthew rush off. She felt shaken. How strongly he still affected her—when she'd first seen him at Larry's door, she couldn't even speak. He looked so well, his marvelous, mercurial face so manly and full of dimension, the craggy lines about his eyes so wise and comforting somehow to behold. His barrel chest appeared proud and masculine accentuated by his broad shoulders, made sensual by his flat stomach and narrow hips. She wanted to throw herself on his chest, hang on his shoulders, and feel him take her in his arms again the way he used to.

But instead he'd glared at her accusingly and mocked her short hair. She felt as if he didn't even find her physically attractive anymore. She hated herself now for cutting off her hair. Making a vow, she promised herself never to cut it again.

Darienne walked to Larry's door and paused outside. She needed to deal with him now, so she must appear composed. Most of all, she had to erase any doubts that Matthew might have planted in his son's mind.

When she walked into his dressing room, she found him pacing. He looked up when she entered the room. He seemed tentative now, as if not sure of her anymore. Perhaps he'd so adamantly stood by her when Matthew was here because he'd wanted to be opposed to Matthew, whatever the issue was. Or perhaps he'd been in the shadow of, and envious of, his father's success, and then felt triumphant realizing that he had attained a woman his father had once admired. But having been alone to think for the last few minutes, perhaps now he felt he merely had his father's leavings.

"How did it go?" Larry asked. "What did he say?"

"He wants me to leave you alone."

"Why? Does he still want you for himself?"

"No," Darienne said slyly. "But he doesn't want you to have me either. Jealousy is like that sometimes."

Larry's mouth curved into a satisfied little grin. "He is jealous then, isn't he? It was written all over his face."

Darienne wanted to ask, Do you really think so? She'd been bluffing, and she would have liked very much to believe what she'd just told Larry. But then she realized it must be Larry's ego and pride that made *him* want to believe such a thing. Darienne could capitalize on this, so she pursued it further.

"That's why he warned you about me and said I was dangerous. I was too hot for him to handle, so he thinks you can't manage it either." She chuckled as she walked up to him and wound her arms around his neck. "Little does he know. You manage very well!"

Larry smiled, but doubt filtered into his eyes. "But you and he were together for three years. He must have . . . handled you well enough."

Darienne felt full of longing inside, thinking of the way Matthew could and had "handled" her. "It was a stormy relationship. He never . . . understood me," she said, embroidering on the truth here and there to suit her purposes. "He only wanted me for sex. He never wanted a real relationship. In fact, he walked out on me, just as he's walked out on everyone else who loved him—like your mother and you. I've met Natalie and I admire her very much. I consider her a brave woman."

Larry's eyes took on a warm aspect as she spoke of his mother. "She *was* brave to kidnap me away from him and start anew in a foreign country."

"Yes, she was. And I can understand why you feel he deserted you, too."

"He was never my father, except biologically. He sent money, but that was probably just to ease his conscience. My mother sent it back. He always put his career first."

"I know. That's just how it was when I was with him. He'd kill himself for the theater, never for me." She hadn't meant to express herself in such a literal way, but she didn't try to correct what she'd said, as it might draw attention. "So you see, we've both been deeply hurt by him. We have that in common," she pointed out to Larry. "I . . . suppose I should have told you I knew your father. But I was afraid, if you knew we'd had a relationship, that you'd reject me before you even got to know me."

"Don't apologize. I think I understand," Larry said with sympathy in his brown eyes.

"You see, I knew you were his son, and . . ." She stopped to blink, as if tears were in her eyes. "I thought maybe you would have the qualities I once admired in your father, and none of his hurtful qualities, that had caused me so much pain. He . . . he doesn't know how to love." This statement carried so much truth that it made her voice break as she said the words. She didn't have to pretend emotion anymore. "I know I told you that I enjoy sex just for fun, and I do. But, after a certain point, even an independent woman like me needs more than that."

"I think I could love you," Larry said, drawing her closer, his eyes full of eagerness. "I can give you what he never could."

Darienne stared at him, a bit stunned. She felt hugely guilty now about leading Larry on, taking advantage of his need to compete with and rise above his father. He seemed so young and idealistic now, telling his father's cast-off mistress, who he'd even assumed was a former whore, that love conquers all. She felt so touched, it almost made her weep again.

She took his hand in both of hers. "You're very sweet and sensitive, Larry. But we need to take things slowly. I know I offered my body to you rather quickly, because I was so attracted. But love . . . that's something we can't jump into, the way we jumped into bed. Do you understand what I mean?"

Larry's expression grew self conscious. "I remember telling you that my parents jumped into their relationship too fast. Looks like I've made the same mistake."

"No, you haven't." Darienne tried to reassure him. "I'm not young and innocent as your mother was when she met your father. And I can't get pregnant as she did. It's an entirely different situation."

Larry nodded, but nevertheless, self-doubt stayed in his eyes. Darienne was going to say more to convince him, but then changed her mind. Perhaps it was best if he realized that he wasn't superior to his father, as he wanted to think he was. Maybe he ought to know he could potentially make the same life mistakes Matthew had made. This self-questioning might be the first step Larry needed to take, in order to better understand, and finally to forgive, his father.

7

If I could pray for you, I would

DAVID PULLED Veronica close to him beneath the covers and held her against him. They had gone to bed early after a weary day at the studio. David had caved in to Solange's demands for more lines for her character, and then when he tried to write them for her, nothing came to him. All he could think of was the possibility that he might once again become a vampire. Veronica had been subdued and looked wan all day. He knew she was worried sick, too. Now, holding her close under the protective, warm bedcovers, he felt more safe, though he knew it was an illusion.

"How are you?" he asked her quietly in the darkness of their hotel room. "You seemed tired today."

"I was," she said as she squirmed against him to find a more comfortable position. "I feel good now. It's so quiet here. I like being close to you."

"I like holding you close," he whispered, realizing, despite all his worries, that the feel of her gentle, warm body against his was arousing him. He needed an escape into the sublime oblivion of lovemaking with Veronica. Lying with her had always made him feel better. But he didn't want to press her if she wasn't up to it.

As if they still had their former bond and she could read his mind, she whispered, "I'd like to make love."

David rose up a bit and looked down at her in the dim light. "Are you sure?"

She smiled. "I'm sure. If we make love, I'll feel that everything's all right again. And then I can sleep more peacefully."

David nodded, understanding. She sat up then to pull off her nightgown. David took off his pajamas. He gazed at her body, shining pale and sensuous in the darkness, her small breasts rounded, ripe looking, the skin taut as if they were slightly swollen, the nipples curiously dark. She looked unusually sexy tonight. He reached out to touch her breast, and she winced as if with pain mixed with profound pleasure. He leaned toward her to kiss her mouth. She responded immediately, and he pressed her down gently under the covers, easing his body over hers. He tenderly fondled her breasts and kissed her body, smiling as she writhed softly in sensual response and sighed with kindling passion. When he slid his hand between her warm thighs and stroked her, she gasped with delight. She was already moist. This surprised him slightly. She'd seemed so tired during the day, he would have thought she'd need extra stimulation. But her fatigue seemed to have disappeared, replaced with a sweet, lustful eagerness for him.

Her breaths were coming fast, and she could hardly speak coherently. "David . . . I didn't realize how much I needed this. Mmmm," she moaned with pleasure as he stroked the quick of her. "No more. I want you . . ." Her voice sounded delicious, arousing him more than she knew.

He moved between her parted thighs and made them one. Her body felt warm and tight around him, moist with the soothing balm of her arousal. An ecstasy of pleasure overtook him as he thrust more and more ardently. In Veronica's arms, it was easy to forget the world around him and the problems he carried in his soul. With her, he was in instant paradise.

She began half laughing, half sobbing as her pleasure consumed her. He knew she craved release, and so did he. Rising up for more leverage, he thrust within her more aggressively, being careful not to hurt her. While he no longer had to keep his former vampire strength in check and could be more free with her, he knew that even as a mortal man he was stronger than she. And Veronica had always been a fragile woman. She didn't seem so at the moment, however, for she responded with eager cries and pressed her hands over his buttocks to push him farther with each forward thrust. Her body felt hot, or maybe it was his own skin. He was sweating and didn't think he could keep up this pace much longer. In his vampire days, he had superior control of his body and could make himself last until she was satisfied. Now he could only hope and pray his body would cooperate, like any other man's.

All at once she arched her neck and chest. She held still for a moment, as if waiting for his next thrust. When he pushed swiftly into her, deep and hard, she cried out, and he could feel her body contracting around him as she held on to him tightly with her arms. His own release came, and he closed his eyes with the mysterious, satisfying pleasure of it. He felt as if he were falling through eternity, a reminder of former days. But when he relaxed and opened his eyes, finding himself lying in Veronica's arms, he knew he was mortal—a mere, happy mortal.

He hoped he'd stay that way. He pushed the ominous thought out of his mind, determined to let himself have a few hours of peace and rest.

Gathering a handful of Veronica's long hair, he pressed the silky strands against her face and neck, enjoying the feel and nearness of her as his body settled down from its intense climax. "I love you," he whispered, then kissed her with all the reverence he felt for her.

"I love you," she whispered back. "Hold me until I fall asleep."

He rolled onto his back and gathered her in his arms as she lay her head at his shoulder. Pulling the covers over them, David settled back in contentment. Before he closed his eyes to sleep, he glanced at the clock. It was almost midnight. Hours before morning. He needed those hours of rest, he thought as he closed his eyes and felt himself drifting into a peaceful sleep.

All at once he heard a knocking sound. It woke him immediately, though he didn't know what the sound was. It seemed to come from the sitting room. Was there someone at the door to their hotel suite? Who could it be at this hour?

Veronica was still breathing softly in the regular rhythm of sleep. He decided to ignore the knock. Maybe he'd dreamt it.

But it came again, strong and clear. Then he heard a distant voice. "David? It's Matthew. Are you there?"

Matthew? David thought. What on earth? And then it came to him. Something must have happened with Larry. Had Darienne come on the scene after all? Oh, God . . . He sighed and gently pushed Veronica from his shoulder, hoping not to wake her. But she did awaken.

"What's wrong?"

"Nothing," David said in a soothing tone. "Matthew is at the door. I'd better see what he wants. Go back to sleep."

"Oh. Okay," she acquiesced, but looked puzzled.

He kissed her, then got up, slipped into his pajama bottoms, and grabbed his robe from the chair where he'd left it. When the knock came again, he called out, "I'll be there."

He turned on the light in the sitting room as he closed the door to the bedroom. When he opened the door to the outer hallway, he found Matthew standing there looking badly shaken.

"I really hate bothering you at this hour, David. But I didn't know where else to turn. Darienne's in London, and she's already seduced my son!"

David tried to steel up his energy as he invited Matthew to come in and sit down. Matthew told him the whole story. He described in a shaky voice how Darienne still wanted him, that she'd threatened to make his son a vampire if Matthew didn't give himself up to her.

"Are you sure?" David asked. "What did she say exactly?"

"She said—in fact she begged me—that if I'd come back to her, she'd do anything and everything to make me happy. When I refused, then she got tough. She said she'd have my son instead. When I asked if she was going to make Larry a vampire, the way she looked at me told me that's her intention."

"So she wants you to be her lover again—as a mortal?"

Matthew swallowed. "I think she wants me as a vampire. When I first walked in and confronted her in front of Larry, she said in an undertone to me, 'You can't stop me. He's mine—forever!' Well, I guessed what that meant, even if Larry didn't. So I said, 'Over my dead body!' And she said, in a vicious hiss that scared the hell out of me, 'Exactly, *mon amour*.' "

Matthew spread his hands and looked at David. "What would *you* think? Am I misinterpreting?"

David's shoulders felt heavy, and he sadly shook his head. "Probably not. She's using Larry as bait, that's for certain."

"And Larry doesn't have a clue. He acts as if he's performed some kind of coup, as if he's stolen something from me that I still want."

"Do you?"

Matthew's round eyes widened. "No! Well . . . I can't deny she still attracts me, physically. But I know better than to get mixed up with her again. I only wish Larry would believe me and stay away from her."

"But if you could manage to go back to her, even for a while," David pointed out, "you could save Larry. She said if you came back, she'd do anything for you."

"That was before I said no and made her angry."

"But what if you pretend to change your mind? What if you tell her you'll take her back, that you'll think about becoming a vampire, but you don't want to be forced into it?"

"Then I'd have to pretend to start a relationship with her again. I'd . . . have to sleep with her, or she'd be suspicious."

"Yes, I suppose you would," David agreed, seeing Matthew's point. "You don't feel you could do that?"

Matthew glanced down at the carpet for a moment, elbows on his knees as he sat in an easy chair. He looked up at David, his expressive eyes curiously bewildered. "The truth is, I'm afraid of myself. She . . . she's cut her hair. You would be surprised at how she looks, David. Can you imagine Darienne with a boyish haircut? She said she did it to spite me, to prove to herself she didn't want me anymore. And the more I looked at her, and those incredible eyes of hers growing radiant as she told me she still loved me—God! What I'm trying to say is, she's hard to withstand. I'd forgotten how alluring she is. Even her short hair began to look sexy to me. If I slept with her again, she might make me willing to do anything, including become a vampire. You know how she is—she can make anything sound logical when she's got a man under her spell. It was all I could do to keep my bearings with her. If I push aside my fear and get involved with her sexually again, I may be lost."

David nodded as he listened, surprised that Matthew had experienced such a strong reaction to Darienne—not to the fact that she was endangering his son, but to Darienne on a sexual level. There must be an irresistible gravitational pull between them, David theorized, just as there was one between him and Veronica. Perhaps it was more than sex. Perhaps Matthew was in love with her and didn't know it.

"What I need is to find a way to get Darienne away from both me and my son. What can I do?"

"I don't know," David said, no ideas for a solution coming to him. "If you like, I can try to talk to her. She doesn't always listen to me, but I like to think that on some occasions in the past, I've had some impact on her judgment—or on her lack of it. Darienne always tries to sound logical, but she really acts purely on emotion. And when it concerns you, her emotions are very strong. She does love you."

"She has an odd way of showing it."

"I agree," David said with a sigh. "Do you know where she's living now?"

"Sheena mentioned Belgravia on the phone."

"Yes," David said, trying to picture what her house looked like. "I remember being at her place many decades ago. I don't know the number or street, but perhaps if I wander around Belgravia, I'll recognize the place. Did she leave the theater when you did?"

"No. I imagine she went back to Larry's dressing room."

"Do you suppose she went home with him?"

Matthew drew in a deep breath. "I hope not, but she probably did. Or brought him to her place. I don't know what arrangements they make. But it was usually Darienne's style to come to the man's place, wasn't it?"

David nodded. "She usually keeps her homes exclusively to herself, sometimes doesn't even say where she lives. But she did invite me and some other writers to her house in Belgravia in the 1890s. She did it because she wanted to meet a shy poet whose underground sensual poems had sparked her interest. She finagled me into inviting him to a pseudo literary soiree she held for the express purpose of meeting him. Belgravia is an exclusive part of London, and she convinced my writer friends that she had connections with the London bluebloods, who might, she hinted, become their benefactors." David let out a long breath, recalling the whole rather comical event.

"What happened? Did she seduce the poet?"

"Of course. He was so shy, she told me later, with disgust, that she practically had to pry his clothes off of him. Apparently his sensuality was all in his head—he was quite inexperienced. She awakened him to the earthy joys of the flesh. After he'd been with her, his poems became so erotic for those days, no publisher would print them. He could no longer find fulfillment in his art, as he had done. And Darienne quickly lost interest in him. He decided to go to sea and joined the navy. I never heard of him after that. Of course, he must be dead by now."

"Amazing," Matthew said. "She's been ruining men's lives all these centuries."

David was inclined not to judge Darienne quite so harshly. "I don't know. She may have done the poet some good. At least he began living in the real world and not in his head." This reminded David of what he'd once concluded about Matthew. As an actor, Matthew was a genius. But he lived more on the stage and with his audience than in his life. David, of course, did not share this passing thought with Matthew.

"Will you talk to her, try to reason with her?" Matthew's eyes were pleading.

"Of course, I'll try. But I can't promise success."

Matthew gave David Larry's address, in case Darienne had gone to Larry's place. Matthew left then to go to his own room. He had an early call the next morning, though he complained to David he wouldn't be able to sleep.

David told Veronica he was going out to find Darienne, and repeated the gist of what Matthew had said.

"You have to go out now? It's almost one A.M.," she said, sitting up in bed as David put on his clothes.

"I have to find her at night," he reminded his wife. "Darienne isn't around in the daytime."

"No, of course not." Veronica hesitated. "Since you know now that she's here in London, I guess I can tell you—I saw her the night we went to *Hamlet.* When I got up to go to the ladies' room, she saw me and followed. We had a long talk."

David was astonished. "Why didn't you tell me?"

"She asked me not to. She wanted to keep her presence in town a secret, because she was afraid you or Matthew would interfere with her plans."

"Which were?"

"To seduce Larry in order to get Matthew's attention. That's what she said. I don't exactly approve of her tactics, but I had to sympathize with her. She loves Matthew so much, she's grown desperate."

"Well, she's succeeded in getting Matthew's attention. He wants me to intercede and try to talk her out of going after either of them. Think I'll have much luck?"

Veronica mutely shook her head.

"Neither do I. But I promised I'd try. You see what I meant about coming to London? I knew I'd get involved with Darienne and her schemes."

"I'm sorry I talked you into coming," Veronica said, near tears. "I wish we'd stayed home, too."

"Shh," David said, reaching out to stroke her hair. "Don't be upset. As you told me, it's their business, not ours. I'll talk to her, but if nothing comes of it, then it's up to the three of them to sort things out."

"How will you find Darienne? You said you didn't know her address."

"I don't. But I have Larry's, in case she's there. And I may be able to recognize her house if I wander around Belgravia long enough."

"If you find her, ask her for Herman's phone number in Switzerland," Veronica said, eyes wide and imperative.

David smiled at her. "I'm glad you reminded me. At least now I've got a reason of my own to hunt all over London for Darienne."

Claridge's called David a cab, and he asked the driver to take him to Larry's address in Knightsbridge first. When the cab stopped in front of Larry's flat, David looked up at the windows of the second floor, where Matthew had said Larry lived. There were no lights on. The windows were open, David noticed. He asked the cabdriver to stop the engine, and David got out of the cab. He walked across the sidewalk and stood beneath the windows, listening. He heard not a sound. No talking, no sounds of lovemaking—Darienne could be quite vocal sometimes. Then, he thought he heard a snore from somewhere. He couldn't be sure, of course, but he guessed that if Darienne had spent time with Larry, perhaps she'd left already. He suspected that after seeing Matthew again, she might have been too distracted to spend an entire night with Larry. Knowing Darienne, she might be off walking and thinking, refining her schemes. But if she were out walking, how would he ever find her?

David went back to the waiting cab and asked the driver to take him to Belgravia. When the driver drove by Eaton Square, David remembered the exclusive area; it looked quite familiar. At his request, the cabdriver slowly passed by large, imposing houses built in the first half of the 1800s. All at once David caught sight of a pedestrian—a woman. An odd sight, to see a woman walking alone at this time of night. She appeared to have short blond hair. David felt a moment of relief, knowing he'd found Darienne. He asked the driver to stop, and he paid the fare. As the cab drove away, he walked up the street, closing the gap between himself and Darienne, who appeared from her gait to be a bit dejected. She usually walked with self-confidence mixed with inviting sensuality in the swing of her hips. Now her wandering seemed a bit aimless.

"Darienne," he called, not too loudly, because of the time of night.

She turned around. Her mouth opened in astonishment when she saw him. "David!" She walked up to him and hugged him. "It's so good to see you. I'd heard you were in town."

"Really? And you didn't look me up?"

"Well . . ."

"Never mind half-truths. Veronica told me she saw you at the theater several nights ago and that you swore her to secrecy."

"She did?"

"She didn't betray your trust. She told me only after I'd heard from Matthew that you were in London. He came to see me tonight."

"Oh. He did, did he? Well, and what did he have to say?"

"I'm sure you know what he told me. Don't play games. You've seduced his son, and you're using him as bait to get Matthew back into your clutches."

"I could have guessed you'd put it like that," she said, turning to start walking again.

"Can we talk somewhere?"

She looked up at him with impatient eyes. But she said, "Oh, all right. I suppose you promised Matthew to do what you could to rescue his son from me. I'll humor you and you can keep your promise. Is that a deal?"

"I don't make deals."

She shook her finger at him and said in a testy voice, "You know, for a mortal, you're pushing your safety limit. Remember I'm three times as strong as you now, puny little man!"

"I'm aware of my limits. I hope *you'll* remember our long friendship," he said seriously.

Her expression calmed. "I remember, David. In fact, I've missed you. I could always turn to you. Somehow I feel I can't anymore."

"Why not?" he asked as they approached her stately stone house.

"I suppose I'm afraid you wouldn't understand me anymore." She turned the key in her lock. "But then," she said as she opened the door and let them in, "you often didn't understand me even when *you* were immortal, too."

"I'll try to understand, Darienne. I promise."

As she turned on the light, she smiled at him. "All right."

David was surprised at her appearance. Her short blond hair shone like a halo in the lamplight, accenting her large feminine eyes, giving her a childlike, angelic appearance. But an angel she certainly was not. He looked around him at the entryway of her mansion then. It looked just the same as when he'd last seen it, heavy with thick purple velvet draperies and an ornate rug. She took him to her living room, filled with big, comfortable overstuffed chairs and sofas, glass lamps, and knickknacks everywhere. She'd decorated it in Victorian times and never changed the decor.

"This is like walking into a museum," he said.

Darienne laughed. "If I had the inclination, I'd get rid of all this overdone finery and redecorate with modern furniture. But I so seldom use this place, I haven't bothered. Can you imagine, we used to like this kind of decor?"

David chuckled, feeling as though he'd taken a step backward into a former lifetime. He sat down in a big, dark green leather chair as Darienne sat across from him on a couch with flowered needlepoint pillows.

"So what does Matthew expect you to say to me?"

"He wants you to leave Larry alone."

"I won't."

"Darienne, tell me the truth, are you really thinking of transforming him into a vampire?"

"I like to keep all my options open," she said in a noncommittal tone.

"Why would you, when it's Matthew you want?"

"An apt point."

"Does that mean you won't transform Larry?"

"I don't know. Do you think I would tell you, knowing you'll tell Matthew everything I say?"

David exhaled and nodded, conceding her point. "All right, I won't ask questions. But think about what you're doing, Darienne. You used to have some sense of fair play. Is it fair to take an innocent young man you don't really want?"

"How do you know I don't want him?"

"You love Matthew."

"Yes, but if I can't have Matthew, then I'll have the next best thing. I must have someone, David. Everyone has deserted me. You've become mortal and you have your life with Veronica. I adore her and I'm glad you're finally together. But I'm something of a third wheel now. It can't be helped, but there it is. And Matthew . . . Matthew doesn't want me. He made that quite clear tonight. Larry, however, does want me. I think as he grows older, he'll become more and more like his father. So I'll settle for him."

David didn't quite believe that she'd settle as easily as she claimed. "Matthew had the impression you were threatening to make his son a vampire, to try to force Matthew to give himself to you instead."

"Now, how on earth did he get that idea?"

"Something you said and the way you said it."

"You men! Always misinterpreting the simplest things we women say."

"Darienne," David said in an admonishing tone. "Be straight with me."

She gave him an innocent look. "Why do you think I'm not?"

"I've known you for too many centuries to be fooled by you that easily."

Her expression took on a look of determination. "All right. I'm after Matthew, not Larry. I admit it. I asked Matthew to come back to me, but he literally pushed me away. I would have been gentle with him, if he'd given me the chance. I don't want to frightened him, or use drastic tactics. But I will. I intend to have Matthew. And to answer your next question—yes, I want him as a vampire."

David sighed. "But has it occurred to you," he said, leaning forward in his chair, "that even if you succeed in making him a vampire, Matthew won't necessarily stay with you? Four centuries ago, I made you a vampiress, thinking you'd share an existence with me and ease my loneliness. Once you were transformed, you took off to enjoy your new independence."

"But I always came back now and then to visit, *chéri*."

"You came back to me for sex," David said with asperity. "But hear my point: If you make Matthew a vampire, he could as easily walk out on you as he did today. So what have you gained?"

"But you've *missed* the point, David," she said with a smile. "I came back to you for sex, because only another vampire could satisfy me. Matthew would always come back to me for the same reason. There aren't many of us left in the world anymore. We've even lost you from our numbers. I only know of a few other female vampires in the world. And I'm certainly not going to give Matthew a list of their names and addresses. So, you see, he'd have to come back to me for complete sexual satisfaction. He'd discover quickly enough that mortal women can't give him the gratification I can. Well, he knows that already. So I'm not worried that he'd run off and never come back, David.
That he'd come back is the one thing I'm sure of."

"But Darienne, if you love him, wouldn't you like to have his love in return? Would you be happy just having him come to you for sex? Wouldn't you feel used? You made me feel used when you came to me, begging."

"Yes, you really suffered," she said, amused as she mocked him. "I don't recall that you ever pushed me away. I remember well our lovely all-night orgies. I wish we could share them again."

David shifted in his seat uneasily. Somehow she always evaded the points he tried to make, and now she was embarrassing him. "I won't deny I needed vampire sex. But afterwards, I did feel used."

"And satisfied!"

"All right, all right. But what if Matthew came to you, from wandering the world as a vampire, and merely wanted to be with you for a night of sex, only to go off again? Would you be happy with that?"

"No. But I'd have decades to woo him, to make him stay longer each visit, even make him love me eventually, so that one day he wouldn't leave. And then we'd have eternity together. I can exist happily enough on that hope, as you existed on the hope of one day attaining Veronica. You've succeeded in gaining happiness in your way. I'll succeed in mine."

"But Matthew doesn't *want* to become a vampire. The idea terrifies him."

"Yes, and why is that?" she snapped. "Because you filled his head with all those awful ideas when he came to you for advice in Chicago."

"He told me that when you showed him your coffin, he almost blacked out with fright!" David argued. "I had nothing to do with that. I wasn't even there. It was his natural reaction."

"Only because you'd already poisoned his mind against the idea. Must we have this argument all over again? I've forgiven you for that, but I haven't forgotten. Please don't open an old wound between us."

David closed his eyes and nodded his acquiescence. She was right. It did him no good to make her angry by reminding her of past arguments over her plans for Matthew. David had felt it was immoral for her to pressure Matthew by whatever means into becoming a vampire. Darienne seemed to see the issue from a different viewpoint, one clouded by desperation and love. Love, he decided, might be the only way he could appeal to her reason now.

"I know you truly care for Matthew. How can you force the man you love into becoming something he so clearly abhors?" he asked her, gravity in his tone.

Darienne was silent for a long while. Her eyes lowered, and she studied her hands in her lap. "You hated being a vampire, David, so maybe this won't make sense to you. I think Matthew will be happier if he's a vampire."

"No, Darienne—" David began to argue.

"Let me finish. Remember how he exhausted himself playing *Shadow* onstage? If we'd let him go on playing the role, as he wanted to, he would have killed himself. He seemed to realize his limits then, and he went back to his ex-wife to try to live a normal life. Well, he couldn't. As soon as he got wrapped up in the *Shadow* movie, she left him again. You see, as a mortal, he doesn't have the energy and time to do both things, to give his career full attention *and* keep up a relationship with another person. He's been frustrated in both areas of his life. He's already lost his family, and he nearly kills himself for the stage, because he barely has the energy he needs to give to a role everything he wants to. That's what's so unique about him. Whatever he does, he gives it his all, his full concentration, his deepest strength and intensity—whether he's in a stage role, or whether he's making love."

She paused and tilted her head. "That's why I can't forget him. No one ever made love to me the way he did. You said if he were a vampire, he'd only come to me for sex. Well, the truth is, when I was his mistress, he only wanted me for sex then, too. But when I was with him, it never felt like he was just using me to satiate his needs. It felt like he was making love, in the most true sense of those words. Maybe he didn't love me. Maybe he never will. But what he gave me was wonderful enough, and I want that back. Or there's no use in my going on existing. High life and dazzle don't impress me anymore. I can't find the enjoyment in them that I used to. Without Matthew, eternity lies before me like a black hole in space."

David studied her poignant expression with a feeling of foreboding. "You aren't saying that you'd . . . you wouldn't destroy yourself . . ."

She blinked back tears and shook her shoulders, as if to throw off a mood. "I don't know what I'm saying now, David. I get depressed sometimes, and I begin thinking things I never thought I would. Don't pay any attention to me. I'm all right."

David felt shaken. He'd never seen her this way. She was always so bright and fun-loving, filled with mischief and sensuality. Now she looked lonely and sad, with her pale face and short hair. He was at a loss—had no idea either how to advise her or further Matthew's cause. He wasn't even sure what was right anymore. What she'd said about Matthew showed a depth of understanding on her part that David wouldn't have guessed she possessed. He wanted her to be happy, to have what she wanted. Yet he didn't want to see Matthew become something David hated having been himself.

Darienne leaned into the side armrest of the couch in a more casual pose. She made an attempt to smile as she changed the subject. "How's Veronica? Is she feeling better? She wasn't too well that night at the theater."

"She's better, I think." David grew morose now, thinking of his own situation. He remembered he must ask Darienne about Herman. "She's very worried, though. About me."

"About you?"

He wet his lips and hesitated. "The sun pains my eyes. I often can't eat. The other day at Harrod's, in the Food Halls, the sight of red meat, the blood . . ."

"Oh, no," Darienne said. "You feel you're reverting? Herman said—"

"Yes, I know. Do you have his phone number or address? I need to see him."

Darienne immediately rose from the couch. "Of course," she said as she found her handbag where she'd tossed it on a side table. She opened it and took out what appeared to be an address book. Having found a scrap of paper in her purse and a pen, she copied something from the book. She gave the paper to David. It listed Herman's phone and address in Lucerne.

"Thank you," David said with relief as Darienne sat down again. "I'll leave tomorrow, if I can."

"I hope he can help." Darienne raised her fingers to her lips then and slowly shook her head, her brows drawn together with apparent concern at a new thought. "Poor Veronica," she said, almost to herself. "She must be terribly upset. If you became a vampire again . . ." Darienne didn't finish whatever thought was going through her mind.

"She is upset. So am I. Though she said she'd stay with me no matter what."

Darienne tried to smile. But David could see tears forming in her eyes. "I know she would stay with you. But it would be so hard for her now . . . Oh, David, if I could pray for you, I would. I hope Herman can help you."

David was grateful for her sympathy, but couldn't help but be rather startled by her reaction. He would have thought Darienne would be happy with the possibility that he might be reverting. She'd even said she was lonely without him, now that he'd become mortal. And Veronica had always been willing to become a vampiress. In Darienne's mind, he'd have thought, there would be no problem: He and Veronica could join her as vampires in her world.

Darienne had changed in more ways than getting her hair cut. He had a hard time fathoming her anymore.

David rose from his seat to say good-bye, thinking he'd said all he could on Matthew's behalf. And he'd obtained Herman's address. The purposes for his visit were accomplished. It was past two A.M. now, and Veronica was probably lying awake, worried, at Claridge's. He needed to make arrangements for them to leave for Switzerland, too. He asked Darienne if he could use her phone to call a cab. As he dialed, he took note of her phone number, in case he wanted to reach her again.

Once the cab was ordered, he hugged Darienne and kissed her on the cheek. "Thank you for hearing me out, even if I haven't convinced you of anything. If you could at least leave Larry alone. He's wholly innocent in all this. Have it out with Matthew and leave the boy out of the matter."

Darienne smiled and squeezed his arm as they walked slowly into the entry hall. "I'll think about all you've said. I don't mean anyone any harm. I told Veronica that. I'm just in love. And I'm not used to not getting what I want. Sometimes, lately, I find myself losing hope."

"Never lose hope," he told her with earnest feeling. "I'm in danger of losing my happiness, too. But I can't lose hope that everything will work out."

"It must, David. See Herman fast as you can." She pressed his arm more firmly. "And tell Veronica to take good care of herself. Will you?"

"I will," David said, slightly puzzled again.

The sound of a car horn came from outside. "There's your cab." She took his hand as they walked to the door. "Good night. Let me know what Herman tells you."

They embraced again, and he walked out to the cab. He waved at her through the cab window as she stood in the doorway, wiping a tear from her cheek. When he arrived back at Claridge's, he found that, indeed, Veronica was sitting up, waiting for him. He got on the phone and called Herman, who he assumed would be up and about at this hour, being a vampire. Herman answered himself, said he'd be happy to examine David, and gave him directions to his lab. Next David phoned the airlines and booked a flight to Switzerland.

Veronica seemed relieved then and fell asleep. David, however, lay awake most of the night, wondering what, if anything, Herman could tell him about his condition.

The next morning, David phoned the studio, leaving word that he had urgent personal business to take care of in Switzerland. He phoned Matthew, room to room, and told him he'd spoken to Darienne but wasn't sure if he'd made any impact. Matthew thanked him for trying. David left him the phone number in Switzerland where he could be reached.

Having taken care of his obligations in London for the moment, he and Veronica packed their belongings, caught a cab to Heathrow, and soon were on a plane to Switzerland.

8

Think before you refuse me

AT DUSK the next evening, Matthew left the movie studio soundstage and drove his rental car to Claridge's. He felt tired from working on the set all day. He'd been shooting *Shadow*'s most well-known song, his trademark, "She Can Never Be Mine," since nine A.M. that morning. The director had finally called it a wrap, but not until Matthew had reshot the scene, using a tape of his singing voice, thirty-two times.

It wasn't Matthew's acting that had made the director unsatisfied; it was the lighting, or the props, or the angle of the shot. By the end of the day, Matthew had lost all his patience.

Tomorrow they were to shoot another key song in the movie. He felt he needed to review the lyrics tonight, because he hadn't sung it since he ended his stage run in Australia.

Matthew thought of the stage with longing as he entered Claridge's and walked across the checker-floored lobby, toward the Causerie for a quiet dinner alone. Making this movie was worthwhile, because it recorded his work for posterity and allowed him to be seen by the widest audience. But he sorely missed being on the stage. Live theater gave him the greatest satisfaction of anything in his life.

But he was growing older, and he knew the number of stage roles that he would be offered would begin to dwindle soon. There was one more marvelous role waiting in the wings for him, however. His agent had called him at the studio today to say that a contract was on its way for a new Broadway musical version of *Wuthering Heights*, casting Matthew as Heathcliff.

He'd already sung the magnificent score for the show's producers and director before he left New York. He'd heard that some thought he was too "mature" to fit the part. But his agent told him the powers that be had finally concluded no one else could dominate a stage the way Matthew could. No one matched his charisma combined with his singing capability, or his ability to portray an overpowering yet anguished character like Heathcliff. So he'd won the role.

He ought to be celebrating with someone, but he found himself alone tonight. The maître d' showed him to a table for two and removed the place setting in front of the chair left vacant. After he'd chosen from the menu, his mind returned to the new stage role he could now look forward to with certainty. He was excited at the prospect, yet he worried if he still had the energy to play such a role. *Shadow* had fatigued him terribly. The role of Heathcliff promised to be physically demanding, too.

They wanted him to climb steep hills, to be built on stage, and jump from a high point to the stage floor. In the last scene of the show, he'd be expected to sing while carrying a dying Catherine in his arms for most of the song. Matthew knew he had the physical capacity to do all these things, though he'd have to go into training to get himself in shape again. But would he have the stamina to continue the role—assuming the show was successful—over a period of a year or more? He'd played *The Scarlet Shadow* for three years, and had collapsed from exhaustion more than once during that time. Once he began playing Heathcliff, he knew it would be the same as with *Shadow:* He wouldn't want to leave the show and give up the role to another actor. He'd want to go on refining himself in the part, perhaps for years, creating a stunning stage character that audiences would come back to see again and again.

Perhaps it showed some idiosyncracy or even deficiency in his personality, but he needed a live audience to connect with, needed to hear applause and shouts of "bravo." He'd come to enjoy having flowers thrown at his feet and mobs at the stage door waiting for his autograph. This wasn't due to an inflated ego. He needed all this affirmation of his talent and his place in the world simply to be reassured that people *liked* him.

All his life, beginning with his humble childhood in Atlanta, he'd thought of himself as average-looking and quiet. He'd lacked friends and hadn't been particularly brilliant in school. He'd always had a high energy level, however, and a creative mind that was easily bored if not challenged.

His parents hadn't gotten along, but had stayed together for the sake of their five children, of whom Matthew was the third. From early childhood, he'd had the feeling he was peculiar somehow, that his mind worked differently from other children's, that he was meant for a more unusual life than his peers. He'd been quite thin, shy, and was considered something of a nerd by his classmates. When choosing teams for basketball, he'd always been left for last.

In his sophomore year of high school, on a whim, he got into a drama class and soon took part in some of the school plays. Suddenly his natural, unexpected talent shone, surprising those around him. A casting agent spotted him in one of the plays. Suddenly seventeen-year-old Matthew was hired to make his first film, *The Boy from Savannah.* With that success, he'd realized where he fit in and knew what he was to do with his life.

Once he'd discovered himself and his unusual talent, his aim ever since had been simply to show everyone what he could do. Over the years he'd learned to excel at comedy, singing, stunt work, and drama. He'd jump through any hoop to win an audience, to get their outpouring of love in return. He'd lost his wife and son in order to have that. This had troubled him deeply, but he couldn't seem to live any other way but to fix his life on his career, leaving everything else to be peripheral, even a wife and son.

Matthew exhaled and leaned back heavily in his chair as he thought of Larry. It was after sundown. He wondered if even now Darienne was with his son, seducing him further into her dark world. Matthew had no idea how to rescue him. Larry wouldn't listen to anything Matthew might try to tell him. And David's appeal to Darienne apparently hadn't been very successful.

Matthew took a sip of water and set the glass back on the tablecloth. He rubbed his forehead in a worried motion. David had said he was flying to Switzerland, but didn't explain why, just gave him a number where he could be reached. Matthew wished he hadn't gone, because David was the only one he could talk to. Even if David couldn't offer a solution, it was a relief to have someone to express his fears to. Yet he sensed David and Veronica were involved in some problem of their own, so Matthew felt he couldn't impose and ask David to stay. He hated even to telephone him.

That left matters up to Matthew to handle. And there was nothing he could do. Unless he wanted to give himself over to Darienne in his son's place. He shuddered. God, there must be *some* other way . . .

While Matthew pondered over dinner in the Causerie, Darienne was climbing an outside wall of Claridge's. Shoes stuffed in her jacket pockets, she inserted her toes and fingers in crevices in the stone wall and pulled herself silently upward toward the window to his room. After David had left her house the night before, she had called Matthew's agent in California. She knew he would remember her from her years as Matthew's companion. Playing innocent, she'd told him she wanted to send Matthew flowers for old time's sake and asked if the agent knew his hotel and room number. The agent hesitated, but soon gave her the information she needed.

Though she despised Claridge's, still remembering the time decades ago when they'd thrown her out for wearing pants, she had walked into the hotel and surreptitiously hunted through it until she found Matthew's room. Of course it was locked. Claridge's had such a famous reputation for discretion, she didn't even bother to try to bribe a maid to let her in, fearing she might be reported and kicked out once again. Instead she figured out which outside wall Matthew's windows were in. Fortunately they did not look out onto the front of the hotel, and under cover of darkness, she could easily climb to his fourth-floor room and not be seen. She'd worn black, however, just to lessen the risk of being spotted. Careful to keep her black nylons from ripping, she steadily climbed, her miniskirt hiked up her thighs, giving her full range of movement. The tight bustier beneath her black silk jacket pinched her waist and rib cage, however. She wouldn't have worn it tonight except for Matthew's benefit.

She reached his window and peeked in. Behind the sheer curtains, the room appeared to be dark. Good, she thought. He hadn't returned yet. The window opened inward from one side. It was latched, but with her superior strength, she pressed the metal until the lock gave way and the window swung open into the room. She pulled herself up through the window and stepped down onto the floor of Matthew's bedroom.

After looking about the bedroom briefly, she walked into his sitting room, where an electric piano keyboard had been set up. Matthew always made sure to have a piano of one form or another in his room in order to accompany himself when he practiced singing. Darienne touched the keys lightly and grew nostalgic for the years she'd spent with him, accompanying him from Chicago to New York, then London, then to Australia as he performed *Shadow* in each city. Those were exciting times. She'd adored attending at least two or three of his performances a week. He used to catch her eye as she sat in the third row and seemed to sing to her alone. The heady eye contact they shared in those moments was an energizing preparation for their lovemaking at his hotel after the show.

No matter how fatigued he was, he always wanted her. Yet his increasing exhaustion from performing was the frightening aspect of being with him, watching him struggle to find the energy to mesmerize his audience each night. In a way he was heroic, and she admired him for that. In another way, he was foolhardy, risking his health, even his life, to such a degree.

But Darienne had a remedy for that. Matthew had refused it once. She would make sure he would not refuse again. In fact, she'd come tonight to give Matthew one more chance to come to her on his own, without undo coercion. When she'd seen him at the theater after *Hamlet,* she'd tried to appeal to him on an emotional level. She'd told him how much she still loved him, hoping this would remind him of how she'd cared for him in the past. She'd even hoped, after all these months apart and after his second breakup with Natalie, he might come to realize that he missed Darienne. Maybe, she'd hoped, he'd come to see that he'd been happiest with her, that he belonged with her.

But he hadn't responded as she'd hoped. So she would try to appeal to him on another level. Maybe he'd never love her, but in their former days, he'd never failed to be attracted to her sexually. She hoped that attraction remained. And if it did, then perhaps she could still win him to her point of view. Perhaps he would do as she wished to have back again that other world sexual relationship they used to share. He must miss it. Certainly he must. If she could give him a vivid reminder of what he was missing, then perhaps he'd come back to her for that reason. And in time, she was fairly certain, she could convince him that his career and their relationship would be even better if he would let her transform him into a vampire.

But if he resisted her tonight, then she would have no choice but to take measures to ensure she'd have what she wanted, even putting Matthew to the ultimate test to make him give in.

Tears rose in Darienne's eyes as she thought of the extremes to which she was willing to go to have Matthew. She didn't want it to be this way. It pained her to put him under duress. But if he continued to make the wrong choice for himself, then Darienne felt she had *no* choice but to force the issue.

With a long sigh, she wiped the bit of wetness from her eyelids and walked back into the bedroom. She took off her jacket and reclined on his bed to wait.

When he'd finished eating dinner, Matthew left the Causerie and took the elevator to the fourth floor. He walked down the hall to his room and unlocked the door. After turning on the lights in the sitting room, he took off his jacket and sat down at the electric keyboard. He needed to run through the song he'd be filming tomorrow. As he began to sing, rememorizing the lyrics, a part of him wondered if he ought to skip practice and go visit Larry to try to talk to him again. But then he remembered that Larry was performing tonight and wouldn't be home until later. He assumed Darienne must be at the theater watching him.

Matthew's fingers stopped on the keyboard, and he left off mid-note. The memory of Darienne's face in the *Shadow* audience watching him with adoration as he sang this very song came back on him quite suddenly and vividly. He couldn't forget the way she made him feel, just by looking at him—

"Don't stop, *chéri*."

Matthew turned in shock at the voice that came from behind him. The room had been empty, as it should have been, when he walked in.

Darienne was lounging sideways on an easy chair, her long legs thrown nonchalantly over one armrest, her bared shoulder against the back of the chair, her arm across the top of it. Her large breasts, pushed up by the tight black lingerie she wore under her miniskirt, plumped like rounded hills beneath her collarbone.

Matthew was transfixed. Fear mixed with desire rose within him. "How did you get in here?" His voice sounded sharp from apprehension.

"I have magic ways, my darling, as you well know."

He rose from his seat. "I'm calling hotel security," he said as he moved toward the phone.

With her vampire agility, she rose and lightly stepped in front of him before he could even get near it. "No, *chéri*, we don't want company. I want you all to myself."

He tried to move around her, but she was always faster than he. His heart began to pound. "What do you want?" His shirt collar was open and he could feel his neck exposed.

But Darienne wasn't looking at his throat just now. Her eyes followed her hands on his chest as she moved them up and then sideways over his pectoral muscles. "I remember how we used to be together," she said, stepping closer so that her breasts jutted against his ribs. "Remember those nights we shared, when we couldn't get enough of each other? I remember the way you used to touch me," she said, taking his hand and covering her breast with it. "The way you held me and kissed me. The way you came inside me and gave us both such ecstasy. We were so good together. I want to share that with you again."

Matthew's fingers trembled over her rounded, soft flesh. He realized how tempted he was and drew his hand away, trying to keep his head. "You disgust me," he said with seething anger. "You'd actually go from my son to me."

"You went from me to Natalie," she pointed out without resentment. She smiled then, taking hold of his hand again. "Larry is sweet, but he can't compare to you. I needed *someone.* You must be wanting, too. I know Natalie left you. She never could replace what you experienced with me anyway. Let's give each other what we both need, darling."

"How can you think I'd want to be with you after all you've done? I *don't* want you! I can't think of a word bad enough to call you."

"How about 'irresistible'? And *chéri,*" she purred, "I think you do want me." She fondled his hand as she pressed it into her cleavage. "Your hand is shaking."

He jerked away. "The shock of finding you here. Get out!"

She smiled again, as if she hadn't heard him. "Your voice was so beautiful and sensual as you sang a moment ago." She reached behind her, apparently unfastening her clothing. Matthew began to panic and tried to move around her, but she was too quick to let him by. Meanwhile, she kept up her chatter in her throaty French accent. "It reminded me of old times, when I used to watch you from the audience. Your voice kindled my desire until I couldn't wait till the show was over, and I could be alone with you. You still affect me that way."

Suddenly her bustier loosened. She unfastened her skirt, and both garments fell to the floor. Now she wore only a thin black-lace garter belt and stockings. As he stood there in mute shock, looking again at the gorgeous female body that had curves like no other he'd ever seen, at the woman with whom he'd shared so much unbridled passion, she took his hand in hers once again. She placed it beneath one naked breast, making him feel the sensual weight of it against his hand, making his fingers slide over her nipple as she gasped with pleasure. She pushed his hand slowly downward along her rib cage to the garter belt at her waist, then over her belly button toward the blond froth of hair between her smooth thighs.

"I want you here," she whispered with an ache as she pressed herself against him. "Don't be afraid. I won't trick you into anything more. Just joyous, fulfilling sex, the way it used to be between us. We shared something so special."

Matthew felt torn between the raging desire she'd evoked and his deep fear of her. Her thigh pressed against his zipper, and he knew she could feel his arousal. The triumphant smile on her face proved she knew her success. Her breaths came faster, and she leaned up to kiss his mouth.

Fear won out, and he turned his head to evade her. But she settled her lips on his jaw, and then, as he closed his eyes in sensuality and panic, he felt her mouth slide down the side of his neck. Once again, he remembered with frightening vividness how her mouth, her sharp teeth, had fixed on his jugular when she'd attacked him in Chicago.

Using all his strength, he broke free and ran toward the door. But she tackled him, and he found himself hitting the floor with a thud. She turned him onto his back, her breasts pendulous over his chest as she kneeled astride him.

"Are you going to rape me now? Or kill me?" he asked, pushing at her shoulders, trying to keep her at bay as he breathed hard. "You claim you love me. Is this your idea of love?"

The look on her face seemed chastened, and she leaned back a bit. Then she moved off of him and stretched out beside him on the carpet, on her side, facing him. "I want you to come to me, to choose to be with me." Her expression seemed repentant now, as if she were truly sorry and wanted to please him. He remembered in times past how she used to do anything to please him. Her breasts jutted from her chest like round pillows, from which her nipples stood out, taut and pert, as if appealing to him to be touched. She stroked his face and then his chest as she said in a meek, almost endearing tone, "Take me, Matthew. Make love with me the way you used to."

Her soft body, now so pliant, felt warm as she leaned against him. Her fingers tantalized him. Her breasts and thighs beckoned him. She was so eager. It would be so easy to roll on top of her and satiate his driving need.

If he did, he knew he'd be lost. Though he might save his son, as David had pointed out. Still, he felt he couldn't give in. It would be disaster to let her win. He had to be strong and try to find some way to save both himself *and* Larry.

"No!" Matthew said in a resolute tone as he quickly got to his feet.

"Think before you refuse me," she warned, rising from the floor, too.

"There's nothing to think about. I won't cave in to you. I'll fight you every step of the way!"

"There aren't many more steps to go, Matthew." She calmly took his arm and stood beside him. "I told you I intend to have either you or your son. I prefer you, but I'll go to him, if you insist on turning me away."

He glared at her. "Get this straight: You won't have me and you won't have him! If you threaten him again, I'll find out where you live." He trembled with rage as he said these words. "And one morning when you're resting in your coffin, I'll come with a stake and hammer and take you out of our lives permanently!"

Darienne visibly paled and stepped back from him. She bowed her head and seemed devastated. When she looked up, tears stood in her eyes. "You could destroy me? Drive a stake through my heart?" She lifted her hand and pointed to the valley between her exquisite breasts. "Pierce my skin and watch the blood run out, knowing I would turn to dust? You could do that to a woman who cared for you when you were sick and depressed, who gave you courage when you had none, who provided you with more pleasure than any one man should have? A woman who has loved you as I have? You could do such a thing?"

As she pleaded with him, her short hair wispy as a child's, her feminine curves looking so soft and vulnerable, Matthew found himself almost overcome with an inexplicable compassion for her—for Darienne, the woman who had almost transformed him by force, who had only a moment ago been about to rape him, who still threatened his son. He had to remind himself she was dangerous. She was a vampire!

"I'll do whatever I need to," he said, trying to sound strong, but his voice came out subdued.

She lowered her eyes and breathed in deeply, as if coming to a new resolve. "Then I'll take that chance. If I can't have you, and you keep me from your son as well, then I'd just as soon perish. I'd rather it were you who struck the blows that destroy me. At least I'd know you were with me at the end." She turned and picked up her clothes, apparently having said all she had to say.

As she fastened her skirt back into place and put on her bustier again, Matthew watched her, speechless and in shock. She was willing to let herself be destroyed over this?

"Aren't there other men in the world you could pursue, besides me or Larry?"

She smoothed the bustier into place from her breasts to her waist, then looked up. "No. There's no one else I want anymore. You've spoiled me, Matthew. I've lived too long, had too many men, to settle for less than what I want." She said this matter-of-factly, as if she'd already thought it over and made up her mind. "So. You've made it clear I must cross you off my list. That leaves Larry." She smiled. "I think Larry will make a different decision. And I'm sure I can train him to suit me. In time, he'll reach your level as a lover. In fact, he'll be even better, because I'll give him the means to be all he can be."

"You mean you intend to transform him," Matthew said, his breath caught in his throat.

Darienne smiled one of her winsome, coy smiles. She moved past him and into the bedroom, and in a moment came out wearing a jacket and stiletto heels. Pausing as she opened the door that led to the hotel hallway, she said sweetly, "Good night, Matthew." She walked out then, shutting the door behind her.

Matthew stood helpless for a few moments, trying to think what to do. He must go to Larry and warn him, he thought. He checked his watch. The play would just be finishing now. Larry would be driving home. Matthew got on the phone and asked the hotel staff to bring his car around. Then he rushed down to the lobby.

He didn't see Darienne about anywhere as he left the hotel and drove off in his car. But he had to assume she was on her way to Knightsbridge. Matthew hoped that he'd reach his son first. Since he had a car, and she probably didn't, it should be easy.

When he got to Larry's building, he parked and ran up to the front door to ring the bell. Larry quickly came down to answer, but looked annoyed when he saw his father.

"I've got to talk to you," Matthew told him. "It's a matter of life and death—yours."

Larry opened the door wider and let him in. "What are you talking about?"

Matthew waited until they had walked upstairs to the second floor and were in Larry's flat before replying. And then he didn't know how to begin. "I told you Darienne was dangerous."

Larry exhaled with impatience.

"Listen to me," Matthew said before his son could interrupt. "She's not a normal woman. She can do you grave harm."

Larry eyed him incredulously. "Are you trying to tell me she's insane or something?"

"Not insane, but physically different from other women. What she wants from you is not what you think. She wants more than sex. She wants to change you forever, to make you into something you can't even imagine."

"I think you're the one who's lost his marbles!"

Matthew didn't know what to say. If he told Larry that Darienne was a vampire, that she wanted to drink his blood and make him one, too, he'd truly believe his father was crazy. Matthew decided to try a different tack. "Why do you trust her? She'd had a long relationship with me, and she never told you. In her mind, you're a replacement for me. She even admitted that in front of you. Do you want a woman who considers you a consolation prize?"

"She told me later how you'd hurt her and left her. I can give her the love you couldn't. I'll be the best consolation prize she could ever have. And I don't need to defend my relationship with her to you!" He glanced at the clock on the wall. "I'm expecting someone. I'd like you to leave."

Matthew felt a sickening chill. "Whom are you expecting?"

"None of your damn business!"

"Larry—"

His son physically took Matthew by the arm and began pulling him toward the door. "Out!"

"You've got to listen to me. She came to me tonight. I know what she's up to."

Larry stopped in front of the door and let go of his arm. "She came to you?"

"At my hotel. It's me she really wants. She's still in love with me."

Larry laughed. "Jealous fantasies!"

"I wouldn't lie to you!"

"I'm not saying you're lying. I'm saying you're hallucinating. You imagine she still wants you, just because she came by to talk. She probably wanted to tell you to leave us alone."

"She did more than talk," Matthew said in heated desperation. "She all but raped me!"

"Rape?" Larry said with angry amusement. "You've lost it, Dad. How can a woman rape a man? It just doesn't work that way biologically."

Matthew was at a loss. Larry opened the door and placed his hand strongly at Matthew's back to urge him through it. "Go back to your hotel and get some rest. Better yet, find a psychiatrist."

"Larry, she can kill you!"

"You bet she can—with love. Go home, Dad. You're not well. I'd be seriously concerned about you, if I gave a damn." He pushed Matthew out the door and closed it behind him.

Matthew stood outside and raised his hand to knock again, then reconsidered. What was the use? Still, he had to do something. All at once he heard footsteps, the sound of high heels, coming up the stairway. Matthew quickly looked about, then softly ran down the hall to where it turned into another hall, leading to other apartments in the building. He hid around the corner and listened.

He heard a knock, and then a door opening. He heard Larry say, "Darienne, I'm glad you're here."

"What's wrong, *chéri*?" she asked. "You look upset."

"You wouldn't believe—"

The door shut then, and Matthew could no longer hear their voices, except very faintly through the walls. Quietly, he walked back to Larry's door. He could hear their voices better and could make out what they were saying. His heart thudded against his rib cage as he pressed his ear to the varnished wood.

9

A hapless moth

MATTHEW STRAINED to hear their conversation through the door. He heard Darienne saying in her soothing way, "Don't let your father distress you. He's just jealous of what you and I have."

"I know that," Larry replied, sounding exasperated. "But I didn't realize how unbalanced he was. He said you were dangerous, that you weren't a normal woman."

Darienne's laughter sounded like chimes. "Well, you know, in a way he's right. You've never met any other woman quite like me, have you?"

Larry's voice grew quieter, more comfortable. "That's for sure."

There was silence then. Matthew suspected they were kissing. His stomach tightened, and another chill ran down his back, as he sensed the danger Larry was in. She might be moving her lips down his throat, toward his jugular, at this moment. And Larry hadn't a clue. She could take him and never tell him what she was doing, change him into a vampire before he'd realized what happened.

"God, you excite me," Larry said in a low, thick voice. Matthew could barely make out the words.

Darienne's voice was much more clear and vibrant. "Do I?" Her tone carried a high degree of intimacy. "I can excite you even more—"

"I know," Larry said with amusement.

She chuckled briefly, then said, "No, listen a moment, Larry.

I have a knowledge of the world that other women don't. I even have special powers. Ancient powers. I can bring you into a higher plane of existence."

Matthew shuddered as he heard these words and had to brace his shoulder against the closed door to steady himself. His breathing grew shallow, harrowed, as he realized in a flash that he had no choice now. He had to act. The realization gave him a sudden infusion of strength as adrenaline pumped through his system.

He tried the doorknob, but the door was locked. He pounded the wood with his fist. "Larry!" he shouted.

"Sounds like my father," he could hear Larry saying.

"Stay away from her!" Matthew yelled through the closed door. "Don't let her near you!"

"Get out of here," Larry's voice came back at him. "Leave us alone!"

Matthew turned sideways and rammed his shoulder into the door. "I'll break this down if you don't let me in!"

"Better let him in," Darienne said. "Someone may call the police."

"*I* will myself!" Larry said, but Matthew could hear his footsteps hurrying toward the door.

In a moment it was open. Larry glared at Matthew. "What the hell is the matter with you?"

Matthew pushed past him and stepped into the room. Darienne stood a few feet away, still dressed in black, staring at him, her eyes a bright green, expectant and almost triumphant. Her lips parted sensually, and she began to breathe through her mouth, her chest rising and falling with each deep, fast breath of anticipation.

And then Matthew realized he'd fallen into her trap.

She must have guessed he would come directly here, blinded with worry about his son, thinking he had one last chance to save Larry. She might even have somehow arrived here first and watched him go into the building. He sensed now that she had guessed he had been listening at the door. She had even raised her voice so he could hear her plainly as she broached the subject of "a higher plane of existence" to his son. Clearly, she had maneuvered them all into this situation to force Matthew into making an irrevocable choice.

And by banging down the door in a panic, he'd made it. He'd flown like a hapless moth into her spider's web, and now there was no way to escape. If he refused to give in to what she wanted from him, she might take his son out of revenge, if not as a consolation prize.

"If you don't leave, I'm calling the cops," Larry warned him hotly.

Matthew ignored him, his eyes fixed on Darienne. "You've won," he told her, his voice hoarse and defeated. "Take me instead."

Her eyes quickened, but she seemed to hold herself back. "How do I know you're not just saying this now to save him? Once you think Larry is safe, you might evade me."

"What?" Larry said, looking from one to the other.

Matthew barely heard him. "I won't," he told Darienne. "I give you my word."

"You'll go through with what I want for you? You won't threaten me with immortal suicide the way you did before?"

Matthew trembled. A deadly chill made him feel faint. "I promise I'll go through with it."

Darienne stood absolutely still for a long moment. She took in a shaky breath, and her shoulders fell as she let it out in a sigh. She seemed to sway slightly. But then she looked at Matthew very directly, her eyes beginning to grow iridescent with a vibrant inner emotion. She walked up to him, quickly closing the space between them.

"You won't regret it, my darling," she said in a whisper, full of feeling. Sliding her hands to his shoulders, she closed her eyes and rested her head sideways against his collarbone. Her body seemed almost limp as she hung on him.

Matthew felt too numb to react.

Larry watched them in deep, disillusioning shock. "What's going on here?" He studied Matthew's face. "You're pale as a ghost! Why are you trembling?"

"Nothing's wrong now," Matthew said, trying to sound as if he meant the words.

Larry's brows drew together, and he looked increasingly troubled. "There *is* something wrong here. I can feel it!" He looked at Darienne. "What did you mean about him saving me? What's immortal suicide?"

"Nothing for you to worry about," Darienne said quietly, lifting her head from Matthew's shoulder. "Matthew and I understand one another." She drew away from him and placed her hand lightly on Larry's arm. "I'm sorry, Larry. I used you. It was wrong of me, but I did, because I needed Matthew so much. Forget me. Go back to Sheena. She loves you."

"Your eyes," Larry said, backing away from her. He looked from her to his father.

Indeed, Matthew saw how ablaze with unearthly, radiating iridescence her eyes had become. They were brighter than he'd ever seen them before. Her vampire desires were aflame with the knowledge that she would soon satiate herself with his blood and then transform him into her vampire consort to satiate her sexual needs. Matthew understood this all too well, and the knowledge made him quake. He felt like a fainting coward inside, but he had to be brave for his son. Larry must never understand.

"We'd better go," Matthew said to Darienne.

Darienne, who had lowered her eyes, turned to him again and took his hand. "Yes, darling."

Larry appeared stunned and frightened. "You're going with her?" he asked Matthew.

"Yes."

"But you said she's not normal. I can see she's not." He swallowed convulsively. "She's crazed or something. How else could her eyes be like that? Don't go with her! You warned *me* to stay away from her."

Matthew stared at his son, whose face was a youthful mirror of his own. "I'll be all right. I . . . may not see you for a long time. Not because I don't want to, but because I . . . I may not be able to. Just know that though I wasn't the best father I could have been, I always loved you. I love you now, more than you may ever understand."

Matthew turned and walked toward the door, pulling Darienne by the hand, wanting to go now as quickly as he could, since he had no explanation his son would ever accept.

But Larry followed. "Wait! I don't feel right about this. Why won't you see me again? Where are you going? What will happen to you?"

Matthew was touched to know that Larry did care about him, now that he was about to lose him. He let go of Darienne and grasped his son by the shoulders. "We may meet again one day. Don't be concerned about me. Live your life and don't make my mistakes. Marry Sheena. Center you life around her. Keep in touch with your mother. Build a family, and don't let your career get in the way of your relationships. It's what I should have done and failed. I'm lost, but you can still find yourself." He hugged his son roughly as tears burned his eyes.

When he let go, he glimpsed the totally bewildered look in Larry's eyes. With renewed determination, he turned away. He took hold of Darienne's arm, opened the door, and rushed her through it, fearing Larry would follow. As he hurried her along the hall and then down the steps, he heard Larry calling, "Dad, come back!"

Once outside, he unlocked the car door for Darienne, then raced around the front to the driver's seat. He turned on the ignition and drove away blindly, not even knowing where he was going.

"Matthew," Darienne said, leaning toward him and rubbing his shoulder lightly with her hand, "calm down. Drive more slowly, or you'll get us into an accident."

"Just as well!" he said, feeling cold, numb and blind with fear and sorrow.

"No accidents, Matthew. I won't let you commit mortal suicide either. You promised me."

He nodded grimly, wondering if he should keep his promise to give himself up completely to her, or if he should ram his car, driver's side first, into the nearest lamppost. Better to do that than let Darienne turn him into a vampire.

"Matthew, slow down." Darienne's tone showed increasing concern because he was driving at the same maniacal speed down London's streets. "Please! I know you're afraid and you'd rather end it all, but you mustn't." She grabbed hold of the dashboard to steady herself as he raced the compact car around a curve, tires screeching. "Matthew, stop this! You may *like* being a vampire. Give me a chance to give you this gift—don't be foolish and kill yourself out of fear of something you may be very grateful for."

He glanced at her momentarily as he held the wheel tightly. Her eyes were pale now, blond wisps of her mussed short hair covering her eyebrows. She clung to his shoulder and arm like a pleading wife. He felt an odd knot begin to form in his stomach, and before he realized he was doing it, he put his foot on the brakes. The car glided to a stop along the side of a residential street. He turned to her again.

"What do you want me to do?"

Darienne was sighing with relief. "Just drive carefully and take your time. There's no rush."

No, he thought morbidly, no need to rush toward a satin-lined coffin. "Where do you want me to drive? Not Claridge's." The thought of leaving bloodstains in that immaculate hotel made him want to avoid the place.

"No. My house in Belgravia. I live on Eaton Square. I'll tell you how to get there. Will you drive slowly now?"

"Slow as a funeral procession," Matthew muttered as a strange, icy calm came over him. His fate was near. All he could do was accept it.

"Don't be so dismal, Matthew," she said in a soothing tone as he drove off, more slowly this time, down the street. "You aren't going to die and disappear. You're going to die and then go on existing in a much more exciting way."

"Isn't the transformation dangerous? You told me once you'd consume a large quantity of my blood. How can I come back after that?"

"Because you'll drink some back from me, your blood mixed with mine. When you consume our comingled blood, it will give you the vampire gift," she said in a comforting tone, as if that were supposed to reassure him. He was surprised, though, that the thought didn't make him ill and ready to faint the way it had the first time she'd described the process to him.

"What if something goes wrong?" He felt a grim gallows sarcasm settling over him. "What if it doesn't work? What if you botch the job?"

Darienne appeared a bit indignant and squared her shoulders. "I know what I'm doing, Matthew. I've done it several times over the centuries, each time successfully. It's very simple, really. There's nothing to it."

Matthew chuckled sardonically. "Nothing to it! It's just my life you're taking."

"I'll be giving you a better life, not taking it, *chéri.* I'll be giving you immortality, superhuman strength and agility, the capacity for sexual passion beyond your wildest dreams."

"Now we're getting down to what you really want."

She raised her hand to the back of his head and curled her fingers into his hair. The feeling gave him light, not unpleasant goose bumps. "Yes," she readily agreed, "that's what I want. And soon it will be what you want, too."

"What if it isn't?" he asked, making a turn at her direction.

"Then you'll be free to leave me," she said in a blithe manner, as if she weren't worried.

"I will?" He glanced at her with surprise.

Her eyes sparkled as she smiled at him. "Of course. You'll be my equal, Matthew. I won't be able to keep you prisoner. You'll be free to roam wherever you want, do whatever you want. I'm sure you'll want to explore all your new powers. But," she laid her head on his shoulder, "you'll come back to me eventually."

"Why?" he asked, wary of the answer.

"Because I'll make your existence worthwhile. Just as in our former days I provided you with companionship. I comforted you with sex. I understood you when no one else did. Just as I understand you now, better than you understand yourself. You'll always come back to your Darienne, *chéri.*"

Matthew felt claustrophobic suddenly as he turned down Belgrave Place, heading toward Eaton Square and her house. He felt as if this small car were turning into the burial box that awaited him.

David and Veronica's plane landed in Zurich. They rented a car and drove to Lucerne. Following the directions Herman had given David, they found the quiet street at the edge of town on which Herman's lab was located. The two-story brick building appeared well kept, though modest in size. David remembered Darienne once telling him that Herman's lab took up the entire first floor, and he lived above it on the second floor. Apparently he had a guest room; when David had telephoned him last night, Herman had invited him and

Veronica to stay there. David had accepted the offer for the sake of convenience.

It was still daylight, so they found a small restaurant for dinner, since it was unlikely Herman, being a vampire, had the means or desire to prepare food for them. As they sat at their table, looking out the window at the sun sinking behind the buildings across the street, David wondered if Herman would be able to find a way to keep him from reverting.

"You're not eating," Veronica said, concern in her hesitant voice.

David realized he was only picking at his food. "Too nervous to eat," he said with a dry chuckle.

"I know. I'm making myself eat, but I'm not really hungry either. I hope Herman can help us."

David smiled, feeling touched that she had said *us* when it was really his physical condition that was causing their uncertainty. He sometimes worried that she would leave him, but clearly she saw her life intertwined with his, and this comforted him. Though, if Herman could find no way to stop him from changing back into a vampire, then Veronica's life would be irrevocably changed, too.

This prospect upset him the most. He didn't want her to become a vampiress in order to be with him forever. Nor would he want her to remain a mortal if he were a vampire again, because he would have to watch her grow old and die one day. He wanted them both to stay mortal and live out normal lives. Herman must be able to help them . . .

"You really should try to eat," Veronica said, breaking into his dark reverie. "You're beginning to look too thin."

David nodded and toyed with his fork. "I'll try."

By the time they left the restaurant, the sun had gone down, so they walked back to Herman's place. David rang the bell, and in a minute the door was opened by a wiry, bald man of medium height. He wore a white lab coat over his gray trousers and held a clipboard in his left hand. His quick, intelligent, gray eyes narrowed and focused on David's face.

"David de Morrissey?" he asked, extending his free hand before David could say a word.

David shook hands. "Yes. You're Herman?"

"I am, indeed. And you must be Veronica." Herman bowed

just slightly toward Veronica in a crisp, Germanic way that conveyed old-world civility. "Darienne speaks of you both every time I see her. Come in, please."

They entered a room that was set up like an office or reception area, with a desk, file cabinets, and two chairs. The walls were painted pale blue. Herman asked about their flight and if they had had dinner, as he led them through to another room, which looked very much like a classic laboratory. Bunsen burners, glass vials, petri dishes, and elaborate electronic and medical equipment David could not identify lined long stainless-steel counters beneath white cabinets. As far as David could tell, everything looked quite up-to-date and modern. And the place was immaculate.

Herman led them through the lab to another, smaller space, which looked like a doctor's examining room. David had never seen one, of course, but Veronica had once described to him what they looked like. When he'd caught a bad cold soon after they were married, she had wanted him to see a doctor. But David had refused, fearing a doctor might detect his unusual past somehow.

"I assume you'd like to get down to business," Herman said.

"Yes," David replied, growing nervous.

"Then please sit on the examining table," Herman said. "Veronica, you may sit in that chair." He pointed to a small leather-upholstered chair to one side of the examining table.

Veronica sat down as David pulled himself up to sit on the edge of the padded table, which was covered with a white sheet. Herman took a stethoscope out of a drawer and slipped it around his neck.

"Would you take off your jacket and shirt?" he asked David in his clipped accent. As he helped David off with the jacket, he said, "Over the phone, you told me the sun hurt your eyes. Is it only sunlight, or would a strong lamplight at night also bother you?"

"I'm not sure. I've only noticed it with the sun."

As David unbuttoned his shirt, Herman pulled over a metal lamp from one corner. The lamp had a large, flat bulb, accentuated by the metal hood at the back and sides of it. "I'm going to shine this in your eyes," Herman told David. "Tell me how it affects you."

David nodded. Herman tilted the lamp up toward his face and turned on a very strong light. Immediately David shut his eyes and averted his face as pain, like knives, stabbed the backs of his eyes.

"It's as bad as the sun!" David exclaimed.

Herman turned the light off. "All right. Let's check your heart and lungs." He positioned the stethoscope at various places on David's chest and back, had him breathe in, cough, then breathe normally.

"Everything sounds fine internally," he said as he folded up the stethoscope and set it aside. "I'll need to take a sample of your blood."

"All right. How do you . . . ?"

Herman smiled. "A needle in your arm. Not my teeth at your neck."

David chuckled, trusting Herman because of his reputation and his methodical, scientific demeanor. Darienne had said that Herman always supplied her with blood bags when she was in Europe, so David knew he had his own supply, probably obtained legally as part of his lab research.

As Herman swabbed his inner arm with alcohol, David asked, "Have you done any more research on the formula that made me mortal again?"

"I've analyzed all the herbal ingredients," Herman replied, "including the poisonous mushroom that neutralized the vampiric agent in your bloodstream. I can now replicate the formula easily. I'm grateful to you and Darienne for sending me the ingredients to analyze. I'd been searching for a cure for vampires for centuries, and this was quite a breakthrough."

"But it may not have worked," David said. "You warned me then that there was a five- or ten-percent chance I might revert." He winced as Herman poked the needle into his vein. When he saw his own blood rising in the syringe, he looked away.

"That's what I'll try to determine, whether or not you are in fact reverting." He removed the needle and placed a piece of cotton on David's arm, then made him bend his elbow to hold it in place. David turned his eyes forward to see what Herman was doing. Herman held up the syringe in front of David's face. "Does the sight of blood affect you?"

David gazed at the ruby liquid, then turned his head away

as a shudder overtook him. "Yes."

"How?"

"It . . . makes me feel ill . . . inhuman."

"But," Herman asked carefully, "do you want to taste it on your tongue?"

David turned back and looked at the full syringe again. "I . . . I don't know. It's my own blood. As a vampire, I never craved my own blood."

"Good point," Herman said, setting the syringe on a metal tray and covering it with a white napkin.

"What about you?" David asked with curiosity. "Isn't taking a blood sample difficult for you to do?"

Herman turned back to him, his gray eyes still, as only a vampire's could be. "I fed before you came. But if I weren't satiated just now, yes, I would crave it. I test blood all the time in my work. I research mortal human viruses as well as search for remedies for vampires. I've learned always to feed before I begin."

"I understand," David said. "What will you test my blood for?"

"To see if it has any traces of the vampiric agent. Your liver may have harbored remnants of the agent, and if you are reverting, it may have found its way back into your bloodstream."

"If it has, is there any way to stop it? Can I drink the formula again?"

Herman's expression seemed grave. "I remember what you described to me on the phone, after you'd taken the formula and become mortal. You said you felt as if you were burning up under the sun's rays and could see vapor, probably water vapor, rising from your fingers. You said you collapsed."

"Yes," David said, remembering the horror, the sensation that his blood was boiling, the fear of imminent destruction. He'd blacked out and awoken in Veronica's arms with Harriet at his side. "Veronica and Harriet did mouth-to-mouth resuscitation," he said, glancing at his wife, who was watching and listening very intently.

Herman turned to Veronica. "Would he have survived if you and Harriet hadn't been there to resuscitate him?"

Veronica's face grew pale. "I don't think so," she said in a near whisper. "When I came in, his complexion looked gray. He wasn't breathing." She raised her fingers to the side of her forehead. "I thought he was dead."

"It must have been a great shock to your body," Herman said, looking back at David. "I don't know if it would be wise to try the cure a second time, if you do revert. Your body might not stand the shock again."

"Can I take, say, half a dose now? Before I revert completely?"

Herman shook his head. "You must remember that the vital ingredient is the poisonous mushroom, a tiny amount of which can kill a mortal in a matter of minutes. If you can still go about in daylight, even though it hurts your eyes, and you're eating food, you're still basically mortal. To take the formula, even a reduced dose, would, I believe, be highly dangerous."

At this point, Veronica stood up unsteadily, her hands shaking. "I'm not feeling well," she murmured. She tried to take a step, but her knees gave way. Herman and David rushed to steady her, each taking hold of one arm.

"She hasn't been well ever since we left Chicago," David told Herman.

"Perhaps you should lie down on the examining table for a moment," Herman said. "Are you dizzy?"

Veronica nodded, apparently unable to speak. David lifted her in his arms and stepped to the table on which he'd been sitting. Herman pushed aside the shirt and jacket David had taken off. As David laid her upon the table, Herman found a pillow and placed it beneath her knees. He covered her with David's jacket, then rushed into the lab and came back with a glass of water. David placed his arm beneath her shoulders and helped her drink it.

"I feel okay now," Veronica said after a moment. "Sorry. I didn't mean to be so dramatic."

"It's all right," David said, holding her hand. He turned to Herman, who was studying her face. "Maybe you can help her. She seems to have caught a virus. Often she feels ill in the morning and doesn't eat much. This is the first time she's fainted, though."

Veronica averted her eyes, as if embarrassed. Herman was looking at her with curiosity. He took her other hand and felt her wrist. "Your pulse is a little fast. Maybe you'd better lie here for a few moments until you fully recover." He turned to David. "I'll need to analyze your blood before I can tell you anything further. Oh, yes, I need a hair sample, too." He reached into a drawer behind him and took out a small pair of scissors. "I'll try to clip some from underneath, so it won't show." David bent his head and heard the sound of his hair being cut. Herman showed him the small lock, about an inch long, which he'd cut off. "I don't think you'll miss it." He walked over and set the lock of brown on the white napkin, on the tray where he'd put the syringe of blood. Then he handed David his shirt.

As David slipped on the shirt, they both turned to look again at Veronica, who smiled at them wanly.

"Are you all right?" David asked.

"I'll be all right," she assured him, her voice stronger now. She lifted the jacket covering her and gave it to David.

"Her color is better now," Herman said. He turned to David. "Do you have luggage?"

"Yes."

"Why don't we let Veronica rest a little longer," Herman suggested, "while you and I bring your luggage up to your room?"

David agreed. He squeezed Veronica's hand and followed Herman out.

Veronica lay on the examining table and listened to their footsteps as they walked through the adjoining lab and beyond. She twisted a bit on the table and sighed. She wished she hadn't almost fainted like that. Pregnant women always fainted, according to popular myth. She didn't want David to guess her secret. He had enough on his mind right now, without adding a pregnant wife to his worries. But being reminded of David's near destruction when he took the formula, and then listening to Herman describe the dangers of taking it again—well, it had proved too upsetting for Veronica's delicate state, both mental and physical. She'd felt suddenly queasy, the air seemed too close, and all at once she began to see spots of light as the room seemed to darken. She'd have to hold up better than this, or Herman would start examining her, too.

All at once, she heard the footsteps of only one man coming back toward the examining room. In a moment, Herman appeared at the open door. "How are you feeling now?" he asked with a gentle smile.

Veronica sat up and swung her legs over the side of the table. "I'm fine now. I just got upset hearing all that."

"I know. Perhaps I shouldn't have had you sit in the room while I spoke with David about his condition."

"No," Veronica said quickly. "I want to know. I want to be here and hear everything."

Herman stepped into the room. "Your husband says you have a virus?"

"Well, that's what I thought it might be. It's nothing, really."

"Could your queasiness in the morning be from something else?"

Veronica looked into his still, gray eyes. "What do you mean?"

He smiled again. "I'm very interested in David's case. He's the first vampire I know who has become mortal again. One of the things I wanted to find out was whether he'd regained his ability to reproduce, as a normal human can. I wondered if David . . ."

Veronica quickly realized there was no use hedging. He'd apparently already guessed. "I'm pregnant. Does that answer your question?" Maybe it was just as well that Herman knew all the parameters of their situation.

He patted her hand. "I thought that might be the case. You have a certain look about you, and you seemed to be describing typical morning sickness."

"If David doesn't stay mortal, we're in a desperate situation," she told him, near tears.

"I understand. I'll do whatever I can. But the truth is, so little is known."

Veronica bowed her head a moment, then looked back at Herman, preparing to ask a question that lingered at the back of her mind. "Since David was once a vampire, will our baby be normal?"

Herman's face sobered. He paused, apparently thinking. "I know of no reason why your child shouldn't be normal. Have you seen a doctor? You ought to."

"I didn't know who to see in London."

"I know of a fine obstetrician here in Lucerne. I've done some lab work for him now and then. He has an excellent reputation." He turned, opened another drawer, and took out a card. "Here. Call in the morning and make an appointment."

"But David doesn't know yet, and—"

Herman appeared startled. "Hadn't you better tell him? It's his child, too."

Veronica took the card. "Thank you. Would you hand me my purse?"

Herman walked over to the chair where she'd been sitting and brought her the handbag. She opened it and dropped the card in just before David walked into the room.

"We're all settled upstairs," he told Veronica. He smiled. "You look much better now."

"She'll be just fine," Herman said. "Perhaps you'd both like to rest now. You've had an eventful day. I'll get to work analyzing the samples I've taken from you. A full analysis takes a few days, so the sooner I get started, the sooner we may have some answers. There's a TV in your room. I'll put on coffee and leave some croissants on a tray outside your room before I retire at dawn. Spend the day as you please, and I'll see you tomorrow evening."

Veronica and David thanked him and walked up to the guest room. The large bedroom was comfortable, with a queen-sized bed, a color television, and a small refrigerator filled with milk, cheeses, and fresh fruit. As they relaxed on the bed together and watched an old American movie, Veronica thought about Herman's advice.

But after watching David fall asleep from exhaustion in the middle of the movie, she decided she just could not burden him with the news that he was going to be a father. Not yet. They both needed to find out what David's future would be before they dealt with their impending parenthood. But Herman was right; she should see a doctor. Harriet had told her that, too. And Veronica knew she should, for the sake of her child. At least she had a recommendation to go by now.

But how would she see this obstetrician without David wanting to come along? She could tell him she thought she should see a doctor about her "virus," but he'd want to come with her. Even if she could convince him she wanted to go on her own, he'd want to know what the doctor said. She had to think of some other excuse.

A facial. Weren't the Swiss famous for skin care? David wouldn't want to go to a beauty clinic with her. Yes, she thought with relief, she had found a solution. She would tell him she wanted a facial because it would be relaxing, and she'd been under so much stress. He'd agree to that.

She glanced down at David, lying sound asleep next to her. He'd gotten so little rest last night, she was glad he had finally fallen asleep. She decided not to wake him to change out of his street clothes. It was more important that he got his rest. Quietly, she got up and turned off the TV, then changed into her nightgown. She found an extra blanket in the closet and put it over David, then got under the covers herself and turned out the light.

In the darkness she closed her eyes and prayed, a new habit she'd learned from David. She prayed for her husband, for her unborn child, and for herself. Their future seemed so precarious. She just wanted everything to be all right again.

10

What's that musty smell?

EXCITED WITH anticipation, yet nervous, Darienne unlocked the door to her Belgravia home. Matthew followed her in. When she turned on the lights, he looked about him at the Victorian decor.

"This is straight out of Bram Stoker," he said. "How fitting. Did you choose this ambience especially for transformations?"

His sarcasm annoyed her. "I could have just as easily transformed you in my ninety-fifth-floor condo in Chicago, but you wouldn't let me." She softened her sharp tone. "I don't use this place much anymore. Sorry if it doesn't appeal to you. Please," she held out her hand, "come into the living room and sit down."

She reached for his hand when he did not take hers. When she felt how icy his fingers were, she realized his sarcasm was covering his deep fear. Feeling empathy for him, she sat next to him on the couch and warmed his hand in both of hers. "Try to relax, *chéri*."

"Does a man on death row relax before he goes to the electric chair?" Even his voice sounded raspy from tension and fright.

"That's not an apt comparison, Matthew," she told him gently as she stroked his arm. "This is more like . . . perhaps like going through surgery would be. You'll fall asleep, and when you awake, you'll be better. Think of it as a healing experience. You'll never be sick again. Never exhausted. You'll be stronger than you can imagine. You'll be able to be yourself to the fullest degree. Forever."

Matthew said nothing. His hand seemed not quite so cold when she touched it again. "What are you thinking?" she asked. "You're so silent."

He shrugged slightly. "I can at least be thankful I was finally able to do something right, as far as my son is concerned. What happens to me now . . . I don't care anymore." He bowed his head. "The movie's not finished. That's one work commitment I failed to complete. But they can hire some other actor."

Darienne smiled. "They know, as I know, there's no one who can replace you. And you'll be able to finish your film."

He turned his head abruptly to look at her. "You mean, as a vampire?"

"Of course, *chéri*. Why not?"

"Won't I look different? My teeth will change, won't they?"

"Your incisors will become slightly sharper, but not so that anyone would notice. You never noticed mine or David's." It occurred to her, however, that filming him might be a problem after all, since, in still photos, a vampire always photographed bluish. "Do you wear a lot of makeup for the film, the way you did onstage?"

"Quite a bit. Why?"

"Then I doubt that there will be any problem. Although you will have to tell them you can only work after dark from now on."

He laughed in a hopeless way. "Oh, sure. They'll agree to that right away!"

"But you're their star. The film is half-made, and there must be lots of money riding on it. They'll give you anything you want."

He seemed unconvinced. "How can I go on acting when I'll be so utterly changed? David hated being a vampire. He wrote his angst into the *Shadow* character I played."

"Now, Matthew," Darienne said with quiet assurance, taking his arm and nestling closer, enjoying just being with him again. "David's not at all like you, you know."

"How do you think I'll react?"

"I'm not sure. But you aren't given to doleful self-searching as he is. If you were, you'd understand yourself better. You go through life more on instinct, as I do. When you want something, like a choice role to play—*Shadow* for example—you go after it with all you have. You devote all your time and attention to it until you've mastered it, and then you thrive on the reward playing the role brings you. Well, I'm the same. Only, instead of roles to play, I go after men to play with. When I saw you, I stopped at nothing until I'd attained you, and then I devoted all my time and attention to you—and *thrived,* my darling, on the lovely reward you brought me every night. So you see," she said as she ran her fingers up his broad shoulder, "we're rather alike. That's why I think you'll react to your new existence as I did. You'll embrace your new way of life and see how perfect it is for people like us, who need to experience things to the fullest degree possible."

Matthew sat still and did not respond, though she sensed from watching him that he'd heard what she had told him. "What's the matter, *chéri*? Don't you believe what I say?"

He shifted uneasily, and when she leaned forward to look at his face, his expression was bleak. "It sounds too fantastic," he said. "This whole thing is . . . surreal. I feel like I'm in an old horror flick, not just watching, but playing out the plot. Already, I'm beginning to forget what living a normal life among normal people was like."

"Who wants to be normal, *chéri*?" she asked in a soothing tone. "You and I weren't like average people to begin with. We weren't meant to have average lives. Now you can be superior, as I am." She squeezed his hand, showing her strength. "You'll be my equal, Matthew. You'll be a magnificent vampire."

Matthew extricated his hand from her grasp and flexed his fingers. "I don't want to be a bloodthirsty freak!" he declared in a harsh whisper, sitting up tall again. "If you had any moral decency, any sense of justice and fair play, you'd let me go."

"My morals and sense of justice are as strong as yours, Matthew, just different. As for decency—well, I do enjoy being delightfully indecent, I admit. No, I won't let you go. You made a bargain with me—you, in place of your son. I'm holding you to your word."

"It wasn't a bargain," he argued. "You set a trap. I'm his ransom payment."

Darienne smiled and stroked his springy gray-and-brown hair. "You're very noble," she told him in an admiring voice. "Heroic."

He jerked his head away from her touch. "Spare me your twisted admiration!" He laughed gruffly. "Apparently the only way I can ever escape you *is* to become your equal." He turned to her, eyes blazing with fear and rage. "Go on then, get it over with! Either kill me or transform me. I don't want to be your prisoner anymore!"

Darienne drew in a long, deep breath to calm herself. The moment was at hand. In minutes, Matthew would become the dazzling night creature she'd always known he must become, ever since she saw him play a vampire on the stage. Now he would thrill her as never before.

She got off the couch, slipped off her black jacket, and knelt on the floor in front of him. She was breathing so hard the bustier hurt her ribs, and she reached in back of her to remove it, too. As she did, she said, "Stretch out on the couch, my darling."

He complied, but eyed her suspiciously as she took off the bustier. Now she was bare-breasted, wearing only her miniskirt and hose.

"I thought you were going to transform me, not have sex," he said with new anger, half rising from his reclining position.

"Shh," she said, pressing her hands to his chest to make him lie back again. She grabbed a needlepoint pillow and placed it beneath his head. "We can do both, *chérie,*" she offered. She began unbuttoning his shirt. "If I begin the transformation while we're in the midst of coupling, you'll forget your fear in the joy of our union. I'll take you over the threshold in the sweet bliss of passion." She pulled his unbuttoned shirt apart and leaned over him, allowing her breasts to softly glide across his chest. But his chest was rising and falling heavily with his increasingly harrowed breaths. He set his hands against her shoulders, as he had early in the evening in his hotel room, to once again keep her at bay.

"I agreed to let you transform me. I never agreed to sex!"

"Matthew," she said, using her greater strength this time to push herself closer to him, "I'm doing this for you. It will be less frightening for you this way. I love you." She whispered the words with sincerity as she lay fully on top of him now, looking down into his face. "Let yourself get lost in my affection, and you'll be transformed before you know it. I don't want you to dread each moment. Use my body and my love to forget where you are and why. Soon you'll awake a wondrous and fearsome male—the man I've waited so long for. And you'll thank me. We'll be so happy!"

She drew her lips near to his and kissed him gently, yet with kindling passion, on the mouth. A whimpering sound escaped her throat as she felt her love for him almost painfully in the depths of her abdomen, in the trembling of her hands.

With surprising strength, he twisted his head away from her mouth, grabbed her by the shoulders, and gave her a forceful shake. "I don't want your deadly affection!" His harsh voice carried a depth of rage that hurt her to the core. "You've got me now. I've surrendered. Get it over with!" He let go with one hand and pushed his open shirt collar away from his neck. Then he turned his head slightly and arched his throat, exposing his carotid artery. "Go ahead—do it!"

His chest was heaving with his deep, ragged breaths, and his pulse point made a tantalizing little drumbeat in the smooth skin of his throat. Darienne felt the lust for his blood rise suddenly, and her mouth began to water. She almost wanted to cry, that he was tempting her this way, for she'd longed to taste his blood for years, but had always kept herself from doing so. She'd wanted to make this experience sweet for him, and he wouldn't let her. He made his throat so appealing, the desire to coax him into sex began to wane. She swallowed. "Matthew—"

"Do it and put me out of my misery," he whispered with desperation, "you heartless—"

He stopped short as she fastened her mouth onto his pulse point, tasting his skin with her tongue, smelling the blood flowing beneath, feeling the little jumps with each pulse and heartbeat. She paused, took in a little, shaky breath, then drew her upper lip back from her teeth, opened her mouth wider, and, as gently as she could, pierced his skin with her incisors. His body jolted beneath her, and he gave a little cry as immediately blood began rushing from the two small holes she'd made. She fastened her lips quickly and closed her eyes in a delirium of pleasure as she drank from him. Between swallows, she breathed slowly and deeply through her nose, keeping alert through her ecstasy, for she dared not get lost in her lust and make a mistake.

In a little while, Matthew's breathing grew more relaxed, and his chest beneath hers rose and fell in an easy, marvelously sensual rhythm that made her wish once again that they were enjoying sex, too. But perhaps it was just as well they were not. Tasting his rich blood while coupling with him might have been too heady an experience for Darienne to deal with in this delicate situation, where timing was all-important. When he lifted his arms up and around her in a warm embrace as she drank from him, tears came to her eyes. This was enough. This was just right. She felt almost as if he loved her, he held her so sweetly.

She drank for a long time, gorging herself. He was bigger and heavier than she, and she had to take enough of his blood to cause his natural death. When his arms slowly slipped off her back and fell to his sides limply, she knew the time was near. His breathing had grown shallow, fast, and raspy, as if he couldn't get enough air. These were the moments she did not like. Though it was necessary, she nevertheless hated to watch a person die, and always suffered a bit as they did. And it was during these moments that timing was crucial and a cool deliberate mind was a necessity.

She drew away from his neck and looked over his deathly pale face. He was slowly slipping into unconsciousness, and she had to act quickly. She got off of him and knelt on the floor beside him. Next to the couch was a small end table. She opened a drawer and took out a pair of scissors. Wincing, she pierced the inner curve of her breast. She made a cut to lengthen the wound and make the blood flow. A small wound would heal too quickly, so she had to make it large enough to keep bleeding the needed length of time.

She set the scissors aside and leaned over Matthew, cradling his head in her hands. Turning his head, she separated his closed lips with her thumb as she pressed her wounded breast to his mouth. "Drink, Matthew," she told him.

He did not respond, and her blood slid down his cheek. "Drink!" she said in a more commanding tone, shaking him a bit. She ran her hand over his throat, to encourage him to swallow. When he did, she sighed with relief. "Yes, my darling, drink more." He swallowed. "Again, my love. Again. My blood mixed with yours . . . take it, Matthew. Yes, good. Oh, good." She closed her eyes, feeling his lips at her breast as she gave him nourishment, her own blood, containing her vampire force, comingled with his blood within her. With this last act of the transformation process, she would save him.

His swallows grew weak and then stopped. She took his head from her breast and looked down at him. His eyes were open, but unfocused. He was breathing, just barely. Stroking his forehead, she spoke softly. "It's all right, Matthew. I'm here with you. You can let go. Just let go." He took one more half breath. His eyes closed, and he exhaled as his head fell slowly toward her. He did not breathe again.

She ran her fingers lovingly through his hair and kissed his forehead. Smiling, she said, "Just a few moments. You'll be with me again." Her heart began to beat eagerly. She took note of the blood on his face and on her chest. It wouldn't be good for him to see blood immediately upon waking up as a new vampire. She hurried into the kitchen, got some towels and wet them, then grabbed a dry one. As she walked back to the living room, she wiped the blood off her own mouth and breast. The wound she'd made with the scissors had stopped bleeding and was already healing. Now it looked like a pink line on her white skin. Good. She wanted her breasts to be beautiful for him when he awoke.

She reached the couch where he lay, kneeled beside him again, and cleaned the blood from his throat and mouth. When she was done, she took the towels back into the kitchen, so he would not see them. She did, however, open the refrigerator and take out two blood bags. He'd lost a lot of blood. He'd be ravenous, so she anticipated he'd need two bags. Usually most vampires drank one bag a few times a week to look normal, feel their fullest potential strength, and have a sense of well-being.

When she came back into the living room again, she hid the blood bags behind a large needlepoint pillow at the other end of the couch, by Matthew's feet. She put the scissors into the drawer from which they'd come and took out a small mirror, which she set on the tabletop. Then, taking his lifeless hand in hers, she sat beside him on the couch, at his hip, and waited.

There was blackness. Then a sudden surge of energy flowed through his body. Matthew's eyes opened to a world of new clarity. The low lights from the lamps, the rich, deep greens and purples of the wallpaper and upholstery, the shining green of the eyes smiling down at him, the sensuality of her exquisite feminine body, the bright blond of her hair—all these colors and images met his eyes with a vivid, vibrant force he'd never experienced before.

In one fluid movement, he sat up. Even that felt different—the strength in his back alone carried him to a sitting position, with no need to push himself with his arms. And then he realized, remembered, what had happened to him and why he felt different. Matthew knew he was a vampire now.

"*Bonsoir, chéri*!" Darienne smiled and held up a silvery round mirror in front of him. "Look. You can't see yourself. You are like me now."

He took the mirror and held it in front of his face. He should have been able to see his eyes and nose and mouth, but instead he only saw the heavy draperies over the windows behind him. Matthew felt unnerved and sat stunned.

Darienne took the mirror from him and set it behind her on the couch. "My love," she whispered with shimmering emotion, her eyes shining as she held her arms out to embrace him. The warmth of her body, the soft swells of her breasts, came up against him as she threw her arms about his neck. Matthew forgot the mirror. Instinctively he drew her close, pressed her forcefully against him, relishing all her feminine vitality, beginning to crave more.

"Oh, Matthew, you *are* magnificent! I can feel your new strength."

"I want you" were the first words out of his mouth, as he felt incredible stirrings in his groin.

"My darling, yes!" Darienne's rib cage expanded with her excited intake of breath, causing her breasts to press more firmly against his chest. Inside he felt wild, and he wanted to push her down and tear away her skirt. But she kissed him hotly on the mouth, and the new sensation distracted him. He kissed her back with heated urgency, grabbed hold of her breast, and kneaded it, feeling her soft, firm flesh mould to his grasp. He suddenly felt the deep urge to bite, to sink his teeth into that feminine softness.

As he drew his mouth from hers to seek her breasts, his gaze crossed her neck, and the pulse point in her throat transfixed him. Instead of her breast, he now wanted to devour that tantalizing pulse. As he moved in to do so, she quickly drew away and pushed her hand against his chin to stop him. She seemed to need all her strength to keep him from biting.

"No, Matthew!" she said, breathing hard with exertion. "It's taboo for one vampire to drink from another. I'll give you something to quench your thirst. But I'll have to let go of you," she warned. "Don't overtake me when I do. Can I trust you?" She eyed him as if she weren't sure.

"Yes," he said, feeling resentment. His need to bite was so strong, it made him angry to have her forbid him his desire. Who was she to tell him what he could and couldn't do? While she was turned away, he reached to grab hold of her.

"Matthew, stop! Look." She held up a labeled plastic bag filled with a dark red liquid. "For you." She offered it to him, obviously wanting him to take it. He did. "Bite into this," she instructed. "I know you want to bite flesh. But you must do this first. Drink from here. Then you will feel satisfied. You'll calm down a bit. And then," she smiled, "you may bite me. You can be rough as you want in our loveplay. You and I will spend the whole night coupling, over and over. After that, you'll be very pleased you've left mortality behind."

Dazed with her promises to satiate all his throbbing needs, he bit into the plastic and was surprised to find he'd easily made two holes. She showed him how to tip and hold the plastic bag, so that the liquid ran smoothly and neatly into his mouth. The thick liquid was cold, but it tasted rich and satisfying. He swallowed it down quickly.

But there wasn't enough in the bag. He wanted more! His intense frustration fired a resurgence of anger. Quickly Darienne produced another bag for him. As he finished it, he felt his hunger satisfied. He paused to get his bearings, recovering from his overpowering need. He looked at the empty bag with curiosity and read the label. On it was printed the name of a blood supply company and the type—O.

Matthew realized with a start that he'd just drunk human blood. His hands grew numb with shock, and the bag slipped from his fingers.

"Matthew? What's wrong?"

"What kind of horrible creature am I?" he cried out, feeling revulsion. He wiped his mouth and saw a small smear of blood on his fingers. He wanted to throw up, but couldn't.

"You knew vampires drank blood, Matthew. I drink it. David used to drink blood, too. And he and I are both quite civilized."

"I knew you had the lust, but—I never *saw* either of you do it," Matthew said, backing away from her. He hated her now. "The first person I've ever seen drink blood is . . . m-me! I don't want to be what I am! What you've made me!" He shifted his legs off the couch and got up. Pacing the room like a caged animal, he felt increasingly claustrophobic. He tore at his hair, wishing he could jump out of himself and escape his vampire body. Frantic, angry tears clouded his eyes, and he cried out in a tormented voice, "I can't stand this! Why did you do this to me?"

"Because I love you," she said, her voice sounding weak and confused. "A moment ago you wanted me." She walked toward him carefully, her tone now artificially calm. "Come and enjoy sex with me, darling. You'll feel better. I always used to make you feel better. Remember?

"Stay away from me!" he warned, turning on her.

"But you wanted me so much only a little while ago," she pleaded, "just as I want you."

"I never felt the murderous lusts I feel now—for blood—for sadistic sex. I want to be *human* again!"

"Matthew, when one is first transformed, the needs feel very strong. But that will calm down with time. You'll learn to control them. You don't have to attack anyone to get blood. That's the beauty of living in modern times. And the sex we can enjoy now isn't sadistic."

"I want to bite you and draw blood!" he exclaimed, barely keeping himself in check. "I want to throw you to the floor, rough you up, and force you."

Her eyes glazed with need. "Biting is normal for vampires, *chéri*. The punctures heal quickly. Look." She pointed to the inner curve of her breast, where he vaguely remembered a wound and blood . . . and swallowing that warm blood. "It's healed already! See? The biting doesn't harm us. It only brings increased pleasure. And if you want to throw me down and take me, then don't resist the temptation. I'd love to be ravished by you."

"I drank blood from your breast," Matthew said, feeling a sense of horror at the memory.

"It's what transformed you, *chéri*." She stepped closer to him, settled her hands on his shoulders and pressed herself against him. "And now you can fulfill me as no other man in the world can. Lie with me. Let me give you appeasement in that way, too. I can take care of all your new hungers." The warm mounds of her breasts quickly brought back his earlier arousal in an overpowering way. He felt obscene and pushed her away with such surprising strength she fell backward onto the couch.

"I'm like some crazed animal full of lusts!" he exclaimed with horror, backing into the draperies. "I don't *want* to be a predator looking for victims. David warned me it would be this way." He ran toward the front door. "I've got to get out of here, run away, before I hurt someone!"

Darienne got up from the couch and rushed after him. She caught him at the door and tugged at his arm. "No, Matthew, you can't leave. You don't know everything yet! I have to teach you how to live as a vampire."

He scowled at her. "I'm not *going* to live this way. I'm going to find some safe place where I won't hurt anyone, and I'll stay there until the sun comes up."

"Matthew, no!" she cried in horror, grasping him tightly. "You promised me you wouldn't do that. You promised! You gave me your word!"

"My word? As if there's a question of honor here?" He laughed harshly. "I'm a vampire now! I'm no better than you. You trapped me into this. I don't see why I need to answer your duplicity with some kind of moral integrity. The lusts you've give me have taken away my integrity. I'm not human anymore!" He pushed her away roughly, sending her flying backward.

Matthew heard her body thud into the wall behind her as he raced out the door and into the street.

Darienne got up, recovering her equilibrium. She'd fallen to her knees after being thrown against the wall. That Matthew should treat her this way wounded her. But she forgave him, knowing he was frightened and didn't understand his own strength yet. She had to find him and bring him back.

Realizing she couldn't run out into the street half-naked, she rushed back into the living room and picked up her jacket. She slipped it on and buttoned it down the front as she ran out the door.

The street appeared deserted, no sign of movement anywhere. Matthew's rental car was still parked in front of her house. Perhaps, in his frantic state, he'd forgotten it was available to him. He must have run off on foot. But even on foot, a vampire could cover distances marvelously fast. Where would he have gone? Which direction?

If he wanted to avoid people, he wouldn't go toward nearby Victoria Station, which was always busy, nor toward Buckingham Palace, where there would be guards. Though perhaps Matthew was too upset even to be thinking about where he was going. Still, he had a plan—to avoid people and meet the sun. Darienne asked herself, If she wanted to avoid people in London, where would she go?

Hyde Park. It wasn't too far and was generally deserted after dark. She ran down the street, heading toward Hyde Park.

When she reached Belgrave Square, a small park, she caught a glimpse of Matthew far ahead. He'd stopped, as if lost and trying to decide in which direction to continue. She kept running, realizing she might have an advantage because she knew London better than he. When he saw her coming toward him, he fled onward in the direction of Hyde Park Corner.

Darienne managed to keep him in view most of the time from then on. When he reached the vast expanse of Hyde Park, which was very dark at this time of night, he headed into a small stand of trees. Soon she couldn't see his white shirt anymore. He'd somehow disappeared.

Soundlessly, she walked into the grove, among the old trees, hoping he didn't know she was still behind him, so she might come upon him unawares. She walked around one tree and then another and could not find him. There was only a quarter moon, and the light was dim. She scanned the park in each direction. Then something, a feeling of being watched, made her look up. Matthew was staring down at her from a high branch of the tallest tree. Obviously he'd discovered his new vampire agility.

"Matthew!" she called up to him, grateful she'd not lost sight of him after all. "Please come back with me. There are so many things I must tell you."

"Go away!"

"I won't leave you."

"You will when dawn comes."

She placed her palms against the tree trunk to balance herself as she looked up at him. "I won't leave you," she insisted. "If you meet the sun, then I will, too. I won't continue in this world if you're not in it."

"Then neither of us will survive the night." His tone was cutting and decided.

Darienne rested her forehead against the tree for a moment. She knew how strong willed he was. How could she convince him not to destroy himself? Persistence was the only answer she could think of.

She looked above her and saw a branch she could reach if she jumped to grab hold of it. Springing upward, she wrapped her hands around the branch and pulled herself onto it, then twisted into a sitting position. She looked up at Matthew, who was sitting on a much higher branch.

"This is my tree," he said. "I got here first. Can't I even destroy myself in peace? Do you have to dog me to the last minute?"

Darienne bowed her head. His words hurt. "I love you. I want to be with you."

"You have the strangest way of showing love of any woman I ever met!"

She blinked back the rebuff and tried to inject humor into

her tone. "I never claimed to be typical."

"That's the understatement of the century!"

"How do you feel?" she asked, trying a new tack.

"Feel?"

"You climbed this tree so easily. Aren't you impressed with your new strength?"

He sat silently in the darkness for a moment. She could see his face behind clusters of leaves which shifted now and then in a soft breeze. "Yes, my strength is remarkable. Frightening! How easily I could kill someone to slake my need for blood." His voice carried resolve. "That's why I must destroy myself."

"But Matthew, *I* crave blood, and I don't go around killing people. That problem is easily solved. Remember the blood bags I gave you? I can tell you how to obtain them."

"You attacked *me* once," he pointed out.

"That was different."

"Yes, a different lust. You wanted to turn me into a vampire so I could take care of your other insatiable need. Now you've heightened that need in me, too!"

"But that's the best aspect of being a vampire, Matthew. We can enjoy sex to a degree mortals don't even imagine."

"Or want. I was perfectly happy with normal human desire. What I feel now is . . . unnatural."

"*Super*natural," she corrected him. Through the leaves she could glimpse the vampire glow now in his eyes, like two lights focused on her. "Don't you want to experience that at least once before you . . . before you throw the chance away? Lie with me now on the grass. Let me ease those fierce desires. And then you can decide if you still want to destroy yourself."

"No."

"Why not, Matthew?"

"I don't want to give you the satisfaction, or reward you for transforming me. And I don't want to be swayed by animal lust. I don't want to know the experience, so I won't want to live only for that."

"But that would be just a part of your existence. You have your career, Matthew."

"You've destroyed my career! I can't finish the movie. I'll

never play Heathcliff on Broadway. How could I appear before a packed theater as I am?"

"They would never know," she argued. "You knew me for three years—and quite intimately, too. You never guessed I was a vampire until I told you."

He didn't seem to have an answer for that.

"What's this about playing Heathcliff?" she asked. "You've been offered the part in a new play?"

"A new musical version of *Wuthering Heights*. I might have equaled my success in *Shadow*."

"Of course you would. Oh, Matthew, you're perfect for Heathcliff. You can be brooding and powerful, filled with unrequited love—some of the same qualities you portrayed in *Shadow*. And your voice—Is the musical score well done?"

"It was great," Matthew told her. "But I'll never sing it."

"Why not?"

"I won't appear as a vampire."

"No one will ever know!" she repeated.

"I'd know. Besides, how can I do the rehearsals? They're in the daytime. I can't even finish my movie for the same reason."

Darienne grew a bit impatient. "I told you how to handle that. You just need to learn to be a little more demanding. It wouldn't be a problem for *me*. Just make them schedule everything to suit you."

"*You* never worked for a living. They'd fire me. It's unprofessional for an actor to be so demanding."

"But you're the star," she argued. "They need you. They'll learn to accommodate you. You know how to be demanding when you want to be. You lay down your rules to me easily enough—No, Darienne, I won't have sex with you. No, I won't stay with you a second longer than I have to. Use a little of that selfish will on the movie and theater people!" she told him with some anger.

He turned his head and appeared to look beyond the park, at the distant buildings.

When his silence lasted a few minutes, she asked, "What are you thinking?"

Her voice seemed to intrude on his ruminations, and annoyance crossed his face. "None of your business." With that, he pushed himself off the branch and leapt all the way to the ground, landing easily on his feet.

"Excellent, Matthew!" she called down to him as he began to walk away. "You could never have done that as a mortal." She followed suit and leapt to the ground, too. Hurrying, she caught up with him as he walked across the grass. "Where are you going now?"

He seemed even more annoyed. "I don't know. Do you have to keep following me? Can't I think over my situation by myself in peace?"

"Do you mean you're reconsidering?" she asked with new hope. "You won't destroy yourself?"

He clenched his jaw and made a huge show of patience. "I *don't know,* Darienne." Pausing in his steps, he added, "But I promise you this: If you don't leave me be, I'll *eagerly* destroy myself just to escape you!"

She nodded, trying to be patient with him, too, and understand. "I'll leave you alone until an hour before dawn. I'll stay nearby so I know where to find you, but I promise I won't bother you. And then you must come back with me to my house before the sun rises. Or you'll turn us both to dust."

He met her eyes with his, their glow showing all the new strength his vampire condition gave him. "I don't want to see you or hear you," he said in a deceptively quiet voice. "And what I do at dawn is up to me. What you do is up to you. You try anymore tricks to get me to do what you want, and I'll break you in two." He took hold of her arm and twisted it painfully. "I'm stronger than you now, I can tell. Male is still more mighty than female, in any form of existence. You'll never twist *me* to your will again!"

He let go. She rubbed the place where he'd held her arm and swallowed hard as tears filled her eyes. "You were always stronger than me, Matthew," she whispered, looking at him, tears and all. "That's why I fell in love with you. In my mind, you were always superhuman. I just wanted that to be a reality. You're unbeatable now, in the theatrical world and the real world."

Matthew's expression changed as he listened.

"If you don't want me in your life," she went on, "then you certainly have the strength and wits to keep me out. Don't destroy yourself to escape me. I'm putty in your hands. Roll me in a ball and throw me away if you must, but don't throw yourself away. You have so much talent to give the world."

He looked a bit dumbfounded as she finished, and his eyes glowed with an inner light that was not entirely vampiric. Perhaps she was mistaken, or perhaps it was just her blind hope, but she thought she saw a hint of appreciation in his face. She considered asking him again to lie with her in the soft grass, but then decided not to risk re-igniting his wrath.

"I'll leave you alone now," she said. "But I'll come to you again before dawn. You must let me take you back to my home. You'll be safe there through the day."

He turned his head to one side, and his shoulders came up in an involuntary flinch, as if he'd been reminded again of what he was. "I'll let you know my decision in a few hours."

"All right, Matthew." She didn't press things any further, but left his side and kept out of his way. He began walking again, and she followed some distance behind in silence. When he reached The Serpentine, a long, curved lake in the park, he sat down near the edge and looked out over the water. She watched and waited, crouching on the ground near some bushes. Hours passed and he did not move.

When she knew dawn was soon approaching, she got up and walked over to where he was still sitting, on the ground, near the water. "Matthew," she said softly as she touched his shoulder. Startled, he looked up abruptly. "It's time," she told him. "You must come with me now."

He turned his head and looked back out over the water. "I haven't made up my mind yet."

"There's no more time. We've wandered quite far into the park. It will take a while to get back to my house, even if we move fast."

He shifted restlessly and threw aside a blade of grass he'd been rolling in his fingers. But he said nothing.

"Look, Matthew," she said, kneeling beside him, "if you need more time to think, then come with me now, spend the daylight hours safely in my house, and then you'll have tomorrow night to think more about your future. You really don't have to make such an irrevocable decision now, if you're not ready to."

He turned and stared at her, statue-like, for a long moment. He'd already acquired that curious stillness characteristic of vampires. "If I come with you," he said at last, "what happens during the day?"

"You'll fall into a deep sleep, that's all. You'll get a good rest. This has been a difficult night for you. By tomorrow night, you may be much better able to put things into perspective, after you've had a day's rest."

"And I sleep . . . where?" he asked as if wary of the answer.

"In a coffin, *chéri,*" she told him with a careful straightforwardness. "You knew that."

"I remember the night you showed me yours in Chicago."

Darienne remembered that night, too. He'd reacted with such horror. She hadn't expected that. "I know the thought of lying in a coffin upset you a great deal then. But you see, that was merely your mortal's fear of death. You're immortal now. The coffin is nothing. Merely a comfortable chamber which will protect you from the sun's rays."

"But I don't have one."

She smiled and stroked back the short tendrils of curly hair that hung over his forehead. "I purchased one for you, *mon amour*. When I found out Natalie hadn't come to London with you, I . . . began to think ahead. It was delivered to my house a week ago. I wasn't sure what you would want, so I had it made up in oak, which always has a masculine appeal. The inside is lined with a light, moss-green velvet. I chose that color because it matches your eyes."

He stared at her mutely, and she couldn't read his reaction. So she continued. "I put some soil from my back garden beneath the velvet. The soil and the coffin together are what protect us from the sun's rays. Of course, you'd rest best if there were some earth from your birthplace beneath the lining. We'll have to arrange to obtain some for you from Georgia. I don't know why, but earth from our homeland gives our kind the most profound sense of peace when we close our eyes for the day."

"You planned my future to the most minute detail, I see!"

"*Chéri,*" she said in self-defense, "if my hope for your transformation succeeded, I had to make certain you would survive as a vampire. I didn't know for sure if we would ever reach this point. But now that we have, I'm glad I prepared so well. You should be glad, too."

"Sure. A velvet-lined coffin. That's just what I'd always hoped for!"

Darienne looked askance, not enjoying his ironic humor. "Dawn is coming, Matthew. We must go now." She reached for his hand. "Come with me," she said, rising to her feet. She tried to pull him up by the hand, but he wouldn't stand.

"If I manage to get in this . . . this terrific coffin you've got for me, what happens then?"

"You'll awake at dusk," she said, looking at the sky. The color was changing slightly.

"And then what? I'll crave blood?"

"If you do, I have some—plenty."

"So I will have to drink more blood, or risk wanting to kill someone? I don't want to experience that horrible, inhuman craving ever again."

She dropped to her knees once more and placed her hands on his shoulders. "Matthew, I promise you, you won't be a danger to anyone. But you're a danger to yourself and me if we don't leave right now. Please, come home with me."

He wrenched himself away. "No. I can't go through that again!"

"You just need time to get used to your new condition. Please, come with me now. Think more about all this tomorrow night."

"No tomorrows. I want this to end."

She took hold of him again and made him face her. "Do you want to be responsible for ending my existence, too? I love you and I won't leave you."

"More emotional blackmail!" he said in a vengeful tone. "It won't work this time. I became a vampire to save my son, but I won't continue in this state one more night to save you."

Darienne felt weak, thunderstruck. Her hope for happiness was disintegrating. He hated her. "You never loved me, even a little, did you? Well, I shouldn't be surprised," she said with a heartsick laugh. "You never said you did, never acted as if you did. You kept me around for the easy pleasure I gave you. I've moved heaven and earth to be with you again, forgiven you for leaving me for Natalie, and you still are unmoved. You died for a son who doesn't even respect you, much less love you. But I, who love you with all my heart, I'm just a nuisance, a thorn in your side."

He turned on her, cold fury in his glowing eyes. "You've attacked me. You've tricked me. Used my son to get me. You made me into a sordid creature I never wanted to be. Your brand of 'love' is evil!"

Darienne drew back. "Evil? You think I'm evil? Maybe . . . maybe misguided or too impetuous. Maybe I'm just too much in love. I was withering without you. I needed you back. I'm sorry for the desperate lengths I've gone to. But you kept your distance from me, and I didn't know what else to do."

Matthew exhaled and ran his hands roughly through his hair. "Then your mistake was to fall in love with me," he said in a less accusing but still bitter tone. "I never expected you to or wanted you to. It wasn't part of our bargain when we began our relationship."

"I know," she whispered. "I told you I wanted to remain independent. I actually meant that when I said it. But then, after we'd made love that first time, I lost my need to be independent. I discovered a new longing—to be with *you* forever."

Matthew shook his head in a hopeless manner. "Women always wanted more from me than I could give them. I never mean for that to happen, but it always has." He looked up at the sky and sniffed the air. "What's that musty smell?"

"Dawn, *chéri,*" she said gravely. "Vampires can smell it, the way animals can."

"You'd better go," he said. "I'll . . . stay here." He swallowed and looked grimly up at the sky again.

"I won't let you perish all alone," she told him with feeling. "I'd rather be turned to dust with you than go on without you. The dust from my body will mingle with yours in the morning sun, and we'll be together then in that way forever." She looked out at the still water of the silent lake. "This is a peaceful place to finish an existence."

"What are you saying?" he asked with something akin to anger in his voice. "You know how to enjoy yourself and the world. That was always the best thing about you, your sense of joy and vitality. Go! I don't want you here."

She bowed her head as tears gathered in her eyes. She felt heavy and old. "I have no joy left in me without you. If you don't want me here, then I'll walk to the other side of the lake."

"Darienne," he said, rising to his feet and lifting her forcefully to hers, "go home!" He grasped her upper arms and shook her. "You'll get over me. I'm bad news for any woman. You'll find someone new."

She grew angry through her tears. "How can you trivialize my feelings for you? I've lived four hundred years. You're the only man I've ever loved. I'm not going to go on another four centuries in the hope there might be some man someday who could replace you in my heart."

Matthew's eyes grew frantic as he looked at her, then glanced up at the sky, from which stars were disappearing, and back at her again. "I'm telling you to go back to your house!" he ordered with military-like authority.

"No!" she shouted.

He chewed on his lip, not realizing his sharp teeth caused them to bleed a bit. "For the last time—"

"No! I'll perish with you. It's too late now. Dawn's almost here."

Panic set his eyes afire. He grabbed her by the hand and began to run across the park in the general direction of her home.

Pulled along by Matthew, her feet almost flying beneath her, Darienne saw trees, then buildings rush by in a blur. She'd never run so fast. Indeed, Matthew had greater strength now than she; he ran faster and gripped her so tightly, she could not have gotten loose if she'd wanted to. And all the while her heart danced with a new exhilaration. Matthew wanted to save her! The time was so short, she wasn't sure he'd succeed, if they'd make it to her house in time. But even if they perished in the first rays at dawn, she'd know he cared enough to try to bring her to safety. And they were moving so fast, he just might succeed! The reborn hope that they might still somehow be happy together gave her new energy.

They came to a street corner, and he hesitated. "Which way?"

"That way," she said, pointing toward Belgrave Square. "Then to the left."

Soon they were on her street. The door to her house was still open, and they ran inside. She locked the deadbolt and turned to him. "Your coffin is next to mine in the back room," she said, leading him across the living room.

"I feel . . . odd," Matthew said, uneasiness in his voice. "Like a vibration is going through me."

"The sun, Matthew. It's coming over the horizon."

They hurried into the small back room, and she locked the door as she always did for safety. Inside, her Victorian coffin with red velvet lining lay beside the oak coffin she'd ordered for Matthew. She opened the lid of his. The lush, soft green lining looked inviting. But when Matthew peered into it, he backed away. Startled by his reaction, she quickly grabbed his hand.

"Matthew, get in."

He mutely shook his head, eyes ghostly pale, and tried to back away. "I . . . c-can't."

"There's no need to fear it. You're already dead!"

His eyes widened with apparent shock, as if this were the first time he truly realized he'd died.

"Matthew," she pleaded. She took hold of him and, with all her strength, pulled him downward until, awkwardly, he almost fell into the thick, richly varnished casket.

"No!" he protested as she lifted his legs and put them in. When he tried to push himself out, she shoved his shoulders down to keep him there. She could feel the power of the sun's rays vibrating all around her, though they were in a darkened room. There was no time now and only one thing to do to keep him still. She climbed into the coffin and lay down on top of him, face-to-face, chest-to-chest. Reaching up, she quickly pulled the heavy lid shut over them.

Now they were finally, absolutely safe, and Darienne breathed a long sigh of relief. But she felt Matthew's body writhing in terror beneath her.

"It's so dark!" Matthew said as his deep chest expanded and contracted. "I can't breathe. this is horrible!"

In the blackness, Darienne felt for his face with her hand and stroked his cheek, then his ear. "Calm down, my darling.

We're safe now. The sun can't hurt us. A lovely lethargy will come over us very soon. We'll fall asleep and wake up together at dusk. Everything will be better then, you'll see." She paused, listening to the silence, listening to Matthew breathe. His body seemed to relax beneath her, and his breathing slowed.

This situation felt unusual to Darienne. She'd seldom ever shared a coffin. Maybe once, at some distant time in the past, for some expedient reason, with David. Lying close to Matthew, experiencing their deep vampire sleep together, would be something she wouldn't want to give up, she knew already. She wished now she hadn't gotten him his own coffin. Then there would have only been hers and no choice but to share. Well, there would be time to work that out—if Matthew stayed.

Exhausted from running and from struggling to get him in the coffin, she snuggled against him, adoring the masculine warmth of his body. "I didn't think you'd be afraid of the dark, *chéri,*" she teased him. Then she said in a truly grateful tone, "Thank you for saving me. I didn't expect it of you. Why did you?"

To her surprise, she felt his arms come up around her to hold her. "I don't know. You've always been so shimmering, so effervescent. I couldn't stand to think of someone so beautiful vanishing on my account."

She would have liked to hear him say that he'd suddenly realized he loved her, but she was more than happy with his reply. Settling her head on his shoulder, she felt the heaviness of the day coming over her. "Are you all right now?" she asked, before she grew too drowsy to think coherently.

"Fine." his thickening voice carried a nuance of surprise. "This is . . . just fine . . ." His voice drifted off, and she knew he'd fallen into the deep sleep of the undead. In the next moment, Darienne drifted away, too. Her last conscious thought was the realization that even in his sleep, his arms were still around her.

11

The beginning of forever

MATTHEW OPENED his eyes, suddenly alert in the eerie silence and the close darkness that encased him. Where am I? was the first thought that came into his mind. He became aware of the soft weight of a woman's body on top of his. And then he remembered. Darienne. The coffin . . .

He was a vampire.

The sun must be setting right now, he realized. That's why he'd awakened. Good, he could get out of this damned, claustrophobic casket.

He felt Darienne's hand at his shoulder move. She must be waking, too. It was too dark to see her, but he felt the shift of weight as she raised herself up a bit.

"How do we get out of here?" he asked, his rising panic sounding in his voice.

"Simple," she replied. "We lift the lid." Again he felt her weight shift over him, her thigh sliding near his groin. He heard a slight creak, and all at once fresh air swept over his face. He looked up and could just manage to make out the crystal ceiling light fixture in the darkened room.

"Better now?" she asked, still half sitting up on top of him. He could see her smile and her blond hair in the very dim light that filtered through the heavily draped window, from the street lights outside.

"When I get out of this thing, I will be."

"You're still claustrophobic?" she asked, sounding amused and puzzled. "I've never met a claustrophobic vampire. Most of us cherish our private chamber, knowing the protection it gives us."

"Mine wasn't very private," he pointed out, her voice and feminine body arousing him. Again it was the urgent arousal he'd experienced last night, that feeling of wanting to overpower her, pin her beneath him with force, bite her and savagely ram all the wily impudence out of her.

"I had to do something to make you stay in here," she said softly, leaning over him and stroking his cheek with her fingertips. "You may have it to yourself tomorrow, if you really prefer it. But I rather like sharing your chamber and awakening with you like this. Don't you?" Her thigh moved over his swollen member. "Oh, *chéri,*" she cooed with delight. "You want me."

"I want to get out of here," he insisted, ignoring her words and his own obvious desire. He began to sit up, which caused her to slide to one side. Grabbing hold of the edge of the casket, he pulled himself up and out. He walked to the draped window, leaving her to get out on her own.

He was avoiding nearness to her on purpose—though he wasn't entirely sure what his purpose was. Partly it was the raging urge for sexual conquest he felt boiling inside him. He was afraid to give in, acknowledge and set loose his fierce need, unsure just what it would take to satiate it. He felt more animal than human. Darienne ought to be afraid of him.

But she wasn't, and that tantalized him even more, Matthew admitted to himself as he pushed the velvet drapery aside and looked out the window, at the street. David had once told him about the biting, the primitive, overwhelming lust that overcame two vampires during sex. He'd never forgotten David's horrific description: *Can you envision*, he'd once asked Matthew, *a sexual encounter with two humans ramming each other with dreadful, bone-jarring power, biting each other to feel their fangs sink into flesh, to see and lick the blood, going on like this hour after hour because it takes so much to satiate their heightened needs? Do you want to become a creature who has the unending lust to copulate in such a fashion?*

Matthew had become such a creature, and now he could instinctively understand what David had described. The intellectual side of him that remained didn't want to experience it. But his transformed body did. David was lucky, Matthew thought as he looked out at the empty street. David had escaped this burdensome need for angry sex. He was mortal now.

Matthew grabbed hold of the drapery as the thought rocked through him. David had been cured! How could he have forgotten? Why hadn't he thought of this already? All he needed to do was to find out how to get the potion or whatever it was David had taken and use it himself. Thank God! He could escape this destiny Darienne had forced on him. There was hope.

All at once he felt Darienne twining her arms around his elbow. "Matthew, what is it? You look shaken. Are you all right?"

"I'm fine."

"Do you need blood? I have plenty—"

"No." Never again, he hoped.

"Are you sure? Perhaps after losing so much, what I gave you last night wasn't enough to sustain you."

Even the thought of blood was making his mouth water. He despised himself. "No, I feel quite strong enough." Strong enough to pump you into a pulp, he thought. The angry lust he felt still threatened to undermine him.

Then again, perhaps his anger had nothing to do with vampire sexual needs. He had every right to be angry with her for making him into the creature he'd become. If he became mortal again, he still would have to find some way to outwit her, to protect himself and his son from her wiles.

She slid her hands down his arm and took his hand. "I want to thank you again for saving us last night." There was almost a shyness in her voice. "I wanted you to do it for yourself, but it seems you did it for me. I . . . I know that you don't love me, and I realize I can't ever expect you to. But it makes me happy that you cared enough to save me from oblivion."

Matthew bowed his head. Why had he done that? He didn't have a good answer for himself. This was the other part of his reason for keeping his distance from Darienne. His feelings about her confused him. He was angry with her, despised what she'd done, and yet . . . yesterday he couldn't let her perish. And, damn himself, he still liked the feel of her body next to his.

Well, whatever it was he harbored for her, anger or lust, he mustn't indulge his feelings. He had no intention of becoming part of her vampire world any more than he had already. A liaison with her now might be too addicting if his goal was to become mortal again. He had to put all desires aside and pursue that goal. He had to get in touch with David.

And Darienne mustn't know.

"You're so quiet," she said in that teasing, totally feminine, French way of hers. He'd always enjoyed her voice, he thought as he kept his eyes focused blindly out the window. "Cat got your tongue?" She edged closer. He could feel the swell of her breast against his arm, and his own swelling grew more acute. He ached to take hold of her and subdue her. He tried to control himself by breathing slowly. "I'd like to repay you for saving me." She reached up, and he felt her fingers softly circling his ear, then toying with his hair. His forehead broke out in sweat. "You deserve to be properly thanked," she purred, "and I know just how—"

He abruptly stepped away from her and into the room. "I need to go to Claridge's," he said, putting a businesslike matter-of-factness into his tone.

"Claridge's?"

"All my things are there—my clothes, papers, money. I left in a hurry, remember?"

"You can go later, *chéri,*" she said, following him. "Let's enjoy each other first." When she reached for his hand, he moved toward the door.

"I'll attract less attention if I go now instead of the middle of the night." He twisted the doorknob, but the door was locked. Turning the key she'd left in the old-fashioned keyhole, he unlocked it. His heart was beginning to beat faster. Freedom from her—from wanting her—was almost at hand.

"I'll go with you then," Darienne said with a reluctant sigh.

"No. I want to go by myself. I have my things to sort through. Besides, the studio must be wondering what happened to me. They may have people or even the police looking for me. I'd rather you weren't with me if they see me."

"But I could help you come up with an explanation. I'm good at that sort of thing."

"Darienne," he said in a firm voice, turning to her. "I'm going alone. Remember, I'm stronger than you now. I won't let you stop me."

The sadness in her great, luminous green eyes caused an odd pang in his stomach which annoyed him. Why did women always give him problems?

"When will you come back?" she asked. Before he could answer, she added, "You must be back here by dawn, you know. Your coffin is here."

She was right; he'd momentarily forgotten. He would have to preserve himself until he got the remedy to cure himself from David. That could take days, since David was in Switzerland. "I'll be back by dawn," he said in as impersonal a way as he could.

"All right." She looked up at him. "Kiss me good-bye?"

He stared at her, his jaw clenching. Should he humor her by giving her a little kiss? "No," he said, without thinking further.

Her chin trembled. The sight raised Matthew's hackles. Another emotional female, trying to cling to him. Practically every leading lady he'd worked with in *Shadow* had gotten like this at one time or another. Even Natalie used to get teary-eyed and begging. Until she dumped him.

"What have I done, Matthew? Last night you saved me. And now in the quarter hour since dusk, you've grown cold again. What have I done in this short time to annoy you?"

"It's not anything you've done in the last fifteen minutes. It's all the things I was angry with you about last night. You turned me into a vampire. You keep asking for a relationship. I don't want one with you. Never have. I don't know why I saved you last night, and to tell the truth, I'm beginning to regret it!"

Tears were standing in Darienne's huge eyes, but now defiant sparks from their green depths jumped out at him. "Maybe I regret it, too! Go to Claridge's. Do what you want. I don't deserve your hatred. And you don't deserve my love. If you have some plan up your sleeve to be rid of me, then by all means, go to it! I'll never ask you for anything again!"

He tried to be unmoved. "Is this another suicide threat?"

She shifted her stance and rested her fist on her hip. "No! You aren't *worth* destroying myself over. There are plenty of men on the globe. There's got to be *one* out there who can appreciate me. It's just a matter of looking harder. And to think I've wasted these years pining over you!"

Matthew was stunned by this sudden change after all the things she'd said last night. But Darienne always had switched gears without warning. Why was he surprised? And yet he couldn't help but notice that this was a repeat of a pattern in his life. Women in his past who said they loved him always seemed to wind up angry and disappointed with him: Natalie; actresses with whom he'd had relationships; even women he'd never slept with who had still inexplicably fallen in love with him. He never looked for deep attachments, and he tried to be honest and make that clear to them. What did they expect? They still grew angry with him because he didn't provide what he'd never promised to give. He'd admired Darienne because she seemed to prize freedom as much as he. But she had turned out to be more clinging, more manipulative, and now more angry, than any of them. To hell with women!

He blinked at her, unable to think of a damn thing to say, and not caring to share his private thoughts with her. Maintaining his dignity, he simply nodded, then walked out the door and out of the house.

Still in a muddle, he began walking up the sidewalk, thinking he should find a busy street and flag down a cab. And then he realized his rental car was parked out in front. He walked back a few steps while searching his pocket for the keys. As he unlocked the car door, he realized he might have escaped Darienne last night if he hadn't been so crazed when he ran out of the house. He'd forgotten about the car. He might have driven out of London, found some remote English moor somewhere in the countryside and met the sun as he'd wanted to.

But then he'd no longer be existing, he reminded himself as he got into the car and started the engine. Darienne's interference had caused him to be here again tonight. And now, in a much calmer frame of mind than last night, he'd thought of a way out of his dilemma. He only hoped he could get hold of David tonight and make arrangements to get the cure. He drove off, heading toward Claridge's.

When he reached the hotel, he climbed the stairs to the fourth floor, not wanting to cross the lobby to take the elevator up. He'd rather not be seen by anyone just yet. He got to his room and closed the door. Immediately he went to the drawer beneath the phone. He found the scrap of paper on which he'd written David's number in Switzerland.

David sat in Herman's office, his head pounding. Herman was asking him a lot of questions about his symptoms when the phone rang. The scientist answered it, then handed the receiver to David. "For you."

"The studio?" David asked with fatigue.

"It's Matthew McDowall. Isn't he that actor Darienne pursued?"

"Matthew?" David reached to take the phone from Herman, muttering, "Yes, she's probably gotten him into another predicament." He brought the receiver to his ear as Herman politely left the room.

"David?" Matthew's voice sounded anxious.

"What's she done now?"

"Transformed me."

David slumped in his chair. "No, don't tell me that," he said with desperation. He didn't need any more bad news.

"She was threatening Larry. I played right into her trap. What choice did I have? I couldn't let her do anything to my son!"

"I'm so sorry," David said in a wretched whisper. His shoulders and chest felt heavy as lead. "I know how lonely you must feel, how cut off from humanity."

"It's the unbearable cravings I can't deal with. I feel like a sordid, human predator out looking for blood and sex, with nothing left to give back to the world. All I can do is take."

The words pained David, knowing how gifted and intelligent an artist Matthew was. The burden of being one of the undead would be that much greater for such a man. But he had to find something to say to give Matthew reassurance. "The lusts will subside, or rather, you'll find that you can subdue them. You have superior strength now, and that strength can be channeled in self-controlling ways that will make you feel almost human again. I'm sure you're capable of controlling your need for blood. As for sex, Darienne will certainly accommodate you."

"She begs for it," Matthew said, resentment in his voice. "I don't want to give her the satisfaction. But, David, I didn't call for advice on how to adjust to this existence. I called to ask how I can get the formula that cured you. I don't want to stay this way. I want to be mortal again."

David's heart sank even further. "I'm reverting, Matthew. The cure wasn't permanent."

There was a dreadful pause. "What do you mean, wasn't permanent?"

"That's why I'm here in Switzerland. The man who answered the phone is a scientist vampire. I came to him to see if he could help me. He hasn't gotten the results of his lab tests yet, but he hasn't seemed very hopeful. When I ask questions, looking for reassurance, all he says is that little is known. I'm the only one he's ever heard of who has taken the formula. He has nothing to go by. Meanwhile, my symptoms have only gotten worse. I have a constant, severe headache. The sight of blood does things to me. I can't eat food. I've had to stay in a darkened room all day today because I can't stand sunlight."

"No . . ." Matthew's voice trailed off in a hopeless moan. "Have you needed a coffin?"

"Not yet, but Herman says he has an extra one. The time when I'll need it is coming soon, I'm sure of it. I'm growing weak from lack of eating. I can't sleep. I'll either revert soon or . . . or die."

"You can't *die,* David!" Matthew exclaimed with shock. "Be a vampire again, if you have to. Have the scientist transform you, so you won't risk dying as a mortal."

David paused. That *was* a last resort, he supposed. "But what about Veronica? I'd have to make her a vampire, or she'd grow old and I wouldn't. I can't abide that thought. She's very upset over all this, too. She's been ill and even fainted the other day. It's probably stress. Though . . . it's odd . . . she went out today on her own and came back looking quite beautiful. Radiant. She said she'd had a facial." He made a confounded chuckle. "Women. They do odd things to help themselves cope. I wish I could do something so simple and feel better." David rubbed his forehead, realizing he barely knew what he was saying, his head hurt so much. "Sorry I'm running on like this. It's just that she looked so beautiful today, whole and serene, and the thought of having to turn her into a night creature so she can be with me . . ."

"I'm sorry, David." Matthew sounded guilty. "I called for help, and you're in a worse situation than me."

"And I have no solution to offer you," David said sadly. "I certainly can't recommend that you take the formula."

"No," Matthew agreed. "All I can do now is adjust . . . to drinking blood and living at night."

David's head was throbbing, and he felt he needed to lie down. "Look, I have to go. I need to rest now. But call again. Let's keep in touch."

"Of course. I hope you'll recover. If not, let Herman transform you. You're my only friend now. I can't lose you. Veronica wouldn't want to lose you."

"I know. Good-bye, Matthew." David hung up the phone. He realized they hadn't even discussed the studio and the movie they'd both been working on. Clearly the film didn't matter to either of them anymore. David slumped forward, placing his throbbing head in his hands. "Herman," he called.

The door opened in a moment, and Herman stepped in. "Finished with your phone call?" He looked down at David in the chair. "What's wrong?" he said, alarm in his tone.

"My head's splitting. I feel so weak . . ."

Matthew sat on the bed in his room at Claridge's, staring at the phone he'd just hung up. David is reverting, he thought. There's no hope for me either. Tears of pain filled his eyes and his vision grew blurred. Then he heard an odd noise that seemed to come from his window, and he turned to look.

There appeared to be a face peering into his fourth-floor window. He must be seeing things, he thought as he blinked hard to clear his vision. Looking again, he saw a woman's face and blond hair.

"Darienne!" he exclaimed with outrage, rising from the bed. Damnation! Couldn't he have a moment to himself? He thought she was angry with him. Through with him. Why was she here? *How* was she here?

He walked to the window and opened it. "How did you get up here? What are you standing on?"

"I climbed the wall," she said, her chin just above the windowsill. "How do you think I got into your room the other night?" She looked down and seemed to adjust her position. "I'm hanging on by my fingernails and toes. You might offer to help me in!"

"I don't particularly want you in!"

"Matthew—"

Exhaling with exasperation, he took hold of her arms and helped pull her through the window. "You got in all by yourself before," he muttered, showing his annoyance. "I thought you were done with me. What does it take for you to *be* through with me? I'll do anything!"

When she had her feet on the floor, she looked up at him with a flash of anger. But as she gazed at his face, her expression changed. "You have a tear running down your cheek."

Matthew turned from her and hastily wiped it away. "I just got through talking to David."

"In Switzerland?"

He turned back to face her. "You know?"

"He came to talk to me on your behalf. He feared he was reverting, so I gave him a vampire scientist's address there. What did David tell you? Is he all right?"

"No. So far Herman—that's his name, isn't it?—hasn't been able to help him. David's symptoms are getting worse. He's afraid he'll revert soon or . . . or die."

"No!" Darienne's eyes widened with alarm and fear.

"I told him to let Herman transform him, rather than let himself die."

"Good." She took Matthew's arm. "Just what I would have told him. What did he say?"

"He started talking about Veronica and how he didn't want to have to transform her, too."

Darienne bowed her head and brought her hand to her cheek. "That's right. Veronica." She looked up at Matthew. "She's pregnant."

Matthew was stunned. "She is? David didn't mention that."

"I don't know if she's told him yet."

"Oh, my God. And I thought I had problems."

"Exactly," Darienne said. "I hope your tears were for David, not yourself. I love David and feel for him, but he would have been better off remaining a vampire. Veronica could have become one, too. She would never have become pregnant, and they wouldn't be in this situation." Her tone softened, grew introspective. "Though, I have to admit, I almost envied her having a child by the man she loved. Still, it's not working out. Now what can they do?" Her voice became choked with emotion. "If he reverts, he can transform Veronica. But then how could she raise her child, if she can only be about at night? And they couldn't transform the child. It would never grow up."

Matthew was a little astonished to see Darienne's hand tremble as she wiped away tears from her lashes. He wouldn't have guessed she'd have any maternal feelings, concerns about a child she hadn't even seen, that hadn't yet been born. Despite her manipulative designs on him, she did have a side that was genuinely unselfish.

As she finished wiping her eyes, blotting dampness with the sleeve of the black jacket she was still wearing over her miniskirt, she looked at Matthew. "Why did you call David?"

Matthew paused, then decided to be blunt. "To ask if he could give me the formula to cure me."

"Oh," Darienne said, her expression of concern fading. "I see. You still wish you weren't a vampire."

"I'd give anything to be mortal again. For obvious reasons, David didn't recommend I take the formula." Matthew scratched his nose. "And if I may ask, why are you here? To repeat, I thought you were through with me."

Her lovely mouth flattened with annoyance. "I am. But I realized there is one more ability you have now as a vampire that you haven't experienced yet. And I'm afraid it may take you too long to discover it on your own."

"I'm not interested in sex!"

Darienne gave him a deadpan stare and then broke into a throaty chuckle. "Don't you wish! No, that's not the ability I mean. I want you to sing for me."

"Sing?" he repeated, incredulous. "Oh, yeah, I'm in just the right frame of mind to start singing!"

She ignored him and walked into the sitting room, where the electric piano keyboard was set up. Matthew reluctantly followed and watched as she found the switch to turn on the instrument. Looking through the music from *Shadow* Matthew had brought home for practicing, she found the score for "She Can Never Be Mine," the song that had made him famous as a singer. He was in no mood to recall his past triumph now that his future looked so dim.

"Play it and sing," she said, setting the music up on the built-in stand.

"No."

"Matthew—"

"Why should I get more depressed than I already am?"

"I'm going to show you a reason to be happy." She sighed at his impassive face and turned to the keyboard herself. "I once learned harpsichord. I suppose I can pick out the melody."

She toyed with the black-and-white keys, hit a few wrong notes which made Matthew wince, then found the melody. "Is that the right key for you?"

"Darienne, I'm not going to sing."

She stopped playing and looked at him. "Do you want me to leave?"

"Yes, I'd like that very much!"

"All right. Sing for me and I'll leave."

Matthew raised his eyebrows in surprise. "Is that a promise?"

"I promise."

He doubted he could trust her, but he was willing to take a chance just to get rid of her. "It's a deal," he said, walking up to the keyboard. He edged her out of the way and sat in front of the keys to play. His heart wasn't in it, but he played the introduction to the song. Then he began to sing the lyrics he'd sung on stage so many times. It was the only song he'd filmed so far for the *Shadow* movie he'd never finish.

"Louder," Darienne prompted. "Sing out, as if you were on stage again." She sat down on a nearby chair and crossed her legs. "Pretend I'm the audience."

Annoyed, Matthew took in a deeper breath, got up, stepped away from the keyboard, and sang without accompaniment. As he reached a perfect high note, he began to be astonished. He delivered the note so easily. And his voice sounded unusually clear and pure, the way it did on the best nights of his stage performances, nights when he was really "on" and nothing could go wrong. Those nights a performer dreamed of and lived for.

As he came to a difficult passage, where his voice had to bound from low to high and back again, he was amazed at his voice's flexibility and accuracy. It was as if all his years of training had fused together, as if everything he'd ever learned had flooded into his mind and automatically flowed straight into his voice—all without strain or the need for acute concentration. His voice poured forth like a miracle. Stunned at himself, he stopped singing mid-note.

"Please don't stop," Darienne whispered with awe.

He found her eyes shining up at him with wonder and adoration, the way she always used to look at him. But now there was an even more profound aspect in her gaze, a new humility, as if she quietly knew she'd given him a gift beyond price, beyond herself.

"I can't believe my voice," Matthew said, struck breathless. "I have such control! If my technique is this good, I can learn to sing flawlessly."

Darienne smiled. "I thought you already did."

"Oh, no." He shook his head. "But I bet I can now, if I keep at it."

"That's it, Matthew. You must keep at it. You must finish the movie and then play Heathcliff on Broadway. Don't you see? It's what you were meant to do. It's what I wanted for you. It's what you can give the world."

Matthew sat down by the keyboard and shook his head. "How?" he asked, feeling despondent again. "Stage rehearsals are during the day. Films are shot during the day."

Darienne leaned toward him, eyes eager. "Make me your secretary for five minutes. I'll make a few phone calls and fix everything for you."

"My secretary!"

"Trust me."

"Oh, sure."

"Did I not make it possible for you to have this voice you're so excited about? Well, I'll find ways to make your career possible, too."

Matthew looked at her askance and spread his hands in the air. "What can you do? Who would you call?"

"The movie producer or director—whoever's in charge. I'll tell them you've gotten an incredible recording offer you can't turn down. You'll work evenings to finish the film so you can record during the day. If necessary you'll take a salary cut to make things go more smoothly—say half of what you were contracted for."

"Salary cut!"

"Matthew, you've already made plenty of money during the three years you did the stage show. I read what they're paying you to do the movie. Half that would be a fortune for the average person. Don't be greedy. Besides, half is more than you'll get if you quit the film."

He supposed she was right. "But there isn't any recording offer. They'd find that out eventually."

"By that time, the movie will be finished. You can say the deal fell through."

Matthew felt uneasy. "I don't like to lie. I've always been honest in my business dealings."

Darienne nodded, as if she empathized with his feelings. "I know. But, darling, a vampire has no choice sometimes. We must get on in the mortal world and yet keep our secret from them. The lie doesn't really hurt anyone, does it?"

Matthew lifted his shoulders. "I suppose not," he replied with reluctance. "I hate to imagine what my agent will think of this arrangement, even if the movie people accept it. He won't like getting less money."

"Make *me* your agent."

He looked at her incredulously. "You? What do you know about the entertainment business? Besides, it's my agent that got me the opportunity to do *Shadow*. He even managed to talk them into hiring me to play Heathcliff when they thought I was too old for the role. I don't like to desert him. I've been with him a long time."

Darienne pondered this a moment. "Well, if you feel you can trust him, tell him your secret."

"He'd never believe it."

"Then make him a vampire, too."

"What!"

"All I'm saying is that there are many ways to get around these problems. Think over different options and decide how these matters might be best handled. You're in the middle of the movie right now, so you must do something immediately about that. And you'll need to warn the *Wuthering Heights* production company that you'll only be available nights. You need to invent some plausible reason. Or even an implausible one." She paused, then her eyes brightened. "You can behave as if you've become highly eccentric from your success—say you've gotten very superstitious and think it's bad luck to rehearse during the day. I'm sure stories have gotten around about your old habit of lighting green candles for health and all those odd diets you tried. This will just seem like a new eccentricity, that's all."

Matthew rolled his eyes, not enjoying the thought of what people would think of him if he followed her advice. On the other hand, her suggestions just might work. He knew famous performers who had made some incredible demands and gotten them. It was just that his demands would be more incredible than any anyone in the business had ever heard of before.

He took a long, contemplative breath. "All right, then. You're my secretary. Call the movie producer and director. See what you can do." He found the phone numbers for her, feeling odd giving the matter over to her and not handling it himself. But he knew she'd be more skilled at inventing ideas and talking people into the impossible than he would be. She *was* a master manipulator.

As she made the phone calls from the bedroom, Matthew listened to Darienne's end of the conversation from the sitting room, trying to distance himself from her maneuvers on his behalf, though he knew very well he was a party to them.

A half hour later the issues about his resuming the *Shadow* film were virtually settled. When he heard her hang up from her conversation with Nolan Wolf, Matthew walked into the bedroom feeling guilty and yet impressed and pleased.

"You're incredible!" he told her as she sat smugly on the edge of the bed, fluffing her short blond hair with her fingertips in a preening way.

"It was easy. Nolan seemed to like my French accent."

"That's understandable. He's having an affair with Solange, the actress playing Marguerite. She's French."

"Your leading lady?" Her eyes narrowed. "I'm surprised she hasn't fallen for you, like all your other leading ladies."

"She's ambitious, and he can do more for her career."

She clicked her tongue in the French manner. "Is your ego bruised?"

"Not in the least! She's sometimes more of a handful than you are."

"A handful?" Darienne repeated in an arch tone. "Of what?"

"Trouble."

"Insults, after all the effort I've gone to on your behalf!"

Matthew smiled. "Yes, but you gave me the problem in the first place by making me a vampire."

"What I've turned you into is the world's greatest entertainer, *chéri.* Your voice is now unmatchable. You have all the strength and energy you need to perform any role you wish for as long as you wish. Generation after generation will revere you. Your acting talent will be honed to perfection as you learn and gain experience with each new decade. You were already extraordinary. Now you're beyond anything, Matthew. This is all new to you, but in your heart you must already sense what your future can hold."

Her words thrilled him, though he tried not to show it. She was right. He felt he was on the verge of a magnificent future. He felt all-powerful, as if he could do anything. All this he felt so strongly that he couldn't wait to be in front of a live audience again. How they would love him! The thunderous applause, the shouts of "Bravo," the fans flocking to the stage door to get a glimpse of him—how he'd missed all that. He needed to know that his public still loved him. He was anxious to be done with the film, so he could go to New York and begin rehearsals. He couldn't wait for the opening night of *Wuthering Heights.*

And Darienne, he had to admit, had made all this possible. Against his will, yes. But now, he couldn't help but be grateful. She was always right about him, it seemed. No one understood him the way she did. She understood him so well, it made him uneasy.

"Thanks for making the phone calls," he said, his simple words seeming inadequate, and yet he hesitated to give her any more approval. Somehow he feared showing too much approval would give her even more power over him than she already had.

"You're welcome," she said, studying him as if trying to make him out. "By the way, when you go back to work at the studio tomorrow evening, if the producer or director give you any further argument about your not working during daylight hours, you have the ability to hypnotize them."

"I do?"

"Yes. It's quite simple. You fix their eyes with yours, concentrate, and plant a thought in their mind. Once you do it, you'll understand what I mean and fall into it easily. For you, this technique will only work with mortal men, however. Just as for me, it only works with other women—sometimes. Women's minds are more complicated. A male vampire has it much easier, because men have such simple thought patterns. Anyway, if one of them gives you an argument, you can change his mind that way and keep it changed. Of course, this is a power you should use with discretion."

Matthew was astonished, but believed her. She'd been right about everything else—his superhuman strength, his vocal and physical agility. "Anything else I can do that I don't know about yet?"

"Well, yes, *chéri,* but you won't let me give you a demonstration of that."

He realized she was talking about vampire sex again. He was beginning to get curious, despite David's horrific description. But he broke eye contact and looked away rather than show his interest. He wasn't sure what sort of relationship he wanted from Darienne now. She was outrageously manipulative. And she was in love with him. She'd been a problem in the past and probably would go on being one, wanting more from him than he could give. He had his career to pursue. Still, she'd given him his new abilities. He owed her, in a way. And yet, she'd thrust it all on him. He hadn't asked for it.

She stood up. "I'll leave now," she said in a straightforward, easy tone.

Matthew felt instantly confused. He'd thought she was going to pressure him again for sex. "Leave?"

"I told you I would." When he looked at her blankly, she said, "I promised you that if you would sing for me, I'd leave. Well, I'm keeping my part of the bargain." She began to walk toward the window.

"But . . ." He followed her. "You don't need to use the window. Can't you leave by the door?"

She paused. "Yes, you're right. I always risk snagging my hose when I climb a stone wall. I came by the window because I was afraid you wouldn't let me in. But I'll leave by the door," she said, pivoting to go in the other direction.

Her tone was calm and full of equanimity, and it bothered him. "You . . ." He followed her again. "You don't have to go. I won't hold you to your promise."

She turned and smiled, but kept walking. "Thank you, Matthew," she said in a cordial tone, "but I think I should."

"Why?"

"Because if I stay, I'll be in your way. You have your belongings to sort through, or whatever it was you were going to do. Perhaps you want to rehearse your song, the one they'll want you to shoot tomorrow night. You probably want to get accustomed to the dynamics of your new voice. I'll see you later, anyway. You'll have to return to my home at dawn."

They were at the door now. "You can stay and listen to me sing," he found himself saying, part of him wondering why he was saying it.

"Oh, no, Matthew," she said sweetly, pausing to look at him, with her hand on the doorknob. Her eyes were softly flashing and beautiful. "You know how your voice arouses me. If I listen to you sing any more, I'll only want you. And you don't want to indulge your sexual needs for some reason, so I'd better go. I don't want to be accused again of trying to rape you," she added with innocence.

He stared at her a long moment, growing exasperated and amused. Why was he fighting? She knew how to outmaneuver him at every turn. And sometimes he even enjoyed it. His eyes traveled down to her black silk jacket, beneath which she wore nothing. He could see the inner curves of her lush breasts where the lapels crossed above the top button. The animal hunger came back on him so fast he had to catch his breath. When he looked at her face again, her eyes were luminous with a wondrous otherworld glow, gazing at him with such longing, she made him feel like the most potent male on the planet. Maybe he was. He wanted to get inside her and find out.

He didn't say a word, but lifted his hands to her lapels and swiftly ripped open her jacket, causing the buttons to fly in all directions. Her revealed breasts looked sumptuous as swollen grapes, their voluptuous contours accented by the smooth midriff they shadowed and her small, neat waist. Just looking at her never failed to thrill and arouse him.

She gasped and closed her eyes in ecstasy as he took hold of her breasts, cupping a hand beneath each one, pushing up on them to make them plump beneath her collarbone, while her pink nipples hardened to delightful peaks. Breathing unevenly with pent-up need, he licked and suckled them, enjoying the feel of each pert peak against his tongue. His sharp incisor accidentally scraped her skin and drew a small thread of blood. He could smell it and taste it. All his senses suddenly heightened. He couldn't help himself; he needed to feel her flesh beneath his teeth. As he opened his mouth and bit into one white breast, she gave a little cry of joy.

"Oh, Matthew!" she breathed as she ripped open the front of his shirt, then pushed it and the jacket he was wearing off his shoulders. She slipped off her own jacket, and when her hands were free, she slid them up over his bared shoulders. Pressing her breasts against him, she bit into the muscled flesh over his collarbone. He winced at the stunning, pleasurable pain.

They kissed and bit feverishly, and fondled each other in a frenzy, all their repressed passions now overaroused. He couldn't get enough of her flesh, her feminine softness, her vampire strength and hot desire.

She unbuttoned her miniskirt, and it fell to the floor, where she kicked it out of her way. As she stood before him wearing only black hose and a black satin garter belt, which contrasted with and accented the white skin of her slim, smooth upper thighs, he felt a huge stirring in his groin and his heart began to beat like a drum. Her blond froth of pubic hair drew his attention, and he slid his fingers downward, playing with it, then reached farther to find and tease the quick of her. He smiled when she closed her eyes and moaned with pleasure, leaning softly against him, her forehead at his shoulder.

"I've missed your touch," she said in a voice that brimmed with emotion. "I've needed you so." She reached down and unzipped him. His erection felt enormous, and his hard member thrust out toward her the moment his clothes were undone.

"You're so huge now," she whispered with aching admiration. "Your vampire strength makes your need so much more powerful. Your body adjusts . . . enlarges." Her voice sounded breathless with desire. She took him in her hands and fondled him, squeezing the sensitive crest between her thumb and fingers. The sensation rocked his nervous system like a shock wave.

"Damn you!" he whispered roughly, angry at needing her so much. He pushed her backward with aggressive impatience, and she immediately complied by falling with him onto the carpet. There, smiling with eagerness, her breasts rising and falling with her quick, deep breaths, she parted her legs for him. He drew himself over her and, with a forceful thrust, slid into her.

As he closed his eyes at the huge sensation of unbearable pleasure, she gave a shriek of joyous anticipation. The heated moistness of her inner body felt marvelously tight about his throbbing manhood. When she moved her pelvis toward him slightly, making him slide even farther into her, the sensation almost overcame him. He moaned as if suffering from acute pain, but he would not have traded this experience for anything. He'd always thrived on sex, but no past experience, even with Darienne, had ever prepared him for this. This threatened to be more pleasure than his body could tolerate.

And yet, he felt *so* powerful. As Darienne writhed beneath him, her lush, plump breasts shifting against his chest as she squirmed with pleasure, he wanted to ram her wondrous, wanton body to pieces, devour her with erotic bites, ravish and conquer her until she begged him to let her be his slave. A fantasy quickly formed in his mind as he drew back his full length and forcefully thrust into her quivering femininity. He'd solve his dilemma about her by battering her with sex, until she promised she'd never make another demand of him if he'd only come to her and satiate her with raging sex every night. That might be a relationship he could be comfortable with for eternity!

"Matthew!" she cried as he thrust hard into her again, so hard it would have broken a mortal woman. Her legs came up over his back tightly, urging him with each thrust.

"Am I hurting you?" he asked.

"No! You can't hurt me, my darling. I love it! Oh, Matthew," she breathed as he thrust again, "I've dreamed of this for years. Only you can satisfy me. Only you . . . ," she said between ragged breaths. "You always made me feel so special. But now your strength matches mine. Now . . . ohhh . . . it's perfect."

Matthew thoroughly enjoyed hearing this. It fit his fantasy. Only *he* could pleasure her fully. She'd said it herself. She didn't have David as a sex partner anymore. Now she only had him. He'd explore his new potential and learn to satiate her till her senses were numb. He'd make her crave him so, she'd never ask for more than this from him, out of fear of losing him. This fit Matthew's newly forming career plans very, very well. As Darienne had just said, now everything was perfect!

As he adjusted his weight on his elbows to support his increasing force, the momentum of his own desire spiraled ever higher, making him almost wild with need. Darienne felt this, too, judging by the incredible iridescent glow in her eyes, her shallow, quick gasps, her hoarse cries with each plunge into her. Matthew was amazed at his own ability to control his body. He could keep himself on the edge of orgasm far longer than he ever could as a mortal. This gave him a new sense of freedom and erotic power. He grew certain that from now on he could make Darienne beg him for sex, anytime he wanted. Yes, he'd save that for future use, sometime when she was trying to manipulate him again. He'd show her just who could manipulate whom.

But right now he wanted this experience to be mutually fulfilling and without ulterior design. She'd given him this new power, and he wanted her to enjoy the profits of her gift to him. Besides, he was beginning to wear down. He needed to climax soon or he'd lose his mind.

Apparently she felt the same overwhelming need to end this beautiful torture, for she raised her arms to her head and plunged her fingers into her tousled hair, as if to pull it out. "Matthew," she said in a voice weak with overindulgence, "I can't resist anymore." He could feel small, preliminary orgasms in her body, and her response excited him beyond his own edge of endurance. Slowly, with deliberation, he drew out almost his full length, looking down at her face as he loomed over her.

She began to gasp quickly, as if in a panic of anticipation. Her eyes held his, wide with iridescent wonder, deep with awe. "Use all your strength," she whispered. "Punish me with love."

Her words thrilled him. Slow and steady at first, he began his final thrust, knowing it would bring his aching member huge relief. As he poised to "punish" her, as she'd asked, he became aware of rising feelings churning inside him. His urgent desire was indeed sharpened by his remaining anger at the way she'd taken control and altered his life, his resentment because of his helpless lust for her body. He *wanted* to punish her, in more ways than she'd meant. But as he looked down into her beautiful face so full of yearning for him, he saw what could only be called worship in her eyes. He felt a strange clutch in the pit of his stomach that almost broke his concentration.

He shut that feeling away and centered on his anger and raging need to climax. *Bitch!* he said to himself as he thrust with all his might into her. She cried out, arching her neck and chest beneath him. He felt her inner muscles contracting tightly and rhythmically, as if pulling him even farther inside her. And at the same time his own organ convulsed, spewing hot liquid into her, the feeling like proverbial cannonballs shot once and then again and then again.

Matthew felt delirious when it was over. He gasped for breath and felt slightly dizzy as his super-tensed body began to relax. But his still swollen member continued to give Darienne pleasure as her convulsions continued, seeming to build on one another as she writhed in a powerful rhythm against him. He helped her, continuing to thrust as she rose against him. Incredibly, her orgasms kept coming, each more powerful than the one before. She was weeping now with ecstasy, tears streaming from her opalescent eyes, flowing back into her hair. Her breasts felt firm and soft as they pressed into his chest with each arch of her body against his. And her face, transfixed and overcome with the satiation of her desire, looked incredibly sweet, almost naive. Childlike with wonder. He'd never seen a woman look so feminine and beautiful. The image of her face at this moment, he knew with a sense of uneasiness, would stay locked somewhere in his mind forever, a haunting epiphany.

Watching as her orgasms became further apart and gradually subsided, he felt oddly protective of her; she looked so helplessly spent from lovemaking. When her body quieted, she gazed up at him with sweetly devastated eyes, apparently too limp and happy to speak. She smiled at him and her lips soundlessly formed his name. Her trembling fingers reached up to stroke his face and touch his mouth.

He felt ashamed now at the ugly name he had called her in his mind a few moments ago. He felt guilty about his anger. Gently he slipped his arms beneath her back and allowed his weight to settle over her, covering her with his body and holding her in his arms, his head next to hers. He wanted to be close as he could to her, and he smiled as he felt her arms come up snugly around his back. He didn't think he'd ever felt so completely and sublimely happy. It almost equaled, or maybe more than equaled, those nights onstage when his performance had gone well and the audience had responded with resounding applause. Onstage, he'd met his challenge with prowess and had been awarded with adulation, just as he was rewarded now, in a much more private way, with Darienne.

Only, these moments in the aftermath of sex with her had an added quality he couldn't quite define. There was a profound, unexpected feeling of peace and wholeness he wasn't used to, and frankly, he found it rather overwhelming, almost claustrophobic.

He drew away slowly, stroked her tear-dampened hair as he moved off of her and lay on his side next to her. "You were right," he said, keeping his tone light. "Vampire sex is the best." Though, as he looked down at her breasts, he grew troubled, seeing the dried rivulets of blood that had trickled from puncture wounds he'd made with his teeth in her soft skin. He reached to touch one healing wound on the side of her breast. "I'm sorry," he whispered.

She took his hand and brought it to her lips to kiss his fingers. "No, darling, don't be sorry. I loved every bite, every moment. They'll heal, just as yours are already healing." She reached out to touch bloodied bite marks on his shoulder. Matthew had forgotten. He fingered his wounds himself and found they didn't hurt in the least. In fact, the blood caked off, and he could feel no scar beneath, as if he'd never been bitten at all.

Darienne, meanwhile, was running her hand over the breadth of his chest. "You were so magnificent! Oh, my love—I've never experienced sex quite this way before. Your new strength, your unique sensitivity—it's more than any woman deserves."

He knew he should compliment her in return, but he felt strangely tongue-tied. "I'm happy, too," he said finally. Since he couldn't find more words, he leaned toward her to kiss her on the mouth. She met his lips with sweet, quiet eagerness. But just as he felt a renewed sensual energy spark between them, she drew away.

"Why don't you check out of Claridge's permanently and bring all your things to my house? Your coffin is there, so you'd have to come back there every morning anyway."

Matthew thought it over and found her reasoning logical. He'd only be here in London a while longer anyway. "All right." Languidly, he stroked her breast, gently teasing her nipple. He could feel a new erection kindling. "I can do that later on."

She took hold of his hand to stop his fondling and smiled. "It's best if you pack and leave now. It just looks better if you check out at a respectable hour in the evening, rather than in the middle of the night. You're a famous person. The less gossip you stir, the better."

"You're right. But we could have one more go-round before—"

"No, *chéri,*" she said, sitting up and taking his hand off her breast. "You don't realize yet that vampires tend to enjoy sex with one another in all-night orgies. This first time together was . . . mind-boggling. We needed these few moments to recover. But if we start again, we may not want to stop. Our couplings through the night will build on one another. We may accidentally break furniture as each coming together grows more frenzied and physical, because we forget our surroundings and our superior strength. You wouldn't want to wreck your room here."

Matthew was breathless at her description. "No . . ."

"At my house, we needn't worry. And if we lose track of time, as often happens, we'll be near our coffins if dawn comes upon us unexpectedly."

He was eager for the experience she described. He could almost envision it, for he felt new sexual energy pouring through him, needing to be sated, and he could believe that everything she said was quite possible. He began to rise to his feet. "Help me pack, then."

Together, they quickly thew his clothes into his suitcases. After washing the streaks of blood off themselves, they got dressed. Matthew found a new shirt, since the one he'd worn had gotten ripped. Darienne collected the buttons of her jacket and put them in her pocket. She kept the lapels closed by folding her arms across her chest. Matthew eyed her as they waited for the bellman to come for his luggage, and he thought how uniquely adventurous and sexy she looked.

She waited in the hotel lobby in this potentially provocative state of dress while he checked out. That done, they got into his rental car. He drove fast as he dared to her house, his pulses racing, his vampire desire demanding appeasement again.

When they reached her house, Darienne carefully pulled together her jacket before getting out of the car, onto the street. She was pleased with the way Matthew was ogling her, obviously eager for more. She was eager, too. And yet there was really no hurry. Tonight was only the beginning of forever.

Matthew was hers now. Their moments of sensual bliss mixed with undeniable emotion made her sure of him. He wanted her now for more than just the pleasures of her body and her sexual expertise, she told herself. She'd felt something in his embrace in those precious moments after lovemaking. Heard it in his voice, too. Perhaps he wasn't even aware of it, but she sensed his inner emotion had begun to make him unsure. She liked that. The more unsure he became, the more their relationship-might progress.

Oh, he was smug and impressed with his newly acquired male virility, as well he should be. She'd been impressed, too. Even humbled. And like him, she craved more. But along the way, she hoped to show him there was more to their stunning compatibility than mutually satiating, supercharged sex. There was something there called *love,* too, though she'd learned to try to be careful when, if, and how she used that word with him. She wasn't sure if he was capable yet of defining or even recognizing that singular emotion in himself. Perhaps he didn't want to recognize it.

When she'd first fallen in love with him, she'd had trouble recognizing the feeling, too. So, in a way, she could understand him. But he seemed a lot more resistant to catching on than she'd imagined he would be. She had to take into consideration, however, that he was a man. Some men were like that, shut off from their own emotions, unsettled at the idea that they might have tender feelings lurking beneath the facade of self-control and authority they worked so hard to create. But she'd chip away at Matthew's inner barriers. She'd make him feel his feelings for her sooner or later.

They brought his luggage in from the car and set it in a corner of her living room. He moved toward her, but she made him wait while she cleared the middle of the room of antique Victorian tables, lamps, and vases. She pushed the couch and chairs to one side. "Vampire sex takes space," she reminded him, and he helped her move the remaining furniture to the perimeters of the room.

She stood in the middle of the room then, facing him, and slipped off her jacket. He took off his, and they quickly removed the rest of their clothes. They fell to the floor together and resumed their interrupted night of torrid, super-energized sex. The dizzying surprise of their initial union over, they fell into an intuitive rhythm with each other. Darienne relaxed as she grew more sure of his desire for her and sought out new ways to appease it, while Matthew seemed to become ever more confident as he explored his new vampire strength and power.

Through the night, they satisfied the intense drives of their bodies, bringing each other to spiraling heights with bone-jarring thrusts and searing bites, rolling about the room in sexual abandon, until they cried out in thrilling climax, only, after a few minutes, to begin all over again in a new position, with renewed energy. Orgasm built on tumultuous orgasm, until at about four A.M., both lay in a momentary stupor from the powerful, shared climax to which they'd brought themselves.

"God, Matthew," she said weakly, smiling as she slowly sat up and the room still seemed to spin softly around her. She felt encompassed by a warm glow as the sensual throbbing below her stomach and between her thighs sweetly ebbed. This last orgasm had been so powerful it had almost frightened her, but now she was delirious with the tingling warmth pouring through her extremities from its aftermath. Matthew reached up to touch her shoulder as he sat up beside her. She took his hand and kissed his fingers with reverence.

"No one has ever thrilled me as you have," she told him as he smiled at her. She knew it was because she loved him, though she didn't tell him that. David had been equally capable of satisfying her. But the sublime heights she reached with Matthew, she knew, were due to her profound feelings for him.

"I couldn't have imagined sensations like this existed." He kissed her then on the side of her forehead, with affection this time rather than as a prelude to another copulation. "Thank you for making this possible."

She looked at him with delight. "You mean, you're beginning to *like* being a vampire?"

He grinned and bowed his head, running his fingertip along the carpet, tracing the outline of her hand as she rested her weight on it. "Yes, I'm beginning to like it. In fact, I don't think I could give this up. We can do this every night? We have that much strength?"

"Sure. Time will be the problem for us rather than strength. Tomorrow night you'll go back to work, and you'll have to rush off as soon as you rise at dusk. But perhaps they'll quit at one or two A.M. and you can come back here to me."

"You'll be waiting?" His gray-green eyes had a soft remnant glow amid the gentle lines that curved upward around them in a smile. His hair hung in short, haphazard, gentle twists over his forehead and gave him the effect of a slightly aged, comfortable teddy bear. She'd never seen him look more appealing. And he'd rarely been this sweet. Looking at him now, she almost wondered how he could be the same man who had just pleasured her with such powerful sex. But he'd always struck her as something of a paradox—a performer with a comedian's face, who moved and sang onstage with more elegant sensuality than she'd ever imagined a man could; an actor who could create profound emotion in a stage play, but couldn't find that emotion in his own life.

"Of course I'll be waiting for you," she answered with feeling and kissed him softly on the mouth. He responded warmly, with a vibrant affection she could feel down to her toes, and it brought tears to her eyes. She glanced away so he wouldn't see the tears when they ended their kiss.

They were near the heavy couch, and Matthew shifted to lean his back against it. He pulled her to him, held her tenderly in his arms, and kissed her again. Their breathing soon deepened, but as if intuiting each other's mood they kept the kiss easy and languid. Perhaps they were just too exhausted for any more raging passion.

Nevertheless, in a few moments Matthew had acquired another erection. When Darienne felt it, she moved over him without breaking the kiss, stradling his hips and taking him inside her. Though she was already thoroughly satiated, it still felt good to be filled with his flesh again. He slipped his arms around her back and drew her close until her breasts softly met his shoulders. He tilted his chin up to maintain their kiss while she began to slowly move upward and downward over him. She curled her fingers into his tousled hair while he spread kisses along her chin and down her neck. No biting this time, just soft, sensual gliding of flesh against flesh, lips against skin. Sometimes they stopped kissing and just gazed at each other, losing themselves in each other's eyes while their bodies continued to undulate in a subtle sexual rhythm.

They went on like this for quite some time, perhaps thirty minutes or more. Darienne really wasn't counting. But after such a seemingly long length of time, she began to realize she'd never had sex like this before with another vampire. This slow sensuality without the heated rush to climax reminded her of when she and Matthew first made love, when he was still a mortal. He'd had a mortal's gentleness, and she remembered how treasured he'd made her feel, as if he appreciated her for the person she was and not just for her voluptuous body.

This was the foremost and best reason why she had fallen in love with him. And now he was behaving that same way with her again, only with more ease and casualness, because they'd known each other for years and because they had just finished a much more intense sexual experience than they'd even imagined possible that first time they were together years ago. They knew each other thoroughly now, which made this languid lovemaking so very comfortable.

"I could go on like this forever," she whispered.

"I could, too," he said, his voice sexy in its breathy softness. "But dawn will be here soon."

"Oh . . . yes," she said, realizing she'd lost track of time. "We'd better finish."

He smiled, drew her close and increased the back-and-forth motion between them. They kissed again, harder, but still with the gentle passion they'd been sharing. He ran his hands up and down her back, over her buttocks and her thighs, spread wide over his. When she glided against him, he pressed her thighs toward him, his member going deeper within her. He extended his fingertips between her thighs, to touch the quick of her. The stimulation quickly brought her to the edge of orgasm, and soon she gasped and held him close as the sweet spasms overcame her. She felt his flesh pulse inside her as his breathing grew ragged. Sighing with pleasure, she leaned back from him a bit and pressed her forehead against his, closing her eyes.

This wasn't the most explosive sexual encounter she'd shared with him, but somehow it was the most meaningful, because of the intimate warmth and comfortable familiarity she felt from him. She hesitated, and then she decided to say what she wanted to tell him.

"I love you, Matthew." She drew her head away from his to look at his face.

His eyes were luminous, and yet the warmth she saw in them changed gradually to a caring confusion. "I know you do," he said, his tone genuine, as if trying to be reassuring. "I don't know why you should, but I know you do. You've always been special to me. You put up with more from me than any other woman has. And you've given me more sweetness and pleasure . . . ," his mouth quirked, "and exasperation than any woman I've known. It means a lot to me, that you care for me the way you do, even after I've hurt you. But . . . ," he hesitated and Darienne's heart began to sink, "I don't think I can give you all you seem to want. I'm not even sure what it is you want from me."

"Your love."

He studied her a moment and slowly lowered his eyes. "Well, I suppose I . . . I do have feelings for you. This is different from what I felt years ago when I fell for Natalie. I was young and far more romantic then. I'm older now."

But not much wiser, she thought. "You're still romantic when you sing 'She Can Never Be Mine,' " Darienne pointed out, settling her hands lightly on his shoulders.

"That's just a song. That's acting."

"But your emotion seemed so real every time you sang it on stage."

He shrugged. "I'm a *good* actor. I'm not thinking of anyone in particular when I sing it," he insisted.

"But the emotion is there within you."

He shook his head. "It's . . . it's just acting. It's not real. I make the audience believe it's real, but it's not. It's just a job."

She nodded quietly and didn't pursue the matter any further. Dawn was coming anyway. "We'd better go into the other room and retire. We only have five minutes or so."

His expression was still serious, even a little sad, perhaps because he knew his answer hadn't pleased her. "I'm sorry to disillusion you about me . . . about acting."

"I'm not disillusioned," she told him with a little smile. "I still love you."

She saw a trace of moisture rise in his eyes, and he glanced away as if in some inner confusion. "Thank you," he said with awkwardness, as if he didn't know how else to respond.

Darienne kissed his cheek tenderly and then got to her feet. She turned out the light in the living room and walked into the small room in which their coffins were. Matthew followed. She locked the door behind them, walked to her casket, and opened the lid.

He stared at her, looking disappointed, almost hurt. "You aren't going to rest with me?"

"Yesterday you said you felt too cramped with both of us together in yours."

He smiled. "That was yesterday. We've just made love all night."

She was touched to hear him say *made love*. Even she didn't tend to use that expression, calling it *coupling* or *having sex* instead. "You want me to share your chamber?"

He nodded. "I might have another panic attack in there and want to jump out again. Besides . . . I like waking up with you."

She bowed her head as tears threatened. Getting hold of herself, she looked up as she walked toward him. "You're not afraid of a theater full of people, but a long box made of wood scares you," she teased.

He grinned and opened the lid. She could see him stiffen as he stared into the empty, velvet-lined casket. Running her hand over his back, she said, "You'll get over it. Go on, get in."

He swung his legs over and lay down, panic flickering in his eyes. She turned out the light on the wall and then carefully climbed in on top of him. Immediately his arms took her, as if claiming her, while she settled herself against him. She pulled the lid shut just as she could feel the first rays of the sun vibrating the atmosphere.

As he held her close, she felt him kiss her hair in the darkness. "I really do need you," he murmured.

She smiled and rested her cheek on his chest. This was a beginning. "I know you do," she whispered back.

Soon the deep sleep of day overcame them as they lay in transient peace in each other's arms.

12

I need a vacation

IN SWITZERLAND the next evening, David sat nervously in Herman's office. His head still ached, and he felt very weak, even short of breath. The scientist vampire sat behind his desk analyzing data from the tests he'd run on David's blood and hair samples. Veronica was upstairs in the guest room waiting. She'd wanted to come downstairs with David and listen to what Herman had to say about David's condition, but David hadn't allowed her to. Last time she'd fainted, and he felt it best if she didn't hear all the details. Whatever the extent of the bad news Herman had for him, he'd find some way to try to soften it before telling Veronica.

She'd been quite serene the last couple of days. He didn't know why exactly, in the face of their predicament. Perhaps she'd put it out of her mind and wasn't dealing with the reality of their situation anymore. He feared it had all been too much for her. But he was glad she wasn't suffering from anxiety the way he was, for whatever reason.

"All right," Herman said, looking up from the computer data he'd been studying. His tone was dry and devoid of emotion, his usual manner.

"You've come to a conclusion?" David asked, bracing himself for the worst.

"Yes," he replied. Then he began shaking his head in a negative way as he arrayed all the results of David's tests in front of him on the desk. "I don't find a single indication in any of these results that shows there is anything wrong with you."

He picked up one sheet. "Your blood is absolutely normal and healthy. No hint of the vampiric agent I was looking for. By the way, your cholesterol and blood sugar levels are fine." He searched for another data sheet. "The hair sample also shows no trace of the vampiric agent. The only thing left would be to biopsy your liver, but that seems to me to be taking things to the extreme. I believe your reversion to the mortal state is permanent. You are *not* turning back into a vampire."

David could hardly believe his ears. This didn't make sense. "But *something* must be happening to me. I can't stand sunlight. I can't eat food."

Herman leaned back in his chair and nodded. "Yes, I'm not denying you have some serious symptoms. As for your lack of appetite for food—do you crave blood?"

"I . . . I don't know. I've avoided thinking about that possibility because . . ."

"Because the thought upsets you?"

"Yes."

Herman smiled and nodded to himself, as if he were on to something he wasn't sharing yet. "I'll tell you what: Let's do a little experiment. Be back in a second."

He left the room for a moment while David sat in his chair wondering how Herman's tests could have come up with nothing to indicate he was reverting. Perhaps his tests were simply inadequate. Herman had said all along that little was known about a human who had gone from mortal to vampire and back to mortal again.

Herman returned carrying a blood bag and a teaspoon. David looked away at the sight of it, fearing it as a harbinger of his future.

"Hope you don't mind my teeth," Herman said, making punctures in the tough plastic bag. "This is the quickest way. Now," he said as David turned with great hesitance to watch, "I'll pour you a teaspoon."

Carefully, he squeezed the bag while holding the teaspoon to one of the two small holes he'd made. When the teaspoon was brimming with the garnet-colored liquid, he held it in front of David's mouth. "Go on. Take it."

As David opened his mouth to ask why, Herman slipped the spoon between his lips. The cold, slightly salty liquid flooded onto David's tongue, and he almost gagged at the taste before he swallowed it. While he still had his eyes closed in revulsion, Herman said with a bit of humor, "I don't see any vampire craving for blood, judging by that reaction."

Swallowing hard again to rid himself of the taste, David could see Herman's point. "You're right, I don't crave it in the least. When I was a vampire, I would have wanted more—that whole bag. Now the thought that I swallowed even a teaspoon—"

"Yes," Herman said, eyeing the bag, "watching you drink has awakened my craving. I fed yesterday, but who's counting? I'll step out of the room so you won't have to watch." He left with the bag. In a minute, he came back without the bag. David noticed that his coloring was marvelously healthy and pink now, as if he'd just come in from a hike in the nearby mountains.

"What about my sensitivity to sunlight?" David asked, desiring to get back to the questions he wanted answered.

Herman, businesslike again, took his seat behind the desk. "But your sensitivity isn't only to sunlight. When I shone my lamp in your eyes, you flinched with pain, too."

"That's true," David admitted, puzzled.

"And you have terrible headaches."

"Yes!" That was the next thing David wanted to ask about.

"I've done some reading in some of my medical texts to see what might cause those symptoms. Have you ever heard of migraine headaches? Many mortals suffer from them."

"Migraines . . . ," David said, turning the familiar word over in his mind. His memory flew to the distant past.

Herman continued. "Some individuals who suffer migraines have an acute sensitivity to light, and nausea when their headache comes on. They feel so ill, they lose their appetite until their symptoms subside. Many spend a day or more in bed."

David's mouth dropped open as light dawned in his mind, then he began to laugh at himself. "Of course! I had them four hundred years ago, before I became a vampire. Migraines ran in my family. I'd forgotten!"

"Another indication that your body has changed back to its original mortal state."

"Still," David said, not yet entirely convinced, "I don't remember my symptoms back then being this severe."

Herman pulled on his earlobe as he studied David in a rather abstract way. "You're a playright, and obviously you must be a highly imaginative, creative person. I'm somewhat the opposite. I gather facts, analyze them, and draw logical conclusions in the scientific tradition. I've trained myself not to be carried away by an idea or notion. But in your line of work, you take an idea and refine on it, milk it and enlarge upon it until it's a poem or even an entire play."

David lowered his eyes and smiled to himself. He guessed what Herman was leading up to, but did not interrupt.

"I believe your fear of reverting into the vampire state," Herman continued, "combined with your active imagination caused you to draw a conclusion that wasn't backed up by fact. The more you focused on your symptoms, the worse they seemed, because you feared what they meant. When you saw blood, even on meat, you feared you would crave it and then imagined you did. I've heard of mortals who listen to a doctor talking on TV about the symptoms of some disease, and the next day they think they have the disease, when in fact they're as healthy as they were the day before."

David nodded. "Veronica has mentioned the word *hypochondriac* a time or two since we've been married."

Herman grinned. "I like her. She's got both feet on the ground, hasn't she?"

"Nowadays she does," David agreed, knowing how she'd evolved from the innocent dreamer she used to be. Though the last couple of days she seemed to have returned to her dream world.

Herman went on. "But I don't mean to minimize your symptoms. Migraines can be quite severe, and you had a valid excuse for enlarging them in your mind and misinterpreting them."

David felt himself relaxing, almost going limp with relief. Even his headache wasn't pounding anymore. "Thank God I'm not reverting! You're quite sure I'll stay mortal?"

"As sure as I can be," Herman said.

"You can't imagine how relieved I am."

"I'll recommend a doctor here who specializes in migraines. I believe he'll be able to prescribe some drug that will relieve your headaches."

David immediately straightened up a bit. "I've been afraid to see any doctors. Afraid they might be able to tell that I haven't had a normal past."

"Don't be," Herman said. "No doctor would be able to tell that you were once a vampire. As I said, your blood panel is absolutely normal. Physically, you're completely normal. Your teeth, I notice, are no longer sharp. There's no iridescence in your eyes, and their color doesn't change. And you're no longer sterile. You're as normal as a mortal can be."

David wondered how Herman had ascertained that he was no longer sterile. Perhaps something in the blood test. "I'm monumentally grateful. I appreciate the time you've spent on this for me."

"I was happy for the opportunity to study you. As I've mentioned, you're the only vampire I know of who actually became mortal again."

David chuckled dourly. "A mortal hypochondriac," he said with dry humor. "What I never anticipated when I wanted to become mortal was that I would feel so vulnerable to disease and accidents. Once you get used to the vampire strength and immunity to disease and injury, it's hard to go back to feeling comparatively helpless."

"I can transform you back to a vampire, if you wish," Herman offered with a smile that suggested he knew David wouldn't take him up on the offer.

"No, thanks!" David replied. "But how do mortals cope?"

Herman leaned his head on his hand over the desk. "That's not my area of expertise. I suppose that's where philosophy and religion come into play."

David thought about his answer. "You're right. Long ago, in my youth, I was quite religious. For a time, I even considered becoming a priest. I lost touch with my faith because when I was a vampire, I felt separated from God." He looked at Herman. "Don't you? Doesn't that bother you?"

Herman blinked. "I don't believe in God. Science has never proven God exists."

"Oh." There was no use discussing this any further with Herman, David realized. But in his own mind, David felt things beginning to fall into place.

"Go on," Herman prompted when David stopped talking. "I'm interested in your ideas, just out of curiosity."

"Well, I was thinking that I haven't been relying on that faith I once had, which is available to me again. You know, I once traded my mortal life for immortality to preserve Shakespeare's works. I considered them more important than myself. I forgot that God thinks everyone is important. Now I must resume living that mortal life I gave up, which has been so miraculously restored. Perhaps God never abandoned me after all. I feel as though I have a purpose again. I'm . . . beginning to understand."

"And you'll have your child to live for, too," Herman said.

David drew his brows together as he replayed Herman's statement in his mind, not sure he'd heard correctly. "What?"

"Your child that's on the way." Herman's expression grew alarmed. "I thought . . . Didn't Veronica tell you? I told her she should."

David sat perfectly still, though the room seemed to sway a trifle. "Veronica?"

"She's going to have a baby, David. I'm sorry. I foolishly assumed she'd told you by now. Well, that's what I get for sticking my nose in a mortal's affairs. Why should I assume a pregnant woman would do what I thought she'd do? This is quite embarrassing. She should have been the one to tell you."

As Herman chattered in chagrin, David felt a joyous new energy surging through his body. His head cleared. "My wife is *pregnant?* My God—" He got up and rushed to the door. "Thanks for telling me, Herman. I've got to see her!"

Veronica was sitting in an armchair, leafing through a Swiss magazine, barely looking at the pictures. What was taking so long? Herman must have told David something by now. Was David really reverting? Was he so upset that he was delaying telling her?

All at once she heard footsteps bounding up the staircase with such speed it startled her. She dropped the magazine. What was going on?

The door opened and David burst in. Anxiously, she stood up and took a step toward him. His posture was tall, he seemed full of energy, and his face looked radiant. This couldn't indicate bad news, certainly. And yet his eyes focused on her with intense expectation, and he said nothing.

"What did Herman tell you?" she asked. "Are you reverting?"

His head went back slightly. "No." He seemed to regroup his thoughts. "The tests he took are all normal. He thinks my symptoms are from migraine headaches." He grinned. "I'm still mortal, God's in his heaven, and everything's going to be all right!"

She smiled while choking back a sob and ran to him, throwing her arms around his neck. "Oh, David, what good news! I had a feeling everything would turn out okay, if we just held on."

He hugged her with gentle strength. But then he took her by the shoulders and held her at arm's length while looking her squarely in the eyes. His tone was a bit reprimanding. "Do you have something to tell me, young lady?"

She stared at him wide-eyed. How did he know? Had Herman said something? She smiled a sheepish half-smile and took her bottom lip between her teeth. "I'm going to have a baby," she told him at last. "I would have told you right away, but you were so upset—"

"Afraid you would add to my worries?" he said with understanding. "Well, I suppose you were right. If you had told me yesterday, I might have taken the news as if it were the end of the world. And that would only have upset you. But today, I'm so happy! Are you all right? How do you feel? Shouldn't you see a doctor?"

"I did, here in Lucerne. Herman recommended him. The doctor told me everything looked fine. He sent me to a pharmacy to get vitamin and mineral tablets that are specially formulated for pregnant women. I'll need to start seeing an obstetrician at regular intervals, but I'm fine for now. The morning sickness should go away in another couple of months."

David listened intently, nodding now and then as she spoke. Then he said, perplexed, "When did you see this obstetrician?"

"Yesterday."

He seemed to put two and two together. "When you told me you were going to get a facial. So that's why you came back looking beautiful and serene. You'd just learned you were pregnant."

Veronica lowered her eyes, feeling a trifle guilty now about the secrets she'd kept from him. "Actually, I found out in London. I used one of those home pregnancy kits."

"You knew as long ago as that?"

She nodded. "Several times I considered telling you, but you always looked so burdened, it just seemed wiser to me to wait. When we arrived here, Herman deduced that I was pregnant after I fainted. I admitted I was, and he said I'd better see a doctor. I wanted to go alone, so I said I was going to get a facial so you wouldn't want to come along."

"I never imagined you could be so devious," he said in a teasing tone.

"All with good reason," she reminded him, touching his chin. Now that his careworn look had disappeared, he appeared remarkably young and handsome. "Besides, I wound up having a facial, too."

"So what you'd told me wouldn't be a lie?" he asked with mock suspicion.

"Partly." She paused, recalling what an unusual day yesterday had been. "After seeing the obstetrician, I was relieved to know that I was all right, that my pregnancy seemed to be normal. But, of course, I was still concerned about your symptoms and what would happen if you became a vampire again. I walked around town a little, thinking, and I passed by a quaint old church. It was open, so I went in. Inside, the church was simple, with carved wood and high windows. Since it was empty and quiet, I sat down in a pew for a few minutes, looking for some peace of mind. I found myself saying a prayer, a heartfelt one. And after that, a calmness settled over me. I felt as though I knew everything would work out all right. I didn't know how or what would happen. But I felt that even if what you feared most came to be, we would find a way to cope with the situation. I left feeling much more easy about our future, whatever it was, as if there were answers I didn't know yet but would learn soon enough. And look—today we have those answers! Wonderful answers."

David's blue eyes seemed to marvel at her. "It seems you discovered the faith I'd lost."

"Did I? This is new to me. I have a lot to learn."

"A person doesn't understand faith. You feel it." He smiled, as if not wanting to get into a deep discussion at that moment. "So when did the facial come into it?"

Veronica chuckled. "Well, I happened to pass a skin care salon on the way back here, and I figured, why not? A facial would be fun, and, yes, it would make what I'd told you the truth—or at least the partial truth. So I had one. Complete with a mud pack of Italian mud—very expensive."

"Mud?"

Veronica lifted her chin. "Didn't it do wonders for my skin?"

"You look absolutely beautiful. No wonder you came back looking so radiant and serene yesterday after all you'd done. You looked so calm about everything, I was afraid you'd lost touch with reality. In fact, you found it."

She gave him a hug. "David, everything has turned out so well! Except—Herman said you have migraines. Should *you* see a doctor?"

"He's recommended one. He also assured me no doctor could detect I was once a vampire. I'll call for an appointment tomorrow."

"I'm sure they have medications that can help your headaches. And then everything will be back to normal: Except for the baby, of course," she added.

David looked down at her in wonder. "Who would have imagined? Me, a father. This is incredible. I'll need time to adjust."

"You have about eight months yet," she said with a grin.

"I have an idea." His eyes widened with new excitement. "Why don't we spend a few weeks here in Switzerland? We could both use a vacation."

"That's a great idea!" Veronica said. "It'll be harder to travel once the baby is born. But—what about the *Shadow* film? Aren't they expecting you to go back to London?"

"Hang the film!"

"But, David, it *is* based on your musical. And they asked for your input."

"But they don't want to listen to me. The director has control of the film, and Solange has control of him. Every question became an uphill battle. I'm tired of fighting. My stage musical won every possible award and will stand on its own. Let the film be a flop. I can't stop them from destroying it. I'll just make sure they don't list my name in the credits as one of the script writers."

Veronica understood his feelings, but was sad even so. "It's a shame, because Matthew's in it. A bad film might put a damper on his career."

David's face grew solemn. "He's a vampire now, Veronica. He called me last night. I felt so ill afterward; it's why Herman had to help me upstairs to bed. My head hurt too much to talk anymore, so I didn't tell you. But Darienne transformed him."

Veronica felt a chill run through her. "She did? He's really a vampire? What did he say?"

"He was distraught. He despised Darienne for what she'd done. He wanted me to give him the formula, so he could change back. Of course, last night I thought I was reverting, and I told him the formula hadn't worked. I'll have to get the cure from Herman before we leave, so I can send it to Matthew."

Veronica nodded, thinking of Darienne. It looked as though her plan to get Matthew back had failed. She'd made him into a vampire, and now he hated her. Veronica knew Darienne's tactics were questionable, but she felt sorry for her all the same.

"Don't look so sad," David said, stroking Veronica's hair. "We'll have Herman duplicate the cure. I'll call Matthew to tell him that I'm not reverting after all and that he can become mortal again. He'll be fine."

"But what about Darienne?"

David's expression grew blank. "What about her?"

"She'll be all alone again."

David sighed, and his tone was patient. "Darienne has created her own situation, Veronica. I care about her. I know you do, too. But there's nothing either of us can do." He let go of Veronica and moved toward the telephone extension in their room. "However, I can do something for Matthew." He picked up the phone and dialed long distance.

In a few moments, he put down the phone, his face puzzled.

"What's wrong?" Veronica asked.

"Claridge's says Matthew checked out of the hotel last night. It must have been after he called me. He didn't give them a forwarding address. I wonder where he's gone. And why?"

Veronica thought a moment. "Should we call Darienne?"

David looked askance. "No, I'm not opening that can of worms again! If she knows where he is, at least he's strong enough to deal with her now that she's made him a vampire. Perhaps I can find him somehow later on." He walked back and drew Veronica into his arms. "I've just let go of my problems. I don't want to take on theirs. I need a vacation! How about you?"

Veronica smiled at him. "Sounds good to me." She stretched up to kiss him, and he responded ardently. He swept her up against his chest as if he would never let go. She kissed him back with deep emotion, grateful to see him so happy again. His body felt strong, warm, and masculine as he enveloped her with love.

"You know what I think we should do?" he asked, his mouth hovering near hers.

"What?" She hoped he was thinking along the same lines she was.

"Have dinner."

"Oh," she said, a trifle disappointed. "Sure."

"I haven't been eating much lately, and I suddenly feel famished. We can go to that restaurant down the street."

Veronica understood. She hadn't seen him eat a full meal in days, and he'd grown too thin. He was, after all, only human. She was glad to know he had his appetite back. "That sounds great!" she told him with a smile.

"We can talk over our vacation—what we should see and do here in Switzerland."

"Okay."

"And then when we get back . . ."

The hint of sensuality creeping into his voice made her catch her breath. "Yes?"

He paused, his face clouding a bit. "Is it all right, now that you're . . . ?"

"Doctor said no problem."

David's slow grin became stunning. "This is going to be the start of a marvelous vacation!"

13

Where little fears grow great

"MMMMM," VERONICA moaned softly with pleasure as David thrust with gentle force deep within her. She opened her eyes briefly to the dazzling blue sky above as the sun shone down on them. The altitude of this secluded alpine meadow, to which they'd hiked for a picnic lunch, kept the summer midday temperature moderate and pleasant. They were lying on the checked tablecloth that had been packed in with the boxed lunch prepared for them by their hotel in Zermatt. Grass and alpine flowers surrounded them, butterflies fluttered here and there over them, and she could hear the humming of insects.

"You know what this reminds me of?" she asked, a bit breathlessly, looking at David's face over hers as he shifted his weight to his elbows.

"What?" As he smiled down at her, his eyes, which matched the sky, filled with sensual adoration.

"The pattern you chose years ago for the draperies and upholstery in the living room." She was referring to the busy green, coral, and yellow pattern of large flowers with entwined stems and leaves, interspersed with butterflies, dragonflies, and bees. She'd been fascinated by it when she first met him and had decided to keep it when she redecorated. He'd chosen the pattern himself when he was still a vampire, with no hope of becoming mortal. "I remember you told me you chose it because it showed the exuberance of nature and sunshine, and it reminded you of the joy of a summer afternoon in a meadow. You said when you looked at it, you could almost feel the sun warming you, even at night."

He lowered his gaze slightly, as if recalling the time when they first met and he'd told her this. "You remember all that?" he said, looking in her eyes again with wonder.

"I remember everything. There was nothing you said that wasn't fascinating."

He hesitated in his lovemaking. "And now that I'm an ordinary human . . ."

"David," she chided, stroking his bared back, for they'd taken off their clothes, "I still find you fascinating."

"But you remember our past with such reverence, as if you miss it."

Veronica contemplated this. Deep down she wondered if he were right, if she did long for the days when he was a vampire and she was under his power. But she wasn't sure that she missed it all that much anymore, especially now that she was pregnant and their future together as two mortals held so much life and promise.

She reached up to stroke back his hair from his forehead. "David, the only reason I brought this up was that here we are in a beautiful meadow, on a lazy afternoon, surrounded by busy insects and flowers, and the sun is beating down on us and warming us. It's everything you missed as a vampire, and why you chose that pattern to remind you of what you couldn't have. You have it now."

A mist came into his eyes, and his expression grew tender. "You're right. You're sweet to think of that for me and remind me. I have even more: I have you. I have these moments, these long, beautiful days with you." He touched her cheek. "I forget to live in the moment. I get caught up worrying about us and our future. I cast a shadow on what we have, don't I?"

"It's all right," she said, stroking his back again as she lay beneath him. "You haven't been mortal all that long. You're still adjusting. And we just came through a bad spell. But everything *is* all right now, and you must try not to have so many doubts and cares. I love you, and I'm happy with you. I'm thrilled about our baby. This is the best of life. Be happy, David."

"I'll learn," he said, smiling, his voice taking on a positive tone. "Thank you for your patience. And your wisdom. Our roles seem to have reversed," he added with humor. "I used to counsel you."

"We nurture each other. I think that's what marriage is supposed to be all about." Her body softly ached since he'd stopped his ardent thrusts. She made a little pout and looked at him with longing. "I need more nurturing now."

His eyes darkened sensually, and he resumed lovemaking. The sensation made her languidly spellbound, and she closed her eyes and lay back to enjoy the pleasure he gave her. Having all afternoon, they took their time, touching and caressing each other, assuring each other with low, whispered murmurs of their profound, building desire. Veronica adored the weight and manly force of his body as he loved her with increasing passion. She breathed in long, deep sighs as she felt herself spiraling upward to the peak of erotic tension.

Long minutes later, she trembled in his arms, in sweet ecstasy as she felt his virile seed pulsing into her. He might no longer take her to otherworld heights. But Veronica was sublimely aware that he had a new power now that had already affected her in a profound and much more lasting way. He'd begun the creation of a child in her womb.

As the sensations of satisfied desire ebbed away, they relaxed together and shared some more bread, cheese, and grapes. And then after a pleasant hour of doing nothing but breathing in the mountain air and watching butterflies and bees flit from flower to flower, they fell into love-making again.

Afterward, they dressed, packed up their lunch, and hiked back down the trail to Zermatt, where their small hotel, built like a classic Swiss chalet, was located. Veronica smiled to herself and was patient when David resumed admonishing her to be careful not to trip on a rock. Hiking had caused him to come up with a new worry: breaking a bone or spraining a limb. And he worried doubly because she was carrying their baby. Though she'd encouraged him earlier not to worry so much, he'd quickly lost track of her advice.

Unfortunately, at the end of the idyllic afternoon, David discovered a new danger he'd never anticipated and which Veronica was sorry she hadn't thought of herself: sunburn on his back. They visited a Zermatt drugstore, where she found a product made with aloe which quickly eased his discomfort.

Despite his lingering worries, Veronica was pleased to see David truly enjoying himself most of the time. They wound up extending the time they'd planned to stay in Switzerland and then extending it again. They were in the Alps for a full month before they reluctantly decided it was time to leave. Veronica suggested they fly directly to Chicago, thinking that was what David would want to do. But David, apparently feeling some obligation to see how the filming of *Shadow* in London was going, decided they'd better return to England, at least briefly, before flying home.

Veronica did not mind. Actually, she was glad he hadn't totally lost interest in the film. For his sake, she wanted the movie version of his greatest and most popular stage show to be a success, and she knew his input was needed to make it one. No one understood the concept of the show or could keep its script on track better than David, its creator.

Of course, as David had reminded her, Matthew understood the concept and characters, too. But David was concerned about what had become of Matthew. He speculated that if Matthew had chosen to disappear because Darienne had turned him into a vampire, then they might have even replaced Matthew with a new actor in the show. "That's why I feel an obligation to go back to London," David told Veronica in a weary tone as they packed their bags. "I owe it to Matthew to find out what happened to him and to give him the cure, if I can locate him. And I ought to see what's happened with the filming. I'm afraid everything will be in a shambles."

"What will you do if it is?" Veronica asked.

He exhaled sharply and shrugged. "If they agree to give me creative control, I'll see what I can do. If not, I wash my hands of the entire project!"

David walked into the London movie studio in the late afternoon. Veronica had come along. They located the soundstage being used that day. The red light above the door was not lit, so they walked in and found the lighting and camera crews getting the historical set ready for a shoot. Nearby they saw Nolan Wolf conferring with Solange, who was dressed in eighteenth-century splendor. When the director saw David, he appeared surprised but pleased.

"I was wondering if we'd ever see you again!" Nolan said, shaking his hand. "Hello, Veronica," he said, turning to her and giving her a kiss on the cheek. Solange smiled and greeted them warmly, too.

David was pleasantly taken aback by their equanimity. He'd have thought Nolan would be angry at him for being away for so long without much explanation. Nolan asked if David's personal business had been taken care of, then asked how he'd liked Switzerland and made small talk for a while.

"How's the film going?" David eventually asked with inner trepidation.

"Fine! We're ahead of schedule, and have only a week or two more of work. Oh, there'll be some background shots and transition shots, that sort of thing. And then the cutting will begin. But we're in fine shape."

"I see," David said, amazed. "And Matthew? How's he . . . doing?"

"Marvelous. He'll be here in an hour or so. He's switched his shooting schedule. He only works evenings—well, often he keeps the crew going into the wee hours of the morning, but no one seems to mind."

So Matthew had continued making the film after all. "The crew doesn't mind working so late?"

"No," Nolan said, shaking his head as if it were no great matter. "No one seems to complain."

David was beginning to have the strange feeling he'd stepped into some never-never land. "What about the script? There were so many problems and disputes over it when I left."

"All pretty much settled," Nolan said. "After you left, Matthew took a strong hand in studying the script and sorting out problems. It's very smooth now, tightly written, and powerful. Would you like to see?"

"Yes," David said, afraid to imagine what had become of it. "Solange is happy with it?" he asked, looking at the beautiful French actress.

"*Oui,*" she said with a Gallic shrug of her shoulders, as if wondering why he'd asked.

Nolan gave David an updated copy of the script. David and Veronica sat down together in an out-of-the-way spot and skimmed it while the movie makers shot a scene with Solange and another actress. By the time he'd reached the end, David had grown absolutely astonished. The script was virtually the same as the one he'd submitted when they began the film. Some scenes already shot, in which dialogue had been added for Solange, were back to their original form. David wondered if they'd played some trick on him and given him the original. Yet the date on it was current.

Nolan came by to ask David how he liked it.

"I'm very pleased," David said with hesitance. "But some of these scenes, particularly the ones with Solange, were lengthened and filmed. In this script, they're shorter."

"We reshot those. Matthew correctly pointed out that Solange's role was overshadowing everyone else's and throwing the film off balance."

David wanted to say that he'd pointed out the same thing, made the very same argument, but Solange had always gotten her way, since Nolan was a pushover for her every demand. "Solange had no objection?"

"Oh, at first. But she quickly saw that it was to everyone's benefit to put the quality of the film first, to have a balanced script that stuck to the main story line and did not weigh it down."

"She did?" David marveled at this. Solange seemed to be cut of the same cloth as Darienne and not the sort to give up her ideas and ambitions easily. It had occurred to him by now that since Matthew was a vampire, he might have exerted his new mental powers to get the director and crew, who were all men, to do what he wanted. But he wouldn't have been able to influence Solange in this way. Unless he'd initiated her. But David hadn't noticed any marks on her throat.

David asked no more questions, deciding it was best to wait until Matthew arrived to find out just how this miraculous turnaround on the movie set had come about. He and Veronica went to the studio commissary to get something for dinner, then they returned to the soundstage. Matthew, David was told upon arriving, had just come in and was in his dressing room changing into costume. It was shortly after dusk.

David knocked on his dressing room door. "Matthew? It's David and Veronica."

The door quickly opened. Matthew, in costume, but not yet in makeup, greeted them with a warm smile. David noted immediately the subtle sharpness of his eyeteeth and felt a renewed sorrow for the actor. This he tried to hide.

"Nolan said you were here. I'm so glad to see you two again!" Matthew exclaimed, opening the door wide for them. "Come in! I want to talk to you." He shook hands with them both.

After Matthew asked about David's health, David told him the whole story, that he hadn't been reverting after all. "I got a medication from a doctor for my migraines, and I feel fine now. I tried to call you and tell you, but Claridge's said you'd checked out."

"I did," Matthew said, buttoning the waistcoat of his costume. "I'm living with Darienne now at her house in Belgravia." At David's stunned look, Matthew added, "I know what you must be thinking. I'd never have believed I could reconcile with her, either. But she showed me all the powers I have now as a vampire—powers that she'd given me, really. You won't believe my voice, David." Matthew grew animated and excited as he spoke. "I can sing now as if I were a . . . a god! My new strength and agility are a constant amazement to me. I can't wait to do a stage show again—I'll wow the audience to kingdom come! And I never get tired. Although after a night of passion with Darienne, I'm a little dazed, I admit."

David couldn't help but look stunned again.

Matthew noted his reaction and smiled. "I know. I said I wouldn't give her the satisfaction. But after she made me discover my singing voice, I was so happy, I gave in to my own desires. Our relationship is incredible now."

David saw the hint of iridescence in Matthew's eyes, indicating the actor's inner passion at merely thinking of his times with Darienne. David felt a mixture of emotions within himself: sadness, for he hadn't wanted to see Matthew become a vampire; and pleasure, for he could tell that Matthew was genuinely happy.

David glanced at Veronica, to note her reaction to all this. A twinge of cold anxiety twisted in his chest when he saw her gazing at Matthew with a faraway look of longing. When she realized David had noticed her, she quickly looked down to hide her eyes.

Matthew had been adjusting the lace at the wrists of his costume, pulling it out of the sleeves of his lavender satin coat. "I'll be glad to be done with all this finery," he muttered. He looked up at David. "Anyway, as happened to you, everything changed around for me, too, after our phone call. I've actually come to enjoy being a vampire." He hesitated, showing sensitivity to David. "I know you didn't like being one, and I can understand that. At first, I almost destroyed myself, I was so horrified at my bloodlust. I still hate that aspect. But as you told me on the phone, I learned fairly quickly to control my craving for blood. Darienne keeps me supplied, of course, so it's not really a problem. I feed at her house when I need to, and then I put it out of my mind and concentrate on my craft, using all the new powers I have at my disposal."

David nodded, trying to understand how Matthew could be so satisfied with his situation, but he couldn't quite. "By the way, I brought you the cure." David took a packet wrapped in a large envelope out of his jacket pocket. "Perhaps you no longer want it."

Matthew stared at the packet. "No, I don't," the actor said quietly. Yet he took the packet from David and turned it about in his hands. "But maybe I should hold on to it, in case someday I change my mind." He looked up, his eyes genuinely appreciative. "Thank you."

"I feel better knowing you have the cure as an option," David said. "The directions are inside. If you ever decide to use the ingredients, make sure someone is with you when you do. Veronica and her cousin had to revive me just after I'd transformed to mortal, or I might not have survived."

Matthew seemed to listen intently. "All right. Thank you again," he said with some gravity and turned to place the packet in the duffel bag David used to see him carry to the studio every day when he was still mortal.

David glanced at Veronica. She returned his look, her large brown eyes a trifle guilty, even apologetic. He placed his hand on her shoulder, wanting her to know he understood that she'd been swept up by Matthew's talk of his new relationship with

Darienne. Being in the presence of a male vampire again, especially hearing him refer to his superhuman passion, must have made her long once more for that brand of passion from David. He could forgive her. But his spirit sank a bit.

"By the way," Matthew said, turning back to David, "the film's nearly finished."

"So I hear," David replied. He told Matthew what he'd learned from Nolan and that he'd read the final script. "Nolan indicated you took a leading hand in all this, which struck me as odd, since he's the director. Have you discovered your ability to plant ideas in men's minds?"

Matthew's grin was smug. "Maybe I ought to feel guilty, but I don't. I know that bending people's minds is something I should do sparingly. Perhaps you wouldn't have done what I have, out of moral consideration, and I respect that. But I've always been pragmatic. I saw the chance to save your original concept from the dustbin and restore it to the film. And once I got started, it was so easy. I'd look Nolan in the eye, plant the thought that this scene should be changed a certain way, and he'd think it was his idea. It was beautiful! The film fell back on track. We fixed what was wrong. I'll show you the rushes later, if you want. I think you'll be very pleased."

"I'm sure you did whatever you felt was prudent," David said politely. Matthew was right; David would not have felt it morally correct to go to the extent the actor had to have his own way. Though, David had to admit, in his own past there had been a few occasions . . . "I've used that power for my own purposes, too. But tell me, how did you manage with Solange? You can't control a woman's mind, can you? If so, you're a better vampire than I was!"

"Darienne took care of Solange," Matthew explained. "When I first went back to work on the film, Darienne came with me a few times to watch. She doesn't anymore because she got bored with all the waiting. But at first, when Solange was still making demands for more lines, it got to be an even bigger problem than it had already been. I'd gotten Nolan and the crew all on my wavelength, but Solange always threw a wrench into things. Darienne got annoyed watching her and asked me if she could help. I told her what I wanted from Solange—a nonegotistical, cooperative attitude. So Darienne took her aside. They spoke in French, and I think Darienne started out by complimenting her on her hair and so on. Next thing I knew, Solange was the picture of humility and cooperation."

David grinned and shook his head with amazement. "You and Darienne make a good team, after all."

Veronica smiled at this. "I'm happy you two have patched things up," she said to Matthew. "She was so sad when you were apart."

Matthew seemed to grow more serious, and he studied Veronica a moment. "I know you always understood her point of view. Maybe you could make an effort to see her while you're in London."

"I'd love to," Veronica said. "David and I will go visit her."

"I'm sure she'd like to see David, too," Matthew said. He glanced at David. "She'll be happy to know that you're all right. She knew Veronica was going to have a baby, and she was quite concerned for you both."

David felt dumbfounded. Did everyone know Veronica was pregnant but him?

"But," Matthew continued, speaking to Veronica now, "maybe you could talk to her alone. She confides in you. I think she's upset about something, and I can't figure her out. I'm getting ready to go to New York to do another stage show when the film is finished, and she was anxious that I do that. At first. But now she's unhappy with me, even though I'm doing everything she'd envisioned for me when she transformed me. She says I just don't understand. It's true, I don't know what she wants. Maybe if she can hash things out with another woman, she'll feel better. I try, but . . ." He spread his hands in a helpless gesture and looked at David for sympathy.

"Darienne has her little fits and tantrums," David said. "They always pass."

Veronica caught David's attention with a compelling look, and he was surprised to see the impatience in her dark eyes. She turned to Matthew. "I'd love to see her again. Is she home tonight?"

"Yes, she said she was going to stay home and figure out arrangements for transporting us to New York so I can begin rehearsals there. I haven't learned yet how these things are done."

"I'd like to see her," Veronica said to David.

David nodded, not exactly looking forward to getting involved with Darienne's problems again.

Matthew mentioned then that he needed to get into makeup, so they said good-bye.

"Thanks for saving the film," David told him, feeling genuine gratitude even if he couldn't quite approve of Matthew's method.

"It was worth saving!" Matthew said, his broad actor's grin returning. "See you later."

They left the studio and got into a limousine that Nolan had called for them. David agreed to Veronica's request that they visit Darienne now. As they rode down London's streets in the plush back seat of the sleek vehicle, David thought over Veronica's earlier reaction to Matthew. He hesitated, then decided to address the issue squarely. If he wanted to keep his wife happy, he couldn't turn a blind eye to her desires. "You long to be loved by a vampire again, don't you?" he said softly in a nonaccusing tone. "You still miss that experience."

Veronica's eyes were wide and full of regret as she gazed up at him in the low light of the limousine. "I'm sorry, David. I couldn't help it. As he spoke and I sensed the power in him, I . . . I did remember how I felt with you when we first made love." As David looked away to hide his pain, Veronica took his hand. "But David, everything's changed now. I cherish what we have together. I enjoy being your equal now as well as I once adored being under your power. Those moments of superhuman ecstasy don't make up for the family we'll have together. If I miss anything, I miss most your old sense of sureness and wisdom. You seem so full of doubts and worries now. What can I do? What can I say to make you feel more sure of me and our future?"

David pondered this a long while, holding her hand as he did. "I don't know. I can see it's my problem, that there's nothing more you can do than you already have." A quote from *Hamlet* came to his mind. " 'Where love is great, the littlest doubts are fear; Where little fears grow great, great love grows there.' "

"You're quoting Shakespeare again!" Veronica said, her eyes shining. "That's a good sign."

"You've been very sweet and patient. I felt I was making progress after I saw Herman. I was beginning to understand. But . . . now I've lost track again . . ." He turned to her. "Can you keep on being patient with me?"

Veronica kissed him. "Pregnant women have lots of patience." She chuckled. "But we don't have eternity."

"No, indeed," David said.

Darienne was surprised to glance out the window and see a limousine pull up in front of her house. She looked at the clock. It was much too early for Matthew to be returning, and he always drove his rental car anyway. She smiled and her heart lifted when she saw David and Veronica get out of the car.

"I'm so thrilled to see you!" she exclaimed after she'd met them at the door and hugged them both. "Come into the living room and sit down."

Darienne listened on the edge of her chair as they sat on the couch and caught her up on all Herman had told them. She was quite relieved for their sake that David would remain mortal, though deep down she still missed him as a fellow vampire. She asked Veronica about her pregnancy and was pleased to learn she was doing well, too. They seemed so happy that Darienne began to feel sad for herself again, and left out.

"Can I make you some tea?" she offered, wanting them to stay awhile. "I have chamomile."

David looked at her with amused puzzlement. "You rarely live here, yet you have tea to serve? How old is it? Did you buy it when you bought this furniture?"

Darienne indulged him with patient good humor. "Sometimes when I rise at dusk I use chamomile tea on my eyes to take away the puffiness from resting all day. I bought it about a month ago."

"It's an old beauty secret," Veronica assured David.

"Well, then, I'll have some, thank you," he said. "As long as I can drink it and don't have to put it on *my* eyes."

Veronica was laughing. "Can I help with the tea?" she offered.

"I'd enjoy that." Darienne looked forward to talking to Veronica alone. She hadn't been around women much lately, except for Solange, whom she'd thought a grasping, self-involved narcissist. She'd understood the actress perfectly, but hated her on sight. On the other hand, she'd always adored Veronica.

David picked up a newspaper Darienne had left on the couch. "I'll read," he said with arch resignation, "so you two can enjoy the pleasure of trading secrets about Matthew and me."

"Only little ones," Veronica said, giving him a kiss on the cheek before rising from the couch.

"Those are the only ones left," David replied with asperity.

Darienne shared a grin with Veronica. They walked to the back of the house, where the kitchen was located. Like the rest of the house, it hadn't been changed since Darienne bought the place in the days of Queen Victoria. There was no refrigerator or dishwasher, and the stove had to be lit with a match.

"I wouldn't even know how to light a modern stove," Darienne told her as she put a kettle of water on to boil. She invited Veronica to sit down at the kitchen table, covered with a dusty linen cloth for which Darienne apologized. "When I'm here, I try to keep the living room dusted, but I rarely use the kitchen."

"That's all right," Veronica said as Darienne got out a bone china teapot and some cups from a cabinet. They, too, were dusty, so she set about rinsing them in the antique sink. "How are things going between you and Matthew, now that he's a vampire?" Veronica asked. She explained how she and David had stopped by the studio and spoken with him.

"In his mind," Darienne said, drying the rinsed teapot with a clean towel, "everything is wonderful. He's thrilled with our new sex life and ecstatic about going onstage again to show off his new abilities. I was as thrilled as he, at first. I was so happy to show him all his new powers. Now I'm beginning to wonder if making him a vampire was the best thing after all."

"Why?" Veronica asked. "You needed him to be a vampire so you would both be on an equal level. *I'm* glad to be the same as David now, even if we *are* mortal."

"Are you really?" Darienne said, setting the teapot on the counter and coming to the table to sit down with her until the water boiled.

"Yes, because now, sometimes I lean on him, and sometimes he leans on me," Veronica explained. "He really needs me for my talents and strengths, not because I'm trusting and dependent on him. I'm discovering that a relationship between two people who are equal and support one another is more worthwhile, whether it's eternal or not."

"I think you're right," Darienne said, surprised at the maturity Veronica had acquired. Darienne tended to remember her as the young innocent David had taken under his wing to nurture and with whom he'd fallen in love. But clearly Veronica had become her own person, in her quiet and unassuming way.

"You agree?" Veronica asked with interest. "You always loved your freewheeling, unattached lifestyle."

Darienne lowered her eyes as she pondered a moment. "I thought I did, too—though to be honest it wasn't always that fantastic. Until I met Matthew. But then, I wasn't free anymore, because I devoted myself to him. In return, he left me." She placed her chin on her hand, elbow on the table. "Now I have him back, and here I am devoting myself to him again. Even tonight, before you came, I was making arrangements for us to be shipped to New York a few weeks from now, when he finishes the film. I give him everything—sex beyond his wildest dreams, companionship; I act as his secretary when he needs one, his travel agent, his confidante. And what do I get in return?"

"Has he been seeing his ex-wife again?" Veronica asked with concern.

"Oh, no. That's not the problem. I don't worry about competition, at least not from another woman anymore. Natalie was the only real threat, because he once loved her. He went back to her, because he thought he could rekindle that love. Deep down, I believe he really wants a close relationship with a woman. But he ruined it for himself, as he had years before, because he became sidetracked with his career. And that's exactly what's happening now. The stage is his true mistress. The rest of us are all expendable."

"You honestly believe that?" Veronica asked. "He seemed sincerely concerned about you tonight. In fact, he asked me if I would talk to you. He sensed you were unhappy. He thought maybe if you talked to me, you'd feel better."

As Darienne listened, chin still resting on her hand, her shoulders began to shake with laughter. "Well, that's a typical man for you! They don't want to take the time to figure out what's wrong themselves, so they send in a woman to do their work for them."

Veronica laughed, too. "I suppose you're right. But he did seem worried. What would you like from him?"

"I'd like him to work on our relationship as hard as I've worked on it," Darienne replied, taking her hand from her chin and sitting up straighter. "I moved heaven and earth to win him. I gave him the gift of eternity and made him my equal. I've made him happy as can be. And he's about to leave me again!"

"But aren't you going to New York with him?"

"Of course, I'll be there with him. But he'll be away from me in thought. I know I'll be pushed back to second place on his priority list. I can see already how preoccupied he's getting with this new Broadway show. It's all he talks about and thinks about. I'm beginning to feel peripheral. I've finally learned that a real relationship is more worthwhile than a fantastic sex partnership. But he has no concept of that. Our sex life is all he wants or expects us to have."

She shifted her position to lean toward Veronica as she spoke. "When he worked to correct the movie script, he understood perfectly what the delicate relationship should be between the hero and heroine of the movie. Fantasy he understands. Because fantasy isn't real and it doesn't frighten him. But a meaningful relationship with me, well, that apparently scares him witless. He won't even deal with the idea. He ignores the potential of what we might have together to the extent that he probably honestly *doesn't* know what I'm talking about or what I want. And I don't know how to get through to him. I used to think men were simple to deal with, but Matthew leaves me stumped."

"You want him to love you and put you first," Veronica summed up, obviously understanding perfectly. Her quick empathy made Darienne feel even more justified in her point of view. Veronica smiled then, her lovely face growing tender. "David does that for me. He really tries hard to understand me. I guess I'm lucky."

"You have no idea how fortunate you are," Darienne said, her voice wistful. "I envy you. I may never have a relationship such as you have with David. I might even give up immortality for it, as David did, if I thought it would do me any good. But even if I had taken that cure and become mortal, instead of making Matthew a vampire, it wouldn't have made any difference. Mortal or immortal, he's still *the same*. I should have realized that. I'm not so different from any other woman, Veronica. I want to be loved, too, just for myself. The way you're loved by David."

"I'm sure Matthew cares for you," Veronica said, reaching across the table to touch Darienne's arm. "Probably more than he knows. At least now he'll have all the time in the world to figure out how he feels."

"If he ever bothers to put his mind to it," Darienne said with dry humor. The teakettle began to whistle. "The water's boiling." She got up to go to the stove. "I may be reaching my boiling point, too," she muttered.

Veronica got up from the table and watched as Darienne put tea leaves in the pot and added the steaming water. "I like that outfit," Veronica said, eyeing the low-cut azure-blue sundress Darienne was wearing. Apparently she'd decided to switch to a more cheerful topic.

"I've had this dress for years," Darienne said. She paused after she put the kettle back on the stove. "You know, I haven't been shopping once since I arrived in London. I've either been depressed or scheming to get Matthew back. And these last few weeks I've been with Matthew again, I've been too busy. No wonder I'm in such a mood! Maybe I just need to go out and buy myself a new wardrobe."

"You always wear such wonderful clothes. I never did get to see your closet. I always wanted to."

"Then you shall!" Darienne said with delight as she put the tea things on a tray. "David can read his paper some more. The tea needs to steep anyway."

She took Veronica upstairs to a large room that decades ago she'd made over into a walk-in closet. There, Veronica marveled at the vast array, rack upon rack, of her designer gowns and expensive Paris dresses and suits, her long shelves of shoes to match each outfit, and her racks of casual clothes, most of which were American.

"Gosh, this is like going into a department store! You have a wonderful eye for clothes. These things are so beautiful and unique," Veronica said, shifting through some of the gowns hanging in front of her. "But you move around a lot. Do you have your clothes shipped to each place you go?"

"It depends. I have heavy winter coats, for example, that I leave in my apartments in Chicago and New York. But these things," Darienne gestured to indicate the clothes hanging all about them, "I usually have shipped from place to place. I never know what I might want to wear when I move, or how long I'll be in the city I go to, so it's just simpler to pack it all and have it travel along with me."

"Incredible," Veronica said with admiration. "And David thinks *I* buy a lot of clothes! Has he ever seen your closet?"

"*Mon Dieu,* why would I show it to him? He'd just have some dour remark to make about my frivolous existence. Even Matthew peeked in here the other night and came away speechless. They just don't understand," she said, smiling as Veronica chuckled. "They're only men, after all. I suppose we must have patience."

"I suppose," Veronica agreed, her wide, delighted grin showing her thorough enjoyment of their conversation. "But we'd better go back and have tea with David. *He's* been patient waiting for us."

"You're too good to him," Darienne said as they went back down the carpeted wood staircase. Thinking again, she added, "But it must be working for you. You and David seem so happy. I'm too good to Matthew lately, and it doesn't get me *anywhere*."

As Veronica went back to the living room to sit with David, Darienne got the tea tray from the kitchen and brought it in to them. She poured them each a cup but, of course, poured none for herself. She sat down again on a chair opposite the long couch on which they were seated, the couch where Matthew had lain while she transformed him.

"What did I overhear you say about being 'too good' to Matthew?" David asked in the dour tone Darienne had mentioned to Veronica. "Was that before or after you forced him to become a vampire?"

"Are you still clucking your tongue over that?" Darienne said with impatience. "You spoke to him tonight. What was your impression? Did he seem happy with his new existence?"

"He seemed thrilled with it," David admitted. "It took me aback, I must say. I'd never have guessed."

"Because you think everyone's as serious and righteous as you," Darienne said. "Once he realized the advantages he has now, he was eager to make use of them—without the attending guilt you always suffered."

"I'd have thought that he'd be conscious of being so different from everyone else," David said, shaking his head in puzzlement, "of being separated from humanity. That always made me feel so alone when I was a vampire."

Darienne traced the flower pattern on the upholstered arm of her chair with her fingertip. "I think Matthew was already accustomed to feeling alone and different, because of his rare talent. Becoming a vampire didn't make much difference for him in that regard. Now he knows his audiences will love him more than ever. It's *their* embrace he longs for. He probably thinks as a vampire he'll be closer to humanity now, not more separated from it. That's made him rededicate himself to pleasing his audience. All so they'll give him the adulation he craves." She sighed unhappily. "It's sad, if you think about it."

"True," David agreed. "I've always thought he lived more in his art than in his life."

"Precisely," Darienne said. "So where does that leave me?"

David blinked and quietly set his cup on the side table. Elbows on his knees, he leaned forward and looked at Darienne. She wondered what he was about to say; he appeared so thoughtful and deliberate.

"Darienne, do you think you're putting too much expectation for happiness on Matthew?" he asked.

"Apparently so," she replied with irony.

"His career always was of overriding importance to him."

"I know. The fool!"

"Have you ever thought of finding some career of your own?" David asked.

Darienne had to stop to think what he meant. Even Veronica turned to look at her husband.

"A career?" Darienne repeated with disdain. "I have money from the jewels and property I inherited from my family. I've always been wealthy, and my investments keep me that way. I don't need to work."

"We both came from aristocratic families," David said. "I didn't *need* to work either, if you put it that way. But I devoted myself to playwriting. That purpose of improving my skills from decade to decade and century to century is what kept me going."

"Because you never knew how to have fun," Darienne said with a shrug.

"But are you still having fun?" he asked point-blank. "When I saw you here a few weeks ago, you said you had moments when you contemplated ending your existence. All because you wanted Matthew. Now you have him, and you still don't seem happy."

"Because I don't have the relationship I want from him." Darienne was growing weary of explaining herself. "He's too preoccupied to put me first."

"Put yourself first."

"I always have!" Darienne retorted.

"Not now."

"But . . ."

"Find some new purpose for yourself, some raison d'être besides Matthew. Before you met him, your purpose was to live a dazzling, jet-set existence. And partying, meeting new men, traveling, and so on satisfied you. You used to have a joie de vivre that you radiated in such a way it was catching. That used to be your gift, your effervescence and lighthearted manner. You made others feel good. You brought me out of my doldrums many a time over the centuries, and I'll always be grateful. But I think you've grown beyond that way of life. Love for Matthew has deepened and expanded your expectations. Dazzling lights and new adventures aren't enough to keep you happy anymore. Am I right?"

Darienne found herself staring at David, who had known her

for so long, with widening eyes. A frightening emptiness came over her, and she had the odd feeling of having no future, as if they'd forgotten to print her month in the horoscope column of the newspaper. "You're right," she said in a fearful whisper.

"Don't look so hopeless," David chided, the way she used to chide him. "I've wondered for centuries when you'd reach this point. You're at a new threshold, that's all. You're the child who has finally finished with playtime and needs to figure out what she wants to do when she grows up."

"But I don't want some stupid career," she argued. "I want Matthew."

"You have Matthew."

"I want his *love*. He can't give me that."

"Maybe he has some growing to do yet, too. In the meantime, if you had some purpose other than your obsession with Matthew, your need for his love and attention wouldn't be so all-consuming."

"Is this some male conspiracy to get women to stop nagging?"

"Look," David said, gesturing with one hand, "if you had a second focus in your life, it would give Matthew the breathing room he seems to need. He might appreciate you more if you had other things to accomplish than worrying about what he's thinking and doing. You've always been independent, but it might help if you added a new dimension to that independence. Become a woman with a full agenda of her own, a career, goals to meet, plans to make. Matthew might begin to worry when *you'll* have time for *him*."

This last statement made lights go on in Darienne's head. Maybe David had something here after all. Hadn't she once told Matthew she'd never pine away for him again?

"All right," she said to David. "Let's say I want to begin a career. What do I do first?"

"You have to decide what sort of career you want."

"Oh." Darienne didn't have a clue what career would suit her. "Any suggestions?"

David shook his head, apparently also at a loss. "Let's see. What have been your interests over the centuries? Men. Jewels. Theater and opera. Travel . . ."

"Clothes," Veronica added. "You could start your own line

of women's clothes, like evening clothes maybe. Have your own designer label."

Darienne sat as if transfixed while a vivid picture instantly formed in her mind of a boutique full of exquisite, sensational gowns. The image shimmered in her brain, like a colorful foreign country she wanted to visit. Her imaginary eye, like a movie camera, did a swift close-up of the label on the nearest dress. The label read, *Scandaleux,* French for scandalous.

Darienne smiled slowly and with dawning pleasure. "I think you may have given me an idea."

14

What do women want anyway?

MATTHEW DROVE back to Darienne's house in Belgravia around four A.M., after another full night at the studio. The movie was shaping up beautifully, now that he had everyone jumping to his tune. Matthew was discovering he had more talents than he'd realized before this. He'd never tried his hand at directing, but he was finding that it came naturally to him. Of course Nolan still had the title of director and believed himself to be the director. Only Matthew knew the truth. But someday, like Orson Welles or Gene Kelly, Matthew might do a film of his own, for which he was the star, the director, and perhaps even the producer. The opportunities that lay ahead of him now seemed endless, like a tantalizing yellow brick road leading to mythical Oz. Someday he'd be the most accomplished entertainer on the planet. Maybe they'd nickname him the Wizard.

Of course, the Wizard of Oz had turned out to be an ordinary man. He ought to remind himself of that now and then, just to remember to be humble. But then again, vampires *were* superior, and why should he feign a false humility and deny his superhuman talents? Still, he had to be careful. His public wouldn't love him if they thought he'd become egotistical. Matthew hadn't yet found a comfortable way of regarding himself in this new existence. He was still defining himself as a vampire. But that was all part of the fun.

By the time he'd pulled up in front of Darienne's house, his mind had drifted back to his current favorite topic, his upcoming role as Heathcliff on Broadway. He hoped Darienne had made all the necessary arrangements for them to travel to New York. Without her, he wouldn't know how to get himself safely across the Atlantic, casket and all. He'd asked her to find an apartment or hotel for them to live in close to Forty-Fourth Street, where the theater was located, so he could walk to work. Apparently she had an apartment she kept on Central Park West but, curiously, she hadn't invited him to live there.

He turned off the car motor, got out, and used the key Darienne had given him to unlock the door to the house. Inside, he found her upstairs packing her vast array of clothes into several huge trunks that she'd pulled from somewhere into the narrow upstairs hallway.

"Packing already?" he asked, looking down at her as she knelt in front of a trunk. "The movie's nearly done, but it'll still be about two more weeks before we leave. Of course, you do have a lot to pack . . ." His voice trailed off as he took in the look of impatience she was giving him. God, was she still in this mood of hers? When would she snap out of it and be her old self?

"Does it occur to you that I might have plans of my own?" she said, standing up from bending over the trunk.

Her cleavage looked delicious in her low-cut blue dress. He'd come in very late tonight, and they didn't have as much time as usual for their passionate rounds of sex before dawn. "Plans?" he said absently, thinking they shouldn't waste time talking.

She drew in a deep breath and exhaled it slowly. It made her cleavage plump and deepen, and at first he thought she was breathing in like that on purpose, to tantalize him. But when he gazed up at her eyes as his masculine member began to stir, he saw that her deep sigh was from exasperation. With him, apparently.

"Did I say something wrong?" he asked.

She lowered her eyes, and her shoulders slumped a bit, as if some of the starch had gone out of her. "Come downstairs with me," she said in a quiet voice. "I need to go over the list I made up for you."

"List?"

"A list of the things that need to be taken care of to get you safely to New York and set up in the apartment I found for you."

"You found one?" He followed her down the stairs.

"Yes, within walking distance from the theater. It's small, but private. I think it will suit you."

"Great!" he said as they reached the living room.

She picked up a piece of paper she'd left on a side table and sat with him on the couch. "Here," she said, handing it to him. "I've written down everything, step by step. I think I've gotten every detail, every address and phone number you'll need to check on arrangements. But you'd better read it through to make sure you can decipher my handwriting and you understand it all."

Matthew read the list through as she had asked, but the way she was behaving began to trouble him. "What do you mean, *I'll* need to make arrangements? You said you'd do it for me."

"It *is* all arranged. But it's always safest to double-check with the shipping company to make sure they've got the dates straight, and to make sure the transport company in New York knows when to pick up your casket and your belongings."

"And yours, too."

"No, Matthew. I'm not going with you."

"Not going?" he said, slowly putting down the instructions. "Of course, you're going!"

"I've changed my mind."

He began to feel cold, as if someone were throwing ice water on him. "Why?"

"Why did Natalie not come here to London with you?"

"Natalie?" What did Natalie have to do with anything? "I'm through with Natalie, you know that. You don't have to worry about her coming between us again."

Darienne shut her eyes, as if growing even more impatient. "Think and answer my question. Why did Natalie leave you just before you came to London?"

"Because she thought I was too preoccupied with the movie and not giving her attention."

"Yes. That's exactly why I'm leaving you now."

"Leaving me . . ." He studied her face, looking for some hint that this was all a joke.

"*Oui*. I'm leaving," she said, her tone and eyes steady and serious. "Natalie wouldn't settle for second place in your life, and neither will I."

"What brought all this on?"

"Your obsession with your new Broadway show. It's all you think about."

"That's my job! You have to allow a man to have his career!" Matthew couldn't believe this. He'd gotten used to this argument from Natalie, but had never expected it from Darienne. He'd thought Darienne understood him. "Why did you make me a vampire? You told me over and over that I'd be able to perform with superhuman skill, that I'd thrill my audience as never before. Well, that's exactly what I'm about to do! I'd have thought you'd be happy for me, not ready to leave me! What the hell do you want?"

"If I could believe that I was more important to you than your audience, I would be happy for you. I thought that once you had a vampire's strength, you'd have more energy left for our relationship. I thought you'd have a more balanced existence." Her voice grew cool. "But I see that's not the case. Where am I supposed to fit into your life?"

Matthew shook his head in growing anger. "You're incredible! After I've taken you back and forgiven you, after listening to you beg and threaten immortal suicide if you couldn't have me, now you're going to leave?! What do you mean, where are you supposed to fit in? We're together. We're lovers again. You've gotten carried away with some idea about a 'meaningful relationship,' but it seems to me we already have one. What we have together means a lot to me."

"Does it?" she asked. "What does it mean to you, exactly?"

He looked at her blankly, no words coming into his mind. "Well, I . . . It means a lot. I like coming home and finding you here. We have fantastic sex. We satisfy each other's needs. Why would you want to leave?"

"Am I supposed to be pleased that you want me to be your sex toy? That was good enough for me before, because I was in awe of you and happy just to be with you. But then you left me. It made me realize how little I meant to you. I won't go back to being your patient mistress while you go out and woo your audience every night. I deserve more than that!" She pulled down on the waistband of her dress as she sat up straighter. "Besides, I have a career to pursue now, too. Maybe it will be as all-satisfying to me as yours is to you."

"A career?" Matthew repeated in astonishment. "You never mentioned a career!"

"David and Veronica came by to visit earlier. David suggested the idea. I've been thinking about it ever since they left, and I've come to the conclusion it's something I should try."

"David gave you the idea," Matthew muttered, wondering why his friend had come up with such a notion. Maybe he'd said it to be humorous, and Darienne had taken the idea seriously. At any rate, he couldn't imagine her new ambition would last long. He couldn't imagine Darienne as a career woman. "What sort of career?"

She gestured toward the staircase and the trunks upstairs she'd been packing. "Clothes. I'm going to start my own line of evening creations. I even know what I'll call it. I have money and connections. I have a sense of style and centuries of experience with clothing. I'm anxious to get started."

He looked at her, incredulous. "Just like that? Where will you go?"

"I'm not going to tell you that."

"Not tell me?" he said, hurt that she was shutting him out like this. "Are you imagining I'd chase after you, the way you chased after me?" He took on a threatening tone to hide his anxiety. "Look, if you go, it's over between us! You forced me into becoming a vampire, and now you're setting me adrift. If you leave me now, I'm through with you forever."

Her smile startled him. "Make no mistake, *chéri*. I was through with you first. As for leaving you adrift, poor helpless thing, well—I think you've been adrift all your life." She tilted her head to one side. "I have been, too, I suppose. Maybe that's why we were attracted to each other. But I'm setting out to find my rudder, my career. As for you, you have your career. You need to discover that people are important, too. I've already learned that part of the equation. I know love and you know work. I need to discover the value of work, and you need to learn the value of love. We did have sort of an incomplete balance between us, didn't we? Too bad it's not enough for me anymore. I did treasure our nights together, *chéri*. I'll remember all those hours of ecstasy we shared and be sad it couldn't continue. But it just wasn't enough. I'm leaving tomorrow."

"But . . ." Matthew was at a loss. "What do you expect me to do? I'm still new at being a vampire."

"Ah, but you learned quickly. I've taught you everything now. You'll find some other woman. Your new leading lady will doubtless fall in love with you. Maybe she'll be willing to be part of the scenery in your life. You can make *her* a vampire. Remember how I transformed you? Use the same method. She probably won't stay with you either, though, once she's realized what an incomplete man you are. Better initiate her instead. Then you'd have what you want, a love slave who'll wait on you and do your bidding and worship you as I once did. Though you must remember, she wouldn't be a vampiress, only an initiated mortal, so she couldn't give you the advanced sort of sex you require now. But one can't have everything, can one?" she said airily.

Matthew was furious. If she thought telling him all this nonsense was going to make him beg her to stay with him, she was in for a huge surprise. She'd wormed her way back into his life and manipulated him once too often. He wasn't going to allow her to manipulate him ever again! Besides, she'd gone to such lengths to get him back, Matthew assured himself, she wouldn't leave him now as she so blithely pretended she would. How often had she declared how much she loved him? And now she was abruptly going off on her own forever? No way!

He knew what she was up to: This was all an act—a way to get *attention*. She ought to get an Oscar or a Tony for her portrayal of a woman who's mind was settled. But Matthew knew better than to play into her hands again. He could be equally uncaring. He made a better actor than she any day.

"All right," he said in an easy, composed manner. "If that's what you want, then go off and have yourself a career. You might try to make my opening night in New York, though. The show will be stupendous. Come backstage and say hello."

He made a point of looking at his watch. "Dawn will be here in another twenty minutes or so. Guess I'll retire early. Unless you wanted one last session of intense passion, just to remember each other by?"

She looked at him so calmly, it nearly unsettled his false composure. He felt a tense, sinking sensation in his chest.

"I don't think that would be wise, *chéri,*" she said with a wistful smile. "Passion has no place for us anymore, unless it's for our work. You know that old song from *Casablanca,* about a kiss being just a kiss and how the fundamental things apply, as time passes by? Well, sex is just sex, and there's not much else fundamental between us." She gave him a small, courteous nod of her blond head. "Good-bye, Matthew. You're a remarkable man. I wish you all the success you long for. I hope it fulfills you."

She got up, walked upstairs, and disappeared from view, apparently to continue her packing. Matthew swallowed, dumbfounded. She was taking this game to the very edge! Well, he wouldn't be fooled. She *said* she was leaving tomorrow. But before he went off to the studio tomorrow night, she would recant everything. Or maybe she'd still pretend she was going to leave and swear she wouldn't be there when he returned. How foolish she'd look when he found her still there when he came home. He'd call her bluff, and then they'd see just who couldn't live without whom here.

To prove he didn't care, he got into his coffin early. He hated the claustrophobic darkness that encased him, but he lay still and waited. She always rested with him in his casket.

Just as dawn arrived, he heard her footsteps in the room. He waited for her to open the lid, but she never did. Instead he heard the slight creak of another lid and then heard it shut. Matthew stiffened at the sound, and suddenly the darkness that surrounded him seemed black, empty, and cold. He lay absolutely still and would not let his feelings get to him. She'd change her mind before tomorrow night was over. No question about it.

Many hours later, when he awoke at dusk, he opened his eyes in the darkness and realized he was alone. And then he remembered. He took a few minutes before rising, despite his eagerness to get out of the stuffy blackness, to compose himself. He needed to show Darienne he didn't care, if she was still going to pretend she was leaving.

When he'd gotten himself together mentally, he lifted the lid and got out of the oak coffin. The light was already on in the room. Her coffin lay a few feet away, parallel to his, but he guessed it must be empty. He walked over and lifted the lid a few inches. All he saw was velvet. Well, she'd gotten herself up and about quickly, hadn't she?

He walked out and looked into the living room, then the kitchen, and the other rooms on the first floor. Darienne wasn't to be seen. Perhaps she'd gone upstairs to continue pretending to pack, he told himself. When he had climbed the stairs, he saw that all her half-packed cases were still in the hallway. He walked into her large closet, still partly full of clothes, but didn't find her there, either. He checked all the other upstairs rooms then, but she was nowhere to be found.

She must be avoiding me, Matthew told himself with a smile. Just another indication that her resolve to leave, if she in fact really had one at all, was weak. He'd find her there, begging him for forgiveness, when he returned in the early morning hours. That would be like her. He recalled how often in the past she'd begged his forgiveness and feared his anger. Well, she was about to learn once more that she couldn't get away with these tactics. I will not be manipulated, Matthew repeated to himself as he bathed as usual, got dressed, and left for the studio.

But when he went out the front door, he found himself locking it behind him because the house looked so empty. Where was she? Why would she hide from him instead of taunting him with more threats of leaving? As he walked to the car to drive to the studio, an unsettled feeling of being abandoned crept into him, and it did not leave the whole time he was at work.

He left the soundstage as early as he could and drove home about two A.M. A sense of foreboding almost unglued him when he turned round a corner and caught sight of her house. The place was absolutely dark; not one hint of light shone through the draperies. He got out of the car and ran up to the door. When he walked in, he felt for the light switch. Once the lights were on, he looked in the living room, but it was empty.

Then he spied a note lying on the couch. He rushed over to pick it up. Darienne's large, graceful handwriting sprawled over the sheet of paper.

> Matthew,
> Please remind the transport company to lock up the house carefully when you leave for New York. Until then, you're free to go on using the place. I'll have the locks changed after you've left. Good luck.
> Darienne.

Matthew crumpled the note in his hand as he raced up the steps. The large trunks in the hallway were all gone. The walk-in closet was absolutely empty. He raced down the steps again, stumbling as he went. Rushing into the room where their coffins were kept, he found them both still there, side by side. He opened hers and found the velvet interior sprinkled with dried petals of flowers and herbs. She'd mentioned once that she had homes all over the world, and she used dried plants to keep the interiors of her coffins fresh and to discourage insects and mildew while they were not in use.

The spiced floral fragrance wafted up to him, and he realized this was all he had left of her. A huge emptiness seemed to displace his lungs and abdomen, and yet he felt heavy. He hadn't thought she'd meant what she said.

He grew upset with himself. Why hadn't he believed her and tried harder to talk her out of leaving him? How had he failed to make her happy? She'd always said she wanted his love. What did that mean? It was just a word. He'd given her all he could. Wasn't that love?

Matthew realized he didn't know. But he knew very well that he'd been through this before—twice, with his ex-wife—and other, less traumatic times, with several women he'd gotten involved with over his lifetime.

He'd heard it said that Sigmund Freud, on his deathbed, asked, "What do women want anyway?" He didn't know if the story was true, but he could believe that Freud, after spending his life studying people, still hadn't figured women out. If Freud couldn't, how could he ever understand what women wanted from him?

Now he was alone again. He clenched his jaw tightly to quell his rising emotions. He'd gotten over Natalie and all the others, hadn't he? He'd get over Darienne, too! After all, he had his new Broadway show to hold his attention. And soon he'd have his nightly audiences back. He'd thrived on their adoration before, and he would again. He had a vampire's stamina now, the energy to give them all they wanted, and they'd again give back to him all their genuine affection. His audiences and fans would make him happy.

So Darienne wouldn't be around this time. So what? He'd lived without her before he met her. He'd surely be able to exist without her again. But like Henry Higgins, whom he'd once played in a summer production of *My Fair Lady,* he'd grown accustomed to Darienne's face. And more.

Matthew sat down on his coffin and recalled then that Eliza came back to Henry at the end of *My Fair Lady*. Darienne might do the same. She'd miss their nights of erotic bliss just as much as he, sensual creature that she was. Surely she'd regret this hasty decision, give up this nonsense about a career, and come back. It might even take less than a week for her to come to her senses. Well, maybe two. Or maybe she'd come to him in New York. Surely she wouldn't miss his opening. Even when she'd made him sing for her a few weeks ago, she'd looked as though she wanted to listen to him forever. No, even if she got sidetracked with this career thing, she'd come to see him perform onstage again. And then she'd come back to him.

All was not lost. In the meantime, he'd just concentrate on finishing the movie and beginning his new show. That made a good plan, didn't it?

Matthew nodded, assuring himself that it did. But he looked at her empty casket again and was reminded that he'd have to get into his own, alone, in a few hours. And that stark reality brought sudden tears to his eyes.

When dawn eventually came, Matthew didn't get into his coffin. He lay down in Darienne's instead.

Almost two weeks went by, and Darienne never returned, never called or left any further message. It was as if she'd disappeared. Matthew asked David and Veronica if they knew where she'd gone, since she'd talked to them about starting a career. Neither had any idea.

"Paris has always been a center of fashion, and she's French, so she may have gone home to her ancestral château," David conjectured on the last day of filming. Veronica was at Claridge's, packing their bags, and David had come to the studio to see the last scene shot. They were sitting in Matthew's dressing room during a break in the shooting. "She has an apartment in Paris, too," David added.

"Do you have a phone number?" Matthew asked. "Can I call her?"

"I might, at home in Chicago. But the number would be quite old and might not be correct anymore. She always visited *me,* you see. I rarely visited her during our centuries as friends."

Matthew brought up something he'd been meaning to ask David. "Why did you suggest to her that she should start a career in clothing?"

"I just suggested a career," David said. "Veronica came up with the clothing idea."

"But why did you suggest any sort of career?" Matthew persisted.

"Because she focused so much on you, she was losing touch with who she was. She seemed to think you took her for granted. I told her to find a new purpose for existing and you might value her more."

"Do you think I didn't value her?" Matthew asked, setting his script aside on the couch where he sat.

David lifted his shoulders in a shrug. "I really don't know, Matthew. If it had been up to me, I'd have kept out of your affair with her entirely."

"Then why did you give her advice?" Matthew said, letting his irritation show.

"Because she's an old friend, and I thought I could see where she'd lost sight of herself. I think she was on the verge of leaving you whether I came up with the idea of a career or not. I just gave her something to leave *for.*"

Matthew looked at the floor a moment, then lifted his eyes to David's. "You seem to understand women—better than me, anyway. What happened? Did I go wrong somewhere?

Or don't women know what they want?"

"Sometimes they don't," David said. "But this time Darienne was quite clear. She said she felt you would never love her."

Not this again, Matthew thought. "Yeah, I know. But . . ."

"But what? It's not an unreasonable expectation on her part. You had a passionate relationship, and she'd hoped to spend her future with you. And she loved you."

"Well, what do women mean by love, then?"

David studied him, centuries of wisdom in the quiet steadiness of his eyes. "She wanted you to put her first in your heart, in your thoughts, in the very marrow of your existence."

Matthew was struck by David's poetic description. No wonder he was such a marvelous playwright. "That's beautiful, David. But be honest, man to man. Have you ever felt such an overpowering, all-encompassing emotion for a woman?"

"Of course! For Veronica."

Matthew stared at him, feeling muddled and lost, as if he'd missed some boat somewhere in his life. "I never have," he admitted. "Is there something wrong with me?"

"Lots of men aren't in touch with their feelings," David said. "It took me a few hundred years to acquire my own insights. I had to put aside all the notions of how men are supposed to behave. In the quest to look tough and in command, we often repress our feelings and barely know they exist."

He gestured toward Matthew. "You tap into yours, I imagine, when you act, because you can become someone else for a while. You're in control of an emotional scene on a stage with another actor because the script is already written. In real life, you can't control what happens. So you don't feel comfortable recognizing emotion, because you don't want to deal with it. Emotions are scary. They make us feel like we might *lose* your control. But if you let go and allow the emotion within to come out and belong to you, you begin to know who you are and what you want." David smiled. "And who you love. And then maybe you can return another person's love without fear or regret."

Matthew felt the weight of David's explanation fall heavily on his shoulders. He wished David hadn't been so thorough. Matthew didn't really want to know all that. "Do you think

I'm in love with Darienne?" he found himself asking.

David lifted his shoulders. "How can I know? Only you can answer that. Ask it of yourself."

"But I've never felt the way you say you feel about your wife."

"Dig deeper," David told him. "Maybe you do."

A wrap party was held late that night. David and Veronica attended, but left early. They were flying to Chicago the next day. Matthew felt sad to say good-bye to them, knowing it might be a long while before he saw them again. His own arrangements to travel to New York were set. He'd double-checked everything on Darienne's list.

The party bored him once David and Veronica had gone, so Matthew didn't stay either. There was one more thing to do before he left London.

He drove to his son's apartment in Knightsbridge. He hadn't seen or tried to contact Larry since his transformation. At first he didn't think he'd ever want Larry to see him as a vampire. But after the intervening weeks at the studio, where he'd worked with people who knew him as a mortal, none of whom seemed to notice any difference, Matthew had more confidence that he could see Larry without his son ever knowing what he'd become.

He hadn't called Larry first, fearing Larry might say he didn't want to see him. So he got out of the car, and seeing lights on in the upper windows of the apartment building where Larry lived, he rang the appropriate doorbell.

In a few moments Larry answered the door himself. He appeared somewhat shocked, but there was a light in his eyes when he saw his father.

"Dad. Are you okay?"

"I'm great. I just wanted to tell you I'm leaving for New York. Can I come in for a few minutes?"

"Sure," Larry said, opening the door wider. "Sheena will be glad to see you."

"Sheena? You're together again?"

"Yeah," Larry said with a grin as they climbed the steps. "It wasn't easy, but she finally forgave me for my mistake with Darienne. Where is Darienne?" he asked, pausing in his upward climb. "I've been worried ever since you went off with her. I even called Claridge's, but they said you weren't staying there anymore. And the studio wouldn't give me any information. I heard you disappeared for a few days."

"I . . . was living with Darienne. But I don't know where she is now. She's out of both our lives for good, I guess."

"Don't sound so sad. That woman was downright strange, not to mention oversexed. She took us both for a spin, didn't she?"

"She sure did."

"But are you all right?" Larry asked again, as they resumed climbing the steps. "You'd told me she was dangerous, and she got that odd look in her eye when you came in the room. You seemed to be giving in to her. Was it to save me from her clutches?"

"Yes, it was."

"I was afraid of that. I . . . I owe you one! But you're all right? She didn't tie you to any bedposts and have at you with whips and chains or whatever plan she had in mind for you? She was downright daft about you, wasn't she?"

Matthew drew into himself, feeling uncomfortable talking about Darienne and her former passion for him. "I'm all right," he told Larry quietly. "That's over now. We can all get back to normal." Whatever normal was for a lone male vampire, Matthew thought.

They reached Larry's apartment, and Sheena rushed up to Matthew at the door, her dark eyes bright, shiny hair bouncing. "Matthew, I thought I heard your voice! I'm so glad to see you!"

"I'm glad to see you!" Matthew replied as he gave her a hug. "Took this guy back, eh?"

"Well, he caught me in a forgiving mood the other day," she said in her thick Scottish brogue. "I'd just been to church. What could I do?"

Larry was grinning. "Want some coffee?"

Matthew's expression changed. "No, thanks. Just came from the movie wrap party, where they had food and drink galore."

"The movie's finished?" Larry asked, motioning Matthew to sit down.

Matthew talked with them both for about an hour, telling them how well he thought the movie had turned out and about his plans to begin rehearsing next week for his new Broadway show.

"Come opening night, if you can. I'll be happy to pay the airfare for you both."

Sheena's eyes brightened and Larry nodded. "We'll see if we can do it." He studied his father. "You're different somehow than before," he said.

A frisson of apprehension ran down Matthew's back.

"I've been trying to put my finger on it ever since you came," Larry continued. "You seem to have more vitality than you did. Have you found some new fad diet that works? Mom said you were always trying them."

"Not exactly," Matthew said. How could he tell his son his new diet was blood? "I think I'm just happy this movie is finally over and I can get back to the stage. The stage is my true love." And then he was struck by his own words. *Was* the stage the only thing he truly loved?

"Is something wrong?" Larry asked.

Matthew realized he'd grown sad for a moment. "No. No. You mentioned your mother a minute ago. Have you heard from her?"

"By phone." He glanced at Sheena. "Mom was the one who kept urging me to not give up on Sheena."

"I always did like that lady," Sheena chimed in.

Matthew grinned, pleased for them. They seemed so genuinely happy to be back together again. "And Natalie's all right?"

"She sounded like it. Apparently she's got a new man in her life." Larry left it at that, as if he felt he might be treading on Matthew's feelings by talking more about his mother's new love.

"Good," Matthew said, not really bothered that Natalie had found someone new. He knew his relationship with her was over permanently now. But he hoped at some point they could at least be distant friends again. "I hope she's found someone who can make her happy," he added quietly.

He asked Larry about his career. Larry described a secondary, but pivotal, role he'd just gotten in a new eight-part British TV series. And he was lining up another Shakespeare play after that. There were other irons his agent had in the fire, too, he explained. Sheena had recently done a series of radio commercials for a brand of Scottish shortbread biscuits and had just been contracted to do more for television.

"Suddenly we're both doing better financially," Larry said.

"Time to get married then," Matthew joked.

"We've been toying with that idea, too," Larry said. He took Sheena's hand and kissed it. "I won't lose her again, that's for certain."

Matthew thought his son seemed more mature now than before. Perhaps the temporary loss of Sheena, and maybe even of his dad, had made him ponder his future and realize what was important to him. Maybe Darienne had done him a favor interfering in his life after all. At least he'd gained some wisdom.

And he seemed to have lost his hostility toward Matthew. That pleased Matthew more than anything. He might be a vampire now, but he had a son who seemed to like him—a son who lived in London, while he was about to leave for New York. Well, maybe he'd take *Wuthering Heights* from Broadway to London as he had *The Scarlet Shadow*. Maybe someday they'd have more time together.

"I'd better go," Matthew said, glancing at his watch. It was almost one A.M., a late hour for mortals on a weeknight. "I need to finish packing."

"You'll be up late," Larry said, looking at his watch, too. "What time does your plane leave? Do you need a ride to the airport?"

"No, everything's arranged," Matthew said, not elaborating. "I'm glad I got to see you both before I leave." He hugged Sheena again, and then his son. "Take care."

"You, too, Dad. Don't overdo it, like you did when you played *Shadow*."

"No, I won't," he said as they followed him down the steps to see him off. His son's concern, now unnecessary, nevertheless touched him. "If you want to reach me," he said as he unlocked his car, "call my agent, and he can get you in touch with me. I've got an apartment lined up in New York, but I don't know the phone number yet."

"All right. Keep in touch!" Larry called out as Matthew got into his car. He waved at them both as they stood arm in arm on the sidewalk, and then he drove off.

When he arrived at Darienne's house, the place looked dark and morbid to him. He'd hoped she might miraculously come back on his last night in London. But she hadn't. As he packed up his clothes, he was glad to be leaving this place where he'd been transformed, where he'd experienced the sensual excesses his vampire body was now capable of with Darienne. The memories weighed on him too heavily, and he wanted to get on with his future in New York.

The next morning, a crew arrived to pick up the baggage and the curious long oak chest, somehow locked from the inside, that looked a bit like a brand-new coffin. They wrapped it in canvas, as instructed, and took it to Heathrow, where everything was put in cargo on a plane bound for New York.

At Kennedy Airport, another crew transported the cargo to an apartment building, where arrangements had been made with the building superintendent to allow them to dump the items in the rented, empty apartment.

When Matthew awoke, he unlocked the coffin and ripped open the canvas covering. He climbed out into a dark room with new carpeting but no furniture, not even a lamp. Walking to the apartment's front window, he looked out on the black buildings and lively night lights of New York City. He could glimpse Times Square. He smiled to himself, feeling freed of his recent past. At least he was home in America now. And Broadway and his public awaited him.

Maybe, somewhere, Darienne did, too.

15

Anyone would have done it

DAVID PICKED up the last piece of Veronica's luggage from the carousel on the lower level of Chicago's O'Hare Airport. Veronica followed as he carried their bags outside onto the sidewalk. Stepping up to the curb, he looked for the shuttle van he'd arranged to take them home. He was so happy to be home again, even the humidity and heat of a late-summer Chicago afternoon didn't bother him. Veronica, however, seemed to be feeling rather limp because of their long hours of travel, a bumpy flight, and her tendency toward nausea due to her pregnancy.

He scanned the cars, buses, and shuttle vans that were steadily streaming by the huge airport, but didn't see theirs. Veronica came up to stand beside him, and he gazed down at her. "You look tired."

She nodded with a little smile. "I need a nap. I'll be glad to get home."

After a moment, David noticed her watching a nicely dressed young woman with a little girl in a pink jumper, who came up to the curb beside them, apparently waiting for transportation, too. The woman held the little girl's hand as she set down her suitcase. The toddler was wearing a pink cap with large mouse ears and a bow.

"Look, David," Veronica said in a low voice as she indicated the little girl with her eyes, "isn't she cute? She must be about two. She's got her mother's blond hair. I wonder who our baby will look like."

"We both have dark brown hair, so I imagine—"

"Well, what about eyes?" Veronica said. "Mine are brown and yours are blue."

"You've got me there," he said with a grin, happy to see her perk up a bit from her fatigue. It amazed him to observe how she dealt with the physical toll of her pregnancy with such equanimity, even joy.

He peered out at the oncoming traffic again, still looking for their shuttle. One passed by, but it wasn't from the company he'd called. The traffic was moving faster now and grew noisy, especially the vans and buses. Fumes added to the unpleasantness of the humidity.

Next to them, the young mother let go of her daughter's hand to get something out of her purse. In the next second, the toddler's hat blew off in a gust of wind and swept across the sidewalk and into the street. The child instantly ran after it.

"No!" Veronica screamed just as the mother noticed her daughter wasn't at her side anymore. Both women froze in horror. The little girl ran in front of an oncoming bus, still chasing her hat.

Without a thought, David bounded off the curb in front of the bus and snatched up the child in his arms. He leapt back onto the sidewalk, stumbling a bit, just as the hot draft from the passing bus blew across his back and hair. He heard the screech of the brakes, which wouldn't have stopped the large vehicle in time had either of them still been in the street. Thank God he'd reached her just in time!

The little girl began to cry as her mother raced up to take her from David's grasp. Once the child was safely in her arms, the mother burst into tears herself. "Thank you! Oh, thank you! I just looked away for a second and—"

"She must like that hat," David joked. He touched the woman's shoulder, hoping to calm her, since she was visibly trembling now. "Will you be all right?"

"Yes, thanks to you. That was very brave of you to run in front of that bus."

And now David realized for the first time himself how close he'd come to disaster. A frisson ran through him. "Anyone would have done it," he murmured numbly.

The young woman shook her head, laughing and still crying

at the same time. "I don't think that's true! But I'm sure glad you were here."

David nodded, feeling confused. "You're welcome. Take care." As he walked back to Veronica, his ankle felt stiff and he found himself limping. But he was more struck by the sight of his wife staring at him, hollow-eyed, looking pale from shock

"David, are you crazy?" she said weakly. "I'm glad you saved the little girl, but—you almost got killed yourself!"

"If I had hesitated, she would have been crushed. I never thought about myself . . ." He wondered why. He paused as he replayed the moment in his mind. "I know. I forgot I was mortal," he said in a soft voice, thinking as he spoke. "For hundreds of years I put myself in situations a mortal never would because I knew I'd recover from any injury. I forgot and just fell back into that state of mind. It didn't occur to me that I was in danger . . . My God, I might have been killed." He felt himself growing a bit pale now.

"I know," Veronica said, weeping as she leaned against him for support. "You're very heroic, but I hope I never have to see you do something like that again."

David held her close to comfort her, but inside he felt odd. He was happy he'd saved another human being from death, but he also felt shaken to the bones at his own cavalier attitude. And yet—he grew aware of a certain exhilaration within him. He felt free in a way he'd never experienced before. He'd felt a vast sense of release when he'd been transformed from one of the living dead into a mortal who was truly alive. But at this moment he felt even more alive—marvelously alive, now that he'd just faced down death and won.

"Part of the adventure of being mortal is that we can die at any moment," he told Veronica. "That thought has kept me cowed ever since I became mortal again. But I see that risk in a positive way now, that I didn't before."

Veronica looked up at him and wiped away a tear. "Great. Are you going to turn into a daredevil now, like Evel Kneivel?"

David stroked her hair. "That little girl might have been our child. Wouldn't you have wanted someone to risk everything to save her?"

Veronica bowed her head. "Of course, I would. But I want our child to have a father, too."

"I'm sorry this has frightened you."

She lifted her chin and managed to smile. "I can hardly believe you. Is this the same man who worried about every headache and sniffle? Who dreaded travel because there might be a car accident or plane crash?"

David looked down at his own body, clad today in a cotton sport shirt and pants. "I think so." He began to feel an ache in his ankle. "I think I twisted my foot, though." He tested it by taking a step.

"You did?" Veronica asked, looking down at his foot.

"It's not bad. It'll be all right." He turned to look at the mother and child again. A car had pulled up, with a male driver, probably the woman's husband, and she and the child were getting in. In a moment the car drove off.

David watched the oncoming traffic again. At last he saw their shuttle van coming. Soon they were riding in the well-used vehicle, windows open and the warm, humid wind blowing in their faces. The driver was listening intently to a Cubs baseball game on his radio.

Veronica took David's arm and snuggled close to him, as if she needed comfort. He couldn't help but recall their ride to the airport weeks ago, when they were leaving for London. David had been the one who had needed reassurance then. He recalled the headache he had had and his sensitivity to light. All that was gone now. He'd felt so well, he wasn't even taking his medication anymore, though he knew he might need it again in the future. He felt well, happy, and secure, something he'd never felt in his centuries as a vampire. And, best of all, he felt loved. He slipped his arm around Veronica.

She looked up at him and seemed to study his expression. Her beautiful face had a hint of childlike wonder in it, the ingenuous quality he'd been so taken with when he met her. He was glad she hadn't outgrown it totally.

"What are you thinking about?" she asked, as if curious. "Being a hero? Saving a life?"

"Actually, I'm contemplating all my old favorite subjects—life, death, and immortality."

"Oh," she said, growing concerned. "You're still worried about our life and future together?"

"No. I'm trying to understand why I'm so happy," David said. "For me, it's rather a new experience."

Veronica grinned, and her shoulders shook beneath his arm as she silently laughed. "I'm glad to hear that. What have you come up with?"

"I'm still trying to work it out. Happiness has something to do with mortality . . . and . . . and also with immortality. But I used to be immortal, and I *wasn't* happy. So I'm . . . still confused."

"How do you know it has to do with immortality then?"

"Because when I saved that child, I behaved as if I were still immortal. And I'm happy now that I did that. Though I'm sorry it gave you a scare."

"Well, now that I'm over it, I'm very proud of you. And a little in awe again, the way I was when I met you. You seem strong and in control now. And full of goodness and philosophy." She smiled softly. "The man I fell in love with."

"Am I? I hope so," he whispered as he leaned down to kiss her. His mind went blank for a few moments as he enjoyed the love he felt in her kiss. And then he lifted his head as an idea, and the words to express it, suddenly fell into place in his mind. He paused, refining the idea mentally for a moment while Veronica watched him expectantly.

"What?" she asked, her eyes wide with wonder.

"I think I've got it: The best way to live a mortal life is to live as if you are *im*mortal."

Veronica pondered this and then nodded. "To take risks and not worry about everything, as if life weren't precarious. I imagine that's what people who are the happiest do."

"That's it!" David said, excited about his discovery. "I may have acquired that attitude when I was first a mortal in the 1600s. But after centuries of immortality, I'd forgotten. Yet isn't that what life is all about, to take risks and live life fully, to do what we can for others, and to love to the best of our ability and the furthest reaches of our soul?"

Tears glazed Veronica's eyes as she gazed up at him in admiration. "That's beautiful, David. I think you're more brave and more poetic now than ever."

He smiled at her. "Well, I'll aspire to that. But I'm glad you think so. No regrets about what used to be?"

"None. I'm thrilled with what I've got now and happy for our future together. Even if it isn't for eternity."

"But perhaps it will be, Veronica. Our souls are eternal, if the great religions of the world are to be believed. As a vampire, I was dead, living an eternal death. But as mortals, even when our bodies die, we still have eternal life. John Donne wrote, 'One short sleep past, we wake eternally, and death shall be no more.' "

Veronica's eyes grew huge. "Will we be together, and our child, too?"

David pondered the question. He'd heard it asked in every century he'd existed, and had explored many theories. "I don't know. That's a great mystery. But I imagine if we want to be together, we can be. And will be. Forever."

The answer seemed to satisfy her well enough. They sat in silence for a while as the driver negotiated the expressway traffic on their way toward the center of Chicago. The city's familiar skyscrapers could be seen against the horizon now. They were coming home.

Over the centuries, David's home had been in many places, beginning with Paris, then London and other European cities. Then New York. Finally, on a whim, he'd come to Chicago almost two decades ago. He began to like the city, its eclectic architecture and down-to-earth citizens. Then he met Veronica and knew he'd never want to be anywhere else but where she lived.

And now he was mortal, and married to her, and happy. He'd carry on with his career as a playwright. He'd accumulate an estate to pass on to his children. He'd create a portfolio of plays to leave to posterity. And he'd finish out his life here, he thought with contentment. All with Veronica at his side.

"Are you going to start working on a new play?" Veronica asked out of the blue.

"I was just thinking about that," he said. "I need to get started on something new."

"What will it be about?"

He thought for a long while, absently stroking his upper lip with his forefinger. Then he lowered his hand and turned to her. "Do you know I've never written a comedy?"

"Never?"

"No. Never. Well, I was always so . . . serious. Yes, I think I'll try my hand at comedy," he said, nodding with resolve as he spoke. "Just for fun."

"Just for fun," Veronica repeated, amused. "The only things I've ever seen you do for fun are dance like Gene Kelly and . . . and . . ." She seemed to be at a loss to think of anything else. "Make love with me," she finally added.

"That's more than fun," David said, touching her nose. "That's an hour in paradise. That's passion sublime."

She grinned and coyly fingered his belt buckle. "I'm glad we'll be home soon."

Her response took him pleasantly by surprise. She'd been under the weather when they got off the plane. "Are you feeling up to it?"

"I feel wonderful. Besides, it'll be nice to be in our own bed again," she whispered.

David drew in a breath of tethered excitement. " 'My heart beats thicker than a fevered pulse.' "

Veronica laughed lightly and wound her arms around his neck. "Now that's the man I fell for—a head full of Shakespeare, and a heart full of love."

He drew her close. "All because of you, my adorable inspiration."

They were still kissing when their driver pulled up in front of their house. The driver had to turn down his radio and clear his throat loudly to alert them that they were home. Veronica was embarrassed. But David rather enjoyed the moment, his creative mind having turned, for the time being at least, from philosophy to farce.

16

A void next to his sorry heart

ABOUT FOUR months later, Matthew stood on a Broadway stage as Heathcliff, carrying a dying Catherine in his arms. He wore a black nineteenth-century suit and white shirt, cut to emphasize his broad shoulders and deep chest. His hair, in this second half of the show, when Heathcliff was older, was left natural, his brown-and-gray tendrils combed back from his forehead. His face had a minimum of stage makeup on it.

An exquisite last, long, tenor note, pure and clear, poignant with emotion, sang forth from his throat. In the darkness of the audience, he could hear people sobbing and could see moving patches of white as handkerchiefs were dabbed at wet faces. This was opening night, and already he could tell *Wuthering Heights* was an unsurpassable triumph, even before the final curtain had come down.

He finished the last note as the actress playing Catherine allowed her head to drop to his shoulder, pretending to expire. Still carrying his leading lady, he bowed his head to one side, over her dark hair, in a tragic pose. The orchestra finished playing the last sad note of the finale.

There was a moment of absolute silence. The stage lights went dark for a few seconds while actors took their places in the wings to come out for their bows. Matthew set the actress playing Catherine on her feet, then raced offstage. Suddenly he heard the jubilant outburst of the audience, the roar of applause, the shouts and cheers. His heart beat faster, and as the stage lights came up and the first actors went out for their bows, he jumped for joy and clasped his hands together above his head, like a track athlete who had just beaten the world record in a race. Other actors nearby came up to clap him on the back.

Soon all the actors with minor roles had gone out for their bows. The applause increased when the lead actress walked out, still in the white, old-fashioned nightgown she'd worn in the last scene. Matthew composed himself and wiped his damp palms on his pants, waiting for his cue. Shoulders squared, he walked out as the other actors stepped back to let him take center stage.

The audience went wild, and the theater seemed to shake with the thunder of their applause. Bouquets of flowers were thrown at his feet, and he bent to pick each one up. Shouts of "Bravo" could be heard above the din, and women were screaming and weeping. The hysteria almost frightened him. His newly enhanced power to sway an audience was more than he had hoped for—or perhaps even wanted. He had wanted his audience to love and admire him again; but this audience, he had the feeling, might follow him like lemmings off a cliff if he said the word.

The applause continued and continued long after everyone had taken a tenth and twelfth bow and the orchestra had been recognized. The actors no longer knew what to do and stood onstage with dazed smiles or laughing. Matthew gave the flowers in his arms to the lead actress and other women in the cast, then raised his hands to ask the audience to quiet down. At first they only clapped louder. But soon they grew silent, realizing he wanted to speak.

"Thank you," he told them, feeling and sounding breathless from triumphant emotion. "I'm so happy to be back onstage."

The audience responded with cheers and more applause. People shouted, "Thank *you!*" and "We love you, Matthew!"

Matthew went on to acknowledge those who had worked behind the scenes. As he spoke, he searched the audience for a familiar face and blond hair, but could not see anyone who resembled Darienne in the first ten rows. Earlier he'd spotted Natalie sitting in the third row, next to Larry and Sheena, and his eyes took in their smiling faces again. But beyond the first ten rows he could not see well enough to recognize anyone. He glanced up at the first balcony, but he could not see faces clearly there either. The second balcony was too high for him to see anyone.

He finished by thanking the audience for their warm welcome. As he stepped back in line with the other actors, they all took a last bow as the curtain came down. It had been decided earlier that there would be no curtain calls, a decision Matthew had not minded. He'd never liked the idea of milking an audience for applause. But now, as he lingered behind the closed curtain and heard the continuing fervent applause on the other side, from an audience who obviously didn't want their theater experience to end yet, he wished they would raise the curtain again. The other actors soon walked off into the wings, but Matthew remained, took hold of the curtain's heavy lining and clung to it, burying his face in it. The audience's adulation felt like a lover's embrace after a long absence, and he didn't want to give it up.

Eventually the applause died away, and Matthew reluctantly let go, reminding himself that tomorrow night there would be another audience. He crossed the stage and headed for his dressing room. There, outside the door with his name on it, he found a bevy of reporters and cameras waiting. He allowed them to film and take photos while he was still in costume. He'd discovered that photos of him did not come out bluish if he had on some makeup. His picture had been on the covers of many major magazines lately, both in anticipation of his return to Broadway in *Wuthering Heights* and because of his movie. *The Scarlet Shadow* had been released a few weeks ago to rave reviews and had quickly become a box office hit. Matthew was now more famous, revered, and sought after than he'd ever been in his already successful acting career. He was no longer an international star. He'd become a world famous megastar.

The crowd of reporters and film crews treated him as such, jockeying for position about him as he stood outside his dressing room, pushing one another's microphones out of the way. He stayed for many minutes, giving grateful, unrehearsed answers about how pleased he was the show had gone well and that his movie was a hit.

When asked why he'd insisted on night rehearsals, Matthew replied that he was superstitious and had come to believe rehearsing during the day was bad luck. Darienne's suggested excuse seemed to do the trick. The reporters eagerly took notes. Matthew had come to realize that appearing to be eccentric would not hurt his stardom and only had to think of Michael Jackson for reassurance.

One magazine reporter asked if he and his former wife would reconcile. Matthew replied that they were still friends, but they had no plans to get back together. To be able to say now that they were friends pleased Matthew. He had called Natalie a couple of months after moving to New York, where she lived, and had gone to visit her at her home on his night off. They talked mostly about Larry and Sheena, who were now engaged to be married. They shared their happiness about their son's plans.

While they spoke, Natalie seemed to study Matthew. She told him how energetic he seemed for being so involved in strenuous rehearsals. Matthew attributed this to a new diet and changed the subject. He asked about the new man in her life, and later she asked about Darienne. Matthew admitted he had no woman currently in his life. "Too busy," he'd told her.

Matthew didn't mention his leading lady, who had fallen in love with him during their long rehearsals, despite the fact that she was married. She'd come to his dressing room one night and point-blank asked him to make love with her.

But Matthew had made it a point to resist her, for several reasons. First, she *was* married. Second, he'd learned from past experience that it wasn't a good policy to have an affair with your leading lady. It could cause a scandal and adversely affect the show. And Matthew always put the show first. Third, she was high-strung and demanding, not the type of woman he favored. Fourth, even though he badly needed sexual gratification—damn well craved it—she was only a mortal, and he would have been afraid of injuring her.

The only woman he'd made love to since acquiring superhuman strength was Darienne. He hungered for their long nights of rough, tempestuous, vampire sex, and feared he wouldn't be able to hold himself in check anymore with a mortal woman. It was safer to go without and channel his pent-up energy into the show, which was how he'd been coping with his need.

So his answer to Natalie's question about his empty love life—"too busy"—was, in a way, sadly accurate.

He'd left Natalie's place that evening feeling good that at least he was on comfortable terms now with both her and his son. He would try to keep in touch with them as the years went by. Until he outlived them.

Feeling he'd given the reporters enough of his time for opening night, he excused himself and went into his dressing room. His assistant was there to help him take off his makeup. Of course, he'd had the mirror removed from the dressing room, and he sat down in his chair in front of the rectangle of lightbulbs that had surrounded the missing mirror. He'd used eccentricity again as an excuse. He'd said that seeing himself before a show threw off his concentration when he was getting into character. A mirror wasn't necessary anyway, he'd pointed out, since his expert assistant applied his makeup for him.

He couldn't help but think that Darienne had been right about everything. He was such a star now, those around him rarely argued with his odd requests. And if anyone did, at least if it was a man, he always had his new power of hypnosis to smooth over difficulties when necessary. Though he tried to use that power judiciously.

The women he worked with didn't tend to disagree with him, though they did seem to find any and all reasons to be alone with him whenever they could manage it. This made his life difficult, because with his sublimated sexual needs, and his lust for blood ever below the surface of his normal facade, he tended to instantly see every woman within reach as a potential object of huge desire. Despite all his good reasons, spurning the overtures of his leading lady hadn't been easy. She *was* beautiful. It had taken a great deal of self-control to resist. He didn't used to look at women merely as objects of lust, and this aspect in himself bothered him, often to the point of shame.

As his assistant removed the last of his makeup, people he knew and some he didn't began to file in and out of his dressing room to greet and congratulate him. Natalie, Larry, and Sheena came in for a while, and it made him feel good to have them there. They left to go to the exclusive opening night party, for which he'd gotten them invitations. Others came in, people he'd known from his days as the star of a TV comedy series and others he'd worked with on previous movies and stage shows.

But with all those who came through his dressing room on that night of his greatest stage triumph to date, Darienne was not among them. He'd been sure she'd never miss his opening night. Had she forgotten him? He had one last hope, that maybe she'd been in some section of the audience where he couldn't see her and had chosen for some reason not to come backstage. Maybe she'd surprise him by crashing the opening night party. She hadn't been invited because he had no idea where to send an invitation, but he knew that wouldn't stop her from coming if she wanted to.

When he'd showered and changed into a tuxedo, he went out to the stage door to greet the crowds waiting for him there. As he stood at the top of the short flight of steps leading up from the street and waved, the crowd, mostly women, began screaming and carrying on as if he were a rock star.

Flashbulbs went off, but he didn't worry about the fact that he was no longer wearing makeup. Thinking ahead, he'd had a blue light bulb installed in the light fixture above the door, insisting to the theater's doubtful maintenance man that it warded off insects and he was allergic to bug bites. Now, when his fans had their photos developed, they'd blame his bluish facial tones in their pictures on that darned blue light above him.

Again he searched for Darienne, in the mass of frantic women, but he did not see her. He gave the crowd a wave and a kiss and went in, not having the time tonight to sign autographs. A limousine sped him to the hotel where the elaborate party was being held. It was a festive event, and he was greeted and congratulated over and over. Though he'd done a strenous show, he didn't feel the least bit of fatigue. He relished this fact, remembering former days when each performance would exhaust him.

The party lasted late, and Matthew stayed until nearly the end of it, waiting, searching the people gathered in the huge room for the one face he was looking for. But Darienne never appeared.

He left as quietly as he could, went out a back door of the hotel to avoid reporters, and walked the several blocks to his apartment. New York's streets were dark and lonely at this time of night, but Matthew knew he had nothing to fear, and the night air felt good. When he reached his tenth-floor apartment, he unlocked the door and went in.

The place was still as empty as when he'd first arrived. The walls were bare. There were no furnishings except for a lamp, a telephone, a small table, and a folding chair, all of which he'd bought himself and carried home over the months since he'd arrived. He'd pushed his coffin into one of the two bedrooms in the apartment. His refrigerator was well stocked with fresh bags he'd obtained from a local blood bank. He'd learned David's old trick of dressing like a maintenance man to steal from the blood bank late at night when the man on duty was reading or asleep.

Matthew felt no urge to buy or rent a set of living room furniture or to decorate the place in any way. He'd only be here for several months, maybe a year, until he took the show to another city. Certainly he had no intention of inviting anyone to see his apartment; in fact, he'd gone to great lengths to keep its location secret.

But the stark emptiness of his place affected him tonight, after all the flurry and triumph at the theater and the party afterward. Despite all the adulation, he came home to this. Now he felt acutely what David had described to him when David was still a vampire: the vast gulf between him and other people. Matthew had always felt a little different, but now . . . now he *was* vastly different. Now he had to live in secret; now he looked upon men as creatures to manipulate and women as potential prey. Now he took sustenance from blood and suffered lusts no human should experience.

He still had the formula David had given him to become mortal again. Should he take it?

No, he quickly decided. His triumph tonight, the waves of love that had emanated up to him from the vast audience at his feet made the dark side of his existence worthwhile. At least for the time being. He had the unsettling fear that, one day, even the adulation of his public wouldn't be enough. Even now, there was a certain emptiness settling into him. He could feel it in his chest, a void next to his sorry heart.

Where was Darienne? Had she really left him for good? Would he never see her again?

The next evening at dusk, before leaving for the theater, he phoned David in Chicago. Veronica answered and immediately congratulated him on his success. "We read about it in the paper!" she told him with excitement and commented on all the magnificent reviews he'd received from critics. Matthew smiled at her enthusiasm and envied David for having such a wife. He asked how she was, and she told him she'd just gone out that day and bought new maternity clothes, she was growing so large.

"I'll bet you look beautiful," Matthew told her.

"David thinks so, but I'm not so keen on my new shape. I'm glad it's only temporary. But I feel good now. No more morning sickness."

She put David on the line then, and he also heartily congratulated Matthew. "Are you pleased with your success?" he asked.

"I'm thrilled and grateful," Matthew replied.

"And content with your new existence?"

"I'm happy with the way I can perform now, but . . . I do feel isolated when I'm not at the theater working. I see now what you meant. It didn't matter so much when Darienne was with me, but now . . ."

"I'm sorry," David said. "Have you heard from her?"

"No. That's why I called. I was hoping maybe you or Veronica had."

"No, not a word," David told him. "Although Veronica saw a photo layout in *Vogue* magazine of a new line of evening clothes by a new designer. The label was called . . . Wait, I'll ask Veronica." He spoke away from the phone and then came back on the line again. "Veronica says it was called *Scandaleux*. That's a French word that means 'scandalous.' She showed me the magazine and asked if I didn't think it might be Darienne's line of clothes. Of course, I had no idea." David's voice showed his amusement. "But Veronica thought the glittery evening dresses were exactly Darienne's style. I had to agree that *Scandaleux* sounds like something Darienne might come up with. I don't know what that's worth. The ad indicated it was a New York clothier. You might try checking into that label and see who owns or runs the company. Though if it is Darienne's, she might keep her name secret."

"You really think she could start and run a company?" Matthew asked.

"Don't underestimate her," David said. "It was always her game to act frivolous around men. She's never shown much interest in business that I know of, but that doesn't mean that she couldn't learn it if she had the incentive. And clothes have always been her passion. Other than you, of course."

"Not anymore," Matthew said. "She didn't even come last night to my opening."

"How do you know? If I remember, that's a large theater. You must have had a packed house."

"Overflowing. But if she was there, why didn't she come to see me? After years of scheming to get me and claiming to be in love with me, how can she have lost interest this way? Is she so wrapped up in her career that she doesn't need me?"

"Are you so wrapped up in yours that you don't need her?"

Matthew stopped short, understanding the underlying commentary of David's question. "You're right," he admitted. "My career isn't enough. Even my success doesn't satisfy me the way I thought it would."

"Maybe she's just been waiting for you to find that out. She has an uncanny sense of when to appear and when to bide her time."

Matthew, in the pit of his lonely doldrums, found this hard to believe and decided that David must be trying to find something positive to say to give him hope. This only made Matthew feel worse, and he decided to change the subject.

"Are you working on any new material?" he asked David.

"I'm trying my hand at a comedy. But the dialogue doesn't sparkle yet. I never realized that comedy is much harder to write than drama."

Matthew chuckled with irony. "An actor on his deathbed once said, 'Dying is easy. Comedy is difficult.' I know that's true, having had experience with both."

"Take heart, Matthew. Remember you don't have to stay in your isolated existence. You *can* become mortal again. If you need someone to be with you if you decide to take the formula, call me and we'll arrange something. You're not alone."

Tears stung the backs of Matthew's eyes, and it was difficult for him to control his voice. "Thank you" was all he could think of to say before quickly hanging up. Of the few friends Matthew had had over his lifetime, David was the one he valued most, though he'd have a hard time finding the words to tell David that.

Matthew mentally stepped outside for a moment and observed himself. He saw an inept man who stumbled when expressing his feelings to someone important to him. He was far different from his alter ego, the actor who could sink himself into a character and emote with abandon. Matthew wondered if he could learn to portray his own feelings for a change.

Almost three months later, Matthew was walking alone in Central Park at about one A.M. He regularly walked in the park after each show, a habit he'd begun mostly to avoid going back to his empty apartment. Here in the moonlight, among the trees and grass, he could wander and let his mind dwell on the audience's applause, thus seeming to prolong their comforting affection for him.

It was early spring now, but the temperature, especially at night, was still cold. Last night it had rained, but tonight the stars were out and the moon was full as he walked along a narrow road that led through the huge park. The setting reminded him, as usual, of the time he'd fled to Hyde Park in London just after he'd been transformed, and how Darienne had followed to bring him back home. Every night he found himself wishing that she'd somehow appear here in Central Park and bring him home. But in the long months he'd been performing on Broadway, she'd never once appeared, and he imagined now that she probably never would. Maybe she'd found another man to transform and become her vampire lover for eternity, a man who showed his appreciation of her more than Matthew had.

Matthew had checked into the *Scandaleux* line of clothes David had mentioned, had even hired a private detective to find out who ran the company. All the detective had managed to discover was that the New York company was managed by a woman of about forty who used to work for Bill Blass. Who owned the company and designed the dresses in their line was a well-kept secret.

The information was useless to Matthew. Besides, it was only Veronica and David's speculation that the company was Darienne's. Maybe she'd never begun the career she'd spoken of at all. Maybe she was in some far-off country traveling. Or maybe she'd gone back to Paris, where she was born, and was at this moment with her new lover.

The thought of Darienne with another man made Matthew angry, with her and himself. If she wasn't so prideful and headstrong, she might have stayed with him to try to work things out instead of abruptly leaving him as she had. But in the end, Matthew had to be angry with himself. She'd wanted *him* to work on their relationship. He'd failed her, just as he'd always done, in all his personal relationships.

Matthew told himself not to dwell on his failings so much, as he continued to walk in the brisk night air. After all, he *was* the toast of Broadway, he thought grimly.

He hesitated as up ahead on the narrow road he saw a lone figure walking in the shadows beneath some trees. Light from the moon and the surrounding city buildings made it possible to see, but not in the night shadows beneath a stand of trees blossoming with new foliage. Walking late at night alone as he always did, he'd encountered his share of muggers. Usually a swift push using his superhuman strength or a flash of ultraviolet from his angry eyes was enough to make them run away. He'd even been stabbed once, but the wound had quickly healed. It had ruined his coat, however. Though he felt safe, he'd just as soon avoid an encounter.

The figure moved passed the trees and out of the night shadows, and he realized for the first time that it must be a woman, judging by the graceful sway of her body. What woman in her right mind would be walking alone in Central

Park at one A.M.? He felt he ought to protect her and picked up his pace to close the distance between them a bit, so he could follow her and make sure no harm came to her.

As he got closer, she took off the long black scarf she was wearing over her head, and he realized she was blond. His heart picked up a beat. Could it be . . . ? But it was too much of a coincidence. The woman didn't know he was behind her. What were the chances that he and Darienne would happen to be walking on the same road in the same city at exactly the same time of night?

And yet the closer he got to her, the more her height and the carriage of her body, the sensuality in her walk, reminded him of Darienne. She appeared to be wearing a long dark dress, perhaps with sequins sewn on, for he could see little sparks of light glimmer beneath the edge of her coat as she walked. Her hair was longer than Darienne's had been when he'd last seen her in London, though it wasn't as long as she used to wear it. This woman's hair was almost shoulder length and smooth, curled under at the ends.

By now Matthew was going mad with curiosity. Was she Darienne or not? He began to run and soon caught up to her. When he walked beside her on the road, she did not even turn and look at him, though she must have heard his footsteps. Or else she was deaf. Maybe she was afraid. Facing straight ahead, she kept walking at the same steady, brisk pace. Matthew ran ahead of her a step or two to get a look at her face. His heart almost stopped with joy. If it wasn't Darienne, then she had a twin!

But she looked past him and kept walking as if he weren't there just in front of her, dodging her forward steps.

"Darienne! It's me, Matthew!"

She coolly shifted her gaze so that her eyes, translucent, calm, and beautiful, met his. "*Bonsoir,*" she told him in an indifferent tone and kept walking.

"I've missed you! Where have you been? How are you?" he asked, breathless and walking backward in front of her now.

"Fine. Excuse me," she said as she stepped around him when his pace slowed and he got in her way.

He rushed to step up to her side again. "How long have you been in New York?"

"Since I left London," she replied matter-of-factly, eyes straight ahead.

"You . . . you've been here all this time?"

"*Oui.*"

"Why haven't you contacted me? You've never even come to my show!" He was feeling hurt now, and his voice showed anger.

"Obviously, I haven't wanted to contact you."

Her cool tone and indifference were getting to him. "Can't you stop walking and talk to me?" he demanded.

"I don't want to stop walking," she told him and increased her pace.

"Why?" He quickened his own steps to keep up. If he hadn't cared about her so much, he would have thrashed her for her callous attitude.

"Because for once in your life," she said, her voice growing a bit tart, "I want you to pursue *me!*"

The instant her words sank in, Matthew began to grin. "All right! I'm agreeable. I'll pursue you," he said, keeping up with her rapid pace. But after several paces, she still had not stopped walking. "What more do you want? What will make you stop so I can hold you in my arms again?"

She turned to give him a stony stare. "You'll have to figure that out for yourself."

Exasperating female! He wanted to pounce on her, but wasn't sure that was what she wanted from him just yet. This wasn't a moment to make a mistake. He'd better stick with words first. "I've missed you terribly, Darienne. In fact, I've been absolutely miserable. Nothing's the same without you. I'm lonely as can be. I want us to be together again—to live together. Have wonderful sex together. Like it used to be."

"No, Matthew," she said, keeping her stride, still facing forward, "I won't have it be like it used to be. I told you in London, I won't go back to being your adoring sex toy while you devote all your attention to your show."

"I'll put you first," he quickly promised. "I won't take you for granted the way I did. I'll . . . I'll try to understand better what you want from me."

She kept walking and didn't reply.

"Well? What's your answer?" he asked with impatience.

"You'd better try understanding better what I want from you *now!*"

Matthew lifted his eyes to the stars, looking for help. "I'm trying, but—what *do* you want? What more can I say?"

Darienne drew in a long breath and exhaled it with slow deliberation, as if doing her best to keep her patience. "Think, Matthew. What do you think I might want to hear you say?"

And then he suddenly realized what she wanted him to tell her. He felt rebellious all at once, as well as embarrassed. To say the words would make him seem weak, put a crack in his masculinity somehow. It would be giving in. Besides, he wasn't even sure—"All right," he snapped. Realizing his tone was all wrong for saying such a line, he softened his voice. "I . . . I think I love you. I'm . . . almost sure of it."

Darienne blinked once and then turned her eyes askance. A humorous twist to her mouth gave her an ironic, impertinent expression. "Oh, rapture," she said, her tone like a deadpan comic's.

Angry that nothing was going right, Matthew grabbed hold of her and with his superior male strength forced her to stop walking. He shook her by the shoulders, making her hair bob back and forth. A new energy seemed to spring up within him. "I love you, damn it! I *love* you! If you don't come back, I'll never be happy again." His voice grew heartfelt as words poured out of him without his mental censor inhibiting him anymore. "Nothing's right without you. Even the applause from the audience is meaningless once it's over. I go home to emptiness. That's why every night I walk in this park almost till dawn, to pass the time and think about you."

"I know. I've seen you," she said, her beautiful eyes growing impish with amusement now.

He stared at her. "Walking in the park? Before tonight?"

"For months. I followed you after the show one night, to see where you went."

"Followed me?"

"I've known where you were every night, Matthew. My apartment here overlooks this park. Once I knew your habits, I could even keep watch over you as I worked on my dress designs. I'd see you passing beneath these trees, looking so solitary."

"Why did you wait until now to—"

"I wanted to wait well past opening night, so that your sense of triumph had time to wear off and you fell into the humdrum of a routine. And I was busy, too, starting my own career. But last night as I watched you, I decided that if you loved me at all, you'd finally be realizing it about now. So I chose to go walking in the park tonight, too—so you could find me."

"You are the most scheming woman," Matthew said, his happiness mixed with outrage. "Did you ever see my show?"

"Oh, *mais oui!* Nearly every night. I wouldn't deprive myself of the pleasure of watching you sing." Her eyes changed color and grew iridiscent. "You're so sensual, the way you move, and the timbre of your voice when you sing. And they let you keep your hair as it is in the second half, so you really look like you now. In *Shadow* you always had all that makeup and the wig. I like this much better." Her expression changed, and her eyes grew a bit accusing. "Your leading lady is in love with you, isn't she? I can tell, even from the second balcony, through my binoculars."

"The second balcony. So that's why I never saw you."

"What about your Catherine, Heathcliff?" she persevered in an arch tone.

"Yes, you're right, she wanted me. But I think she's given up on me by now. I refused her because the only one in the world who could make me happy was you. And not just because of the superhuman desire that only you can appease, but because . . . you're my soul mate. You drive me nuts sometimes, but I love you. I love you with all my heart."

She gave him an impish look of doubt. "You're sure of it now?"

"Absolutely positive."

"Well, in that case . . ." She drew her arms up around his neck. They felt light as they settled on his shoulders, and yet he could sense their possessiveness. As he felt her warm breath on his cheek when she drew close to kiss him, he experienced the acute joy of knowing he finally belonged to her as he wanted her to belong to him. Her lips were warm and sweet as they met his and lingered there. He slid his arms about her and drew her up against him. Even with a winter coat covering her form, she felt sublimely feminine. His frustrated need was so great, a spark ignited inside him and soon raged in his pulsing arteries for appeasement.

"Where can we go?" he asked, breaking the kiss, his breaths heated and fast. "I need you."

Darienne drew away a bit and placed her hands against his chest, as if to keep him in check. "Before we resume where we left off in London, I want to know how it will be between us. You say you love me—"

"I do! I want to love you to pieces!" he said, trying to convey the depth of his feelings at that moment.

"All right, but I want a commitment from you first."

"What do you mean? I'm committed to you already! Natalie and I are finished for good. She's even found someone else. And I've turned down my leading lady because I wanted only you. I'll be faithful."

"My main rival is your audience, Matthew."

Ah, so that's what she was getting at. He hastened to reassure her. "Your love means more to me than theirs. I've come to realize that. What I get from my audience is fleeting and ephemeral." He took hold of her hands. "But you're true and real."

She looked at him as if puzzled.

"What do you want?" he asked when she didn't respond. "Do you want me to quit the show for you?"

"Well—"

"I'll do it!" he said, making the decision on the spot. "I don't need the show anymore. My initial contract's ending soon. I'll quit. I'll do something else instead. I'll become a director. That way I won't have any audience for you to feel jealous of."

Tears filled her eyes. "Oh, Matthew," she whispered. "You would quit your show for me?"

"Shows come and go, but there's only one you. And I want you to stay with me forever."

A tear spilled down her cheek as she looked up at him with great, wet, luminous eyes. "Then you really do love me more than your audience. I was afraid you'd never love me that much. I was afraid you'd never love me at all."

"I love you," he said with assurance, finding the words easy to say now. "I suppose I have all along. I was just too preoccupied or too oblivious to know it." He wiped the tears from her face. "I want to make you happy. I can go on without my audience, but I can't survive without you. Will you stay with me and live with me? Love me?"

She answered with a sudden, bold, heated kiss that took him by surprise. But he answered with equal passion, and soon he could feel unleashed desire vibrating through her. He responded in kind, ripping apart her coat to hold her body close. He found her thinly clothed breast and cupped it in his hand, fondling her as he bent her back in a deepening kiss.

All at once she broke free, confusing him for a moment. Hair disheveled, eyes bright with iridescent desire and a wild smile, she took his hand.

"My place is near," she said with excitement. "Come with me!"

They took off running through the trees toward Central Park West. She led him to a handsome apartment building where a doorman opened the door for them. An elevator took them up to the top floor. She brought him into an elegantly furnished apartment, with traditional furniture upholstered in blues and corals. Beautifully draped windows looked down onto Central Park. Matthew noted a desk facing one window, with dress designs scattered over it. Expensive paintings hung on the walls, and art nouveau carvings and vases decorated the tables. A large Aubusson rug covered the floor.

"This is incredible!" he said as she took his coat from him and put it with her own in a closet. "How long have you lived here?"

"I've had this place for decades. I use it whenever I come to New York, which is fairly often. I lived here when you were doing *Shadow* in New York. You never knew where I went, when I left your place before dawn every night. I keep my coffin there in the other room," she said pointing to a varnished door. "There's room in there for yours, too."

Matthew broke into a smile. "You're inviting me to move in?"

"*Oui*."

"I'd love to live here with you," he said, taking her in his arms. "I don't necessarily have to have my own coffin, either."

She laughed as she tangled her fingers in his curly hair. "I'd love for you to share mine. But you ought to have yours brought here, too, just in case we have a fight one night."

"Us, fight?" he said with a grin. "After I've finally told you I love you? What more is there for us to argue about?"

"Something's bound to come up over the first few hundred years."

He looked down, noticing for the first time her clinging, sequined black dress, cut exquisitely low to make an exhibition of her marvelous cleavage. He drew in his breath, trying to keep his rekindled desire from raging. "This dress makes my heart stop. And a strategic area below my belt is going crazy."

Darienne smiled with pleasure and ran her hands in a lingering way up his shirt front. "I designed this and had it made to wear especially for you for tonight. I thought if you still couldn't love me, at least I'd make you want me enough that you'd value me more than your audience."

"I do," he said as he unbuckled his belt. "I want you so much I can't see straight. I don't care if I never perform in front of an audience again. But I do need to perform for you. Now! And I don't mean singing."

"Matthew," she whispered, the spaghetti straps holding up her dress, slowly slipping from her shoulders. "You sang so beautifully tonight and looked so manly in my binoculars, I could have fainted, I wanted you so. My heart pounded because I planned to let you find me in the park afterward, and I wondered if it would end like this. And it is." Her eyes glistened moistly as the dress slipped off her arms, baring her sumptuous upturned breasts. She unfastened something in the back, and the dress slipped off her nude body to the floor. "My heart is thudding so hard now I can't even breathe," she said in a voice so soft he could barely hear her.

She swayed slightly, and he took her in his arms. As if of one mind, they fell together onto the thick carpet. He covered her body with his and kissed her roughly. Her eager hands ripped off his shirt while he unzipped his pants and freed his engorged manhood. At the sight of him, she whimpered with desire and parted her thighs. Panting with fierce need, he found her delicious, moist recess of heat and slid deep inside her.

Both moaned in immediate pleasure as he filled her. Her tightness fit him like a slick glove. He began bucking motions, hard, driven with need, and rough with unsatiated passion. She arched her firm breasts against his chest, and her beautiful eyes closed as if in delirium as she moaned with each thrust he made. Her response made him feel incredibly powerful and fully male, and yet caused such an intense ache of caring and joy in his chest that he nearly wept for her and for this moment.

Her climax came as a surprise, perhaps even to her, for all at once she arched her neck and cried out his name as if in agony. He felt the pulsing sensations around his thrusting member as her body wracked in convulsions. She held onto him tightly. The throbbing of her flesh around him brought on his own orgasm as he thrust deeply one last time. He cradled her against him as he felt his semen spring forth inside her, giving him such an intense release that he thought for a half moment he might not survive the sensation.

They lay close for a long time, not saying anything, just recovering their breathing and their equilibrium. Matthew's head spun, and he couldn't remember for a moment what city he was in or what planet he was on. All he knew was he was with Darienne. She had finally given him again what no other woman could, a pleasure so vital, a love so potent, he might have died of it if he weren't a vampire.

He rolled to one side and gathered her against him, looking into her glazed, worshiping eyes. "Why did you have to take so long to meet me in the park?" he asked, half accusing, half adoring. "I needed you months ago. Since the night you left me."

"So did I," she admitted. "But I wanted you to know you missed me. And it was worth the wait, *n'est-ce pas*?"

"It was worth the wait. But don't ever leave me again."

"I won't as long as you love me."

"Then we'll be together forever."

"*Mon amour*," she whispered, stroking his face. "I love you so much." She smiled as if with a new delight. "I can't wait to see you from a third-row seat! The second balcony was pure misery. I had to struggle so to see you through the binoculars. I cried sometimes, it was so frustrating, trying to focus them on you while you were singing, and not managing very well. My hands would shake, and the image of you would bob and not stay still. I hated it."

"Serves you right for keeping yourself away from me."

She ran her hand up his chest, over his pectoral muscles. "I've suffered my punishment long enough. Can you get me a good seat? A permanent one, third row center? I want to sit there for as long as the show runs."

Matthew drew his brows together in puzzlement. "All right, but there'll be another actor in the role once my contract is up next month. I promised you I'd quit the show."

She smiled comfortably, squirming her beautiful, lush body closer to his as he leaned over her. Absently toying with the contours of his collarbone, running her forefinger along it until it disappeared into the thickness of his shoulder muscles, she said coyly, "I never asked you to quit the show."

"Yes, you did."

"No, *chéri*, you must have *thought* that was what I wanted, and so you said you would. I was thrilled that you were willing to go to that extent to make me happy. It did prove to me that you cared more for me now than for your career." She ran her fingers lightly over his bicep, giving him pleasant little chills. "But, Matthew, I don't really want you to quit, unless it's what you really want for yourself. Why would I want to put an end to the pleasure of watching you sing? I want to sit in the theater and swoon over you every night like all those other women in the audience do."

Matthew took in a slow breath of relief. He'd begun to wonder if he really would enjoy directing as much as acting. "Are you sure?"

"Acting is a part of who you are, a part of what I fell in love with. I wouldn't want you to abandon something so important to you. I just want to be most important to you, that's all."

"You are. I love you and need you more than anything."

"But you will keep on doing the show?"

He nodded. "I'd like to. My biggest payoff for doing a show well was seeing you in the audience giving me that private little look of yours that said, 'Just wait till after the show, big star, and I'll give you something you'll like a lot better than applause.' "

She chuckled and jabbed his belly button. "Is that really how I looked at you?" she asked with innocence.

"You knew it, too," he accused her lovingly. "Sometimes I nearly went blank on my lines. I'd try to school myself not to find you in the audience, but it never worked. I love to look at you, provocative wanton wench that you are. And sinfully beautiful, too."

"But you have such willpower," she whispered, admiring his bicep again with her fingertips.

"It always wilts against your temptations."

Her eyes drifted down the length of him. "I see something of yours that's definitely not wilted."

He grinned and pushed her down into the soft carpet.

They made love until dawn, and then he shared her casket through the day. The next night, she sat in the third row and beamed at him while he sang, feeling the power of the gods within him, his voice carrying easily to the rafters. The audience went crazy, but it was her secret smile for him alone that was most important. Afterward, at the stage door, she quietly stood to one side, as she used to during his run of *Shadow,* watching as he signed a hundred or more autographs.

This began a new routine for them, repeated night after night. After finishing at the theater, they'd go home to the Central Park West apartment. Sometimes she had work to take care of for *Scandaleux.* Or else they'd walk for a while in Central Park. Or else they'd spend the whole night in lovemaking.

"Are you happy with your existence?" she asked him one night after they'd shared their erotic vampire passion.

"Very," he replied. "Why do you ask?"

"I just was wondering if you have any regrets about being a vampire."

He toyed with her hair, still growing longer and more beautiful. "Sometimes I'm conscious of being so different from everyone, the separation from humanity David used to speak of."

"Does it really bother you?" she asked with concern. "Are you going to brood about it the way he did?"

Matthew considered the question. "Oh, not for another century or two. I'm having too much fun."

She gave him a little smile, but then asked, "Do you wish we could have a child, the way David and Veronica are? I called her yesterday, and she's due any day now."

Matthew had never even considered the question, since he knew it was impossible. "I already have a son. I don't mind not having more children. Do you wish you could have one?"

"Not yet," Darienne answered. "But . . . I'm not sure. Maybe someday I'll come to a point where I would like to have your baby. Veronica seems so happy, it . . . it intrigues me."

"But we'd both have to become mortal again."

"I know." She shrugged. "Well, it's something to consider some day." She touched his hand. "But Matthew, if you ever should decide you don't like being different, that you don't want to be a vampire anymore, then . . . well, I'd take the cure along with you. I'd become mortal, too, to be with you. I just wanted you to know."

Matthew marveled at her words and kissed her forehead. "I love you. The way you'd do anything for me has always moved me, even when I thought I hated you. I'll cherish you forever, whether we stay immortal or not."

She touched his face, her eyes wide and radiant as if struck with a wondrous thought. "Our love is so strong, being mortal or immortal doesn't really make any difference, does it?"

"No. Though immortality stretches out a little longer."

She grinned softly and kissed him. Then she lay back, her honey-blond hair spreading out on the plush carpet, her green eyes bright, looking as pleased with herself as a pampered Persian cat, and welcomed him into her arms. Matthew sank down onto her voluptuous body and decided this was a marvelous way to spend the next few centuries or more—loving Darienne.

Epilogue

MATTHEW WON his second Tony Award for his performance as Heathcliff. Tickets for the show were sold out for a year in advance, and he decided to stay with it in New York for a full year before taking it to London. Darienne's line of clothes, *Scandaleux*, was discovered and favored by several Hollywood actresses, who wore her creations to the Oscars. She soon had more work than she wanted, stealing hours from her nights with Matthew, so she sold the company, but stayed on in the role of creative consultant. She continued to attend Matthew's performances, wearing one of her stunning dresses every night, and shamelessly flirting with him whenever he glanced at her while singing onstage. After spending the rest of the night together walking, talking, and making love, they retired to the hidden room in their apartment in which their coffins were kept side by side, though they always used only one. Their only bone of contention nowadays was about closet space, most of which Darienne had appropriated for her vast and ever-increasing wardrobe.

On a sunny morning in Chicago, Veronica safely gave birth to a healthy, perfect baby boy. They brought him home from the hospital to the nursery room Veronica had prepared. David, though thrilled, grew nervous for a while about every little cough and gurgle his infant made, fearing it was a sign of illness. But Veronica gradually eased his fears, and he soon began to take his new fatherhood in stride.

David finished his next play, and it opened in Chicago to

excited reviews from surprised critics, who were used to his more serious works. They labeled the show a "fantasy comedy" since the plot revolved around an anxiety-prone vampire who must adjust to being a mortal after taking a mysterious elixir.

The angst that had troubled David's former days was gone now, and he was happy with his work, his life, and most of all with his beloved Veronica and their child. Veronica was also thrilled with her new role of mother, and remained deeply and proudly in love with David. The restless longings of their obsessive love, of their former vampire bond, were gone forever now; replaced with a more serene, but still everlasting, mortal love—a love that fulfilled their days together and made their nights restful, after lovemaking, with a comfortable mortal's sleep.